I Am Here

I Am Here

A Novel

Marlys Beider

I Am Here

Published by Wheatmark®
2030 East Speedway Boulevard, Suite 106
Tucson, Arizona 85719 USA
www.wheatmark.com

ISBN: 978-1-62787-694-0 (paperback)
ISBN: 978-1-62787-695-7 (hardcover)
ISBN: 978-1-62787-696-4 (ebook)
LCCN: 2019937016

Bulk ordering discounts are available through Wheatmark, Inc. For more information, email orders@wheatmark.com or call 1-888-934-0888.

In Memory of Bella and Sidney Miller

You left your fingerprints of love, courage, wisdom and dignity on all the lives you touched.

It is not more surprising to be born twice than once; everything in nature is resurrection.

—Voltaire

Chapter One

"Do you want to hear my theory of why I was misdiagnosed with Asperger's syndrome before I was five years old? Shall I clue you in as to why I was incorrectly identified with autism spectrum disorder by yet another pediatric neurologist? Have you read those parts of my file that elaborate on the voices that spoke to me in languages I couldn't understand? Or how about the dark and distant hallucinations I endured for more than a decade? Did or did I not have schizophrenic episodes? Or...could it be that I might have been acting and lying all those years?"

Kuri Berger paused and, for a brief moment, reclined into the sofa in the psychiatrist's office where hues of pale green and warm pink in the upholstery complemented the tones in the area rug and the tint of the painted walls; the subtle glow from two table lamps spread across the cozy room during this early evening hour.

Still staring intently at her new therapist, Kuri leaned forward again. "But...what if my life really has been stranger than fiction?" A forced lopsided smile formed on her lips. "Doc Clayson believes that you'll be able to help uncover what's been haunting me all these years." And, barely audible, she added, "Can you?"

Right then, Kuri felt her body going into a familiar half-conscious state. She didn't expect the icy wave that drew her into darkness, and as the first raw chill bit into her bones, she shivered inwardly and envisioned her skin changing to blue gray. She could sense her fingers turning numb, her muscles stiffening. Because this had happened to her many times before, she had developed the ability to slow her pulse and replace her shallow breathing with deep inhales and soft exhales. The third exhale freed her from the cold darkness, and she embraced returning to the warm reality around her. Throughout the brief episode, she deliberately maintained eye contact with the therapist.

Dr. Melanie Brichta had not stirred during this brief nonverbal communication. Surprised by a strange uncertainty, she was unable to interpret her immediate instincts. Never before in her long professional career had she experienced personal flashbacks from her own past while listening and observing a patient. She was particularly startled when, even during Kuri Berger's momentary distress, their eye contact was never broken.

The therapist cleared her throat. "After I spoke to Dr. Clayson, I read most of your clinical reports," she said calmly. "I believe I can help you."

Chapter Two

Met with Kurisutaru (Kuri) Berger, June 8, 2018, between 2:15 and 3:45 p.m.

Patient came referred by Arnold Clayson, MD

Patient is a 22-year-old female of mixed race

Patient looked healthy and alert

Patient has history of mental illness (???), first diagnosed at age five

(June 5, 2018: Received evaluations and information regarding past psychiatric history, including hospital summaries and clinic records from Boston and Milwaukee)

Father:	*David Berger (white American).*	*Age:*	*78*
Mother:	*Teruko Berger (Japanese).*	*Age:*	*66*
Siblings:	*Aimi*	*Age:*	*40*
	Gavin	*Age:*	*38*
	Ethan	*Age:*	*36*

No known family history of mental illness. (Received family reports 2002 to 2010)...

Melanie Brichta stopped and leaned back. She stared at the screen; the flashing text cursor kept prompting her to continue typing or at least be mindful of the large file she'd downloaded only two days ago. Having read a few of the evaluations and records between 2002 and 2005, she was able to compare them to the hospital summary from 2010. Certain parts of the years in between still needed to be read—there had not been enough time.

Her eyes wandered from the screen to an empty spot on the desk. Whenever in deep thought, her right index finger gently massaged the tip of her nose.

She noticed the desk phone lighting up; as always, its ringer was turned off. She recognized the name and hit the speaker button.

"Arnold? You're supposed to be in Europe relaxing."

"We're in Stockholm, but our ship's not leaving port till midnight—in exactly twenty-five minutes. Vacation only starts when city noise is replaced by sea, solitude, and starlight. How did it go, Mel? Did Kuri Berger keep her appointment? She's known to cancel."

"She was here for ninety minutes. I am still processing what I learned today."

"Mel, I must thank you again for helping me out on such short notice. I almost canceled our trip because of my interest in this patient." Arnold paused. "Believe me, I had difficulties admitting that I'd come to a dead end, but I have high hopes that your expertise will help her."

Melanie felt a familiar tightness in her neck and slowly rolled her head. The usual soft crack brought the desired release. "Go on," she said.

"You saw in the records that two reputable therapists have tried hypnotherapy on the patient. Both felt she was not a good subject; she refused to follow their instructions. Knowing her so well, I'm convinced Kuri was unable to get in tune with them and their therapy. So, she simply resisted. I immediately thought of you and made her aware of the many favorable outcomes your special technique has achieved. I was surprised when she agreed to the referral, despite the fact that you're in another city. However, with her traveling so much and her family living in the Chicago area—"

"Excuse me for interrupting, Arnold. Kuri said she's leaving for Europe either late tonight or early tomorrow. She thinks she'll be done filming in three weeks—maybe less than that. She then plans on being with her parents in Lake Bluff for a while. We tentatively set aside some dates, but when I mentioned that a few sessions were needed prior to starting hypnotherapy, she reacted anxiously. I can't guarantee she'll stick around."

"I expect she will. I know she's ready to go beyond what she calls same old same old." Arnold paused. When a brief announcement from the ship's PA system passed, he continued. "So what was your overall first impression?"

"Well, she definitely stirred my curiosity. She was…" Melanie hesitated. "She was a blend of opposites—simultaneously distressed yet unconcerned, impatient yet indifferent. Her intelligence is stunning, yet she claimed ignorance when asked simple questions even though it was obvious she knew the answers. It seemed to me she enjoyed the confusion she was causing. But what fascinated me most was her constant insistence on maintaining eye contact. It didn't bother me, but I imagine the intensity of her gaze could terrify others." Melanie paused, recalling the scene in her memory. "Her stare is almost numbing, and it piqued my curiosity."

"Oh yeah…I know that look," Arnold agreed with a chuckle. "It's like the holy grail of a bionic lens with a direct sightline into your soul."

"Nice analogy. She also surprised me with a captivating sense of humor. There's a puzzling contrast between her and herself—if that even makes sense."

While talking to her colleague some five thousand miles across the ocean, Melanie gazed sightlessly through the interior of her tranquil office; in her mind's eye, she pictured Kuri. "Even her physical appearance has an unusual range of striking differences," she said.

"Agreed! My wife and grown children are great fans. Before Kuri became my patient, my family and I saw her in *Freya's Fate.* Her performance was outstanding. I always believed her unusual looks on the screen or on magazine covers were due to cosmetic enhancements, but meeting her in person almost took my breath away. Not a trace of makeup; her hair was tousled when she took off her cap. She wore almost colorless, loose-fitting clothes—yet she sparkled! Her beauty is not only physical; it almost borders on mythopoeia." Arnold paused. "She's like a flower that manages to blossom in the arctic sun."

"Interesting." Her colleague's analogy drew Melanie's attention back to the screen in front of her. She scrolled and found what she was looking for. "You met her parents. Is there anything that's not in the file?"

"Well..." There was a second of silence. "Teruko found herself pregnant again at age forty-four; she and David were worried and took advantage of every available medical test. When all proved normal, they were excited—as were their older children...well, two of them, anyway."

"What's your impression of the parents?"

"They're humble despite their wealth. Their children are their highest priority. They traveled all over the country, seeking only the best medical attention, as soon as Kuri's episodes started. They were shocked and baffled when they received one devastating diagnosis after another."

Melanie scrolled to another page of medical records on her screen. "I notice suggestions for rather powerful medication when she was just thirteen."

"Teruko and David fought the idea of medicating such a young child. They only gave in because the ongoing trauma made them fear for Kuri's life. When neither the medication nor any new research brought results, they decided to stop all treatments—much to the chagrin of the specialists. Yet within a relatively short time, Kuri's episodes stopped. Her trauma and angst subsided and she began to recover; no medical explanation was given."

"She got her first role in a movie the following year. How did that happen?"

"During the years when she was in and out of hospitals and in therapy, she was tutored privately. Then Teruko and David enrolled her in Lake Shore Country Day School. Academically she shone, but socially she had difficulties blending in. When she tried out for a school play, she got the lead! The parent of one of her costars was a famous actor-turned-film-director, Hal Radis. He saw her performance, and the rest is history." Arnold suddenly accelerated his speech. "Listen, Mel. I promised to meet my family on the upper deck when we start sailing out of port—it's a tradition."

"No problem," said Melanie. "Safe travels to all of you, and we'll hook up after your return."

"Oops, hang on—one more thing, Mel. For about eight years, Kuri's episodes were completely gone, but they've recently returned with even greater intensity than before. This time she's reached out for help herself, and I'm convinced she's ready to get at the root of her fears and anxieties. Please finish reading my last report—Kuri had some new recollection and recognition and…"

Arnold stopped talking when loud horn blasts indicated the cruise ship was ready to leave port. "Hold on!" he shouted over the noise.

Then Melanie heard the voice of Louis Armstrong singing "What a Wonderful World" and envisioned a beautiful white ship sailing on unbound cornflower-blue waters. Memories of her own travels to far lands flashed by.

"Mel? You still there?"

"Yes."

"Guide Kuri to talk about her relationships, especially with her brother Ethan."

As soon as the call ended, Melanie searched her files for more information on Kuri's siblings. With growing interest, she began to read.

Chapter Three

Ethan Berger left his family's office building in a hurry, oblivious to his seething smirk. "What the fuck?" he grunted as he spotted Stan, the chauffeur, standing by the car across the busy street. "Fuck this shit," he grumbled as he dodged traffic coming from both directions on LaSalle Street.

Stan held the door open and apologized for not being able to park in front of the tall White Birch building because of ongoing street repairs. Without looking at the older man who had driven the family for over twenty years, Ethan brushed by him and threw himself into the leather seats. As the door closed, he felt himself disappear behind the dark tinted windows. He brusquely ordered Stan to make a stop at Tavern on Rush. "We're picking someone up! Then to my house! I'm in a hurry!"

Ethan was unable to control his fury and hatred over what had transpired in the past two hours.

"Son, I love you very much, but under no circumstances can I put my name to this! I've suggested before to find another venue interested in your ideas. I cannot jeopardize White Birch's dignity—not now nor ever!"

The powerful voice of his eighty-year-old father kept echoing in Ethan's mind, and he remembered how abruptly his carefully prepared ten-page presentation had been cast aside. It was no surprise that his two older siblings were in full agreement with their father; like two bobbleheads, they kept nodding in unison.

"Fucking imbeciles," Ethan snarled under his breath, sensing an unpleasant burn in his gut. *The old man's getting too long in the tooth,* he thought. *Gavin is a total pussy, and fucking Aimi remains oblivious. They don't have the capacity to understand my visions for the future! Fuck 'em all! I'll take my ideas to...* he was unable to finish the idea—what if other venture capitalist firms refused to show interest as well? How would he handle another rejection? And then he remembered his father's other announcement, and the tightness in his chest worsened.

"Last but not least, I have wonderful news to share with you," David Berger, the founder and senior partner of one of the most prominent venture capital companies, had said at the end of the two-hour meeting in his large corner office on the fifty-fifth floor.

Looking at his three children, David continued. "It gives your mother and me peace and comfort knowing that you and your families are financially secure for the next three generations. Therefore, like many other billionaires all over the world, this morning I signed a pledge to give the majority of my wealth to philanthropic causes. Part of it now, the rest after my death."

Ethan was appalled when his siblings catapulted from their chairs to embrace their father and congratulate him on what they called an extraordinary decision. Ethan had to force himself to do the same. In order to hide fury, shock, and anger, he buried his head into his father's neck; the desire to bite through the old man's carotid artery was intense.

Only moments before, his father had loudly dismissed Ethan's prototype for a virtual reality headset with 3-D-printed sex toys—cutting-edge stuff, the future of the VR porn industry. Developing the prototype alone had already cost Ethan most of his own investments, and he had been counting on the family fortune to recoup the financing.

How could he not be outraged when he heard the colossal amount of money his old man would throw into philanthropy? Ethan ignored the fact that he and his siblings had received large monetary gifts in the past and that his father's investment strategies had more than tripled these gifts that were designed to outlive Ethan and his descendants—offspring he never intended to have anyway.

He paid no attention to how his lavish lifestyle, grandiose ideas, and addictions had depleted much of his own fortune. He actually took pride in the way he managed to hide his opulent spending habits from his family. Ethan had always believed the financial flow from the immense Berger fortune was like the mighty Mississippi—never ending.

As his angry teeth almost bit into his father's neck, Ethan saw his multicolored dream of fame, wealth, and privilege disintegrate into a pile of gray ash.

When he limply disengaged from the embrace, Ethan could not look his father in the eye. "Why wasn't Kuri here today? I bet she's been told before us!"

"Kuri already is on her way to Europe, filming the last episode of *Quorum*," his father replied, still all smiles. "I wanted to bring her in via FaceTime while we were all together today, but she surprised your mother and me last night and flew in from New York. It made me very happy I could tell her in person."

"Why does she come first all the time?" Ethan's face was crimson with fury. He slapped his folded prospective in his hand. "Clearly, she never got to see my proposal!" His already dry throat made his voice sound more growly. "Let me guess...you'll continue giving to her but not to us, huh?"

"How dare you, Ethan?" Aimi had raised her voice. "All four of us have always been treated the same. You should know better."

"Yeah, shame on you," Gavin chimed in. "Aimi and I have worked our butts off at White Birch while you were missing in action! And yet...haven't you always received the same financial benefits?"

"I was missing in action? Really? What about Kuri—she's never worked a day in this firm, yet she was given more than any of us." Ethan spat his words into his older brother's face.

"Ha!" Gavin jabbed his index finger toward his younger brother. "What kind of stupid reality are you living in? Kuri is a megastar in film and television. Do you have any idea what a shitload of money she makes? She's become wealthy all on her own."

Gavin stepped closer, so close that Ethan could feel the anger radiating from his brother's chest.

"None of us were able to accomplish as much at her age, especially after all the years she underwent treatments. Can't you ever give her credit? What's wrong with you?" Gavin glared at his brother. "Seriously, Ethan, what's wrong with you?"

"You fucktard!" Ethan hissed, grabbing at his brother's shoulders, shaking him violently.

"Stop it!" Aimi forced her way between her brothers. "I can't believe what I am hearing!" Then she turned to her father. "Dad, I wish you wouldn't have to witness this! You and Mom have been beyond fair to all of us."

"Don't apologize for me, Sister Dearest!" Ethan shoved Aimi aside. "I know what I know! And I feel what I feel! For years, you and Gavin have been blind to what's going on, and look at you..." He sneered at them condescendingly. "The management of this business is like Barbarism 101, and the two of you play deaf and dumb to what's happening."

Ethan didn't realize that his father had risen from his chair until he stood tall and proud like a solid tree. From behind his desk, he eyeballed Ethan. "I thought I would never have to say this to one of my own family, but after what I just saw and heard, I am asking you to leave! Get yourself help and clear what's wrong in your head. I do not want to see you again—not until you have come to your senses and have changed your ways!"

Ethan tried to control his boiling blood, but he could tell his face was glistening with sweat; he felt moisture exuding through the pores along his breastbone when he confronted his father. "You want me to apologize, huh? What the fuck? All of you need to apologize to me! I've been the one who—"

He couldn't finish the sentence when his father, brother, and sister stared at him in silence. Nothing in their expressions gave him a clue. They stood there as if painted with neutrality, all cast from the same mold. Ethan knew he had gone too far but couldn't express regret for what he had said. "Say something!" he shouted at them. "Don't stand there like you're waiting for the fucking bus to stop. I'm not an object—I'm your flesh and blood!"

"*Enough!*" his father bellowed. He came around his desk. He took a few steps toward Ethan. He pointed his finger at the door. "You are excused…get out!"

"Fuckfuckfuckfuckfuck…" Ethan muttered to himself in the back seat of the car as his mind replayed the scene over and over.

He realized the car was slowing down before coming to a stop. Through the tinted window, he saw Irina talk to a tall, good-looking young woman behind the outside hostess stand. Despite his misery, Ethan perked up when he watched her. The stylishly short dress almost looked painted on her twenty-five-year-old chiseled body. Shoulder-length platinum-blond beach-style waves framed her pretty face, and her naturally long legs looked even longer in metallic ankle-wrap stiletto sandals. He liked when Irina dressed in a style where sophistication confronts seduction—it turned him on.

Stan walked around the car to the passenger side, prepared to open the door, but Irina paid no attention to the black custom-built Mercedes-Benz S-Class—Ethan assumed she'd expected him to pull up in his yellow McLaren 570S.

He had met Irina the previous year at a party in Lake Geneva where she and three other attractive young women were hired to bartend the event. He found out she was Ukrainian and had come to the States at the age of fifteen. Ethan did not mind that she spoke with a strong Slavic accent—it actually was another turn-on.

"Oh my gosh! I wear many hats," she had told Ethan after delivering several drinks to him and his friends. "I do bartending. I do part-time modeling. I do housesitting…and not only for dogs and cats…" Even her giggle immediately had appealed to him.

Later during the party, Irina had sought him out again. "Hey," she whispered, "you better be careful! I wasn't only one who see you and friends doing coke! The hosts here not like drugs on their premise; already I hear people talking." She handed him another dirty martini and leaned even closer. "But if you ever need good stuff, call me. I have friend with connection. I also am very discreet." She winked at him, slipped a piece of paper into his hand, and disappeared in the crowd.

Gazing through the tinted limousine's window, Ethan realized a minute or more had passed; Irina still seemed oblivious to the driver by the car.

"Dumb bitch!" he muttered. He rolled down the window, and in the same way he ordered his dog to come, he let out two short whistles. He noticed Irina's perplexed expression, but then she quickly air-kissed the other girl on both cheeks, picked up her imitation Goyard tote, and in a few long strides came toward the car.

"Oh my gosh," she said. "Who this car belongs to?"

Ethan did not bother to explain. "Did you get my stuff?"

"Huh? What stuff?"

"What the fuck? I told you three days ago! Dammit, I gave you a lot of money," he hissed.

"Oh my gosh!" Irina grinned like a Cheshire cat. "*Durnyy khlophchys'ko.*" She smirked and reached into her tote. "Silly boy! I have it." She pulled out a colorful cosmetic bag, slowly opened the zipper, and showed him a wide assortment of recreational drugs in individual packets. "I really not like you take these pills! And you know that I hate run drug errands for you, especially pick up at creepy guy. I not trust him." She looked at him pleadingly. "Why you even take this shit? You not need it."

He glared at her and motioned his head toward the driver. "Shut up," he hissed. "How do you know what I need?"

With two fingers she wiggled a small plastic packet with white powder from her tote. "This is only thing I like…and for special occasion only." She winked at him again. "Me and you? Together? Later?"

Ethan gave her another warning look after making sure Stan had his eyes on the road and not on the rearview mirror as the car entered the courtyard on East Walton.

"Well, Stan," Ethan said as he climbed out of his seat, "better hurry back to White Birch before the old man gets pissed at you, too." With a smug grin, he added, "Tell him…" He paused when he noticed Irina was still sitting in the car, bent over her phone, texting. "Get out!" he snapped at her, then turned back to Stan. "Forget it, man!" Ethan huffed. "Absolutely no need to tell my father anything!"

Every inch of Ethan's spacious condominium was meticulously designed to be perfectly balanced in tone and light intensity. He wanted the mostly open spaces to be practically minimalist, devoid of fuss and clutter, and he liked the hard beauty of marble, glass, and steel partnered with all gray and black décor. Some well-placed modern sculptures and wall hangings—all in a palette of copper, bronze, and rose gold—gave the sharply defined bachelor pad a bit of warmth.

He ordered Alexa to open the motorized window treatments, then told the virtual assistant to play Bruno Mars's *24K Magic.* Out of the corner of his eye, he watched Irina walk toward the guest quarters. It pleased him that she knew better than to throw her tote on one of the Vladimir Kagan iconic sofas and chairs, nor would she kick off her shoes on the white Thassos marble and Otta Pillarguri stone flooring. Instead, she went straight into one of the elaborate walk-in closets. Ethan followed so he could watch her strip off everything except the black lace bra, thong, and high-heeled sandals. After checking herself in the floor-length mirror, she slowly turned, posed, and gave Ethan a questioning look.

"You approve, my emperor?"

He nodded because he liked when she put her body on display for him. He watched her stride across the great room space—the clicking of her heels was overpowered by the state-of-the-art sound system with Bruno Mars singing "That's What I Like."

After pouring himself a drink at the elegantly designed, fully stacked bar, Ethan sat on the edge of the sofa, dumping the pills he'd emptied from Irina's cosmetic bag onto the Armand Jonckers coffee table. He popped a Vicodin, followed by a shot of Rey Sol Anejo. He grinned as his chocolate-brown Labrador trotted over and looked back and forth between Ethan and the pills. He patted the dog and chuckled. "This is my candy, Lolli. You get your treats later."

"Hey! You didn't wait for me," Irina pouted when she saw Ethan snorting a line of coke.

"Well, then get your ass over here," he grunted and, without looking up, snorted the second line. He sank back into the cushion and through half-closed eyes watched Irina behind the bar as she expertly combined gin and vermouth over the ice in the cocktail shaker, then stirred the mixture before straining it into two chilled crystal coupes, adding two olives for Ethan, none for her. "Get over here," he said again.

When she handed him the drink, Ethan looked at her through already glazed lustful eyes. He had just picked an ecstasy pill from the assortment on the table and held it between two fingers. "What d'ya think?" he asked hoarsely before he popped the candy-colored pill in his mouth. "Will this transfer the rest of my misery into rapture?"

"Enough! You already did two!" Irina scolded when she saw him lay out another line of cocaine. "It's my turn!" She snorted half the line in each nostril.

Ethan pulled her closer. "Take that off," he ordered, tugging on her thong while licking the powder off the tip of her nose.

Irina slithered to the floor to pleasure Ethan in the first round of what promised to be a long hot summer night.

Chapter Four

Teruko Berger had taught herself how to maintain equanimity in all situations of life, and so she had been able to sleep through what would have been a restless night for many other women. Trying not to wake up her husband, she tiptoed out of the bedroom and quietly descended the grand staircase. Walking through the foyer, she entered the kitchen, opened the large french doors, and took a deep breath, inhaling the early-morning air on this first day of summer. She watched the sun peek over the horizon and waited until the dark blue colors of the twilight sky began to fade. Lifting her hand, she allowed the soft amber, pink, and orange hues to stream through her spread fingers. She welcomed the warmth and energy of the new day.

After preparing her morning Sencha tea—always making sure she had the perfect leaf-to-water ratio—she put the Japanese iron teapot, the one adorned with two carved bronze goldfish, on a tray and took it outside. Sitting on the terrace, she poured herself a cup. When she took the first sip, she closed her eyes, trying to absorb nature's melodies. But the stillness of her mind was disturbed by the memory of her conversation the previous night with David, when he told her of the encounter with Ethan. She shared her husband's pain but also felt her son's torment—she knew his latest conflict would once again have an impact on the whole family.

Teruko was not known to complain. Rather, she reminded herself of the privileges and blessings she enjoyed during her long life. She was born in Tokyo—the only child to gifted violinists. Surrounded by music Teruko discovered her own talent at an early age and started dancing when she was four years old. Her parents' shared profession took the family to Paris where Teruko continued her studies. All of her teachers praised Teruko's perfect ballet body, the long legs and high arches; prodigious accomplishments soon followed. She won silver in her first dance competition at the age of fifteen and two years later took first prize at the Prix de Lausanne. Major prestigious companies came with their offers, but she chose New York City for her career and home.

In her musing, Teruko looked back on David's tenacity to win her heart. Whenever possible, he would sit in the first three rows of international venues. It was after her guest artist performance of *Giselle* in London when he came backstage with white roses and a diamond ring—their wedding was six months later.

Teruko decided to end her successful career at the age of twenty-six, the year Aimi was born. Gavin arrived two years later, and two years after that, the Berger family welcomed Ethan into the world.

Teruko sipped her tea while reflecting on those years of early parenthood, where love and laughter bounced off every wall in their home. The grand old house and the surrounding forty acres had been a wedding gift from David's parents; the remaining more than two hundred acres of White Birch Farm were donated to conservation and wildlife habitat. Over the years, David and Teruko remodeled and refurbished the old estate into their own dream home, as well as turning the landscape around it into a nature wonderland for their children. Teruko could still hear the excited voices of Aimi, Gavin, and Ethan when David surprised them with a zip line that wound from the high bluff of their land down to the shores of Lake Michigan. Another carved-out path brought shrieks of joy while sledding during winters. Teruko remembered the giggles and shouts as her children tried to hide from their parents in the tall prairie grass. Her own favorite moments were those when the family fed and groomed their horses and ponies after riding them for hours through nature trails. To this day, going to the stables near the main house remained Teruko's preferred activity. On most afternoons, she talked to the horses while brushing them, always bringing ample rewards of bananas and melon rinds.

Of her children, Aimi had formed the closest bond with the horses. She easily learned to master the basics of equine behavior as her riding skills and knowledge grew. Aimi not only shared her father's love for the animals—where genetics were concerned, there was no denial she was David's doppelgänger. "I'm double recessive," the little girl used to tell her friends and teachers. "Look, I have my daddy's white skin and his always-rosy cheeks; I have his green eyes and blond hair." And then, with serious emphasis, she always added, "The only thing I inherited from my mommy are my high cheekbones and a rare blood protein. But my brothers definitely have more of the dominant genes..." Teruko's memories made her laugh out loud, and reflexively, she covered her giggles with the palm of her hand.

Gavin and Ethan had inherited their mother's beautiful Asian features and thick hair. Gavin stopped growing when he was fifteen years old and to this day teased his parents that he should have been a girl with his slender build. At age sixteen he told them he was gay. He said he'd known for some time but was worried about his father's reaction. David embraced his son and said, "You never need to worry. I want to learn with you how to be accepted in what can be a cruel world." Now, twenty-four years later, Gavin was happily married and, with the help of advanced reproductive technology, he and his husband Dale had chosen an egg donor and surrogate. They were the natural fathers of four-year-old Milly and two-year-old Max.

Enjoying the warmth of the early summer morning, Teruko was

grateful that she and David were blessed with four healthy grandchildren. Aimi was given full custody of eight-year-old twin boys after a nasty divorce, and on many occasions the old house once again was filled with young happy squeals and carefree laughter.

When a cloud slowly began to move over the sun, Teruko shook her head ruefully as she recalled Ethan's abrupt change from happy-go-lucky boy to confused, angry teenager. Ethan's metamorphosis began shortly after his fifteenth birthday, right after Teruko had gone to the doctor, concerned her fatigue and tender breasts, coupled with the abrupt end of her period, might be signs of early menopause. Instead, she found out she was with child. When David and Teruko informed their children of her unexpected pregnancy, Ethan ran out of the house and hid for hours in the thicket of the bluff; he meant to worry his parents, and it worked—at least for a while. But when his schemes to draw attention to himself stopped bringing the desired results, his outbursts of anger became more frequent and his schoolwork suffered. He fell in with other troubled youngsters who, like him, had been born into a fortune and struggled to find meaning and self-respect.

Teruko and David tried to prove to Ethan that each of their children had their own special place in the family. On occasion, Ethan seemed willing to accept their reassurances, but the glimmer of hope did not last, and his downward spiral accelerated the day Kurisutaru was born.

"What a beauty! She's my definition of perfect," Dr. Morton had said. "Look at her, your baby got the best from both of you," the obstetrician added when he handed the infant to the parents.

David shed tears of joy when he held his youngest daughter for the first time. He sat next to Teruko as she lay in her hospital bed, pressing his lips to her forehead. "I hear angels sing, and I see the stars dance with the moon," he said softly. "You already have given me so much of everything…and once again you're giving me new purity of love."

That first night of being alone with their baby girl in the hospital, Teruko and David marveled about the mysterious mixture of inherited genes in their fourth child. The infant had David's blond hair and light-green eyes, but there was no doubt she had inherited Teruko's white skin, cheekbones, and nose; she had David's double eyelid and Teruko's large almond-shaped eyes.

"Look at what we made," David had whispered, not taking his eyes off the baby. "You named Aimi, and I chose the boys' names. Have you thought of a name for this little doll?"

"Yes, I want to call her Kurisutaru."

"That's a big name for a tiny girl," David had teased. "What does it mean?"

"It means crystal," she had answered twenty-two years ago.

"Kurisutaru," Teruko whispered as she refilled her teacup. "My crystal child—my Kuri."

Aimi and Gavin could not get enough of their baby sister, but Ethan hardly paid any attention to her. Craving his parents' undivided attention, he tried to fault his older siblings for countless problems that he, in reality, had initiated. When his attempts at deceit failed, as they often did, he became abusive and lashed out at the baby sister he believed had taken the love and affection that was rightfully his. In retaliation, he would purposely overheat Kuri's formula or rock the cradle so hard that the infant would crash against the sides. In another instance, he removed the netting and left his sister in the buggy outside, facing the sun. One night, he snuck into the nursery and turned the baby over on her tummy, placing a pillow close to her face. Luckily, someone was always able to prevent the worst from happening, but Ethan would vehemently deny his actions, habitually trying to shift the blame to his older siblings or the nannies.

Teruko shivered when she remembered the night when she and David had walked into the nursery and found Ethan leaning over the sleeping infant, about to run his cocaine-smeared fingertips across Kuri's lips. David had yanked his son away from the crib, shouting, "What are you doing? What are you doing? What are you doing?"

Teruko had lifted Kuri from the crib, making sure the baby was breathing, when Ethan tumbled down in front of his mother and clutched her legs. "That little freak will never love you the way I love you!" he screamed, slurring his words. "I am your favorite—you must love only me!"

He held Teruko's legs so tight, she was about to lose her balance when David caught her and the baby. He then pulled Ethan off the floor and asked again, "What are you doing?" Ethan pushed his father away and broke into hysterical laughter. Seeing no other option, David called the police to have sixteen-year-old Ethan arrested and soon afterward sent to his first rehabilitation center.

Teruko sighed, wishing she could rid herself of those painful memories. She welcomed the soft clatter and voices coming from the kitchen. Without looking she knew that Sofia, their devoted housekeeper, was about to hand David a mug of coffee. She turned around and saw him standing in the door.

"Did I interrupt your thoughts?" he asked.

She shook her head and patted the cushion on the chair next to her. "Sit, my love. I'm glad you were able to sleep. You had a rough night."

"Things looked too good for a while—I closed my eyes and ears to the inevitable."

Teruko laid her hand on David's. "I also tried to hope against hope." She squeezed gently. "We got through it before, and we'll get through it again."

David shook his head. "I wish I could be that optimistic. Ethan is in a bad place right now. The prospect of his inheritance has always made him oblivious to his simmering dysfunction. I found out that he's depleted most of his own investments and now is trying to contest one of the trusts."

"When did you become aware of this?"

"Yesterday, right after I asked him to leave my office. He'll have to file a lawsuit in the probate court. Unfortunately for him, he'll have no legal grounds to stand on."

Teruko sighed again. "I still keep asking myself what and why things went so wrong with our beautiful boy. Remember how he captivated everybody with his wit and sense of humor? He had so much going for him until..."

"Yes, our sweet little boy could charm a vulture of its carcass," David said wistfully. "You and I tried so hard to keep him focused on the love that surrounded him, but in his troubled mind, he built up this toxic resentment against all of us...mostly Kuri."

"Our Ethan—so forlorn, so unhappy. Envy is due to low self-esteem and lack of confidence. I'm sure he's using again. What can we do?"

"This time we'll wait. Hopefully he'll be able to clear his head and come to his senses. When he does, we'll help him through this again. But if he continues to be stubborn, he'll have to crash emotionally, financially, and mentally by himself. I won't stop him—this time he needs to hit rock bottom."

"I hurt so much when I imagine Ethan's torment. But in my own youth, I was in great emotional and physical pain from endless hours of practice and rehearsals. Things got so bad, I threw my pointe shoes in the garbage and for days refused to eat and drink. I stayed in bed and cried; I was ready to give up dancing forever. My parents chose not to pity me—they practically ignored me. My father's words, 'Your breakdown may be your breakthrough,' made me think. His wisdom gave me a new vitality and restored my enthusiasm." Teruko squeezed David's hand again. "Let's hope for Ethan's breakthrough."

They heard the ringing on the computer in the kitchen and looked at each other.

"Maybe it's Ethan?" There was a hopeful glimmer in Teruko's eyes.

Then they heard Sofia's excited voice. "Mrs. Berger! Mr. Berger! Quick. Your computer is ringing. I see Kuri's name on the screen."

Chapter Five

Kuri looked at herself on the screen of her laptop and adjusted her new hairstyle while waiting for FaceTime to connect with her parents. She heard her mother's voice before she saw her face; in the background her father came slowly toward the computer. She smiled broadly when both of their beaming faces greeted her.

"Hey, you guys. Good morning!"

"What a sweet surprise," her mother said, laughing. "Your father and I were outside. It's such a beautiful summer morning, and now you bring us more sunshine."

"How are you, darling?" Her father's shining eyes reflected joy. "It's only four in the afternoon in Germany. How come you have time to call?"

"We started shooting at four thirty this morning, Daddy. I just got back to the hotel and now have a few hours to rest before heading back for reaction shots."

"Filming at night again?"

"Yeah, it's complicated, Daddy. This last episode of *Quorum* is over-the-top complex."

"If you hadn't filled us in, we would've never understood the previous seasons of this futuristic society where the human brain is the only natural organ, commanding and controlling a mostly bionic body. Maybe we're getting too old to comprehend this advanced and menacing age where humans and machines merge."

"It's highly advanced technology but the theory behind it is really cool. In *Quorum*, there's an underlying realism that combines the past, the now, and the future—it's all about looking at the origin and destiny of life from different angles."

"So... this being the season finale, will your cyborg character survive?" Teruko asked.

"Tsk, tsk, tsk." Kuri grinned sheepishly, waving her finger. "Even though FaceTime is supposed to be secure and encrypted... I still cannot tell you."

"Where are you staying in Munich?"

"We're not in Munich—we're about twenty kilometers away, close to Dachau. Our crew took over this entire hotel called *Bergfrieden*. It's—"

"Dachau?" There was notable surprise in her father's voice. "That's a former Nazi concentration camp. You're filming there?"

"Yes and no; the autobahn is nearby and that's where we're shooting a wild car chase with aerial and stunt shots, always exiting the autobahn at the 'Dachau' sign. The former Nazi prison camp does have an incidental consequence and impact in the script." She paused. "In what little free time I have, I find myself drawn to reading more and more on what happened in Germany decades ago." She paused again. "What's baffling to me is that parts of the monstrosities seem oddly familiar, especially what happened in Dachau."

"Familiar? Perhaps when you were younger, you overheard me talk about your great-uncle Alfred. He was with the US Seventh Army's Forty-Fifth Infantry Division, which liberated Dachau on April 29 in 1945."

"I have a question for you, Dad. The name Berger... is there a possibility of Jewish ancestry in our family?"

Kuri saw her father furrow his brow, his eyes squinting as he thought. "Not that I'm aware of," he said. "Both of my parents were born in the United States. My father's ancestry is German—Lutheran as far as they go back. My mother's family came from Sweden; they were agnostics." He shrugged.

"The reason for my asking is because Diego, our location assistant's last name is Berger too. He's from Argentina, and he told me about his family—they are Ashkenazi Jews."

"Gavin always talks about wanting to do a genealogy on our family. I'll tell him of your interest; maybe it'll give him the needed nudge to get going."

"You do that, Daddy. But in the meantime, I'll do some unearthing of my own while I'm here."

"Be careful! If the paparazzi and fans are as intrusive in Germany as they've been in the other places you've been filming..."

"Don't worry, Mom. The photographers and fans are already camped out near the hotel, but whenever I need privacy, I have a way to trick them. Everything's fine and I—" The buzzing sound from Kuri's phone made her stop in midsentence. She looked away from the camera to read the text message.

"Mom, Dad, sorry. I had a wardrobe malfunction earlier, and now they need me for a fitting. I'll call you tomorrow or the next day."

Chapter Six

She catapulted from the car as it raced down the autobahn, just before it took a direct hit from the drone that divebombed from above and exploded. Taking long, elegant steps, she quickly took position in a cornfield close to the exit ramp. She crouched and pulled out the high-tech laser weapon attached to her skintight uniform and aimed. She waited for the smoke and the shower of drone-debris to subside. When she could see the sky again, she stood and brushed the dust and dirt off her glossy midnight-blue sci-fi combat fatigue. She parted the tall green stalks, searching for the blue exit sign for Ausfahrt Dachau-Fürstenfeldbruck. Assuming a regal pose, she let out a mirthless laugh. "Veni, vidi, vici," she sneered, then turned and strode decisively through the field; the thicket of dark green leaves softly waved their tassels in the silky summer breeze. Like the ghosts of baseball players in *Field of Dreams*, she disappeared between the rows of corn.

"Cut!" John Gibson, the director, ran to her. "Perfect!" He beamed. "I've said it before, this character was tailor-made for you, Kuri. You nail every scene."

Later, when the French wardrobe stylist drove her back to

the hotel, she hovered low across the back seat. "*Merci beaucoup*, Marcel," she said, grateful he had dodged a bunch of reporters.

"*Pas de problème*, but I better drop you by the back entrance," he muttered, keeping an eye on three paparazzi trailing behind them on motorcycles. "Stay down for another moment," Marcel said, and lowered the window. "*Hallo, junger Mann*," he called out. Then, in his lightly accented German, he proceeded to ask the food delivery man to block the driveway with the truck.

Kuri's disappearance into the hotel went as smoothly as the scenes they had filmed all morning. "You did it again, Marcel," she said as she high-fived him. "Can I borrow you one more time today? In, let's say, thirty minutes?" She told him of her afternoon plans and how she needed to be incognito.

"Sure," he said. "Let's pull our womb-mate trick again."

Thirty minutes later Marcel, dressed in tan cargo pants and white T-shirt under a dark hooded vest, knocked on Kuri's suite.

Having donned the same outfit as the wardrobe stylist, she laughed when she opened the door.

"Hello, Slick!" she said.

"Well, hey there, Slim!"

They pulled their faces deep into their hoodies and adjusted their aviator sunglasses.

Marcel left the hotel by himself, stood by the car, and talked to the driver. "I'll be right back," he shouted as he walked back into the hotel. He purposely looked at the photographers and star-struck autograph hunters crowded around the hotel's front doors, but nobody seemed interested in him. Three minutes later, Kuri stepped out and quickly hopped into the car. Since she and Marcel were almost the same height and lean body shape, the throng once again was fooled by their deception, as it had been several times over the last few days.

"I know where to go—Marcel gave me the directions," said the driver. "It's not far."

Through the car's tinted windows, Kuri stared at the houses on cobblestone streets as they drove through a small Bavarian town.

She saw a woman sweep her sidewalk and two men engrossed in a conversation; she saw a black cat run across the street and jump over a picket fence; she saw two German shepherds chase each other—the whole scene seemed ghostlike to her. She shuddered, blinked, and rubbed her eyes. *This is ridiculous,* she thought of her sudden hesitancy to continue to her destination. She blamed the uncomfortable feeling on fatigue.

"We're here," said the driver. "Sorry, Miss Berger, but cars can't go any further. You have to walk to the entrance." He turned around to look at Kuri when he apologized. "When should I come and get you again?"

She exhaled and managed to smile at the driver. "I don't know yet. I will call you."

Chapter Seven

She stood, looked around, and spotted a few people ahead of her who turned left and disappeared out of sight. She watched a car drive by and saw two cyclists pedaling in the opposite direction; she heard their laughter as they passed.

She saw a tall, handsome man—she guessed him to be her age, perhaps a few years older—park his motorcycle on the other side of the road. He released a backpack from the cycle, slung it over his shoulder, and crossed the street. "Hallo!" he called out. His voice was deep, his smile genial. Kuri only nodded in response, quickly lowering her head and pretending to text. She watched him walk toward the entrance with unflinching determination.

For a fleeting moment, there was silence. Then a school bus pulled up right behind her and came to a stop. Soon the stillness was interrupted by young voices. Kuri readjusted her hoodie, lowered her head, and began to walk. The group of youngsters, led by two adults, passed by her. She sensed some of the teenagers glimpsing at her; she hoped they were seeing a skinny young man bent over his cell phone. She heard them speak in a foreign language, possibly Swedish or Danish—definitely not German. She followed their voices but stopped as soon as she had made the turn that everyone else had made.

An unexpected panic gripped her when she looked straight ahead at the wrought-iron gate with the infamous slogan *ARBEIT MACHT FREI* spelled out below the archway. "Work sets you free," Kuri whispered. The night before, she had spent hours on her laptop, reading more about Dachau and other Nazi concentration camps, watching and listening to interviews with Holocaust survivors. She shivered despite the warmth of the summer day. She stood, as if frozen to the ground, and stared at the gate.

"Hi, are you part of the group from Texas?" A middle-aged man suddenly stood next to her, smiling broadly, extending his hand. "I am John Wexler, your tour guide."

She shook her head and lowered her voice. "I'm not part of a tour—I'm by myself."

The man apologized and walked toward a new group of arriving visitors.

The crunching of stones beneath her shoes seemed to echo in her ears as she slowly made her way down the gravel path toward the gate. As everything she had learned about the atrocities of the past ricocheted through her head, she could sense something else, something familiar and deeper, something much darker. Unable to shake loose of these obscure thoughts, she walked through the gate, only to become overwhelmed by her anxiety. Feeling nauseous and dizzy, she leaned against the guardhouse wall. She saw the young man with the backpack look at her and hoped he didn't notice her wobble. Kuri concentrated on her breathing techniques until she had regained her inner equilibrium and was able to walk again.

"We are now in the former roll-call area where prisoners were counted each morning and evening." Kuri heard the solemn voice of the man who had introduced himself as Jerry Wexler. He stood with a group of five people. "Around the camp was a four-meter-wide ditch with water flowing through it, and the barbed wire you see all around the camp was electrified. Nobody could escape. The few who tried were shot." The guide continued to tell the small group that the prisoners could see the faces of the patrols under their steel helmets in the guard towers; their machine gun barrels pointed through the windows day and night, ready to kill. As the tour group walked by Kuri, she heard the guide tell them, "We'll cross this area again on our way to the reconstructed barracks. Right now, please follow me into the main exhibit."

Dazed, Kuri followed the group into the former maintenance building, now the museum where every room gave testimony to the monstrous evil of the dehumanizing system the SS had created here.

Like a robot she walked from exhibit to exhibit, unaware of the visitors around her. She grew oblivious to the passage of time as her thoughts were flooded by the horrors perpetrated against the Romani, the gays, the disabled, the ethnic Poles, the political dissidents, and above all, the Jews. Her subconscious produced faces and voices that gave this nightmare even more weight in her mind. She felt as if she, too, had been stripped of her belongings and of her dignity; she, too, was forced into hard labor, starved, tortured, and subjected to unspeakable medical experiments. More than thirty thousand lives, she recalled, had been taken on these grounds, victims of a horrific ideology.

A glistening stream of tears pearled from her unblinking eyes. As she mechanically wiped her cheeks with either the back of her palm or the fabric of her hoodie, she felt a sudden onset of dizziness and cold. Her breathing became shallow. *Breathe!* she told herself. *Relax! Breathe!* Her legs wobbled, and she had to steady herself alongside the walls as she walked out of the building.

Though shaded by sunglasses, Kuri squinted into the sunlight, welcoming the warmth that banished the cold running through her. Her breathing returned to normal and, despite feeling drained of energy, she willed herself to press on.

Crossing the ominous roll-call ground again, she saw the young man with the backpack enter one of the two reconstructed barracks and decided to head in that direction.

As soon as she stepped onto the bare wood floor inside the

barrack, the terrible sounds and visions rose up in her mind once more. It felt as if these weren't just her imagination but the souls of prisoners themselves desperate to tell her of their suffering. Was it her creative power, or could she actually see their faces, hear them whisper to her? *Stop it,* she ordered herself, blaming these vivid, hallucinatory thoughts on the resourceful drive she called upon to bring life to her acting performances. *Stop it!*

She reluctantly stepped aside to allow another group of visitors to enter. Once again, it was Jerry Wexler's group. She saw him pointing out two areas where doors used to separate the toilets and washbasins.

"There were strict orders and laws requiring cleanliness." Wexler's voice was low. "Prisoners had to remove their shoes before entering and then they were commanded to keep the barracks spotless at all times. After the Kristallnacht in November 1938, things changed rapidly. Almost eleven thousand Jews were brought here." The guide paused. When he continued, his voice was barely audible. "By 1942 more than twelve thousand prisoners were ordered to live in thirty-four barracks that were designed for less than six thousand."

Kuri saw Jerry Wexler run his hand over one of the three-tiered bunk beds. "Each small bunk was meant for one person to sleep, but two to three were forced to crowd together. It wasn't unusual to lie between one fellow prisoner with high fever and another suffering from diphtheria or typhus. Imagine being grateful for someone else's fever to keep you warm during the night…only to wake up in the morning lying next to a cold, lifeless body."

The room blurred as ghostlike images of people appeared in Kuri's field of vision, their voices steadily drowning out Wexler's speech. Her head began to spin, she felt her knees weaken. As she collapsed, she sensed someone catching her; then everything went black.

Chapter Eight

Adam heard a soft, low cry and saw the slim young man next to him wobble. He caught the stranger just before he fell onto the barrack's wood floor.

Other concerned visitors offered help.

"I got him," he assured the group. "I'll take him outside. I'm a doctor."

He saw a shady spot under a tree nearby and gently placed the limp body on its back. With his bulky backpack, Adam elevated the youth's legs and unzipped the vest to made sure there wasn't a restricting belt or tight pants that needed loosening. He gasped when he saw the breasts protruding under the white T-shirt. "A girl!" he murmured, quickly closing the vest again. He studied her face and realized he hadn't noticed the hood slipping off, exposing her white-blond hair with its fluorescent streaks of midnight blue and turquoise. As he took her pulse, he heard her call out in a small, hoarse voice.

"It's so cold, so dark. Where are you?" Her right arm moved through the air, her hand clutching and searching for something. "It's dark! Where are you?"

"I am here!" He took her hand. "I am here!"

The girl's eyes opened wide; a mix of confusion and wonder intensified the gleam in her emerald-green eyes. "No!" She shook her head. "No…it's not…" She tried to sit up. "Where am I? Who are you?"

"Please don't sit up. You fainted. You are safe now. Keep your head down a little longer. I am a doctor. My name is Adam Gold."

He pulled a bottle of mineral water from his backpack. "Try to drink a little. Your pulse is rapid—you may be dehydrated."

"Thank you." She nodded and took a few sips, never breaking eye contact with him.

"When was the last time you ate something?" He pulled a protein bar from his backpack.

"Thank you," she said again, gratefully taking the bar. "I ate…but it was early this morning. It's been a busy day."

He helped her lean against the tree and watched as she took the first bite. "I think you'll feel better once you finish that and have some more water—you can keep the bottle; I have another one."

Suddenly, she reached for the sunglasses lying next to her and pulled the hoodie back over her head.

"Good! I see the boy is feeling better," a woman from the Texas group said as she walked toward them. "Do you need any help?"

"We'll be okay. Thanks," Adam said, and waited until the group moved away. "I don't mean to pry, but are you hiding from someone?"

"Not hiding," she said. "I just don't want to be recognized—and it seems to work."

His puzzled face made her smile. "I'm an actor. We're filming a TV series nearby. I'm trying not to draw attention, especially not here."

He tilted his head and leaned in to consider her more closely. "Well," he exclaimed, his eyes brightening with sudden recognition. "What do you know? You're Kuri Berger!" He shook his head, and an amused expression spread over his face. "That explains the roads near Hebertshausen being blocked and so many people standing around there yesterday. I had to take a less-scenic detour to my destination."

"Try to avoid that area tomorrow—we'll be back there most of the day." She paused and then added with a twinkle in her eye, "Unless you want to do a medical follow-up. In that case, I'll make sure they let you through."

He saw that she was ready to stand and offered his hand. "You feel okay now?" He tenderly kept his hand on her arm, realizing his desire to touch her was stronger than the reflexive urge to help.

"I'm good again. Sorry for causing concern. I'm grateful for your help."

"If you drove here, it may not be safe…"

"I didn't. I'll call someone to pick me up—later, though, when I'm done visiting this site."

"Are you sure you can keep going?"

"I'll be okay. I definitely want to finish what I came here for."

Adam adjusted his backpack. "If you allow me, I'll go with you, just in case. I've been here before, should you have questions or—"

"Yes!" she interrupted eagerly, "that would be very helpful."

They walked side by side without talking until Adam stopped in the middle of the main camp road and quietly explained that the rows and rows of large gravel beds marked the site of thirty-four of the former barracks.

"They forced prisoners to construct the barracks," Adam said. "Each building was called a block; most of them were used to house the prisoners." He signaled to various areas, explaining which one was used as a camp canteen, library, infirmary, prison, and morgue. "Over there"—he directed Kuri's attention to another location—"were punishment blocks, separated from the others by barbed wire."

Adam noticed she had removed her sunglasses and tucked them into her vest. He wondered if she would take off the hood as well. Instead, she pulled it closer into her face. "Feel free to ask any questions," he said in a low tone.

"I read that when the concentration camp was in operation,

there actually were flower beds on the sides of each barrack. Why would the Nazis try to beautify the horror they purposely created?"

Adam shrugged. "Nothing that took place here will ever make sense! Whenever I visit sites like this, I'm overcome by the dark shadow that fell on this earth from the evil of the Holocaust." He took off his backpack and removed a small pouch filled with stones. "I brought these to pay honor to the memory of those who died here."

"I noticed a few other people place small stones on the gravel beds. Why?"

"I don't know how the tradition got started, but there are a number of different stories. Personally, I like the one that explains how most things fade, but that stones, like souls, endure forever."

Kuri's eyes grew wide and in a thin voice she asked, "Would you share one or two with me, please?"

Adam took a few stones from the pouch and laid them into the palm of her hand. His fingers gently closed hers over the pebbles. For a fraction of a second, a dynamic form of energy seemed to fuse their hands together. When he heard her sharp inhale, he released her fist, wondering if his touch had made her uncomfortable.

Instead, her eyes locked onto his like magnets, and without warning, he was overpowered by the mental image of his inner being crossing a bridge to meet her.

"Oh..." Kuri blinked twice. "Oh." She breathed and slowly opened her fist. She only broke the eye contact to look at the stones, then softly excused herself to walk between two of the gravel beds. Adam watched her stop by a small mound to place her stones on it, one at a time, allowing the palm of her hand to rest on the gravel. When she remained in that position, it seemed to Adam as if she was having her own solemn dialogue with the dead.

Without taking his eyes off her, he moved between another two rows of gravel beds. Eventually he stooped down, pulled a rock from his pocket, and added it to the gravel. He lowered his eyes and, for a few moments, the world around him faded away.

As soon as he allowed himself to rise, his eyes were drawn to her as if by a powerful magnet. He couldn't understand this instant connection he felt with her. For years he had sensed an unexplainable constant existence of someone absent, and now, having met her, he wanted to stay in her presence.

"Impossible," he whispered. He shook his head as if trying to obliterate a perplexing concept. "It simply is impossible."

Chapter Nine

The following morning, Kuri was suspended above the Bavarian countryside, hanging from a giant crane. Between takes, she shielded her eyes from the sun as she scanned the roads for Adam and his motorcycle. She had invited him to join her at the location, but she didn't see any sign of him.

While she waited for the crew to prepare for the next scene, her thoughts took her back to the previous day, walking with Adam through the camp; she recalled everything he had told her about the rifle range, the gas chambers, and the crematoriums where so many innocent lives had been savagely taken. Adam's encyclopedic knowledge about World War II and the Nazi-SS atrocities supplied her with a surprising awareness; not that she knew all these facts already, but perplexingly, she somehow felt intuitively familiar with them. She hadn't shared that sensation with Adam, though. When she was younger, nobody had been able to grasp the complexity and profundity of her feelings and thoughts; she had learned the hard way to keep them to herself.

"What does that mean?" she had asked Adam when he recited a portion of the Torah in Hebrew while they laid some more of his stones on the grounds of the prison camp that forever was soiled with blood.

"The soul of man is God's candle," he had answered, and she remembered seeing sadness in his hazel eyes when he said, "I don't know your beliefs, but I always imagine a life in the twinkling dance of a candle's flame. We all need air to live; a flame needs air to glow. Most candles can shine strong and bright, but some, still in the bright beauty of their dance, are extinguished by evil." Recalling the sorrow in Adam's warm eyes made Kuri shiver even as she swayed in the warm sunshine, still wired up to the crane, waiting to shoot the next dynamic scene.

"Kuri? You okay? You ready?" The voice coming through her wireless earpiece snapped her back to the present. She gave a thumbs-up and repositioned herself horizontally. A giant wind machine, mimicking the power of natural turbulence, roared into life ahead of her.

"Action!"

In the skintight silver and burgundy costume that matched the new colors running through her hair, she stretched out her arm like Superman and flew into the man-made wind toward the distant snowcapped Alps.

Later, when the sun already hung lower in the sky—still blinding, but not ready to dip behind the mountains—Kuri returned to the hotel. She wondered if she would find a message from Adam. In addition to inviting him to the *Quorum* set, she'd suggested they could meet for dinner.

I really want to see him again, she thought as she stepped out of the shower and reached for a towel. She looked in the mirror and saw herself blush. She pointed an index finger at herself. "What are you doing?" She giggled. "Are you falling for him?"

The digital alarm clock on the nightstand showed 20:18 when the phone rang.

"Miss Berger? You have a guest waiting in the lobby. Are you expecting Herr Adam Gold?" the receptionist asked hesitantly.

Kuri's heartbeat quickened. "Thank you, yes. I'll be downstairs in a few minutes." She put on her favorite distressed denim jeans and chose a white silk camisole to go with it. She applied some pink lip gloss and quickly tousled her hair, giving the long choppy bob a somewhat messy look. On her way out, she slipped into her Giuseppe Zanotti sandals and grabbed a white linen jacket. Passing the full-length mirror, she nodded approvingly at her reflection.

She immediately recognized him by his height and wavy dark hair. He was leaning against a wood column, watching the people circulating around him in the small, crowded lobby.

"I'm glad you came!" She extended a hand out to him.

"You look…radiant! Obviously feeling better." He held her hand. "I wasn't sure you'd actually see me." He glimpsed at the crowd in the lobby. "It's busy here. Can I take you out for dinner? I know of a good restaurant not too far from here. Quiet, too."

"No, no," she protested. "I invited you! Plus, I'd prefer to stay in the hotel. It's more private—no fans, no photographers." She waved a hand at the people around them. "These are all cast and crew—they won't bother us."

Kuri led the way into the hotel's restaurant, Schnitzel Stube, introducing Adam to friends so she wouldn't have to field questions from them later. She liked how easily Adam seemed to blend in with her colleagues, maintaining his composure even after recognizing some of the other well-known actors who costarred in *Quorum* with her.

"Quite a colorful collection of people," Adam whispered, running the palm of his hand over his hair as they approached an empty table.

Kuri grinned and raked fingers through her silver hair with fluorescent burgundy streaks, the same equally vibrant coloring as some of the other cast members'. "Are you talking about our rainbow heads?" She leaned closer and elbowed him slightly. "These dazzling dye jobs are an essential part of our characters, but they get us a lot of attention…offscreen as well." She grimaced, rolling her eyes. "I can't wait to go back to my natural hair color again when we're done shooting."

They ordered a Bavarian wheat beer and looked at the menu.

Kuri recommended the restaurant's specialty. "It's Schnitzel Stube!" she exclaimed. "You have to try the schnitzel!"

For the next couple of hours, Kuri asked question after question. Of course, she wanted to learn more about Adam, but she also liked looking at this attractive man and listening to his deep, calm voice.

He was thirty years old, an only child raised in Boston. His father taught at Harvard, and his mother worked as a nurse in the city's children's hospital.

"I got lucky with my parents. I am who I am because of their selfless devotion and unconditional love from the moment they adopted me a week after I was born."

His birth mother had concealed the identity of his biological father and then overdosed on drugs and died soon after giving birth to Adam. "Years later, when I was given her name, I traveled to Iceland to search for relatives. But wherever I looked, a Maja Haraldsdóttir never seemed to exist; my biological mother remains an enigma," he said between bites of schnitzel.

Kuri frowned as she put her knife and fork on the plate and pushed it away. "Perhaps she changed her name." She leaned closer. "Have you thought of taking an AncestryDNA test?"

He nodded. "Yep. I discovered that I am of Jewish descent from my paternal line, but so far no match was found to anyone I may correspond genetically to." Adam folded his napkin and placed it on the emptied plate. "My adoptive father is Jewish as well, and my adoptive mother comes from Denmark." He rested his hands on the table and met her eyes. "Serendipity at its best."

Kuri liked how relaxed Adam was in allowing her into his life. She respected his frankness and did not want him to stop talking.

"Please go on," she said.

"Enough about me. I'd like to hear about your life away from cameras and lights."

She rolled her eyes. "I'm sure you know about my childhood struggles—after all, my private life has been dissected in the media over and over again."

"I actually know very little about you. I don't have much time for social media. However, I'm not a social recluse. And even though I may not be up on the latest in film and television, I see the advertisements and magazine covers. That's why I recognized you yesterday."

"You told me you're a doctor and that your reading material revolves around your work. What's your specialty?"

"I'm a psychiatrist."

"Really?" She grinned. "I never seem to be able to get away from shrinks—no offense." She laughed when she saw him leaning forward. "Oh, you're curious? Well... let me fill you in."

She gave an abbreviated overview of the problems that had tormented her during her childhood. "Except for my family and my nanny, everybody believed I had a serious mental illness." She talked about the treatments that never helped, as well as the sudden recovery that left her doctors baffled. Just when she was telling Adam about her first role in a school play, she paused to take a sip of beer. "Yeech, warm beer tastes bitter." She looked at his empty glass. "Would you like another cold one?"

Instead, they decided on coffee, accompanied by house-baked warm *apfelstrudel*.

"I don't mean to pry," Adam said, "but how did you overcome your anxieties and fears?"

Kuri's eyes darted toward the ceiling. "I did, and I didn't. For years, I was pretty free from all that stuff and then... poof... it recently came back. But I'm older now, and whenever I experience these inexplicable dreams and visions, I have found effective ways to deal with these apparitions when they strike."

"So, you feel you don't need therapy anymore?"

"I didn't say that. As a matter of fact, I started with a new therapist. She's supposed to be an expert in hypnotherapy." A vague smile formed on her lips. "I'm so ready to dive deeper; I must find out what's lying on the bottom of my mind's reservoir."

For a moment there was silence at the table.

"Hypnotherapy did help me," Adam said finally.

"You? Why?"

"That's a too-long-and-complicated story," he said hurriedly. "Perhaps we can talk about it another time—on our next date."

"Is this a date?" she blurted, feeling her heart gallop. She plunged forward, not waiting for his reply. "I normally don't like dates, especially not those the studio sets up when I have to wear clothes I don't like and have to wear too much makeup." She looked at her distressed jeans and wiped her hand over her cheeks. "No makeup, simple and comfortable clothes... this is how I like to be. Meet the real Kuri Berger!" She paused, then nodded. "But, yes, I really would like to see you again."

When she realized they were the only guests left in the restaurant, she said, "I could sit here all night and continue talking, but I have to get up at five o'clock. We're changing locations—to a lake called Ammersee." She had inched closer to Adam during the course of the evening, so close she could detect his body heat. "Maybe you have time and can stop by?"

Adam took her hand. "I wish I could; I only have one day left to find what I came here for. My flight home leaves tomorrow night."

"What are you trying to find in this area?"

"It's complicated." He shifted in his seat. "I must make more progress in my search before I feel comfortable talking about it."

Holding hands, they walked under starlit skies, surprised by the crisp breeze of the night. Kuri sank into the warmth of his arms when he pulled her close. As soon as his forehead leaned onto hers, obscure images flashed through her like electrical impulses trying to fuse together. When their lips touched, she experienced an unknown passion—mysteriously familiar in this moment of déjà-vu.

Chapter Ten

Adam took his Breitling watch off the nightstand and fastened it around his wrist. It was 5:37 a.m. He stretched and then sank back into the fluffy goose-down pillow. It had been a restless night ever since he'd gotten back from Kuri's hotel, and his few moments of sleep had been filled with troubling dreams. When he heard a rooster crow somewhere in the faint predawn light, Adam yawned and stretched again. Through the open window, he watched the Bavarian countryside change from night to day. A single bird began his early-morning song, soon followed by a chorus of others, each one signaling their strength and vitality. In the distance, livestock greeted the new day, and as soon as the first rays of sunlight filtered into the room, Adam heard hushed voices and the clatter of dishes near his open window; he knew the proprietors of the pension at which he was staying already were setting the breakfast tables for their guests.

He showered and got dressed, suddenly feeling strangely energized. He hoped it was a sign that, on this last day in Germany, he might finally succeed in his search.

For the past five days, he had rented a room in Gasthaus Huber, the German version of a bed-and-breakfast. On his way out to the terrace, he saw Frau Huber working in the kitchen. He greeted her and, in his broken German, asked if he could leave his packed bags at the reception area until later in the afternoon.

"*Ja, freili.*" Frau Huber nodded and wiped her hands on the apron before she shook his hand.

The Hubers had been more than generous in their hospitality. Adam had rented a VW Golf from Europcar at the Munich airport but was able to return the automobile to the rental agency in Dachau soon after his arrival at the Gasthaus when the Hubers offered their son's motorcycle for Adam's use. "It just sits there," Herr Huber had said, explaining that their son was on a biking trip through Vietnam.

Adam sat on the terrace, cupping a mug of coffee in his hands, enjoying the quietude. None of the other guests had come down from their rooms at this early-morning hour.

When he watched the white cirrus clouds high above him change shape as the wind moved them across the sky, his thoughts returned to the remarkable experiences of the last two days. The moment Kuri had opened her eyes under the tree at the Dachau concentration camp memorial site, he sensed a powerful familiarity—it was as if he had met her before, and not because he recognized her as an international film star.

The previous night, when Kuri told him of her recurring childhood nightmares, filled with troubled voices, he had merely listened, without offering any perspective of his own. When she talked about the visions that filled her with terror and anxieties, he did not question what she had seen and heard. His only suggestion had been that she continue with her new therapist and give the possible benefits of hypnosis a try.

He didn't like feeling dishonest, but he didn't want to risk derailing his relationship with Kuri before it was given a chance to progress. That's why he had kept silent about how he, too, once had been afflicted by awful dreams until a trip to South Asia transformed his life.

For years Adam had suffered through repeated dreams where he was dragged away from those he loved by men in uniforms. Certain scenes fixed themselves in his brain as he kept seeing a young girl with blond hair who he felt might be a sister or another close relative. The girl sang in German, the same few lines, over and over. Adam knew just enough German to make out enough of the words that he could search online and discovered he was hearing a song that had been popular in 1938.

Roter Mohn, warum welkst du denn schon?
Wie mein Herz sollst du glüh'n und feurig loh'n.
Roter Mohn, den der Liebste mir gab,
Welkst du weil ich ihn schon verloren hab?
Rot wie Blut, voller Pracht, warst du noch gestern erblüht,
Aber schon über Nacht ist deine Schönheit verblüht.
Roter Mohn warum welkst du denn schon,
Wie mein Herz sollst du glüh'n und feurig loh'n...
(Red Poppy, why are you wilting so soon?
When, with my fiery heart, you could be in tune.
Red Poppy blossoms for me from my hon,
Are you wilting now because he left and is gone?
Red like blood, yesterday still full of splendor
But to the night did your beauty surrender.
Red Poppy, why are you wilting so soon
When, with my fiery heart, you could be in tune...)

Among his other reoccurring night terrors, he was beaten and kicked by uniformed guards, he saw himself among dead people, he sensed starvation and thirst. He kept seeing a gate with a German inscription, and he felt himself walking under that gate again and again. But the most vivid of these visions was an image of a farmhouse and a barn. Behind the house was a meadow. There was a bridge over a brook and a majestic tree. He was not alone—a girl was with him, a girl who, he somehow sensed, had captured his heart. In his dreams, he could see her pretty face, framed by red ringlets of hair. He would hear her voice. "I can't see you. It's dark. Where are you?" And he would always answer, "I am here."

Adam had written down every detail he remembered from these dreams. He also meticulously drew the images, hoping one day to make sense of it all.

During his graduate studies at Harvard he had befriended Sanjay Argawal, another psychiatry major. Sanjay told Adam how he had suffered from burdening anxieties until a therapist in his native India was able to use hypnosis to lead him to a dramatic revelation. Adam found the details confusing at first, but Sanjay told him that in mostly Hindu India, the belief in karma and past lives was as old as time itself.

Shortly after their graduation, Adam visited Sanjay in Mumbai and wound up enrolling in classes at the Institute of Life, where he learned how phobias, physical illnesses, depression, and anxieties found full resolution as the cause was healed from beyond the current life. The more he discovered about the mind, body, and soul through past life regression therapy, the more he trusted that these amazing techniques would eventually cure him as well.

It was eight months into his studies when Adam experienced his first past life regression. Through the guidance of Darshita Khatri, his mentor and guru, the visions he could never convince himself were simply products of his overactive imagination suddenly gained new meaning. Even though Adam knew the existence of reincarnation was not scientifically accepted, Darshita Khatri helped him understand the apparitions as moments where his soul experienced life in another human body decades before him.

Sitting on the terrace of the Gasthaus Huber in Bavaria, Adam rubbed his hand over his light stubble, remembering an explanation by the Swiss psychotherapist Carl Jung: "We are all inheritors of a collective mythology."

"*Guten Appetit,*" said Frau Huber, placing a tray filled with farm-fresh scrambled eggs, cold cuts, cheeses, and warm bread rolls in front of him.

Adam wasn't hungry, but he didn't have the heart to disappoint

Frau Huber, who smiled broadly, hands on her wide hips, waiting for him to dig in.

"*Schmeckt's?*" she asked.

"*Ausgezeichnet!* Delicious as always, Frau Huber."

Two other guests stepped onto the terrace, and Frau Huber excused herself in order to assist the elderly couple.

As soon as Adam finished his breakfast, he made sure he had everything in his backpack. He walked around the house and got onto the motorcycle. Even though he knew the map by heart, he took it out, unfolded it, and looked at it again, scanning for areas that had not been crossed out. "Forget it," he told himself, shook his head, and folded the map away. "Today I'll follow my instincts." He turned the key in the ignition and pressed the start button. As soon as the engine ran at a fast idle, he said, "Let's do it!"

He headed south, even though he already had searched the areas between Dachau's former subcamps Allach and Pasing, as well as Würmtal and Starnberg. He had also explored the regions between Wolfratshausen and Bad Tölz and traveled as far as Tegernsee. In each community, he had gone to the libraries and archives to do his research but never came close to finding the farmhouse, the bridge over a stream, or the old tree. He had drawn those images from his dreams and later had a professional artist work from those sketches until they almost looked like photographs. He had shown them to many people over the last few days, but nobody was able to recognize the scenes.

After riding some twenty kilometers on roads he had not been before, Adam came to a crossing. One yellow sign pointed right in the direction of Tegernsee, the other pointed left to Kochel am See. He instinctively turned left. After two kilometers on the quiet country road, he stopped. The morning temperatures were quickly rising, so he took off his jacket and put it in his backpack. He drank from a bottle of water, then looked around and listened. The sun spread like liquid gold over the green fields as the hum of bees and the buzz of insects mixed with the chirp of birdsong. The lush colors of the countryside with the alps in the distance reminded him of a Lovis Corinth painting he had seen in an exhibit at the Staatsgalerie in Munich the previous year.

He looked at his watch, idly thinking that by now Kuri must be busy filming scenes, somewhere not too far away. Adam was glad they had exchanged phone numbers—he would call her later. He breathed in the summer air, and a smile spread across his tan face when he recalled their promise to meet in a few weeks, even though they had not settled on a day or a place. He laughed out loud, realizing his heart had begun to beat faster the moment he thought of her; cartoonish images of his adrenaline, epinephrine, and norepinephrine dancing the jitterbug swirled in his head. "Now, that's ridiculous," he reprimanded himself, but couldn't wipe the grin off his face. For a moment longer he sat still, lost in thought. A herd of cows grazed nearby—one lifted her head and looked directly at him, chewing. A flock of sheep gathered near the fence to his right, and some of them also looked in his direction.

He finished the water and pulled out the folder that contained the map and the photos he had made of the digitally enhanced drawings. He became so engrossed by the pictures that he did not hear the clip-clop-clip-clop of horse hooves until they were just a few feet away. He looked up.

"*Brrrr.*" An old man with a weathered face brought the horse-drawn cart to a stop. "*Griaß Eich!*" The greeting came in the unmistakable heavy Bavarian dialect.

Adam walked over to the cart to shake the farmer's hand. "I am lost and wonder if you can help me," he said, apologizing for his clumsy German. He opened the folder and showed the man the image of the farmhouse.

"Does this look at all familiar to you?"

The old farmer studied the picture. He shook his head. Adam quickly handed him the next picture, the one with the big tree and the bridge over the stream.

"*Joh!*" said the man. "*Joh gwihß!*"

Adam realized he had been holding his breath. "You know this place?" he asked excitedly.

The man nodded. This was the Bauer farm, he told Adam. He could tell as soon as he'd seen the picture of the tree and the bridge. And now that he looked at the first image again, he realized it was the original house, before the Bauers had built additions to the structure. He handed the pictures back to Adam and pointed down the road.

"When you go past those sheep there, you'll see another small road. Turn right. Another kilometer and you're there! Ask for Max. Tell him Sepp sent you."

Adam impulsively stepped up onto the cart and hugged the old man. "*Tausend Dank,*" he cried out. "You have no idea what this means to me."

Ten minutes later, he turned off the motorcycle's engine, climbed off, and gaped at the farmhouse a few yards ahead. Now he knew for a fact that this never had been just a dream, never his imagination. It was real. "Oh my God," he whispered, "I found it. I am here."

Chapter Eleven

Adam remained gazing at the old farmhouse, ignoring the two new additions on either side of the original structure. When he noticed movement by the front door, he straightened his back and rolled his shoulders. "Let's do it," he encouraged himself.

He saw an old lady coming out of the house, walking unsteadily until she reached the bench under a window. Her face was timeworn, her winter-white hair neatly tied in a milkmaid braid over the crown of her head. Her bright red sweater matched the color of the hanging red alpine geraniums that were planted in every window box. Adam saw her squinting against the sun in his direction; she lifted her arm and motioned him to come closer.

"*Grüß Gott,*" he said, offering the traditional Bavarian greeting. "I am looking for Max. Is he around?"

The woman responded with a toothless smile and a hand gesture he did not know how to interpret. He returned her smile, bent down, and raised his voice slightly. "Sepp told me I would find Max here."

There was a sparkle in the old lady's eyes when her trembling hand tried to touch him.

"That's Resi Bauer, my mother. She's almost deaf—she also has trouble talking," said an energetic voice from behind. "Can I help you?" A man in his midsixties, wearing a checkered green shirt tucked into knee-length lederhosen, put down a large bucket and wiped his forehead with an already damp handkerchief.

"You must be Max; Sepp told me to ask for you." Adam shook the man's hand. "I'm sorry my German is not very good."

"No problem, you can talk to me in English," Max said. "When I was in my twenties, I lived in Australia for three years." He pulled his suspenders and let them snap back. "What brings you here, and what can I do for you?"

Adam took the drawings from his backpack. He cleared his throat, hoping he would make it through the cover sorry he had fabricated to explain his quest. It embarrassed him to be dishonest.

"My name is Adam Gold. I am a psychiatrist, and I made a promise to help a patient—a Holocaust survivor. He and his son were prisoners in Dachau between 1942 and 1945. They were on the death march on April 26, 1945. My patient and his son were able to escape—he told me of the approximate area. I am Jewish myself, and as you can imagine, I became fascinated with the story. My patient drew these pictures, and I had them enhanced. He passed away, but I'm compelled to fulfill the mission." Adam handed Max the pictures one at a time. "You can see, the house looks like yours prior to the additions; and then there's this tree..."

The farmer separated the drawings on the garden table and stared at them. "That's unbelievable," he said. He turned toward the house. "Eva," he called out to a woman who was assisting the older lady to stand up. "You've got to hear and see this. And please bring Mother."

Once the woman had assisted the old lady to sit down at the table, Max made the introduction. "My wife, Eva. We met in Melbourne—it was love at first sight." Max's broad smile supported his statement. "My Eva is a fair dinkum Aussie; she's the best thing that ever happened to me." Then, Max gave an abbreviated version of the story he had just heard from Adam and pointed at the drawings on the table.

"Holy Dooley—someone drew this from memory over seven decades ago? Well, I never..." Eva exclaimed. She looked at Adam. "You need to go behind the house and see the tree, the meadow, the bridge...it's all still there." She pushed the drawings closer to her mother-in-law. "*Schau, Mama.*" Eva explained to the old lady the drawings were made many years ago.

Eva looked at Adam. "Too bad she can't speak anymore. She could answer your questions in more detail than Max," she said.

Suddenly the old woman cried out. She pointed at the drawings with a trembling finger, then waved her arm toward the back of the farmhouse, nodding and moaning inarticulately.

Max sighed and put his arm around his mother, pulling her close. "She still remembers," he muttered.

"Yes," Eva agreed. "I think mother wants you to tell our guest what she can't."

"Let's go for a walk." Max motioned Adam to follow him as he strode toward the barn. "My parents married in 1941, right before my father had to fight Hitler's war. My mother was only nineteen years old then. She and my grandparents tried to keep this farm alive. Those were terrible years—the Nazis took most everything of value. They brutalized my grandfather for hiding food and terrified the women because they helped hungry neighbors, especially strangers. My father was captured by the Red Army in 1944 and did not return home until 1949. I was born in 1950." Max slowed his pace. "What I am about to tell you came directly from my mother soon after my father passed away and, until she lost her hearing, I listened to her story over and over again."

They had reached the barn when Max stopped walking. He went inside and returned with a shovel, kicking the door shut behind him. "My mother had just turned twenty-three when on April 27, 1945, she found two emaciated young people...teenagers...hiding in this barn, just a few days before the Americans liberated Dachau. Mother later found out that thousands of starving prisoners were heading toward Tegernsee. Many of them were so weak they did not make it; countless other prisoners got shot by the SS henchmen; somehow these two kids managed to escape from this deadly march."

"Did you say... two kids?" Adam's heartbeat quickened.

"Yes. A boy and a girl." Max frowned. "But didn't you say the father, your patient, escaped with his son? My mother never mentioned another man—only the young girl and boy."

Adam swallowed, caught in the half-truth so soon. His mind raced, trying to find a way to clarify the discrepancy. "I... um... my patient said he left his boy behind by this farm, so he could scout out the area. He had meant to come back and get his son but... um... got very sick and collapsed. The Americans found him, and he eventually recovered in a military facility far away from here. Later, he couldn't remember the location where he left his son, but he made the drawings of your property—he never gave up searching."

"So tragic!" Max shook his head. "Well, my mother definitely was unaware of another escapee, and it's strange that your patient never mentioned the girl." He scratched his head. "Anyway, the girl probably had typhoid; she was burning up with fever. The boy was sick, too."

A German shepherd came running from behind the barn, wagging his tail when he saw his owner, then sniffed around Adam's shoes and pants. Both men took turns petting the animal.

"My mother did not want to tell her in-laws that she had given the fugitives food, water, and blankets, but of course my grandparents found out all the same; they were afraid of catching the disease, but their greater fear was the SS thugs. My mother stood her ground, though. She insisted on helping the girl and the boy."

Max moved his head, an indication to follow him around the barn.

Adam gasped as he found himself standing before the green meadow with its rolling hills and the narrow bridge crossing over the brook. He turned his head to the left and became overwhelmed by emotion at the sight of the majestic oak tree. In its divine perfection, it seemed to cast shadows of decades gone by.

As if he'd read Adam's thoughts, Max said, "The tree has grown older and bigger, but it's the same as in your pictures. Amazing that your patient was able to remember all this so clearly. The love of a parent is wondrous..."

Adam blushed; it was unbearable having to deceive this kind man. Without looking at Max, he asked, "What happened to the boy and the girl?"

"My mother said the youngsters, though they were in poor health and terribly weak, were fighters; they wanted to live! She gave them clothes and asked the boy to burn the shreds of prison garb they arrived with. The girl, so sick, slept most of the time, and my mother had trouble communicating with the boy. She didn't know the language he spoke at first; she thought she was hearing some Polish or even German words, but it was with a strange dialect.

"Was it Yiddish?"

"I don't know. Maybe. Anyway, when she asked for his name, she believes he answered Jimmy. Strange, huh? Not really a German, Jewish, or Polish name." Max stopped talking; his eyes lit up. "But, hey, you must know his name! Didn't your patient tell you? What did he call his boy? And what was their last name?"

Adam's face reddened again. "Um, the last name was Gold, same as mine." He felt slightly less dishonest giving his own name. "My patient preferred to speak in Yiddish and referred to his son mostly as *meyn zun,* which means 'my son.'" Adam had never felt as uncomfortable as he did when he gave Max this complete fabrication. He quickly asked, "What about the girl?"

Max shrugged. "My mother called the frail beautiful girl with red curly hair *Engerl.* It's Bavarian and means little angel." Max looked at Adam intently. "Something else you should know. Jimmy asked for papers and pencil. Mother said she watched him write and saw him put the pages in a small metal box he must've found in the barn. He buried the box over there by the old oak."

"Why? I don't understand. You never tried to retrieve the box?"

Max frowned; his lips formed a grim line. "Mother always had somewhat of a sixth sense. She was convinced the boy wanted his writings to be read only by someone who'd come looking for him—after what you told me, perhaps his father? But now you're here, in his place, after all these years." Max paused, as if to consider an idea, then continued. "On April 29, 1945—as you can imagine, my mother remembered the day exactly—she walked into the barn with fresh bread and water but found the girl and boy lying dead in the hay. She said they were facing each other in a tight embrace—so tight, they looked like one body." Pausing, Max raised his head toward the cloudless sky. "Mother said they were surrounded by beautiful light from sunrays filtering through the roof of the barn. She said the youngsters looked like cherubs in paintings...angelic and at peace."

Max sighed deeply. "Living on this remote farm, my mother was unaware the Americans liberated Dachau that very day—she still was afraid the SS would find out my family was hiding Jews. So, that night, my grandfather carried the kids over there." Max pointed toward the brook. "See that tall apple tree? That's where Grandfather buried them. Of course, the apple tree wasn't there in 1945. My mother planted it after I was born in 1950."

Adam had grown still and somber. He felt Max's arm on his shoulder. "Come," he heard the farmer say. "Let's walk over there."

The summer flowers in the meadow were swaying and dancing in the breeze; the rustling leaves of the apple tree sang a duet with the babble of the brook.

"Oh my..." Adam whispered when he saw Max pointing to two Stars of David carved into the tree trunk; he tapped on the inscription below the two six-pointed Jewish symbols.

"*B'hüt di Gott,*" said Max. "It means 'God be with you.' My mother said this every day when she was able to walk here and pray to her angels." Max lowered his head, shifting uncomfortably. "I'm not religious like my mother. But I try to come by here often...it's a peaceful place to think."

Adam's eyes embraced his newfound friend. "Your mother, you, and your family—all of you were born with pure greatness. I'm very grateful we met." He pulled two small stones from the pocket of his pants and explained to Max what he was about to do. Then, he crouched down, placed the stones under the tree, and reflected silently on all he had just learned.

"Here." Max spoke softly when Adam straightened again. "Take this shovel. I believe you should be the one to dig up the box the boy buried by the oak. I'll show you where." Max took him to the oak tree and then excused himself, slowly walking back to the barn.

Fifteen minutes later Adam sat down, leaning against the mature trunk of the oak, brushing rich soil off a small metal box.

He carefully opened the old box and gently ran his hand over the faintly yellowed pages, smoothing out the wrinkles of time. The boy's penmanship was beautifully precise, still legible after all these years.

Grateful that his father's Hasidic parents had taught him Yiddish, Adam began to read: *Meyn nomen iz Shimon Messing. Sei rufen mir Shimmy…*

Adam blinked through tears. "And my name is Adam Gold," he whispered, and clutched the paper to his chest. In a tender yet exultant voice, he said, "As the soul is eternal in the continual law of die and live again, your soul found me. For years I sensed your calling and now…I am here!"

He looked over to the barn and farmhouse. He wished the old woman and Max could hear him when he said, "His name was Shimon Messing. His nickname was Shimmy…that's why you thought he called himself Jimmy." Adam inhaled and exhaled slowly, wishing his breaths would connect with those that were expressed so long ago. He watched his tears fall onto the soil and hoped they could mix with the tears Shimmy had shed when he sat in the same spot over seven decades ago. He raised Shimmy's letter up from his chest and resumed reading:

> *The girl I love is sleeping in the barn—she is fifteen years old. Her name is Judith Rozenblum. We met under cruel conditions. Men and young boys, like horses, were forced to pull*

wagons filled with corpses. We dug trenches and buried the dead—too many to be counted. We were held captive by insurmountable evil—by the unconquerable darkness of slaughter.

First time I saw Judith, we passed each other under the iron gate ARBEIT MACHT FREI. *She was so pale and thin, but her beautiful face and big green eyes captivated my soul.*

Women and men were not allowed to talk, but when she held my eye contact, she renewed my strength.

Later, despite the danger if we were caught, Judith and I would sneak to the fence that separates the women's and men's sections; through the fence, we encouraged each other to be strong and made plans for our future. We knew we'd be shot if we were discovered, but we did not care—we wanted to be together.

Only two days ago, in the middle of the night, all prisoners of Dachau were ordered to march. We did not know why or where the march was going. Many were too sick; they died in less than an hour of walking. Whoever passed out because of weakness was shot. It was in the middle of the second night when Judith and I broke away. We crawled through the bushes and trees. Judith was weak, I carried her most of the way. Too tired to continue, we collapsed in a ditch. In the morning, we moved on. Behind the edge of the forest, we saw a barn and crept inside. Half-starved, exhausted, and cold, we fell into warm hay. Now we keep praying we won't be found by those who hate us, who starve us, who brutalize us.

My parents were Ferdinand and Nanette; both are dead. I have a sister, Golda. To keep her safe, my grandparents sent her to live with a kind Polish couple; their names are Janina and Waclaw Kuczok. Golda had to change her name and pretend to be their daughter. She is Mara Kuczok now. I pray every day that she is all right.

Before it all started, my family lived a prosperous life. First in Breslau and then in Oświęcim, which was annexed by the Germans and renamed Auschwitz.

Judith lived with her parents in Schöneberg. She and her mother were taken to Ravensbrück and later transported to Dachau. Judith's mother, Dora, died in Dachau. Judith does not know what happened to her father, Arthur. She hopes he is alive.

Judith is very sick; I am sick, too. I think we both have typhoid. But we refuse to give up hope. We know fate has brought us together—we know we are soul mates. We want to heal. We want to live and laugh and dance.

After what we have seen and been through, we know there is goodness in German people. The kind young farm woman who gives us shelter, warm clothes, water, and bread is standing by the barn, watching me while I write this. I don't want to give my letter to her because the SS may find it and punish these good people. I will make sure she sees where I bury the box.

In case we won't survive, my writing shall be proof that Judith and I are now here—we live and have real names. We only remain alive because of each other. Our love is eternal.

Chapter Twelve

1936

"Shimmy!" My mother is calling me, but I don't answer. Felix and I press our fists in our mouths so she can't hear us laugh. We just climbed to the top of a tree in our backyard, and I don't want Mama to know. I am not allowed to climb trees anymore—last year I fell from one and broke my foot.

"Shimmy!" Mama's voice is louder; she now is directly under the tree. I see her footsteps on the thick green grass; from up here the grass looks like our velvet sofa. She walks over to one of the rosebushes and inspects the leaves. She motions Gustav, the gardener, to come closer. She's telling him something about black spots and fungal disease.

Felix and I watch her look around. I think she's still searching for me. She shakes her head and walks toward our house again. She tells Gustav, "When you see Shimmy, please ask him to come into the house. His father and I are waiting."

"Did you do something wrong?" whispers Felix.

I shrug my shoulders and snicker. "Maybe it's about the frogs and dead mice in the basement? They say it's great I want to be a doctor, but they never like me experimenting with—"

Felix interrupts, faking a retching sound. "I don't like your dead mice either. I don't even like doctors. I'm going to be an advocate, like my father." When Felix attempts his descent, he slips and clutches desperately at a branch. "Ouch," he cries. "My hand... my hand... I hurt my hand."

I help him from the tree and wrap my handkerchief around his bleeding wrist. "See, I'm already a doctor. No more blood."

Felix is my best friend. We are seven years old.

"Come children," Papa says in our living room, telling my sister, Golda, and me to sit between him and Mama. "This may be hard for you to understand, but we have to move to another city."

When Golda and I start crying, Papa explains that he has made a business decision.

Our father owns a bus company that covers Upper and Lower Silesia. He says he needs to expand to Oświęcim in Poland and Moravská in Czechoslovakia.

"What about Felix? What about my school?" I protest.

"What about my voice lessons? What about Ruth?" Golda sobs.

"We will keep a branch in Breslau. I promise Mama and I will take you back here to visit Felix and Ruth. Of course, they always are welcome to visit us."

Bubbeh and Zaydeh, my grandparents, are moving to Oświęcim with us. Golda and I love them so much. They speak Yiddish with us, but Mama and Papa only speak to us in German. Now we will have to learn Polish, Mama says.

Golda and I don't like Oświęcim. We miss our house in Breslau with the garden and the trees that are full of apples, cherries, and plums. We miss all the colors of Mama's flower beds. Now we live in the middle of the city in a very big apartment, on Bahnhofstrasse 25, right around the corner from the fancy hotel Deutsches Haus.

Learning Polish is too difficult, complains Mama. Golda and I agree. Papa hires a nanny for Golda and me. Her name is Agata, and she only speaks Polish to us.

My Bubbeh teaches Agata how to bake challah and even how to make gefilte fish; Golda and I don't like gefilte fish, but Agata learns fast and soon she cooks all our favorite dishes.

A lot of bad things are happening. Mama cries a lot, but she does not tell us why. Agata says it's because the Germans don't like Jews. On Friday nights, when we have Shabbat dinners, Mama makes sure all the curtains are closed, even though it is still light outside. Golda and I now have to go to a school for Jews only, and Agata has to walk with us every day.

1938

There is sadness in our home. Mama is very ill with pneumonia. Golda and I stand behind the door. The doctor tells Papa the medication does not help anymore. We are not allowed in the room. Papa says we can get sick, too.

It's Sunday morning, and Golda climbs in my bed. She is sobbing and clings to me. When Papa comes in my room, his eyes are red. He sits on the chair next to my bed—the chair where Mama always sits and sings German lullabies. I can hear her beautiful voice.

Guten Abend, gut' Nacht	*(Good evening, good night*
Mit Rosen bedacht	*Covered with roses*
Mit Näglein besteckt	*Adorned with thorns*
Schlüpf unter die Deck'	*Slip under the covers*
Morgen früh, wenn Gott will	*Tomorrow, if it's God's will*
Wirst du wieder geweckt…	*Will you wake again…)*

"Your mother passed away," Papa whispers. He folds us into his strong arms. We all cry.

"You, Shimmy, have to be the man of the house now when I am away on business." Papa says. "Promise you will take care of your sister." I nod. I am only nine years old and Golda is eleven, but I am already taller and much stronger than Golda.

❋

Because Papa travels a lot, we are glad our grandparents are with us. Agata now is our best friend. She knows how to make us laugh, and she invents games we can play inside. Bubbeh and Zaydeh don't allow us to play outside anymore, and Agata is afraid for us when she takes us to school. "You both look very Aryan with your blond hair and blue eyes," she says. "But never count on it. Sooner or later the Nazis will find out you're not German—they're like bloodhounds; they know how to sniff out the Jews."

Golda often is scared. She has bad dreams at night. My grandparents ask Agata to move Golda's bed into my room. Now our Bubbeh sits in mother's chair every night and sings Yiddish lullabies to us.

Shluf, man feigele,	*(Sleep, my birdie,*
Mach tsi dus eigele,	*Close your eyes;*
Shluf sech ois, meyn kind.	*Sleep enough, my child.*
Di shlufst nit fraid.	*You sleep with joy.*
Di weist nit ken laid;	*You know of no sorrow;*
Shluf sech ois gesint.	*Sleep with health.)*

Soon, Golda is not scared anymore. She even eats more because she wants to be strong like me.

1940

Today is my birthday; I am eleven. Agata already baked six different cakes, dozens of *hamantaschen,* and *rugelach* cookies. She also brought bottles of apple juice—it's Golda's and my favorite drink. Agata's father works in an apple orchard and knows how to make delicious juice. Five of my friends and two of Golda's friends come for my birthday party; we know all of them from our *shul.* Their parents are invited, too. Everybody eats so much cake—only crumbs are left.

Agata is having fun with us children; we play duck-duck-goose, and my friend Samuel ends up being the goose a lot; we laugh and laugh because he waddles like a goose. Then we chase each other through the hallway and rooms, playing catch. But we laugh the most and scream the loudest when we play old maid. Agata keeps losing, and her nose and her forehead already are black from paint. We are so loud that Papa tells us we need to calm down; he's been sitting with the other parents and Bubbeh and Zaydeh in the living room behind closed doors. Earlier, when I stuck my head in there, the adults talked in low voices, looking concerned. I heard Papa say he has cancer, and I know that is a bad illness. Zaydeh said something about Papa's lungs and that he smokes too many cigarettes. I am a little worried, too, because he lost a lot of weight. He also has been coughing a lot—just like Mama before she died. But I don't want to think about that now, I am having such a good time on my eleventh birthday.

Papa sits with us in the living room and tells us the Germans confiscated his business. He says the bus company will be given to a non-Jew, and there won't be any compensation for us. Papa has a great reputation as a businessman, and he knows best how to discuss terms with the Germans—until now, they left us alone. But Papa says he doesn't have the strength to negotiate anymore. My zaydeh says it's a miracle the Nazis allowed Papa to run his company for so long.

I know Papa's pneumonia is getting worse, and Agata can't find medicine anywhere. Well, everything is getting worse! We even are afraid to go to shul, it's too dangerous. The other day, Samuel, his whole family, and all their neighbors disappeared. Zaydeh says they were taken on a train to a relocation center. "Why?" I ask. Zaydeh explains it's because of the war and believes most Jews will have to be relocated. I tell Golda I hope the Germans will relocate us back to our home in Breslau, but Golda says I am naïve.

Golda and I sit on Papa's bed through the night, each holding his hand. "Be strong," he tells us when the morning light comes through the curtain. "Never lose hope." Those are his last words.

Golda won't stop crying on Bubbeh's shoulder, and Zaydeh has not moved away from the window. He keeps wiping his eyes. Agata is trying to console all of us, but without Papa our steady and reliable focus is gone. I go to my room because I don't want anyone to see me cry uncontrollably.

1941

More and more Jews are being rounded up and sent away. Bubbeh and Zaydeh tell us we must split up in order to be safe. Golda will move in with Agata's cousin Janina and Waclaw Kuczok. Their thirteen-year-old daughter, Mara, recently died from pneumonia and whooping cough—so many people die from it these days. Mara had blond hair and blue eyes, just like Golda. The Kuczoks are moving to a small village near the apple orchard where nobody knows them. Until the war is over, Golda will have to pretend to be their daughter, so she can pass as a Gentile. Agata swears her cousins are good people and that Golda will be well taken care of; she will be safe!

Tomorrow Golda will be picked up by Agata's cousins. We cry because we're sad, but there are smiles under our tears because we're happy that Golda will be safe. Bubbeh, Zaydeh, Golda, Agata, and I sit in the living room. Bubbeh sits at the piano and asks Golda to sing her favorite song. I love when Golda sings—she has a beautiful voice.

Roter Mohn, warum welkst du denn schon,
wie mein Herz sollst du glüh'n und feurig loh'n.
Roter Mohn, den der Liebste mir gab,
welkst du weil ich ihn schon verloren hab?
Rot wie Blut, voller Pracht, warst du noch gestern erblüht,
aber schon über Nacht ist deine Schönheit verblüht.
Roter Mohn warum welkst du denn schon,
wie mein Herz sollst du glüh'n und feurig loh'n.

Because I also look Aryan, Agata promises she'll find a safe Polish home for me too.

But it doesn't happen. When I walk home from studying with

the old *rebbe,* two Nazis grab me while others of the German SS take hold of more Jewish boys.

"*Wie alt bist Du?*" A skinny Nazi with thin lips and pockmarks all over his face slaps me. I am about the same height as him but definitely brawnier, so I stand up even straighter and stare him down. "I am fifteen," I lie, answering in German. He takes a step back and through slits of eyes looks me up and down. Then he puffs out his small chest and points to a group of Jewish men to my right. "*Weitergehen,*" he yells, and moves on to assault his next victims.

My heart pounds so hard, but I don't want anyone to know how scared I am. "What is happening?" I murmur to the men I now stand shoulder to shoulder with.

"Don't look them in the eye. They will beat you or shoot you," whispers the man to my right.

"Don't even talk," breathes someone behind me.

To my left, another man starts sobbing like a child. I see the skinny Nazi point his rifle and fire. I instinctively turn my head when I hear the dull, heavy sound of a body falling to the ground. I try to bend down to help, but the man to my right grabs my arm. "Don't," he whispers, "or you'll be next."

When the uniformed guards shove us into ominous trucks, I turn around, hoping to see Agata or my zaydeh running toward the trucks to take me home. Instead, the doors of the vehicle slam closed.

"Where are they taking us?" I dare ask.

A stranger says, "Auschwitz."

"The camp of death," says another.

1942

I have no idea what day it is; someone whispers that it's April. Soon I will be thirteen years old, and I think of the day my family set aside for my bar mitzvah. I think of the kind rebbe—I so enjoyed studying with him as I prepared to enter my manhood. But will I have a bar mitzvah when I get out of this gloomy, grisly place? Who will be waiting for me? Mama and Papa are not among the living anymore. Will I find Golda again? The last time I saw my grandparents and Agata was last autumn—the day the SS took me away from those I love.

When I arrived at the camp, I immediately sensed the smell of fear in the air; I saw bodies hanging from gallows, heard the screams and shots, and realized there would be no escape. Like cattle, we were steered into a huge hall where the SS made us strip off our clothes. They cleaned us with disinfectant and shaved our heads. Naked we waited as they pointed at us, jeering and laughing. Eventually they gave us striped uniforms and wooden shoes. Then they tattooed us with a number. Mine is 177404—I no longer have a name.

Chapter Thirteen

Adam sat under the oak tree, caught up in his own visions of Shimmy's life, a life that once was vibrant with love and hope. Still pressing Shimmy's two-page letter against his chest, Adam wished he could remain in this trance, that he could unlock more of Shimmy's memories, but he realized that he no longer was certain how much time had passed in the world around him.

Through glazed eyes he noticed movement at the nearby farmhouse and focused his attention on Max and two other men as they pushed heavily loaded barrows into the barn. Their laughter carried across the meadow. With a sigh, he folded the letter and gingerly closed it inside the metal box.

I will go back in time again, he promised himself. I *will learn more about my previous life.*

Reluctantly, he removed his hand from the trunk of the old oak. He looked one more time at the apple tree with the two Star of David carvings. *I found Shimmy,* he mused. *My mission now is to find Judith. I believe that is my purpose; it is why I am here.*

"You sat under the oak for a long time," Max said when Adam returned to the barn. The farmer finished rinsing his hands, then shut off the outside faucet and faced Adam. "I believe you had your reasons."

Adam had thought about this as he was walking through the meadow. He knew he had to clear his conscience and restore his honor. He cleared his throat. "What I'm about to tell you will be difficult for you to believe," he said. "Perhaps you won't trust what you will hear, but I cannot leave unless you know the truth."

He began by apologizing for his earlier deception and then plunged directly into the real story. He explained how his vivid dreams and recurring visions had led him to be standing on the very site where he believed he had been in a previous life.

"Whoa!" said Max. "That's a lot to absorb." A puff of air escaped his lips. "Maybe I'll never subscribe to your theory, but I must admit…how you managed to draw our farm, the house and the barn, the location of the oak tree, the stream and the bridge…" The farmer shook his head in amazement. "It's otherworldly how you connected the dots. My mother always believed in the mystical forces of nature—maybe I should give more credence to probabilities than just possibilities."

"May I see your mother again? Even if she can't hear me, I still would like to let her know about Shimmy and of what I just told you."

Adam sat across from the old woman, holding her hands, talking softly. "*Danke für alles!*" he said when he finished. "Without you, I would've never found Shimmy."

Both Adam and Max gasped when they heard the old woman speak.

"Shimmy," she rasped, touching Adam's forehead. "*Mein Engerl…bring' sie mir,*" she said, and crossed herself. Then she folded her hands in her lap and lifted her face to the skies. Her lips started to move, but her prayers were silent.

Chapter Fourteen

"Go rest up! You've got another demanding scene to shoot in less than two hours," the assistant director shouted after Kuri as he watched her walk to her trailer.

"You bet I will," she mumbled to herself, lifting her arm, giving him a thumbs-up. Even though the last scene had taken a lot out of her, the sudden onset of low energy still came as a surprise. She couldn't remember the last time she felt like taking a nap. She brushed her teeth, washed her face, and curled up on the small bed. A minute later she was asleep.

Loud knocking on the door woke her from pleasant dreams. She looked at her watch and realized she slept for more than one hour.

"Okay! I'm getting ready," she called out. She yawned and reached for her private phone, its number known only to her family, closest friends, agent, and assistant. She quickly read the text messages from her parents and sister and replied immediately. She grimaced when she saw four messages from her agent, urging her to contact him ASAP because of exciting news; from experience she knew that everything was exciting news in his mind. She kept scrolling and was disappointed that there was nothing from Adam. She looked for the newest entry in her directory and tapped on the telephone number. The sparkle in her eyes faded when, a few seconds later, she heard Adam's recording, asking to leave a message.

"It's Kuri," she answered. "I was hoping to talk to you before your flight. But now I have to go back to work, and by the time I'm done, you'll be in the air. You can text if you wish…but if you can call me, I would love to hear your voice." She smiled as she thought about their time together the previous night. "I really had a great time being with you yesterday. Safe travels, Adam."

"Okay, okay! I'm coming," she shouted when the knock on the door returned, louder than before.

Hours later, rainclouds began to darken the beautiful Alpine sunset. Kuri felt a cool breeze and marveled at this rainbow riot of colors with so many rich and varied hues in the June sky. She already could hear the nearby harmonic thrumming of rain, swiftly drawing closer. As the first sopping drops of moisture fell on her face, she hopped into the van that would take some of the cast and crew back to the hotel.

"Another hot date tonight, sugarplum?" Her costar, Justin Cross, teasingly poked Kuri in her ribs. He was the epitome of an Adonis, tall and devilishly handsome with a rugged physique and a George Clooney smile.

Kuri slapped his hand away and grinned. "Yep, my fat German goose-down pillow and I have big plans to snuggle all night long."

"Mmm! The pillow most likely will end up on the floor." Justin chuckled, attempting to tickle her again. "I hear there's a surprise waiting for you."

"Unless it's you, I'm not interested," she said, giggling and blocking his hand.

Justin winked at her. "I keep telling you, if I was on your side of the shore, you'd totally be my type and I'd be a yestergay." He matched her laughter and moved closer. "Seriously, though, there are rumors someone's waiting for you, sugar lips!"

"Shut up, Justin!" Kuri chuckled and pushed him away. "Busy yourself with tweeting and texting—suits you better than teasing me." She playfully kicked his leg with her foot and then reclined the back of her seat. She relaxed into it and took out her phone to check her messages again. Her heart skipped when she saw Adam's name on her voicemail list.

"Kuri, thank you for letting me hear your voice—I know how busy you are. My flight's about to take off. I can only hope your day was as successful as mine. You have no idea how long I searched for what I finally found... today! No words can describe what I'm feeling." There was a short pause. "Ehm... when the time is right, I'd love nothing more than to share this with you; I hope it will be really soon." Kuri could hear a male voice in the background, reminding Adam to turn his phone off. "Kuri, I have to go. I definitely will call you tomorrow. I can't wait to speak with you again." Kuri replayed his message twice more and then closed her eyes.

When they neared the hotel, Justin nudged her awake.

"Whoa, whoa, whoa...what's going on out there? Look at that crowd—looks like double from the nights before." He looked at Kuri. "Do we really have to deal with this tonight? I'm so not in the mood!"

Kuri peeked through the tinted windows. "If you want the rainbow, you gotta put up with the rain." She grinned and gathered her belongings. Just when she was ready to dash from the van, she stopped, staring in disbelief at the crowd of fans who suddenly screamed from the top of their lungs, running toward the hotel's entrance.

"Ha! Check it out!" Justin pointed ahead. "I told you there was a surprise for you!"

Kuri stiffened. "What is *he* doing here?"

"Why do I get the feeling you're disappointed?" Justin looked surprised. "Isn't he your man? Or has he been replaced by that babe magnet you introduced me to last night?"

"I don't know how to answer that question," she muttered,

staring at the crowd by the hotel entrance. "Okay then, let's go and greet The Supernova," she said, grimacing.

Tommy Nova was a South African–born singer, songwriter, and producer. He and Kuri had been dating off and on for more than a year. The twenty-nine-year-old rock star had achieved fame with an eclectic blend of electronic, pop, and hip-hop that was mixed with swing from the big-band era. Tommy was celebrated worldwide, always admired for his panache. Fashion houses took delight in designing his stage suits, always in the bright colors he loved, matched with unusual shirts and ties.

He stood in front of the hotel entrance, dressed in Comme des Garçons's wide suspended knickers over a CDG T-shirt, surrounded by screaming fans. It was obvious he enjoyed posing with them for selfies, but the second he saw Kuri and Justin emerge from the van, he pushed through the crowd shouting, "There they are!"

Like a clutch of chattering chicks, the squealing horde followed their idol.

Tommy threw his arms around Kuri and lifted her off the ground, twirling her through the air before holding her aloft like a trophy to show the crowd. "Are you ready for me?" he whispered into her ear. "I got some surprises!"

She wiggled out of his arms and waited for the hotel's security staff to come out to escort them into the lobby. When the doors closed behind them, they welcomed the calm and privacy.

As soon as they entered Kuri's suite, Tommy pulled her close. "Oooh, my yummy sugarboo, you feel sooo good." He squeezed her tightly, planting kisses all over her face.

Kuri shook loose from the embrace. "I told you, I don't like when you call me that." She walked into the closet to hang up her jacket.

"Hey, hey, hey! I couldn't wait to see you, but you don't seem nearly as excited as I thought you'd be." Tommy flashed her an exaggerated pout. "I came straight from Oslo so I could be with you for twelve hours before tomorrow's gig in Copenhagen. We haven't seen each other in weeks, and I won't even get back to the

States for another month. And now…where's the love, where's the ecstasy? I'm not feeling it!"

"I'm sorry." Kuri apologized. "It was a long, grueling day." She pecked him on the cheek. "I'm just surprised to see you."

There was a knock on the door. Tommy went to open it, and a table, set for two, with lit candles and rose petals strewn over the pastel-colored cloth, was wheeled in by a young woman and man in their traditional Bavarian costumes.

"I called from Norway to make sure this hotel in the middle of yodeling folks in lederhosen and dirndl dresses could handle our favorites." He poured two glasses of Armand de Brignac champagne. "I know you enjoy fish, so I talked the chef into doing this…" he lifted the warming cover off each plate. "Voila!"

Kuri nodded when she saw the beautifully arranged pan-fried sea bass atop a mound of creamy beans, accompanied by artichoke puree and plated with deep-fried rocket and sun-dried tomatoes. She clinked her flute with his. "Well done, Supernova."

Tommy smirked. "I told you I don't like when you call me that," he said, mimicking Kuri's earlier protest, then gulped the champagne and poured himself a refill. "Hey, while I was waiting for you, I had a few drinks downstairs, and the bartender said he enjoyed seeing you have a really, really good time last night with someone he didn't recognize. Who was that dude?"

Instead of flinching, she leaned closer to make meaningful eye contact. "His name is Adam. He's a doctor; he helped me yesterday after I fainted."

"Fainted? O-M-effing-G! What happened?"

She told him about her visit to Dachau, and how Adam had taken care of her when she was overwhelmed by everything she had seen at the camp. "He not only gave me first aid, he helped me understand."

"Understand what?" Tommy's brows knitted into a frown. "Why the heck would you want to go to that fucking Nazi prison camp in the first place?" He bit his lip and looked away when he saw Kuri's shocked reaction. "Ooops," he said, reaching for her hand. "You know how jealous I get when I think of you being with someone else." He pressed his mouth into the palm of her hand. "Forgive me."

Kuri sighed in relief when Tommy became his usual loquacious self during the meal; it distracted her from missing Adam. She forced herself to pay attention and, at times, actually enjoyed Tommy's stories about some technical mishaps and other anecdotes on his current European tour. The more he talked, the more he drank, the more excited he became.

"Hey, I gotta take this," he said, and stepped onto the balcony as his phone buzzed.

Kuri took the opportunity to cover her plate; although she'd barely touched her dinner, she did not want to disappoint Tommy after he'd taken the time to arrange all this for her. "Go on," she encouraged him when he came back into the room. "Tell me more."

"Damn, I love being with you; every time I look at your gorgeousness, I remind myself how lucky I am." He kissed each one of her fingertips. "My agent has it right, you and I totally belong together." Tommy popped the third cork, refilled his glass, and waved the bottle toward Kuri.

"Not for me—I can't even finish my first glass." She looked at the two bottles he'd already emptied, amazed that the amount of alcohol was having relatively little impact on him.

"Thanks for a delicious dinner, Tommy. A thoughtful treat after a long day."

He grinned and winked at her. "Day's over, but our night's only begun." He motioned her to sit on his lap.

"I really want to take a shower—as I said, it's been a long day for me."

"Good idea! I'll join ya!" Tommy said, and as he jumped off the chair, he spilled the champagne on his shirt. "Motherfucker…" he grunted, and refilled his glass. On unsteady legs, he walked toward Kuri.

"No, Tommy." She took his hand and led him to the sofa. "You're too tipsy already."

He plunged into the seat cushions and, again, motioned her to sit on his lap. "Tell me you love me…I need to hear it," he said.

"I do love you, Tommy, but…I've never been in love with you!" What she had wanted to tell him for some time now finally was out. She was surprised how easily it had come to her lips.

"What?" He looked at her through glassy eyes. "What?" he asked again, this time louder.

Kuri sat on the arm of the chair across from Tommy. "You are a highly talented artist, and it was your music that swept me off my feet. Your flattery flattered me, and I admire your spunk and energy. I love you for all of that, but that's all. The studio and our agents clearly treasure and protect our union because it makes headlines. But they don't care how I feel; they even made sure to hide all your—"

"Hide what?" Unsteadily he got off the sofa and pulled the bottle from the ice bucket. Instead of filling the flute, he poured the champagne into a water glass. He pointed at her. "Hide my flings?" He drank too fast, coughed, and wiped his mouth with the back of his hand. "I have needs when I'm away for so long. I keep telling you, none of those chicks mean anything—they mean shit to me." He shrugged. "What can I do?" He took another gulp and fell into the sofa again. "Come here, sugarboo. How many times do I have to tell you, you're the only one for me!"

"I can't be who you want me to be, and I can't give you what you need. We are too different, Tommy—we are worlds apart. I've told you all this twice before. I really tried my best to feel something more for you. I tried again and again, but it's not working…for me."

"C'mon, baby! Let's give it the rule of three; *omne trium perfectum*; I promise our third time around will be perfect and forever satisfying." He laughed and downed the rest of the bubbly from his glass. "Go, take your shower—it'll make you feel better. And then…I'll make you feel even better yet." He laughed louder.

Kuri looked at him through sad eyes. "Again, you didn't hear a word I said," she whispered as she walked out of the room.

"Hey…did I tell you how madly in love I am with you?" he

called after her, slurring his words. "You're mine...all mine, my little sugarboo."

When she returned from the bathroom, Tommy lay passed out on the sofa. She removed the cell phone from his chest and saw the time was 1:30 p.m. She took off his shoes and covered him with a light blanket. He was breathing evenly, deep in sleep; an occasional soft snore parted his lips.

Kuri looked at him and remembered the few moments where he had been kind and compassionate. "But you have a dark side," she said, and wished he could hear her. "You neither have the patience nor the time I need to understand myself," she whispered. "I met someone...someone who I feel can help me find what I've been looking for."

She closed the door to the bedroom and curled up in bed. Ease spread over her face when she saw his handsome face, heard his modulated deep voice, sensed his spirit. Slowly she drifted into sleep with Adam.

Chapter Fifteen

The meeting was not going well. Ethan had expected to spend the entire day going over his prospectus with executives of Orbit Capital Partners, but the meeting was already coming to an end, only two hours after he had entered the VC firm's tall glass headquarters in St. Louis.

"We were hoping to learn more directly from you about your vision for what you foresee as a unique product," said Calvin Gross, one of the senior partners, "but after looking closer into it, and now listening to you, your material does not justify the large risk we believe we'll be taking."

"I beg to differ," Ethan interjected. "This fresh initiative promises to fill a void in the marketplace! My team's work is very distinct; it clearly can't easily be replicated." He attempted to reiterate the highlights of the demo, but he could tell from the expression on their faces that he was losing momentum. He realized his hurried speech might show them how nervous he was; he forced himself to slow down.

"Why not take your product to White Birch, your own family's enterprise? Why did you come to us?" asked Eric van Dandork, another partner.

A vein popped out on Ethan's neck as he willed himself not to smirk at that question. *You're so dumb witted, no wonder your last name ends in dork,* Ethan thought. "It's a personal decision," he said instead, speaking slowly. "I am certain White Birch would fund my product, but it's time I chart my own path without the help of the family business." The lie rolled easily over Ethan's lips, but the memory of the recent confrontation brought back the fury against his father and siblings. He could feel his chest tightening, hear the gurgling in his gut. He cleared his throat and continued his sales pitch. "My team has developed the perfect product; a product that definitely has the market nailed! I'm so confident in this opportunity, I decided to do this on my own."

Calvin Gross closed the prospectus in front of him and looked at Ethan. "My partners and I have discussed your proposal carefully, and after listening to you, I now speak for my colleagues when I say that we have come to a decision. Given the high level of risk associated with your product, we will not be funding this project."

"Please hear me out..." Ethan pleaded, trying to control his exasperation. "I've gone far and beyond what's already available in the virtual reality field. My brand-new concept of tracking, rendering, and display will project the user into a whole new world...it's truly like physically being together." Ethan fumbled for the VR headset he had brought with him. "Allow me to demonstrate..."

"Sorry," Anna Schroeder, another senior partner, interrupted. "I agree with Calvin. It would be against our strategies to bet on the jockey over the horse—or the other way around." She collected the prospectuses as her partners passed them down the table. She piled them on top of each other, stood up, and held out her hand. "It was nice meeting you, Ethan. You and your team are made up of young, capable movers and shakers. This is a big country; another venture may show greater interest in your startup."

Feeling sick to his stomach, Ethan watched them leave the

meeting room. Three of the partners already were talking about other business. Erick van Dandork stopped in the open doorway and turned around. "Take care, Ethan. Just put the rest of your stuff back in the box. I'll see to it that it gets FedExed back to you in Chicago first thing in the morning."

I gotta get out of here . . . fast! Feeling unwell, Ethan sped down the long hallway and stumbled into the ultramodern men's restroom. He didn't recognize the slumped figure staring back at him from the mirror—pasty, depleted, utterly miserable. Suddenly his vision faded, his knees and hands began to tremble. He looked around for support and staggered into the nearest stall just in time to vomit up whatever was in his stomach; the bitter, stinging substance simultaneously spewed through his nostrils and mouth.

The heaving stopped, but painful spasms continued. Ethan groaned and leaned against the door of the stall. He felt lightheaded; his mouth and throat were dry. Slowly, he opened the door and looked around the stark bathroom. He was alone. He went to the sink and rinsed his mouth. He took a quick glimpse in the mirror and shuddered. He washed his face and rinsed his mouth one more time, then ran his fingers through his hair. When the spasms and blurred vision began to ease off, he looked in the mirror again. "Shit," he grunted, wiping flecks of vomit off his new Prada suit. He remembered the two Xanax he'd stashed in the pocket of his jacket. He gulped them down, chasing them with a handful of water.

When he left the building, bright daylight stung his eyes and the city noises hurt his head. He shot dirty looks at two nearby workmen with their asphalt-drilling jackhammers, he glared at intolerant drivers leaning on their horns. The unpleasant squeals and screeches from brakes and the wailing from nearby police sirens stung his senses. Still standing in front of the glass building, he took one last look at the Orbit Capital sign and spat on it.

A few hours later, he stood on the balcony of his apartment in Chicago and imagined himself jumping. Would death end his torment? Would killing himself pass his pain and misery onto his parents and siblings? They would deserve to feel guilty, he told himself; the thought of their suffering gave him much-needed pleasure.

He leaned over the balustrade and looked at the street, forty-two stories below. Cold sweat formed on his head and he felt drowsy. He gagged and almost lost his balance.

"Oh my gosh! What you are doing?" Irina yanked him backward. "You crazy?"

He gagged again and fell onto the outdoor chaise lounge.

"You white like ghost. I call ambulance!"

"Fuck, no! It's nothing. Rough day—I got dizzy, that's all. Stop overreacting. Get me a drink, will you?"

She returned to the balcony with water and crackers. "No alcohol now. No pills now. You need sleep and get better."

He kicked out at her in fury, causing her to stumble and drop the tray she carried. He watched as the water glass shattered and spilled on the spotless terrace. "What the fuck do you know about what I need?" he yelled. He rose from the chaise lounge and kicked the shards of glass away. Still feeling woozy, he reached for the wall. "How the heck did you get in my apartment, anyway?"

"You gave me key last week, plus door was open, *mudak*!" Irina took a long step over the mess on the balcony. "I not clean this up," she scoffed, and stomped inside. "You want drink alcohol? Fine! You want drugs? No problem. Your choice, as always." With blazing eyes and a lopsided smile, she poured gin into the cocktail shaker, then shoved the glass across the marble. "Will this please the emperor?" She saw Ethan pull a new supply of drugs in a plastic bag from his pant pocket. She shook her head. "Where you get this from?" she asked, but he did not answer.

"I'm sorry, Irina-Czarina." His apologetic grin was slow. He cut himself a line of coke and downed the drink with one swallow. "I really had a miserable day. I need some of these pills and I need you; together you will make me feel better." He smacked his lips, swooped her off the floor, and planted her squarely on the counter.

Later, still enjoying the effects the ecstasy drug had on him, Ethan said, "Yes, your emperor is pleased. You always know what I need, don'tcha, my little sexpot?"

They lay sprawled on the bed, admiring the way their naked bodies glistened in the reflection from the city lights that softly streamed through the windowpanes.

"Oh my gosh!" Irina suddenly bolted up, wrapping herself in a towel. "Why you not tell me Kuri Berger is your sister?"

"What? How the fuck do you know that?"

"Downstairs, I wait for elevator with woman who lives in building. She ask who I am going to visit. I tell her, and she ask if I meet your famous sister yet. I tell her I have no idea what she talking about and then she tell it's Kuri Berger. And—oh my gosh—why you hide that from me?"

"Who the fuck was this woman? I purposely haven't told anyone about the family connection; my sister's never even set foot into this building! Who…?"

"Lady says she and husband are old friend of your parents. Small thin woman with silver hair and very elegant; she wore diamond ring bigger than fist. Her name Freda or something…forgot last name."

"Oh, shit! Yeah, her. She and her arrogant husband own one of the penthouses. They're mostly in Santa Barbara and…pffft…of all things, you had to run into her!"

"Well?" Irina stood wide legged, hands on her hips. "Why you not tell me? You even watch *Quorum* with me—you get pissed when I watch episode twice. I tell you that I have crush on Justin Cross and how obsessed I'm with Nura, the character played by"—she widened her stance, leaned closer, and hissed—"*your sister!* Why you never tell me?"

"Because we can't stand each other. We don't get along. Last time I saw her was…" He snorted. "Fuck, I can't even remember."

"Oh my gosh!" Irina sat at the edge of the bed. "What's wrong with you? If she my sister, I wipe her perfect butt."

"You don't know her. She…she ruined my life," he growled.

"She's the one who put the rift between me and my family. I couldn't give a shit if she's good on the screen because in real life she's a fucking mess."

Irina's mouth hung open. "If she's good on screen? Your sister already win Oscar and Golden Globe! I read about her and love see interviews with her. I admire her kindness and philamo...philanepy? No, what's word for giving shitload of money to poor and sick people?"

"Philanthropy my ass..."

"Yes, that's it! Kuri work in Puerto Rico after hurricane. She help people in rubble of homes."

"Hardy-har-har-har! Don't believe everything you read and hear. I have no clue what anyone sees in her. Nothing makes sense in that face or body. Her eyes are a weird mix of Caucasian and Asian, her cheekbones are too pronounced for the rest of her face, her nose is too small, her lips too full, her legs too long, her breasts..." He waved his hands dismissively. "They clearly don't compare to yours!" He pulled Irina close and ran his hands over her curves. "I don't know what people see in my sister; to me she's like a grab bag that nature tossed aside."

Irina pulled away, her forehead crinkled in disbelief. "What planet you come from? Your sister so beautiful and special." She cocked her head. "You jealous of her fame?"

Ethan smiled, trying to camouflage the mixture of fury and envy pulsing through him. "Maybe I have a right to be jealous. You have no idea what she and my family did to me!"

"What you mean? You want to talk about it?"

"It's too tricky and exhausting to explain." He looked at her, terribly tempted to express his own version of events.

"I am good listener, you know that! But I take shower first, and when I come back, you can tell all night. I am cheaper than psychiatrist." She gave him a subtle wink and dashed from the bed.

He watched her and licked his lips. "Before you shower, bring me a generous shot of tequila and the tray of coke—don't forget the straw."

"If what you tell me is true, then your family is wrong," Irina said hours later, lying next to Ethan.

"Right? They owe me!" Ethan smiled, enjoying the high spirits he had been lifted into by unloading his story onto Irina. "I have to figure out how to make them realize how they've wronged me. Not only how they hurt me emotionally, but by cutting me off financially! Fuck, they all owe me big time…especially Kuri!"

Irritated, he looked at Irina who kept mumbling to herself. "Hey, what-what-what? You're talking Ukrainian again."

"Sorry, it's easier to think in my language." She lifted herself onto one elbow. "Your story is sad, but you want to hear worse?" She leaned closer to him. "My friend Olena had not one but two really bad things happen in one year. First, she lost baby in middle of pregnancy. She lost lots of blood, and in hospital she gets bad, bad infection—she almost die. Her husband, Alex, was nervous wreck, but then Olena get better."

"That's it?" Ethan raised his eyebrows. That's your sad story?"

"No, quiet," Irina scolded him. "It get worse. Right after hospital, Olena get call from some banker and lawyer in Ukraine. They tell her of huge inheritance from uncle she hardly knew. She and Alex get really excited because they save money to buy house. The people in Ukraine tell them what Ukrainian lawyer to see in Chicago and to take personal documents to him. That man show them letters from uncle and how much money Olena will get. Lawyer assures Olena and Alex everything is perfect and legit and they give him all their personal information, like social security numbers, birth dates, bank accounts…everything! Lawyer tells them inheritance of over half-million bucks will transfer into their accounts. Olena and Alex wait and wait and wait. And then they get call from bank. Both their bank accounts are empty! They saved good money to buy house, but all gone in end—even lawyer gone! They go to police—I think FBI get involved too—but Olena and Alex never see one penny again. Their credit score now shit. For months they live with me in my tiny apartment, and I buy food for them and try to help with bills. They move to Los Angeles few months ago and live with Alex sister."

Irina rolled on her back and stared at the ceiling. "Police tell Olena and Alex that many people fall for inheritance scams." Irina turned her head and looked at Ethan. "Now that is sad story, right? Oh my gosh, they have nobody to help. You lucky because if this happen to you, your family will feel sorry and help you again."

Ethan was quiet; his mind was working overtime. Then, he pulled her on top of him. "Mmm. Your sad, sad story just gave me an excellent idea!" He slapped her on the behind and grinned. "My lovely Irina is wiser than an owl, isn't she?" When he noticed her surprise about the rare compliment, he quickly added, "But you know I'm smarter than a rat and more slippery than an eel." He laughed and spanked her again. "Is my little wise owl hungry for some prey? Well…why don't you dive and get it!"

Chapter Sixteen

Kuri sank into the soft leather sofa of Dr. Brichta's waiting room. She hadn't taken the time to look around during her first visit, so she took the opportunity now.

The walls were colored like a sunset in warm shades of orange, pink, and yellow. Mellow lighting spread from table lamps left and right of the sofa. *National Geographic* and *National Wildlife* magazines were evenly spread on the oval wooden table. Photographs depicting various species from the animal kingdom were uniformly framed to decorate the walls. Kuri looked from one photograph to the next and wondered who had taken them—Dr. Brichta perhaps, or someone close to her? Was she married? Did she have children? Kuri got up to take a closer look at one photograph showing a leopard clinging onto her cub, hanging onto a tree branch. Kuri noticed how the animals' eyes were locked and believed she could see the worry in the mother and the fear in the cub.

"I took that photo on one of my trips to Africa."

Startled, Kuri's head followed the voice; the door had been opened without a sound. She nodded at Dr. Brichta. "Then you took all of these. They're magnificent!"

"Thank you. Photography is my passion, and I travel to remote parts of the world where my lens can catch the animals in their natural habitat." She opened the door wider. "Please come in."

"I appreciate that you found time for me today," Kuri said, then asked for permission to take off her shoes and make herself comfortable on the sofa across from the therapist's chair. "It feels good being here without an ocean separating us," she said, adjusting herself in the simple cross-legged Sukhasana pose, looking directly at Dr. Brichta.

"I rarely agree to phone appointments," the therapist said. "The exceptions are emergencies."

"Was I…am I an emergency?" An amused expression spread over Kuri's face.

"I was curious when you called from overseas and talked about psychodynamic therapy. You said your thoughts and feelings recently seemed outside your awareness again." Melanie uncrossed her legs, not breaking the eye contact Kuri had initiated.

Kuri smiled. "Your brown eyes are so warm and generous. I don't know why, but for as long as I can remember, I've gotten to know people through their eyes."

"What do mine tell you?"

"That you want to help me." Kuri relaxed deeper into the soft sofa. "That you are caring and that you love to laugh. You're independent, quite determined, and strong willed. You love nature—those beautiful photos in your waiting room bear witness. But I see something else in your eyes, too—a sense of spirituality, really. Maybe that is what draws me toward you."

Dr. Brichta's eyebrows lifted, almost imperceptibly. "How intriguing," she said, and cocked her head; her hands formed a steeple that slightly hovered above her lap. "When you called, you were very eager to make an appointment today."

"Since I returned from Germany last week, I've been having new disturbing dreams."

"What can you tell me about them?"

"They're about my brother Ethan. You should know that he and

I have had little to no contact over the years. Not because of my crazy schedule but because he always disliked me. From the day I was born, he wanted me gone! When his attempts to get rid of me failed, he would call me ugly names, press my face into mirrors, and say I looked hideous. He told me I was stupid and never would amount to anything. He knew I was treated for mental illness and took every opportunity to let me know I was possessed by the devil."

Kuri paused to readjust herself back into the Sukhasana pose. "Strangely enough, Ethan's hurtful mistreatment did not seem to affect me. As young as I was, I could see he was crying out for love, and I felt sorry for him. His sibling envy had a corrosive effect on his ability to show attachment to anyone. I tried to protect him and even lied to my parents so they would not know how bad things were. The more I shielded and defended him, the more he hated me." Kuri blinked a tear away, then reached for the Kleenex box and put it beside her. "In case I need more," she said, grimacing.

"Do these incidents of your childhood have anything to do with your recent dreams?"

"Yes and no. In my dreams, Ethan and I have found a way to reach a place of harmony and love, but as soon as I begin to feel happy, Ethan morphs into another person, someone who brutalizes me, calls me horrible names, and tortures me. This transformed version of Ethan looks foreign, even the voice is unfamiliar." Kuri dabbed her wet cheeks, then restored eye contact with Dr. Brichta. "These dreams are so vivid, they feel numbingly real. They take me back to the phantasmagorical visions of my childhood."

"You said despite everything that happened in the past, you still long for a close relationship with Ethan. Have you thought of initiating contact with your brother?"

"When I woke up this morning, I had a weird thought. What if my nightmares are trying to give me a message?"

"In your dream, does this monstrous version of your brother have a face? Could it be someone else from your past?"

Kuri lowered her eyes and, after a long silence, whispered, "Maybe." The muscles in her face tightened.

"When we spoke on the phone," Dr. Brichta pressed, "you told me of the impact the Dachau visit had on you. You had trouble distinguishing between imagination and reality; you talked about mental images so heinous they caused you to faint. Can you feel a connection between those and your recent dreams?"

"I think so, but I really don't understand! That's why I am here, Dr. B. I need you to help me discover what's locked up deep inside—something I'm unable to express." Kuri sunk into the sofa, her beautiful face clouded by frustration. "I know you've helped others through hypnotherapy. When do you think I'll be ready for it?"

The therapist leaned forward. She folded her hands over Kuri's. "Soon! I do need some more information for hypnotic strategies to work. When I determine you're ready, though, it may take only a few sessions for the treatments to be effective." She pulled back her hand and reached for her calendar. "Let's make another appointment while you're in the Chicago area. If necessary, I'm also willing to speak with you via phone or FaceTime when you're out of town again. I don't usually conduct appointments that way, but I can make an exception in this case."

"I'll be at my parents over the Fourth of July before I go to New York for a cover shoot and interview next Monday. It's going to be crazy busy because my publicist also lined up several talk-show appearances. I'm glad we will book more appointments now; hopefully we can start hypnotherapy as soon as I return to Chicago."

"We still have a few more minutes left today. When you told me about your emotional experiences in Dachau, you mentioned the bond you formed with the young doctor who had helped you, Adam. Have you kept in touch?"

Kuri buried her face into the palms of her hands. "I can't believe I'm blushing—I get excited just hearing his name," she said, chuckling. "Haven't seen him other than on the screen of my phone or laptop, but every time we talk, it's like there's a mysterious connection pulling me closer and closer toward him." Kuri uncrossed her legs and grounded her feet to the floor. "And guess what? While I'm in New York, he'll visit me." She playacted quivering, as if struck by electric shock. "Look at me." She laughed. "I am buzzed beyond belief!"

Chapter Seventeen

As soon as he finished his strength training in the space that he recently had turned into a fitness room in his house, Adam took off for the Esplanade Run. He didn't bother looking at his watch, he knew how long it would take him to complete the seven-mile loop; he'd have more than enough time to shower and get ready for dinner with his boss.

It was the perfect day for a run—pleasant temperatures and low humidity were always welcome during the month of July. Adam looked forward to each running day, especially on those when he was by himself. Once he put aside routine concerns and other banalities of life, he focused on mentally organizing his schedule for the weeks ahead. There were two patients who needed extra sessions, which meant he'd have to shuffle some other appointments around. Would there be enough time to brief the interim therapist covering for him during September? He also thought about how irritated his boss had been after being informed that Adam was leaving for an entire month for the third year in a row. Regardless, Adam was looking forward to his annual consultancy at Rancho del Sol in

Sedona; it was an extended working sabbatical he had negotiated for himself before he started working at Capps Capital.

Conrad Capperton, the manager of Capps Capital, had heard of Adam while he was still in graduate school and cultivated a friendship with the young psychiatrist in training. Capps referred to Adam as "my young medical genius" and offered him a job as the in-house psychiatrist at Boston's prominent hedge fund company immediately after graduation.

Adam did not like to talk about his achievements, and few people knew that he had graduated high school before his sixteenth birthday. Because he was still so young, it had been more difficult finding a university that would accept his determination to immediately begin studying medicine. The fact that his father had his own outstanding reputation and was on the faculty of Harvard of course was an asset, but Adam's unique qualifications and his excellent academic record were in demand; thus, the oldest institution of higher education in the United States opened its doors wide to Adam.

It wasn't the career he'd envisioned for himself, but Adam enjoyed working for Capps Capital, where a young new strain of alpha males challenged all activist investing. The self-made billionaires were madcap thrill-seekers; at times, Adam even imagined these daredevils capable of trekking up the dramatic ridges of Mount Annapurna in shorts and gym shoes. His patients at Capps Capital considered Adam their performance coach, and during their individual sessions, they seemed to look forward to relieving themselves of their most private and intimate perplexities, and occasionally, they even set free some of the firm's most confidential secrets. Even though Adam was younger by a decade or more than his clients, he had a given talent to ease each patient's personal chaos. But as they were prone to the stress of their jobs, the therapeutic comfort was short-lived—the constant stress of their jobs always brought them back to Adam's office with new burdens.

A female jogger came sprinting toward him, and Adam's heartbeat quickened. Her long legs, her lean, athletic, yet proportionately curvy body, the baseball cap low above dark sunglasses, reminded him of Kuri, and instantly her voice rang in his ear—they had talked again for over than an hour the previous night. He was looking forward to Friday and the weekend trip to New York City to see her again.

During their many conversations, Adam had learned more about her life, her likes, and her dislikes. He had listened with interest to the stories she told about growing up with her family. Her account of her brother Ethan's behavior toward her was disturbing, yet Adam refrained from going into therapist mode with her, he never interrupted and let her talk freely. He also had learned how she got involved in film and television and admired her work ethic. He was awed by her zestful energy when she found a captivating project. She said transforming herself into a new character was a great therapeutic tool that allowed her to deal better with her younger, problematic years.

Adam realized he had passed the halfway mark; as usual, he increased his speed, then returned to his thoughts. As much as he'd learned about Kuri, he also had shared more details of his own life. In addition to talking about his work and hobbies, he had openly discussed the relationship he had with a British woman he had met at Harvard. They lived together but after two years decided to go their own ways when Adam resisted committing to a long-term relationship.

He felt free to tell Kuri everything, except for the most important thing—the real reason behind his trip to Germany. How could he expect her to accept that he'd gained knowledge of a previous life experience, and that it continued to reverberate in his existence even now? To him, of course, everything had become clear when the PLR therapy provided firmer shape to his elusive visions, especially after locating the farm in Bavaria. The moment he found and read Shimmy's letter, Adam had his validation—born decades apart, his and Shimmy's lives were linked by the mysterious force of nature. Yet Adam felt uncomfortable talking about it; he knew that sooner than later people would be open to accept his story rather than stamp him a charlatan. But above all, without understanding why, Adam was convinced that finding Kuri in Dachau was somehow connected to his profound revelation.

An angry car horn and screeching brakes seized Adam from his reverie. He stopped and mouthed an apology to the driver. He turned onto Follen Street, a quiet tree-lined road in the South End Back Bay location. He slowed his pace for this last stretch until he reached his home—a small brownstone his parents purchased after their marriage. After they adopted Adam, the Gold family moved into a larger home but continued renting out the brownstone, gifting it to Adam on his twentieth birthday.

The moment he entered the house, he went straight to the refrigerator and pulled out a quart of coconut water, drinking greedily. The digital clock on the stove showed there was plenty of time before he had to leave again. He showered, used the clippers on his overgrown stubble, then rifled through his closet. He picked out a slim pair of light gray pants and a black shirt to wear at dinner. Since he still had time before having to leave the house, he decided to check his email.

As usual, there were many messages that didn't require his attention; these he simply deleted. He became engrossed in an interesting new study on hypnotherapy a colleague had sent him and almost ignored the incoming text message alert. Then he remembered his boss frequently changed dinner plans at the last minute, but the message was from Sarah Goldstein, a genealogist who specialized in tracing Jews who'd perished in the Shoah. Adam had met her on one of his earlier trips to Europe, when he was searching to make the connection to his visions. Soon after he had discovered the Bauer farm, he emailed Sarah and gave her the names and cities mentioned in Shimmy's letter. He was eager to see what she had found.

Adam, her text said, *I am sending a separate email with detailed attachments containing my findings. I think you'll be pleased with the results. —S.*

He looked at the inbox, but there was nothing. Nervously he refreshed the page over and over again until he heard the ding of an incoming email. Holding his breath, he moved the cursor to the top of his inbox and clicked on Sarah Goldstein's name.

Dear Adam:

I hope this finds you well.

My work in Ukraine, Hungary, and Poland is finished for now, and I'll be returning to California in two days.

Your project kept me on my toes, to say the least. The good news: I have extensive up-to-date results on relatives of Shimon Messing. Unfortunately, my research on Judith Rozenblum's family was less successful.

After reading my summaries, please open each of the attached files for all the details.

"Oh my God," Adam whispered. "There are relatives? Maybe alive today?" With great anticipation he began to read.

SUMMARY—Part 1

ROZENBLUM
Dora and Arthur Rozenblum,
One daughter: Judith
Last known address: Rosenstrasse 20, Berlin-Schöneberg

1938

Arthur Rozenblum and his brother Salomon were arrested and sent to Sachsenhausen. Salomon was killed that year in Sachsenhausen.

1942

Arthur was transported to Dachau. He died January 3, 1943, from high-altitude medical experiments, performed by Dr. Sigmund Rascher. I've attached the details for all of the following years.

A.R.doc

1942

Dora and Judith Rozenblum were arrested and sent to Ravensbrück.

1944

Dora and Judith were transported to Dachau (one of last transports).

Dora died of typhoid December 25, 2944, in Dachau.

D.R.doc

April 26, 1945

Judith Rozenblum was sent on death march.

J.R.doc

Note: I found survivor records from Dachau Death March. Judith Rozenblum's name is not among them.

Dachau-Death-March-Survivors.doc

MESSING

Nanette and Ferdinand Messing

Two children: Golda and Shimon

Ferdinand's parents: Edith and Herschel Messing

Last known address: Bahnhofstrasse 25, Oświęcim.

(Oświęcim was annexed into Third Reich and named Auschwitz. Renamed Oświęcim in January 1945 when Wehrmacht was pushed out by Red Army).

1938 Nanette Messing dies (natural causes)

1940 Ferdinand Messing dies (natural causes)

1941 Shimon Messing prisoner #177404 in Auschwitz

1943 Edith and Herschel Messing become prisoners in Auschwitz II-Birkenau

1943 Shimon Messing transported to Dachau

1944 Edith Messing exterminated in Auschwitz II-Birkenau

1945 Herschel Messing exterminated in Auschwitz II-Birkenau

1945 Shimon Messing was sent on Death March
Messing Family.doc

Note: No record of Shimon Messing found on Survivor Dachau Death March list (see above .doc Dachau-Death-March-Survivors).

Adam:

The list of survivors from the forced march out of Dachau is incomplete. Judith Rozenblum and Shimon Messing may have been among those never identified or among those who died on the march from disease or exhaustion. I tried all of my resources but was unable to find any information about them after April 1945. Sorry.

Because you were able to supply me with the information that Golda Messing was "adopted" by Janina and Waclaw Kuczok in 1941 and took on the name of Mara Kuczok, I had more luck! See below.

The unwelcoming ping of a new incoming message—this one from Conrad Capperton—forced Adam to turn away from the computer screen. He looked at his iPhone.

Hi All: Sorry to cancel dinner on short notice. Something came up. Leaving for London early AM. Back in three days. —Capps.

Relieved and delighted, Adam returned his attention back to Sarah Goldstein's email.

SUMMARY—Part 2

July 1945

Janina and Waclaw Kuzcok with daughter Mara moved from Kety, Poland, to Crakow, Poland.

kuzcok.doc

February 1955

Mara Kuzcok (28) changes her name back to Golda Messing.

legal name register.doc

April 21, 1957

Golda Messing (30) moves to Rivne, Ukraine. Marries Paul Ivanenko.

marriage license G&P Ivanenko.doc

September 5, 1958

Paul Ivanenko (38) dies in plane crash / military exercise.

death certificate P.I.doc

November, 24, 1958

Golda Ivanenko (31) files for legal name change from Ivanenko to (maiden name) Messing.

name register G.M.doc

December 12, 1958

Golda (31) gives birth to Ferdinand Paul Messing.

birth certificate F.M.doc

January 18, 1985

Ferdinand Messing (27) marries Irina Andrukh (23).

marriage license F&M Messing.doc

October 12, 1990

Golda Messing (63) dies in Rivne Hospital (cause: lung cancer).

death certificate G.M.doc

August 2, 1993

Irina Andrukh-Messing (31) gives birth to daughter Golda Messing.

birth certificate G.I.M.doc

May 1, 2007

Irina (45) and Ferdinand Messing (49) die in train collision near Kiev.

Last known address: 58 Soborna Street, Rivne, Ukraine

death certificates M&F M.doc

May 30, 2007

Golda Messing (14) becomes ward of state / Rivne orphanage (no known relatives).

Rivne Orphanage.doc

January 21, 2008

Golda Messing (15) disappears from orphanage.

Rivne Orphanage.doc

Adam:

I located Bela Birinski, a former neighbor of the Messings, in Rivne. Golda was close to the Birinski family and came to them for help after running away from the orphanage.

According to Birinski, Golda Messing met an American citizen with Ukrainian heritage, Anton Korolenko (35). Golda told Birinski that A.K. wanted to marry and take her to the United States. Against Birinski's warning and pleading, Golda left.

Birinski notified authorities because of Golda's age. By the time authorities went into action, Birinski assumed A. Korolenko had taken Golda out of Ukraine.

I searched for Anton Korolenko. See Part 3:

SUMMARY—Part 3

November 11, 2008

Anton Korolenko reenters United States at O'Hare Airport, Chicago.

On same day Golda Messing enters United States at O'Hare Airport, Chicago, with Polish passport on a visitor's visa.

passenger list immigration record.doc

March 12, 2009

Golda Messing (16) marries Anton Korolenko (36) in Chicago.

Address: 5430 Main Street, Morton Grove, Illinois

Marriage certificate G&A Korolenko Cook County Clerk's Office.doc

July 14, 2012

Dissolution of marriage between Anton Korolenko (40) and Golda Korolenko (19).

clerk of circuit court Cook County Illinois.doc

November 1, 2012

Golda Korolenko (20) changes name to Irina Golda Messing.

Address: 1501 N. Honore, Unit 3, Chicago, Illinois

(Something is unclear about the legality of name change and her marriage license. See my comments below.)

Adam:

I found it heartwarming that three generations of women kept changing their name back to Messing—as if to honor the loved ones who perished.

Meanwhile, it took effort and patience to locate Golda Korolenko's whereabouts after the divorce. I finally found her under new name (see my mention above in part 3).

My research resulted in no legal status for either naturalization or permanent residency for either Golda Korolenko or Irina Golda Messing. I don't know much about immigration and naturalization procedures and did not want to spend more of my time or your money on this matter. Should you be interested in finding out about her legal status in the United States, I can refer you to an excellent lawyer in that field.

Also, unless Irina Golda Messing moved from the Chicago address, you should have no problem getting in touch with her.

If you want to continue your own research for possible survivors on the Rozenblum side, I can let you know where to look and who to contact.

You know when and where to reach me.
Always warmly,
Sarah

Adam sat motionless, staring through the computer screen into a mental space where the names and dates he had just read began to blur in his vision and slowly were replaced by indistinct images struggling to take shape. When he began hearing the murmur of voices, he knew the past was reaching out to him again. He let go of all self-focus and embraced complete relaxation so the contents of his subconscious could come to the surface. Adam's deep spiritual gaze took him back in time—returning him to his path of another existence and to the events of Shimon Messing's life.

Chapter Eighteen

1942

The days are long and grueling, the nights are dark and lonely—twenty-four hours are filled with sobs, groans, pain, and death. I close my eyes and will myself to silence the suffering around me by thinking of a place that is pure with light and love—that's where I find Mama and Papa. They renew my strength, they heal my wounds, they feed and nourish me. It's the only way I find the courage to bravely face the block kapo who counts out our tattooed numbers during *appell* every morning at 5:30. Sometimes when the number of prisoners is not correct, we must remain standing in wooden shoes and thin clothing until an SS officer finally makes the numbers tally. This can take hours, regardless of hot or cold temperatures, regardless of rain or snow.

The death rate from slave labor and starvation is growing every day, yet the demand for labor keeps increasing. I see more prisoners arrive daily; I ask many of them if they know anything about Edith and Herschel Messing, my bubbeh and zaydeh. Heads shake weakly and sad eyes look upon me with empathy, because most everybody is looking for their own loved ones as well.

I don't worry about Golda—I feel she is safe with Agata's cousins and tell myself every day that passes can only bring me closer to reuniting with her again.

Despite the meager rations, I manage to stay strong. After morning roll call we get a half liter of boiled water with some grain-based substance they call coffee. I don't like the taste, but I cherish every drop because the next meal is not until lunch, when we get a watery imitation of soup. I always count my blessings when I find a piece of rutabaga or turnip or potato in it. In the evening, the Germans give us a small piece of black bread—on rare lucky days we receive a tearing of sausage or cheese. I chew and drink very slowly—this way I can pretend it is more. And when I'm very hungry, I feed on Papa's words: "Never lose hope and always have confidence in your future. We Jews can't allow ourselves the luxury of feeling despair." When I think of Papa, I feel his comforting arm around me. "All people are like bicycles," he used to say. "They can only keep their balance as long as they keep moving."

I work on the construction site of the IG-Farben factory. Every day I either load excavation debris into railroad carts or, when they send me to another area, I have to overturn the carts and empty them. The work is exhausting to many of us—especially the older ones. I force myself to work fast because I see what happens to those who can't. They get flogged, then forced to work faster even through their pain. I try to help other prisoners whenever I can, but I have to be careful; when the guards see someone assisting others, the punishment is severe.

I have already been beaten many times. One day, I was so hungry, I searched the garbage pail, and a guard caught me. He made me strip naked and gave me twenty lashes with his whip. Another time I saw a potato field across the tracks. After emptying debris from a cart, I managed to sneak into the field and stuff my pockets full of potatoes. I was so happy to share the raw crop with those working near me, but then a guard spotted some of us chewing. He whistled for help, and we were severely beaten—some so severely they had to be taken to the hospital. It is common knowledge that if we do not heal in four to five days, we will be gassed. I stay out of trouble now; I still blame myself having been the cause of punishment or death to others.

1943

I don't know what day it is, but looking at the sky and feeling the warmth of the spring sun, I know it must be around the time of my fourteenth birthday.

Many of us, those who are still able to labor, are moved to Auschwitz III—a camp closer to the IG Farben Buna-Werke near Monowice—the Germans call the village Monowitz. The camp is overcrowded, but we now don't have to walk seven kilometers to and from the worksite every day. I hear we are considered too valuable to be sent to the gas chamber—as long as we can keep up the work, we are allowed to live.

I develop some good electrical skills, and a foreman by the name of Hans Schlichte seems to take a liking to me. He doesn't talk much, but he teaches me how to troubleshoot systems or isolate problems caused by faulty wiring.

"You sure you're not German?" Schlichte asks, watching me splicing wires together.

"I always thought I was," I answer calmly. "I was born in Breslau. I went to German school, and I speak the same language as you."

He hands me electrical tape. "Blond, blue eyes, tall... if it wasn't for the number on your arm, you could've fooled me." He shakes his head and motions me to work faster.

I never dare to strike up a conversation, but when Schlichte checks my finished work, I can tell he's pleased. Sometimes he even mumbles, "*Gute Arbeit*," before he sends me to my next assignment.

One day, I see Schlichte pull a sandwich from his pocket and leave it on a stool nearby. My mouth is watering, but there are workers and guards nearby. I think Schlichte may be testing me, so I choose hunger over beatings.

The next day Schlichte asks me why I didn't take the sandwich and I answer that it wasn't mine. With a faint smile he pulls a new sandwich from his work smock and stuffs it into the pocket of my prison jacket. "Eat!" he commands. "You are getting too thin."

From that day on, Schlichte slips me a thick piece of bread or a few slices of meat or chunks of cheese. On days when we work among other prisoners and guards, he tells me where he has hidden my daily blessing.

We hear the screams from a prisoner when he falls off a scaffold, near where Schlichte and I are doing an electrical installation. A different foreman tells Schlichte he needs someone to help transport the injured man. Another prisoner and I carry the wounded seven kilometers to the hospital—of course, we're accompanied by a guard with a rifle.

As soon as the nurses put the injured on a gurney, our guard barks orders at us to head back. Suddenly he stops and stands at attention. I don't know why, but somehow I smell fear in the air. I look up to see a good-looking man in a white coat—a doctor. His eyes examine me up and down. He smiles. "*Sprichst Du Deutsch?*"

"*Ja.*"

"Why are *you* here?"

"We brought in an injured man from Monowitz."

"I see you are strong! How old are you?"

I lie without hesitation. "I am sixteen."

He pulls a lollipop from his white coat. "Hmm... is sixteen too old to enjoy sweets?" he asks teasingly.

I want that lollipop so badly, but instead I say, "Thank you, but sugar slows down my metabolism. I need my energy to work."

"*Gute Antwort!*" He laughs, obviously pleased with my reply. He puts the lollipop back into his pocket, then looks at our guard, nods his head to the left, and walks away.

Outside, the guard hits me hard with his rifle. "*Du Judenschwein hast kein Benehmen!*" His angry face is close to mine, and he hisses, "Next time Herr Doktor Mengele speaks to you, you had better call him Herr Doktor! You're lucky; he only let you go today because he sees you can be used as a good worker." He spits on my wooden shoe. "Work…that's all you're good for, you Jew swine." He again cracks the rifle across my back.

❋

Month after month, week after week, more and more of us are sent to the gas chamber. Thick dark smoke rises from the chimneys around the clock now. I hear little kids banging on doors, screaming for their mothers; I see traumatized mothers falling to their knees, pleading as their babies are tossed into the air for target practice. My heart bleeds, but it keeps beating; my soul weeps but tells me I'm being tested—I have no choice but to constantly find new ways to survive this hell.

Bubbeh's voice often rings in my ear. One of the many wise things she used to say is, "*Di velt iz sheyn; di mentshn makhn zi mies.*" Oh yes, my bubbeh was so right: The world is beautiful, but people make it ugly. Since I'm unable to change what I can't accept, I have to accept what I cannot change.

I welcome the night when I can lie in my bunk, close my eyes, and escape this dark world. I imagine Mama and Papa surrounded by beautiful golden white light; I hear their healing words and feel their soothing hands. I see Bubbeh in the kitchen taking a loaf of sweet-smelling challah from the oven and handing me a thick warm slice with butter. I pretend I'm sitting next to Zaydeh—our heads are close and bent over a new book. I hear Golda sing her favorite song.

1944

"Why?" I whisper to Schlichte, who is standing behind me, overseeing my work on the electric fence. "Where will they send me?"

"I don't know," he whispers back. "Something is going on—I hear there'll be new resettlements everywhere—transports to other camps."

"Changes for you, too?"

Schlichte shrugs. "Maybe. I hope to be transferred into Germany, closer to my wife and children in Dresden." He takes a step forward, and we stand shoulder to shoulder. With his tools, he pushes the barbed wire away from me, so I can do my work—he's never been so close to me.

"I think it's good to get out of here while you're still strong." He speaks softly, hardly moving his lips. "There'll be a transport of mostly Hungarian Jews to Dachau—I'll make sure you're on it."

❋

I know Schlichte tried to help by getting me out of Auschwitz. Little did he realize he was merely sending me into another hell.

I am among what seems thousands of Jews, forced to march for days with no idea where we are going or for how long we will have to endure hunger, thirst, and severe muscle spasms. The SS henchmen scream and curse when our pace slows. We don't dare step out of line to relieve ourselves, or we will be severely beaten with the butt end of rifles or with iron bars. Anyone who falls from exhaustion and has trouble getting up is killed. Gunshots and piercing screams overpower the cries of pain or prayers for God to take their lives before evil will. And so, we keep marching between faultless rivers of sinless blood.

At night, in between bits of spasmodic sleep, we shovel anything we can find into our empty stomachs—grass, bugs, leaves, even mud. When it rains, we lift our faces to the skies and open our mouths to relieve our thirst. When I hear the never-ending gunshots and see relentless beatings, I tune out everything around me and silently pray, finding solace in thoughts of my family and our happy, carefree times together.

Finally, on the fourth day, we reach a train depot and are loaded onto cattle cars. Weary beyond belief, we realize how many of us were shot, beaten to death, or died from exhaustion along the way; less than a thousand of us remain. In a state of total physical and mental exhaustion, we collapse onto each other inside the cattle wagons. When the Germans slam and bolt the doors from the outside, we hear one of them shout that the train is bound for Dachau.

❈

ARBEIT MACHT FREI—that sinister black iron gate mocks us as we hobble through it. Some of us can barely walk. We're exhausted and scared of what will be next.

The Germans have us disinfected and force us to take cold showers. We are given new prison outfits made from heavy, coarse denim, but we get no hats and no underwear. We are assigned into barracks that are already overcrowded. Someone tells me these rooms originally were designed for fifty prisoners, but I think there are more than two hundred men crammed in here.

Learning new strict rules and regulations distracts me from dwelling on struggles, worries, and more misery. The SS are counting us three times a day in the big square, and no matter what kind of weather, like in Auschwitz, we again must stand at attention for long periods of time. It is already getting colder; on many days dark clouds make sunless skies even more dismal.

We are given a quarter loaf of bread and told to make it last three days. After each morning's barley broth, we receive no more nourishment until the watery soup in the evening. I know I have lost weight, but I must keep strong.

❈

One of the older Hungarian Jews I share my bunk with dies during the night. He and I were unable to communicate, but he was a kind man—he always smiled at me and nodded before I went to sleep. We have to carry his corpse from the barrack to the square for the counting—the dreaded roll call.

"*Wer ist Nummer eins-sieben-sieben-vier-null-vier?*" a guard bellows out.

I move through three lines of men and step forward.

"*Zeig' Deinen Arm.*" A guard grabs me and checks the number on my arm, looks at the piece of paper in his hand, and commands, "*Mitkommen!*" I follow him into the administration building.

I keep my head down as I walk through the warm, spotless rooms with their immaculate furniture, but I'm overwhelmed by the aroma of tobacco smoke and freshly brewed coffee—I cannot remember the last time I smelled such things. But here, surrounded by monsters, even these sweet smells make me want to vomit.

The guard knocks on one of the doors. When a deep voice from inside orders him to enter, he motions me to follow him.

"*Heil Hitler!*" The guard salutes a man in a field gray uniform with silver collar piping and shoulder boards.

"I found him," the guard says, steps aside, and tells me to stand straight.

The SS officer behind the desk commands the guard to wait outside.

"*Jawohl, Herr Unterscharführer!*" The guard salutes. "*Heil Hitler!*" Then he's gone.

"*Sprichst Du Deutsch?*"

"*Ja.*" I force myself to look straight at this German—a big man with broad shoulders—meeting his gaze with my own. His sparse dark hair is precisely parted but strangely low on the right. His reddish complexion and the knit between his thick brows make him look angry.

"Name?"

I'm afraid to give him my name. "*Eins-sieben-sieben-vier-null-vier,*" I say reflexively.

He grimaces. "Name, I said!"

I swallow. "Shimon Messing."

He takes his time writing something on the papers in front of him, closes the fountain pen, and leans back, studying me with a closed-lipped smile. "Interesting," he says, and narrows his eyes. "So, you helped with electric repairs in Auschwitz?"

I immediately think of Schlichte. He must still be trying to help me from afar.

"*Ja,*" I answer.

"I understand you did good work there. I'm willing to give you the chance to do the same here. Understand?"

"*Jawohl.*"

He picks up the phone and barks short instructions to someone on the other end. Then he looks at me again. "You realize you are very fortunate...don't screw it up!"

❊

The German I work with now, Herr SS Schütze Karl-Heinz Blonke, is the opposite of Schlichte. This one talks a lot and laughs at his own jokes that aren't funny. He has a heavy limp, but he still can walk as fast as he talks. He tells me before the war he was an electrician in Stuttgart. While fighting the enemy, he says, he got injured and his lower leg was amputated; he lifts up his pant leg and proudly shows me his prosthesis.

Blonke is a hard worker, and he makes sure I keep up with him. I am grateful we work indoors in one of the armament factories outside Dachau. I am given extra rations of bread and clean water. Blonke is a slight man and often doesn't finish his midday meal; whenever he tosses the rest into a garbage pail, he laughs and dares me to retrieve it. I do it all the same.

Chapter Nineteen

Throughout the hour of grooming and feeding the horses, they had been engaged in a spirited conversation, and as they walked from the stables back to the main house, they pondered about their exchange of views. Before entering the house, they removed remnants of hay from their sleeves and brushed the dust off their pants.

Teruko lifted her head and looked at Kuri. "After everything you told me, I'd feel better if I called Ethan to make different arrangements for getting together." She stopped talking when she pulled a long strand of hay from Kuri's hair. "I could give him the choice to meet us here, or I'll accompany you to his place in the city," she continued.

"Absolutely!" David said, looking at his youngest daughter. "I don't like the idea of you being with your brother by yourself—especially not after such a long time of estrangement."

"Mom, Dad…please! He reached out to me and now I need to know why Ethan wants to see me! Please don't stress out about it. I told you, I've been thinking about contacting him even before his phone call."

"At least it's comforting to know you talked to your therapist about the history between you and Ethan." Teruko pulled her daughter into an embrace. "Now, I simply need to trust that you're making the right decision."

"But I don't trust *him!*" David's brows drew together. "I told you what he did during our last meeting. I'm convinced he has a new Machiavellian plot; he just wants...no, he *will* expect something from you!" David took off his glasses and wiped his eyes. "Ethan is my flesh and blood—having to say these things about him is like stabbing myself."

Kuri touched her father's arm, then took his hand. "I'm sorry, Dad—I know how difficult this is for you and Mom." Side by side, they walked into the kitchen, and she waited until he sat at the table. "I'll get some water for us," she said, motioning her mother to relax as well.

While her father continued trying to persuade Kuri otherwise, she remained insistent. "Please, let me do what I feel is the right thing to do," she said.

She showered, got dressed, and made sure her laptop, phone, and few other necessary items were in her small carry-on; having another extensive wardrobe in her New York City apartment didn't require her to pack any clothes.

"I promise to call you on my way to the airport...right after I leave Ethan!" she called out to her parents. She blew them a kiss through the open window as the car pulled out of the driveway.

Forty-five minutes later, Kuri opened the door and exited the car. "No need to get out, Stan," she said, stepping up to the driver's window. "Don't go too far. I'll text you if I have to leave earlier, but otherwise I'll meet you down here at three o'clock."

"Kuri...your hat."

Kuri laughed and gave Stan a thumbs-up. She pulled the hat close into her face, donned her sunglasses, and walked into the elegant lobby of her brother's condominium building.

"Kim Haynes to see Ethan Berger," she said to the doorman, who nodded politely and called Ethan to announce his visitor.

Alone on the elevator, Kuri did some quick vocal toning—a technique she had learned to reduce stress hormones. She massaged her fingertips and wiggled her toes, then took a deep breath before the door opened on the forty-second floor.

"Kim Haynes? Hahahaha!" Ethan's laugh was unnaturally high and rang falsely in Kuri's ears. "It's good to see you, little sister," he said as he embraced her awkwardly. Keeping his arm limply around her shoulder, he led her into his apartment. "Let me look at you." He stepped back and dropped his jaw theatrically. "Wow! You look sensational!"

Kuri ignored her brother's hyperbole; she could tell he was on edge and knew it would take some work on her part to make him comfortable. "To be honest, I was rather nervous to visit you," she said, "but now that I'm here, it's really good to see you."

"Come, sit down. Relax. You want a cocktail?" Ethan walked to the bar area and pulled a few bottles from the cabinet. "I totally stopped drinking, but I stock only the best for myse—my guests."

"No alcohol for me. If you have sparkling water…"

"LaCroix okay?"

"LaCroix and no ice, please." Kuri watched as he poured two glasses, then handed one to her.

"Here's to new beginnings." She clinked her crystal with his, noticing that his face contorted as he sipped the water. She wondered how long he had been sober. Her parents certainly were concerned that he might still be drinking or using drugs. But she was here to make peace, not to confront him. She looked away from him and walked through the great room.

"Your place is magnificent, Ethan. I'm not surprised—you always had excellent taste." She turned back to her brother, seeking eye contact. "It's been too long! There's so much we need to share. You want to start?"

"Everything is more than chaotic—I'm not even sure where to begin."

Kuri was still trying to figure out why he was rolling his eyes as he said this when he darted over to the sofa, sat down, but promptly got up again. She watched him walk to the balcony doors and open them, only to close them immediately. Her eyes followed him as he paced back and forth like a caged animal, casting an occasional glimpse in her direction.

"Ethan, are you okay?"

"I'm sure you had long talks with Mom and Dad behind my back. Knowing our father, he told you that I am a fucking mess, right? Well, whatever he said, you need to hear my side."

Kuri stepped in his way, forcing him to stop his pacing. "I came here because I wanted to. It has nothing to do with Mom and Dad. You said you wanted to fix our broken relationship; I really want that too."

She noticed fine beads of sweat forming on her brother's forehead; she saw the tension in his muscles and heard his labored breathing. Were those signs of drug withdrawal or simply emotional agitation? She couldn't be sure. She would have to give him the benefit of the doubt.

"I want us to work on being friends, Ethan," she said. "Tell me where to begin. What can I do?"

"Really?" He sniffed. "Will you excuse me for a minute? I have something to get…eh…something to show you." He sniffed again.

She watched him disappear behind a door at the end of the hallway.

Chapter Twenty

"Quick. Where is it?"

Irina pointed to the left of the marble vanity.

Expertly he laid out lines and snorted the white powder. "My drink?" he snapped.

She pointed to the opposite side of the marble vanity.

He washed down an Adderall with a shot of tequila, then bent over the sink and rinsed his mouth with Listerine. Without looking at her, he asked, "You ready?"

"Puh! You need ask? I sit on hot coal here for long time." She smoothed her form-hugging red dress and lifted her chin. "Well?"

"You look perfect! Remember, I'll do most of the talking. Do not interrupt! I have a plan." He pointed his index finger at her. "When you see her, don't get too excited—I know how starstruck you are. Don't fuck this up!" He bent down and tugged on his dog's collar. "Let's go, Lolli-girl. Now you can watch a snake selling snakes to a snake."

It thrilled Ethan to see the surprise on Kuri's face when he returned hand in hand with Irina.

"This is my fiancée, Irina Messing, and this lovable furry beast is Lolli," he gushed—feeling more confident and alert after his secret fix.

"Your fiancée? Nobody told me." Kuri drew closer. "What a lovely surprise." She opened her arms. "May I give you a hug?"

"Oh my gosh. The Kuri Berger hugging me. You are…oh my gosh, you are so gorgeous. I am huge fan." Irina's hands trembled as she leaned into the embrace.

"This is very exciting." Kuri laughed, holding onto Irina's hands. "When did you two become engaged? Mom and Dad didn't say a word. Do they even know?"

"I was going to tell them, but ever since Dad kicked me out of White Birch, I've been too distressed." Ethan pulled Irina onto the sofa next to him. Without looking at his sister, he gestured her to sit down in one of the chairs. He shifted and shoved a pillow out of his way. "Do you have any idea how his insults hurt me, especially since I really counted on his support for my new business venture?" He elbowed Irina. "Tell her…"

In a shaky voice, Irina leapt into the story Ethan had worked out before Kuri's arrival. "Ethan had broken heart—was not talking, not eating, not drinking. I was worried. And I could not help much because I was…well, I…" She shook her head and inched away. "I cannot do this, Ethan."

"Aaawww." Ethan quickly pulled Irina toward him again. He wanted to smack her for veering from the plan, but instead he pressed his lips onto her forehead while he worked to regain his composure. Just then, an idea came to him, and he decided to run with it. "Obviously, my misery was too much stress for my sweet Irina. It got so bad that she miscarried our baby."

"No, Ethan…don't! This is wrong. You have to—"

Ethan squeezed Irina's arm hard, silencing her. He shook his head and continued.

"She's embarrassed because she tried to be brave. It happened in the middle of the night, and she did not want to wake me, hoping the bleeding would stop. But it got worse, and her loud cries finally woke me up." He gave Irina another hard squeeze. "Right, my love?"

It annoyed him when she pressed her lips together and lowered her eyes.

"By then it was too late. She lost the baby and a lot of blood; she needed transfusions..." Ethan sighed dramatically. "We're only starting to get over the trauma now—all of which was caused by the unfair treatment I received from our father and two older siblings." Ethan slumped his shoulders, trying to look deflated. "I really was working hard and actually thought things were finally turning around, but..."

He glanced at Kuri. Her eyes were wide open. Was that skepticism he saw, or was she buying all this? He couldn't tell and quickly added, "What made it worse..."

"Don't tell me," Kuri interrupted, leaning forward. "There's more?"

Yes, Ethan triumphed silently. He had counted on Kuri being stupid and naïve enough to believe whatever sob story he came up with, so she could make a big deal about being a good sister and saving him. It gratified him to see that his instincts were paying off. He gave her a stiff smile and launched back into his story. He talked about Irina's childhood in Ukraine and how she'd become an orphan when her parents died in a train wreck. *At least this part is true,* he thought, becoming more confident.

"Am I getting this right, my love?" Ethan could feel Irina's shivers. He squeezed her arm again. "Maybe you'd like to tell my sister what happened next?" He wanted to slap her when he saw her sink into the sofa cushions.

"No! I can't... Please, Ethan..."

"It's okay, sweetie," he said, hugging her just a little too tightly, willing her to stop sabotaging his plan. "I know it's difficult for you to go through it again. Can I get you some water?" He shoved himself off the sofa and began walking across the room. "Look, if anyone understands what it's like to face adversity, it's Kuri. Right, little sister?"

He looked back from the bar, and it infuriated him seeing Kuri moving from the chair to the sofa, seating herself next to Irina, taking her hand. She wasn't even looking at him when she asked, "What happened next?"

Ethan angrily opened another LaCroix and poured it into a glass, slamming the empty can on the counter in frustration. Before Irina could fuck things up further, he jumped in to seize back control of the situation.

"Irina was left a sizable inheritance by her parents that she was to receive on her eighteenth birthday," he lied, "but got mixed up with this guy who claimed to be her legal guardian. He smuggled her out of Ukraine when she was still fifteen and brought her to this country, where things only got worse."

Ethan felt a boost of confidence when Kuri's eyes shifted back to him, and he immediately spun out an elaborate story, recalling the facts Irina had told him about her friends Olena and Alex.

"Her entire inheritance had been stolen out from under her, and her so-called guardian had disappeared, leaving Irina saddled with a mortgage on a condo, as well as massive credit card debt." He wanted to pause but was afraid he'd lose momentum. "When I met Irina," he continued, "she was working around the clock, trying to pay off all the creditors. Of course, the condo, the car…everything the banks could repossess, they did. But I paid off all the legal fees and the rest of the debt." He slowly walked over to the sofa and put the glass of water on the table. "Here, my love," he said, then reached out to touch Irina and almost lost his cool when she seemed to shrink away from his hand.

"It's okay, sweetie," he said, keeping his voice low. "You don't have to be ashamed—you were too young and hardly could understand or speak English. You fell into the wrong hands. But I took care of everything, didn't I?"

He seethed inwardly as Irina remained silent. With her lowered head, blinking away tears, she reminded him of a stupid schoolgirl caught cheating on a test.

"Well, I'm sure you've spoken to the police and international authorities," Kuri said.

"We've tried everything and lost." Ethan realized he wasn't

going to get anywhere with his stupid sister if he lost his temper, so he immediately dialed things back. "It is what it is," he said, more gently. "Irina can't take the stress anymore. I was happy to help her, but it set me up for a financial disaster of my own." He started to pace through the great room again. Out of the corner of his eye, he saw Kuri crinkling her nose; her perplexed expression was what he wanted.

"I don't understand," she said.

"Shortly after I paid off Irina's debt, I invested most of my remaining assets in a project I'm confident will pay off greatly…but when I needed more funding to keep my venture going, our self-righteous father turned me down. The old man is forcing me to give up my dream…plus everything else!" Ethan made a sweeping motion with his hand, as if to show off the apartment. He paused and turned away, pretending to wipe his eyes. "I'm ready to give all of this up. I'm ready to downsize, but who knows how long it'll take to sell this place—after all, it's in one of the highest-priced buildings in the city."

He went back to the bar and noisily opened another LaCroix, not even bothering to pour it into a glass but gulping it directly from the can. He hated the plain taste and shuddered. "I don't feel very good," he murmured. "Will the two of you please excuse me for a moment?" He fired a warning stare in Irina's direction and mouthed, "Ask her!"

He hurried down the hallway. Slamming the door behind him, he grabbed the pill container, shook out two Vicodin, and swallowed them without water. He feverishly searched for more cocaine, banging the drawers shut when he couldn't find any. He fell back against the wall and slid down, waiting for the pain to go away.

Chapter Twenty-One

"Will he be okay?" Kuri gazed down the empty hallway.

Irina nodded; the color had drained out of her face. "Oh my gosh, I feel horrible about things he told you. I am so sorry." Her fingers trembled when she reached for the glass of water. "I think Ethan is lost soul," she whispered. "I watch him burn bridges with friends and now family, too." She buried her face in her hands. "I make too many mistake myself; maybe I even make Ethan's big problem bigger. He needs—"

"Sssshhhh. I'm here to help," Kuri said softly, trying to calm Irina. "I'll also talk to our parents." Kuri smiled reassuringly. "Before you lost your baby, were you working? What did you do?"

"Baby? What? No!" Irina looked mortified. "Oh my gosh!" She looked down, avoiding Kuri's eyes. "I have many jobs. Not jobs like in office or so; I not have good education—I was fifteen years old when I left school in Ukraine. Here, in America, I work in catering and I do house services when people go on vacation. I register with model agency in Chicago, and sometimes I get small jobs."

Realizing Irina was uncomfortable talking about her tragedy, Kuri used the opportunity to change the subject. "I'm not surprised," she said. "You're tall and have a distinctive kind of beauty. Do you have comp cards, portfolios, or a web profile—any kind of marketing material?"

Irina's eyes suddenly lit up. "Yes. Few months ago, Ethan give money and help me get it. Was really expensive, but then…"

"Oh, I forgot, you got pregnant."

"Oh my gosh, please, not talk about this again." Irina shifted nervously on the sofa.

"Of course, I apologize for reminding you of your loss," Kuri said. "Anyway, can you email your material? I'm on my way to New York, and I know some people who might be interested." Kuri pulled Irina to her feet and asked her to turn around. "You are the perfect size, you have great posture, and your features are distinctive in a natural way."

"Really? That would be dream come true. I'm not too old? I'm twenty-five."

"Forget age—you look younger, and you're beautiful." Kuri took a step back and clapped her hands. "If it works out and you come to New York, you must stay with me." She looked at Irina and with a genuine smile, she said, "You'll be my sister-in-law, but you're already my friend."

"Ahem."

Kuri and Irina turned and watched Ethan as he walked back into the room.

"Ethan! You look better. Sit with us; I may have a solution to your problem."

Kuri then shared her intention to provide Ethan with the financial help he needed. He appeared to be happy with the news, but was there a hint of smugness in his grin? She could not tell and quickly reminded herself to push past such doubts; she was here to restore their shattered bond.

"Until you get back on your feet, you can count on me," she assured him. "I'll run this by my financial guru, and she will get in touch with you to handle the details."

"Fabulous! Thank you, little sister." Ethan went behind the bar and pulled out a bottle of Dom Pérignon. "Champagne to celebrate?"

Kuri and Irina shook their heads.

Ethan slapped his forehead. "Ha! Forgot! And, of course, not for me either."

Kuri watched him opening the wine cooler and noticed his reluctance to return the bottle.

"Please keep this financial arrangement between us," Ethan said, still holding the bottle in his hand. "At least for now. I don't want the rest of the family, especially our sanctimonious father, accusing me of taking advantage of your generosity. I know that's how they all would spin this."

"My financial advisor will handle everything. Her name is Valerie Hopper. You'll hear from her soon. She will…" Kuri stopped talking and looked at her buzzing phone. "Ooops—I didn't realize it's already past three. I'm late." She faced Ethan. "I was really happy when you called me and now, I'm excited about our breakthrough."

"Where are you off to?"

"New York. I have interviews and all kinds of other job obligations starting early tomorrow morning—the week is jammed. I already look forward to the weekend." She felt herself blush when she thought of Adam's visit. The ping on her phone indicated another message.

"Good old Stan," she said, after glancing down at the screen. "Once he realized I'd be running late, he called the pilot to delay the departure. That'll give me a little more time to get to the airport."

"What? The old man is letting *you* use the company jet?"

"Of course. Dad always has been generous and understanding of my privacy when it comes to traveling. He has been so bighearted to all of us."

"Really? Not to me! I can't remember the last time he let me use the plane. But I'm used to getting nothing from him."

The shrill tone that had crept into Ethan's voice made Kuri uncomfortable. She watched her brother's jaw clench and felt pity for him. She put her arms around him. "Don't be so hard on Dad or yourself. Give it time…"

"Time, huh? Well, my first thirty years of time flew over me and only left a damn shadow," Ethan said with a curled upper lip. "But I'm ready for time to hand me a glow of pleasure."

Kuri gave her brother a thumbs-up as she walked down the hallway. "Time gives all of us the chance for new beginnings," she said before the elevator doors closed.

Chapter Twenty-Two

Adam didn't remember the last time he felt as ecstatic as the moment he stepped onto the train that would take him to New York City and to Kuri.

Just the other night, Kuri had told him she thought he might be the conduit in her search for the missing elements in her life. Adam was elated to hear that she, too, believed something more than luck had brought them together. On the other hand, he faulted himself for not having used that perfect moment to tell her how his visions and dreams had led him to Germany, where he had unearthed proof that souls are not extinct, that there's a universal law of continuum—an order of dying and being again. He very much wanted to let her know how he found the evidence that past lives exist; he wanted to tell her that he, himself, did bear witness to another lifetime. *What is it that keeps holding me back?* he thought.

In a few hours he would see her. Over the next two days, he would be near her, hold her in his arms. *Maybe when we're together, I'll get a chance to tell her,* he thought, only to immediately dismiss the idea again. As a psychiatrist, how could he in good conscience put such ideas in her head while she was in therapy, trying to solve lifelong issues? He would have to wait until she made her own breakthroughs. He knew Kuri was looking forward to her first hypnotherapy session; hopefully soon after he would be able to talk freely.

Instead of booking a flight, Adam had chosen the low-stress option of a train that would take him from Boston's South Station into Manhattan in less than three and a half hours. Since there were no assigned seats, Adam chose the first empty table he found, setting his water bottle and laptop down, then stowed his single piece of luggage in the overhead bin. He intended to spend the next few hours working on his presentation for Rancho del Sol. In addition to his lecture on reviving spirituality, he would also get to work with patients at the rehabilitation center. He was looking forward seeing a few old colleagues again and meeting new ones, especially one who was renowned for her work in hypnotherapy and past life regression therapy. Adam had read most of her publications and couldn't wait to be introduced to Dr. Melanie Brichta.

"Is this taken?" An attractive young woman in skin-tight black denim, a white T-shirt, and moto boots stood in the aisle, hovering over the table.

Adam looked around the half-filled car, wondering why she was choosing to sit so close to him when there were other seats available.

"I know," said the brunette with a smile, intuiting his thoughts. She tapped on the seats across from him. "This is the last empty row facing forward. It's the only way I can travel."

"Sure," said Adam as he moved his laptop to give the woman room. He watched her fling her leather jacket into the overhead space, then settle down across from him and open her own laptop. He hoped for a nontalker, but he wasn't in luck.

"Going home?"

"No, visiting," he muttered, not looking up from his screen, expecting she'd catch the drift that he did not want to be disturbed.

"Great weekend ahead. Weather should be perfect. So much's happening in New York." She fiddled with the chord of her headphones and placed them on the table next to her laptop, then took out her phone and, with both of her thumbs began to tap swiftly at the screen. He hoped that whatever she was doing would keep her busy.

Moments later he heard the buzz of an incoming call. Just as he realized it wasn't his phone, the woman snagged her headphones from the table, popped them into her ears, and plugged the cord into her phone.

"Hey there, Dana. I was hoping you'd call. How did the interview go?"

Thank God she speaks in a low voice, Adam thought, but she was still close enough that he could hear every word.

"Really? That's awesome. Congrats!" Pause. "Yep, she's a pure delight to interview—I got her right after the premiere of *Desirée,* the remake that won her an Oscar." Pause. "What? Ha-ha-ha-ha-ha. Only you would do this. Ha-ha-ha-ha-ha..."

Her jarring cackle prompted Adam to look in her direction.

"Sorry," she whispered. "Business. I'm a reporter."

Adam bent over his laptop again. Inwardly, he cursed himself for having forgotten his own headphones; they would've cancelled out all noise.

"Send me whatever you're willing to share—I definitely can use it for my next column. I'm surprised you remembered you owe me a favor." The reporter started to giggle.

Adam sighed. Her light, silly laugh was only somewhat less annoying than her loud cackle.

"That whole thing was a riot, right? Anyway, it happened again. Ha-ha-ha-ha." Pause. "Yup! I wrapped the editor around my pinkie, and he weakened and showed me their rough cut for the final episode!" Pause. "Best over-the-top episode yet. What an un-be-fucking-lievable ending! I held my breath for the last three minutes!" Pause. "Yup, you guessed it. I bet *Quorum* will be nominated for best series, as will Kuri Berger for leading role."

Adam stiffened, his fingers hovering in midair at the mention of Kuri's name.

"I can't tell you any more. You'll just have to see for yourself when it airs. Okay, now...what have you got for me?" Pause. "That's all you got? Well, thanks for nothing, babe. Ha-ha-ha-ha! I'll be in touch. Kiss kiss." The woman put the phone down and began typing furiously on her laptop.

Adam realized he had been holding his breath and quietly exhaled through his nostrils. He couldn't stop dwelling on this odd coincidence and was still thinking about it twenty minutes later when the woman picked up her phone again. She tapped at the screen and waited.

"Billy-Boy! Hope I didn't wake you—what time is it down under?" Pause. "Ha-ha-ha-ha-ha. Beer at eight in the morning? You're incorrigible! You're such a yobbo! Tell me...how was the concert? Did you get your interview with Tommy Nova?" Pause. "Very cool. How was he? Last time I interviewed The Supernova, he was so high, he talked about e-v-e-r-y-t-h-i-n-g; some of it unprintable." Pause. "Uh-huh. Did he tell you anything about his surprise visit with Kuri Berger in Germany?"

What? Adam's body tensed up. Over the last few weeks, Kuri had told him, without much detail, about a few short-lived relationships, but she had never mentioned Tommy Nova. Although an admirer of his music, Adam otherwise was clueless about the rock star's life. Now this woman across from him talked about a liaison between Tommy Nova and—

"Rumor has it, Kuri broke up with him."

Adam realized he was not going to be able to focus on his work anymore. He closed the laptop and leaned his head against the windowpane, closing his eyes. He tried to tune out the reporter's voice. The context of her jabber was like a jigsaw puzzle he was unable to complete anyway. So, Adam thought about the questions he would have for Kuri when he was close to her, when he was holding her hand, when he could look into her eyes—very soon.

Chapter Twenty-Three

Kuri ran into yet another room in her parents' Manhattan apartment, searching for the ivory cordonetto lace shirt that she liked to wear with her favorite stretch denim jeans. She opened more drawers and searched on shelves. She leaned against the wall and looked at the disarray. "I give up," she mumbled, and resignedly reached for a printed cotton tank top.

Kuri loved this apartment—it already had been her mother's when she was a dancer, and her father had moved in when her parents got married. They lived here on and off for another three years before making the estate in Lake Bluff their permanent residence. But they had never given up this beautiful sanctuary with its graceful layout of grand-scale rooms. And after the children were born, the family continued to stay here whenever they visited New York City.

After all these years, Kuri hadn't changed anything in the apartment because the well-designed and lavish décor continued to give her great comfort.

She wandered over to one of the windows and looked down;

sixteen stories below, a steady stream of cars and pedestrians was making its way down Fifth Avenue.

The alarm on her phone sounded; earlier she had set it for 5:15 p.m. In another hour and a half, Adam's train was to pull into Penn Station. She quickly straightened out the mess she had created in some of the closets, then walked from room to room, making sure everything looked good before Adam arrived.

She sat in her favorite chair in the living room. It was time for her phone session with Dr. B.—the nickname she'd settled on for her therapist; Melanie, she knew, was too personal, and Dr. Brichta too *comme il faut*. She tapped on the number, then on the speaker icon.

"Hello, Kuri. How are you?"

"Today I'm doing really, really well, Dr. B. I'm beyond excited because Adam is on his way—I can't believe we'll finally see each other again; it seems like an eternity since Germany."

"I know you've been looking forward to this day. Why did you say that *today* you're doing really well? What happened since the last time we met?"

"Well, I decided to see my brother Ethan." Kuri paused. "The things my brother told me, his overall conduct, and his reactions were a lot to unpack."

"Do you want to talk about it?"

Kuri nodded and began to talk freely.

"I tell you," she said at the end of her monologue, "on one hand, I feel good about my visit with him; on the other, Ethan's behavior has left me in a state of uncertainty and confusion. The more I go over everything I just told you, the more certain things don't seem to make sense."

"Mmmh. What bothers you the most?"

"Well, I don't understand his relationship with Irina. She's a lovely young woman. I can't shake the feeling that Ethan is holding something over her—she seemed terrified in his presence."

"You said that Ethan repeatedly talked about paying off her enormous debt. Could it be she feels embarrassed?"

"If it's true what Ethan said, then I'm sure she does feel uncomfortable, but I think there's more! I just don't know what it is."

"Perhaps you can find out when Irina comes to visit you in New York. That is, if you feel at ease asking her."

"I have to think about how I might approach that kind of sensitive subject."

"While you were in Ethan's presence, how did you react when you noticed some of his odd behavior?"

"I was very proud of myself because I remained in absolute charge until..." Kuri stopped talking, exhaling loudly.

"What is it, Kuri? Are you okay?"

"I felt strong and confident while I was in Ethan's apartment, but then, one hour after I left my brother, I experienced another incident. It happened shortly after the plane took off in Chicago; I had another very unpleasant aura—something I had not felt since I fainted in Dachau."

"Did you faint on the plane?"

"No, but the incident was extremely disturbing."

"In previous sessions you talked about how troubling memories of your brother often were followed by a resurgence of episodes. And now that you saw him in person, it happened again. Can you see a connection between those spells and Ethan's behavior toward you?"

"Absolutely! During these episodes, where Ethan metamorphoses into this evil being, I sense a link; it's the same as the visions I had during my youth and to what I recently experienced in Dachau."

"Interesting," said Dr. B. "In the short time I've known you, Kuri, you've broken through some barriers. Are you able to feel a possible connection?"

"I think so," Kuri said. "I understand now that I should follow those strange visions rather than fight them. But more so, I want to decipher images that remain difficult to be perceived by my physical senses."

"You know, there's a famous argument that Plato laid out in *Phaedo*; he was fascinated by the mastery of some people who were able to accomplish things that they never learned to do. So, according to Plato's perception, learning actually could be a form of memories. In other words, as our minds get piqued by our educators' questions, we come to recall things that might be events from our previous lives."

"Wow! I heard about that but until recently never gave much thought to it," Kuri said. "I remember at an early age I developed attitudes and phobias that nobody understood. I was too young to verbalize what I saw and believed I heard in my dreams. But now I am eager to dig deeper and find out what it all means."

"I believe you are ready for regression therapy! Perhaps under what I consider *focused awareness* you will be able to recover your suppressed memories."

After Kuri scheduled her next appointment with Dr. B., she disconnected the call and walked back to the window. Leaning against the windowpane, she felt growing excitement about the upcoming hypnotherapy. She looked up into the skies, grateful for new tomorrows.

Chapter Twenty-Four

Adam walked under the canopied entrance between extensive sidewalk landscaping, then stepped through attractive cast-iron doors into the prominent, tall limestone-clad apartment house with its asymmetrical roof on Fifth Avenue.

"Who may I announce?" the doorman asked in a precise, neutral British accent.

"Adam Gold, please."

The doorman, wearing an impeccably cut and stylish uniform, walked from behind the front desk.

"Of course. Ms. Berger is expecting you." He opened the elevator door and waved the security fob over the reader to unlock access to the Bergers' residence on the sixteenth floor. When Adam thanked him, he held his hands clasped in front; like a footman from Downton Abbey, he bowed his head slightly at the neck and said, "Good night, sir."

A few minutes later, the elevator door opened onto a sweeping circular foyer, where Kuri was waiting for him.

Without saying a word, they came together like magnets.

"I finally am here," he said, and loved the way she bent her head until it rested on his arm. "How I've waited for this."

"Yes, you are here," she whispered, and then her lips parted.

Their first kiss seemed to last forever, as if they needed to taste the sweet significance of every moment in time.

❄

The night flew by; too soon the morning sun started to soak the large residence with light.

For an instant, Adam believed himself still in a dream, but when soft even breaths warmed his arm, he turned his head. Again, he was dazed by her beauty. He closed his eyes, challenging himself not to look at her for too long. But even behind closed lids he saw her—just like the sun and the moon and the stars, he knew she would always be there.

They did not leave the apartment at all that Saturday—there was so much to tell each other, so much to discover. They did not want the outside world to interrupt their bliss.

They prepared meals together, working side by side as if they had done so for years. When a full bowl of blueberries slipped off the kitchen counter, they crawled like babies searching for the small roundish fruit, jokingly competing with each other to see who would retrieve the most. They laughed until their sides hurt.

During the late afternoon hours, they sat on the terrace, basking in the sun, enjoying the unobstructed views over Central Park. When night fell, they lit candles in the master suite and the adjoining bathroom. They enhanced the bath with essential oils and luxuriated in the warm water; they played with lavender buds floating on top. Later, still watching the flickering flames from the candles, they were mesmerized by the stillness and solitude of the moment.

They only allowed themselves to fall asleep for short periods of time, trying to stretch the hours, craving to learn more of the other, and desiring each other's nearness.

"Can't you stay through Monday?" Kuri pleaded.

"I wish. But neither you nor I can abandon our tight and demanding schedules."

She snuggled into him. "I can't bear the thought that I won't see you for more than a month."

"We'll talk every opportunity we get—and one month is a short time for what I hope will be love that sustains a lifetime." Adam pressed his lips onto the top of her head.

"Something Tolstoy wrote just came to me—it's exactly how I feel," she whispered sleepily. "Everything is. Everything exists because I love."

Adam breathed into the soft strands of her hair. He recalled a quotation by Carson Kolhoff, one he had carried in his heart for years. "I never wanted anything other than to be your everything," he said softly.

Chapter Twenty-Five

The vibration from Kuri's cell phone on the nightstand woke him from deep, dreamless sleep. Adam blinked at the early daylight that filtered through half-closed shades and curtains. Quietly, he climbed out of bed and tiptoed toward the open door into the hallway. When he saw the time on the kitchen stove, he knew Kuri would want him to wake her up.

Thirty minutes later they were strolling through Central Park—in this very early morning hour, they practically had the park to themselves. Hand in hand they walked along the pond, passed statues and monuments, crossed bridges, and relaxed on the grass near Bethesda Fountain. While they strolled and stopped, walked and talked, they shared more of their lives with each other. They purposely left their phones behind in the apartment, not wanting the outside world to interfere with the short time they had left together.

As the sun rose higher and higher in the morning sky, the park began to fill with people. When they arrived at the Great Lawn, several young families already had spread out their blankets; a group of children ran after a ball, and their high voices pierced the morning air. Seven teenage girls sat on the grass in a circle, hysterically laughing as they watched two dogs hump each other nearby. A group of Muslim women performed stretching movements, their arms and legs draped in loose clothing, their head scarves billowing in the breeze.

"Should we head back?" Adam shielded Kuri as a cluster of tourists passed by. "You may get recognized; people may wonder who you are with."

"Are you ashamed to be seen with me?" Kuri teased.

He squeezed her hand.

"Race you home." She laughed and sprinted ahead.

❄

They sat across from each other in matching white robes as they enjoyed a light meal. Adam leaned over the table to wipe a breadcrumb off Kuri's lip. "I have to get going soon," he said, sighing. "What time is your brother's fiancée getting here?"

"Don't tell me… is it that late already?" Kuri looked at her phone to check her schedule. "Her plane gets in around five this afternoon. Depending on traffic, she'll be here around sixish."

"Just about the time I need to leave." Adam began cleaning the dishes off the table.

Looking again at her phone, Kuri read another text and laughed. "My soon-to-be sister-in-law is beyond excited that I got her this interview with a top modeling agency tomorrow. I gave her all the prompts for what to do. She looks exquisite when she doesn't wear makeup… so fresh-faced and natural. She's quite tall—just what the industry is looking for. I know she'll do great." Kuri handed Adam the rinsed plate. "Maybe you'll still meet her."

"Mm-hmm." Adam replied automatically. "Earlier, when you told me about your visit with Ethan, you didn't mention anything about your brother's reaction to the financial assistance you offered him. I don't mean to pry, and it's understandable if you don't want to talk about it."

"Wow, I forgot! Probably because I'm trying not to upset myself again." Kuri drank the rest of her tea and put the mug in the sink. "After Ethan supplied us with the necessary documents, we offered him one million dollars to pay off most of his debt. We even allowed some wiggle room so he can get himself financially reorganized." She bit her lip and shook her head. "Would you believe…it wasn't enough; he asked for more."

"Whoa. And…?"

She shrugged. "When it was made clear that it's all he can get for the moment, he reacted with indifference, totally unenthusiastic. But he signed the papers and that's it." With a sigh she added, "I would've liked to hear that he's happy, but he draped himself in silence. Not a word…at least not yet. My dad is furious, and my mom is heartbroken. I kept reminding them it was my decision, and they promised to stay out of it. I really wanted things to go well with Ethan…" She sighed, then flung her arms around Adam's neck. "You and I had an amazing weekend, I don't want it to end on such a sour note."

One hour later, while drying off in the shower, Adam heard the house phone ringing in the bedroom. A few seconds later he could hear Kuri raising her voice anxiously. "No Albert! Do not send him to my apartment, please." She paused to listen. "I'm sorry for the disturbance, Albert. Please take him to the owner's lounge—I'll meet him there."

Kuri looked pale and distraught when she walked into the bathroom.

"I must apologize, Adam. I should've told you more about my previous relationship with Tommy Nova and how persistent he can be. I told him it's over…that I needed to move on without him. But now he's downstairs and demands to see me." She pressed her face into the palms of her hands. "I can't believe he continues to disregard my wishes."

Adam freed her face. "It's okay…I can leave right now—it'll give you the privacy to deal with the situation." He wiped her tears away. "You can fill me in later."

"I am so, so sorry this is happening…"

The loud banging on the front door startled them.

"Oh no..." Before she moved out of the room, she looked into his eyes and said, "Adam, I love you—I am in love with you! He means nothing to me; he never truly did."

After she walked out of the bedroom, Adam closed the door behind her and turned to pack his carry-on. He realized he felt neither nervous nor jealous, and despite the unexpected intrusion by Tommy Nova, Adam didn't doubt Kuri's love for him. As always, he believed that moving forward with a confident spirit made everything work out in the end. Suddenly, loud voices interrupted his thoughts.

"I don't appreciate you coming into my family's home and invading my privacy, Tommy. I asked you several times to respect my wishes and allow me to move on. This is—"

"Nah! You never said anything about respecting wishes or moving on. You said you had doubts. Doubts about what? It doesn't matter...we'll get through this. You. Can't. Dump. Me. Ever!" Tommy Nova's peppered words were like a burst of bullets. "I. *Won't.* Live. Without. You! You're mine, always mine. You're my sweet sugarboo."

Then Adam heard a loud crash. Alarmed, he moved to open the door, but paused—his palm wrapped tight around the crystal glass lever handle—when he heard Kuri's surprisingly calm voice.

"You are not only drunk, you're also high on something."

"Am I high? Not high enough yet! I'm still on a booster rocket." Tommy Nova laughed. Then there was a thud.

"Please get a hold of yourself and leave. You are making me uncomfortable in my own home."

"No, I'll never leave. You're what I need and you're mine."

There was another loud thump, like a body hitting the wood floor. That was all Adam could take. He rushed through the hallway into the living room and saw Tommy Nova kneeling in front of Kuri, twirling a ring with a big stone around his little finger. He laughed out loud and started singing, "Marry me, my honeybee! I love you, my sugarboo..."

When Tommy caught sight of Adam, he stopped singing. "Who's this?" he shouted, unsteadily reaching for the table, trying to find his balance as he stood up. The ring slipped off his pinkie and rolled onto the floor. "Fuck!" His eyes searched for the ring, but then he turned his attention back to Adam. "Who. Is. This?"

"I'm Adam Gold," Adam said in as calm a voice as he could muster.

"Oh! The shrink who picked up my sweetheart in Germany," Tommy said, sneering. He fell onto the sofa and pointed at Adam. "Are psychiatric bedroom sessions your specialty? Ha-ha-ha." He attempted to get off the sofa, only to collapse back into the cushions. He pointed at Kuri. "I had the ring…where is it?" he slurred. He leaned forward, his eyes searching the floor once more. Then his index finger, still pointed at Kuri, moved downward. "Fifteen fucking flawless karats somewhere on this fucking floor." He laughed again. "Guess what? I showed your engagement ring to the paparazzi downstairs. They sucked up the news. They love me!" he cackled proudly.

"Tommy. You have to leave. Now!"

"No. Never. You're a germ in my bloodstream. I can't get rid of you." He spoke slowly, garbling the words. He looked at Adam, pointing his middle finger at him. "Th-th-that's all, folks. You're excused, Doc. You can leave now." Tommy leaned his head back and closed his eyes.

Wide-eyed, Kuri stared at the intoxicated man on her sofa, then turned to Adam. "I think he's passed out," she said. "How could I ever have been so wrong about a human being?"

"I won't leave you alone with him. What can I do?"

"I'll call my agent. He'll know how to handle this." She pressed the contact on her phone and spoke quickly.

Soon after, a team of paramedics came with a gurney to take the still unconscious Tommy Nova away in an ambulance.

"I can't ask you to forget what happened just now." Her voice was low.

Adam looked at her and smiled encouragingly. "If you and I are meant to be together, then nothing can interfere that tries to tear us apart. If we take hurdles together, we come out stronger in the end."

Despite the optimism in his heart, when they embraced and kissed one more time, he felt a sense of tremendous loss as the elevator doors shut between them. Would he have to wait a whole month before he could see her again?

The lobby was quiet and cool. A different doorman than the one from the morning shift greeted Adam. *This must be Albert,* Adam thought.

"Would you like a taxi, sir?"

"Thank you, but I already called an Uber. It'll be here shortly."

Albert opened the heavy door for a tall, striking young woman to come through.

"Hi," she said. "I hope I'm in right place. Kuri Berger, she live here? I am houseguest for few days with her." She looked around the elegant lobby. "Wow," she whispered.

"Who may I announce?"

"My name Irina Messing."

Adam froze. His head whipped around. *What? Irina Messing? How is this possible? Can this be Golda Messing's granddaughter?* He gaped at the blond woman. *This either is a bizarre coincidence or, mysteriously, I just met Shimmy's grand-niece who is visiting Kuri. Could it be...?*

The young woman smirked when she noticed Adam staring at her. "Hi," she said. "You know me?"

"No. I...I don't believe we met." Embarrassed, he averted his eyes and looked out the door to the street, where his ride was already waiting. Before he walked through the glass doors, without conscious thought, he turned to watch Irina Messing step onto the elevator. As the doors closed, she nodded and waved at him.

Chapter Twenty-Six

1944

New prisoners arrive every day. KZ Dachau has mostly male prisoners, but lately I also see women and young girls arrive—many of them are sent to work in the armament factories. Sometimes I look over to the women's barracks; heavy barbed wire separates them from the men's camp.

I can smell fall is in the air—someone tells me it's September, and I think of those autumn days when my parents allowed Golda and me to climb into the tree to pick apples while they watched us from below.

Every day, after morning roll call, I walk with groups of other prisoners to the armament factory. As we pass through the gate, we see the new arrivals; this time it's only women—hundreds of them—young and old. I steal glimpses of their worried faces; many of the women look completely drained of strength. Suddenly, one pair of eyes connects with mine, and I almost lose my balance. An unfamiliar form of energy jolts through me, and the moment seems to linger. We pass each other in silence, but I dare to turn my head, and at that same instant, she turns too, and our eyes lock again.

From that moment, I can't stop thinking about the pale, fragile girl with red curls. She reminds me of the *Girl in a Straw Hat*—a painting by Pierre-Auguste Renoir—I saw when our family traveled to Dresden to visit the beautiful museums there. Will I ever see the girl I just passed again? And if so, how will I talk to her? The SS have eyes everywhere. But I find hope in remembering what Mama said when she met Papa. *"We don't meet people by accident. They are meant to cross our path for a reason."*

It is getting colder, and I am grateful we are working mostly inside. Blonke is given a new assignment in a satellite camp; he calls it Agfa-Commando. Many women work here. Blonke says they are brought here to assemble ignition timing devices for bombs and for artillery ammunition, also for V-1 and V-2 rockets.

On the first day in the Agfa-Commando factory, I see my Renoir girl. Once again, our eyes lock.

Blonke guffaws when he sees me blush. "*Schon wieder ein Fuchs und keine Flinte.*" Another fox and no rifle. I remember that dumb saying from when I was in school in Breslau and some of my classmates would tease redheaded girls. Back then, I always thought of it as a dull-witted joke, but here, in this slave labor camp, it becomes a grotesque innuendo. And yet, as soon as Blonke says it, he turns to one of the SS officers guarding the women and tells her he needs more assistance; he somehow manages to have the red-haired girl and another female prisoner assigned to work with us. He looms closer to me. "Now's your chance to talk to her," he murmurs, then proceeds to give instructions to the other woman.

With my one free hand, I point to a tool. When the girl hands it to me, our fingers touch, and I feel a mysterious current pass between us. Hesitantly, I look at her and can see she has felt it too.

"*Ich heisse Judith,*" she says softly.

"My name is Shimon; my nickname is Shimmy," I answer. "You're German. From where?"

"Berlin. My mother and I were at KZ Ravensbrück before

coming here." She throws her hand across her face and for a second seems lifeless. When she removes her hand, I see her wet cheeks. "My mother just died," she whispers, swallowing back her tears. "I miss her so." She swallows again and looks at me.

Her voice is warm like sunshine, her breath is sweet like honey. I force myself to concentrate on the wires, stealing only the occasional glimpse. I try not to draw any attention to us, hoping to keep her near me as long as possible. I find out she's just fourteen, two years younger than me. The brief smiles that pass between us as we talk sparkle like stars; we sense each other's luminosity. In this gruesome darkness around us, I suddenly see a light.

It must be December now because Blonke keeps complaining that he is not in a Christmas mood. I don't ask questions, but I listen when I see him talk to other guards. I overhear that the war is not going well for Germany; I hold my breath. Could this horror be over soon? I continue to hope and pray.

Wet snow falls during roll call, the temperatures drop below freezing, and our prison uniforms become rigid with ice. Yet the guards, in their sheepskin coats and warm boots, seem to enjoy our suffering. Whenever I feel my skin turn pale and blue, I go into deep concentration—so deep that I visualize the sun is warming the ground below me, and soon I imagine heat rising from my feet throughout my body. I can't tell anyone I'm able to do this because I don't know how to explain the trust in my spiritual beliefs—who would understand? Sometimes I think the Germans leer at me when they don't see me shiver or flinch like my fellow prisoners.

1945

Despite the deteriorating conditions, I am better off than so many others here at Dachau. I still work with Blonke, and when he's in a fair mood, he hands me extra food. More than ever, I rely on my faith to nurture my hope—that and my feelings for Judith. She is so fragile yet never complains. Word spreads about an outbreak of typhoid fever in the women's barracks and I worry about her.

Blonke has an order to work on the electrical fence. My heart sings when I spot an area near the women's barracks that is partly hidden from the lines of sight in the guard towers all around the camp.

Judith and I now meet there regularly. I always share the food I get from Blonke and often give most of it to her. Even though we only have precious minutes, each time we meet, we whisper to each other with promises of survival. When our hands touch, energy surges through us, and we agree that our lives will be as one, together. "You are my pulse," I tell her, and she replies, "You are my every emotion."

❋

It is April. Conditions have become unbearable and even Blonke seems to get thinner; every day he looks more pallid. His limp is getting worse, and he tells me that the flesh on the stump of his leg is infected and that the prosthesis hurts like hell. Most days, he's in a foul mood but still gives me part of his food—often all of it.

As every morning, I meet Blonke after roll call, ready to go to work. Instead of handing me tools, he informs me that he is about to be transferred. He leans closer and whispers, "It's over. We're done!" I don't dare to ask, but he can tell I'm worried. "The enemy is moving in," he grunts. "All of you—everybody—will be transferred somewhere! I have no idea where to, but I hope you'll survive." He looks around, making sure nobody's watching in the chaos around us.

"*Hier!*" He slips something into my sleeve—I know it is food. "*Deine Henkersmahlzeit!*" He shakes his head, wipes his eyes, and limps away. I shove what Blonke calls *my last supper* further into my prison jacket and stand there, watching him pass from sight.

It is getting dark already when they round us up—thousands of us. They give each of us a half loaf of bread with some fat and order us to make it last. They don't say for how long.

Nobody looks back as we trudge away from this hellhole. Men, women, and children—many are skeletal, depleted of energy, others so sick they can hardly walk. When I see someone collapse, I help them up, even carry them until they walk again. Whoever stays down gets shot. Corpses already line the sides of the road, the bodies of those who had marched ahead of us.

We walk through towns. I see faces behind windowpanes, always just for seconds; the moment they see us look at their houses, the curtains close, lights are turned off.

The SS henchmen never stop with their cruelty. They get a kick out of offering their fresh smelling bread to half-starved prisoners; then they laugh, fire shots into the air, and command their ferocious dogs to chase these undernourished people empty-handed back into the lines.

I ask every woman I pass if she knows Judith. I walk faster and stretch my neck forward—I purposely fall behind and turn around, always searching. My instincts tell me I will find her. It is nighttime; I try to ignore the aches in my body—I don't allow fatigue to slow me down. And then I hear my name; the honeyed whisper is her voice. I grasp her hand in the darkness, and suddenly I know what to do. I tell her. She nods weakly. "Yes," she says, trying to sound confident. "We will make it."

Ahead of us I hear gunshots and barking dogs—painful screams and angry, loud voices indicate mayhem. The two SS near us rush forward, their rifles pointed, ready to join the shooting.

"Now!" I push Judith into the thicket to our left. When I hear her gasp, I lift her up and carry her into the blackness of the forest. The shouting and gunshots, the shrieks and wails ahead, are enough to cover the noise we make as we break through bushes and crack the fallen branches under our feet. I keep moving as fast as I can while gulping for air. I don't know how long I run or how I find the strength, but suddenly the ground disappears under me and I tumble into a ditch, tightly holding onto Judith. Clinging to one another, we lie motionless and shed tears of relief. We are far enough from the road now that all we hear are our pounding hearts and the whispers of a moonless night. Luckily, we landed on a thick bed of moss and leaves. The foliage from autumns past provide the blanket we need for warmth. After I cover our bodies, I pass out, exhausted.

We wake up to the sound of birdsong. I kiss Judith on her forehead—she feels very hot, and I know she has fever.

"Thank you!" She smiles and snuggles into me. "Let's stay here until I feel better."

I tell her that we need to keep moving and promise to carry her until we find a safe place. She cringes when I lift her up, telling me she has severe abdominal cramps. Now I know she has typhoid, but I don't say anything to her. Instead I assure her we will find help.

Judith drifts in and out of sleep. Is her fever getting worse? I pick leaves, damp with rain, off the trees, dabbing them onto Judith's lips. When I can, I hungrily devour Hawthorne leaves and chew on pine needles, cherishing their citrus taste. I tell Judith that I know of their medicinal value, but she shakes her head—she only wants water.

I keep walking; I barely feel my legs, and many times I'm afraid I will drop Judith because the muscles in my arms have begun to spasm out of control. Sometimes I must stop and rest. Eventually, Judith insists she can walk, and slowly we continue picking our way through the woods.

Dusk is falling when we reach the edge of the forest. A small brook courses through a meadow, and I point to a farmhouse and a barn. We see no people and hear no voices as we quietly approach the barn. We slither through the door, and I pull Judith between two haystacks. I cover us with hay—it feels soft and warm. We fall asleep in each other's arms.

A voice wakes me; I hear German words, and I stiffen. A young woman stands nearby.

"*Seid's ihr Juden?*" Concern and worry is in the woman's voice; she speaks in a heavy Bavarian dialect.

My mind addled by fever, I ask her to please help us—I speak to her in Yiddish, and she looks at me confusedly. She steps toward us, but I hold up my hands, gesturing not to come closer.

She points to herself. "Resi Bauer." She wants to know if I understand it's her name.

When I nod, she smiles and asks for my name.

"Shimmy," I say. Before I can tell her Judith's name, Resi Bauer leaves the barn; she returns shortly with fresh water and warm bread. Then she makes another trip, this time bringing back thick blankets, pants, and sweaters for Judith and myself. She tells us to put our worn, dirty prison garb into a bucket outside and burn them. She walks away to give us privacy. When she returns, Judith manages to sit up and smile at the kind young woman. I can't take my eyes off Judith. Her pale, beautiful face is framed by waves and ringlets of auburn hair that reflects the morning sun; the light green sweater matches her glistening eyes. Her mouth moves, but her voice is so weak I know Resi Bauer cannot hear Judith's words of appreciation for the kindness we're receiving.

The young German woman sadly tells us she won't be able to get a doctor or medicine. She is afraid of consequences from the SS. She promises she'll be back with food and water. "*Ihr müßt's schloafen*," she says, telling us that rest will make us well.

Judith talks in her sleep—her whole body is hot, but she shivers. I hold her tight and sing the songs that Mama and Bubbeh used to sing. During her few lucid moments, Judith shares childhood memories, her dreams of becoming a dancer. She kisses my lips and tells me she loves me.

I wake up from a bad dream and know what to do. I tell Judith I will be back. I go to the farmhouse, quickly so as not to be seen, and ask Resi Bauer for a pen and sheets of paper. I rush back to the barn and grab a small metal box that sits on the windowsill. I sneak behind the farmhouse to the meadow. Maybe I only imagine it, but it seems the big oak tree is waving to me, calling me to sit on one of its exposed roots.

In the dream that woke me earlier, Zaydeh warned me of the Germans. "They have wronged the Jews! Never forget and always be proud of your heritage," he said—and so, as I sit under the tree, I write what I have to say in Yiddish. When I'm done, I place the sheets of paper in the box, dig a hole, and bury the box.

Resi Bauer has been standing by the brook, watching me. She nods and smiles back.

My own abdominal cramps are almost unbearable now, and my body rages with fever, but my shivers stop as soon as I lie next to Judith. "I need to rest," I tell her, and promise I will feel better soon.

She turns to me, and we move so close that our noses and lips touch. Unexpectedly her eyes widen.

"The pain, the hurt…all is gone!" Her freed laughter is pure, like vibrations coming from hundreds of crystal bells. "Look!" She weakly points upward. "Look…the light. Can you see it?"

I look to where she's pointing and sense a golden white light that gently lifts me from my physical body; motionless, I begin to float.

"Do you hear the music? I've never heard sweeter melodies." I hear Judith's voice. "Dance with me," she whispers.

I am gliding away from suffering and distress—I am free.

"We are free—we're floating on air," I hear myself say, linking my fingers with hers. You and I…forever."

Chapter Twenty-Seven

Melanie Brichta looked over the room she'd just prepared for the upcoming session with Kuri. It was an interior room, with no windows facing outside; no city noise would disturb the warm, welcoming silence she had worked very carefully to establish. Burning incense sticks released a fragrance that mixed pleasantly with sweet scents from a bouquet of fresh flowers. Content that her stones and crystals were aligned properly, the Tibetan bell was in its place beside them, and calming music filled the air, Melanie dimmed the light, closed the door, and returned to her office.

She sat behind the desk and looked over her notes. The previous day, during a phone session, Kuri had talked about the wonderful weekend she spent with Adam and how their bonding had been momentarily derailed by Tommy Nova's intrusion.

"And now it's all over social media," Kuri complained. "Tommy told the tabloids I kept that insanely huge ring after he broke off the engagement when he caught me with another man. But they have yet to print the statement my agent released immediately after the incident. There's no word that Tommy's and my whirlwind friendship led us in opposite directions, that we already had separated in Germany because of irreconcilable differences."

It was the first time Melanie could recall hearing Kuri so intensely irritated during any of their sessions.

"The truth is," Kuri had continued, "that stupid ring remained on Tommy's own finger until he dropped it in his drunken stupor; it somehow rolled under a chair in my apartment. We found it after the ambulance took Tommy away. My agent made sure the ring was back in Tommy's possession that very night... hopefully, the tabloids will get it right, soon!"

Melanie confessed to her patient that, out of curiosity, she had read the interview with Tommy Nova online in which he shared his version of what happened in Kuri's apartment that Sunday afternoon, portraying himself as a shattered victim, heartbroken by her betrayal.

"You know what really upsets me, Dr. B?" Kuri said angrily. "On top of all of this, Tommy made sure he gave the reporters Adam's name, and now the poor guy is being hounded by the paparazzi."

"How is Adam dealing with the situation?" Melanie had asked.

"He says that it's not bothering him and that his love for me can't be challenged. He even said he thinks that being apart from one another for one month will be good—by then the media will have lost interest."

"Why won't you be able to see each other for a month?"

"This time it's because of his work, not mine. Next week, he's going to work at some rehabilitation center in Sedona—he's done that for the past three years; it's become a routine for him in September."

Melanie instinctively suppressed her surprise. She herself was leaving next week to lecture and train at Rancho Del Sol, the only treatment center in Sedona. She considered telling Kuri but did not think the time was appropriate. Nor would it be proper to bring this up during today's hypnotherapy work. Melanie, still deep in reflection, jumped to her feet when she heard the soft ring of her doorbell announcing Kuri's arrival.

Melanie opened the door to the waiting room and saw Kuri again standing in front of the picture where the leopard cub was clinging to its mother.

"I love this photo, Dr. B. The animals' eyes speak volumes." Kuri turned and walked toward Melanie.

"Good to see you, Kuri."

After they shook hands, Melanie held onto Kuri's to lead her into the office.

"How are you feeling? You seemed troubled during our appointment yesterday. We can postpone our session if you still feel nervous."

"Absolutely not! I'm ready!"

Melanie made eye contact with Kuri. "There is no proof that past life regression is possible. As ever, it is individual free will to believe in the existence of souls."

Kuri nodded. "I am ready," she said again.

Melanie led her patient into the small room and pointed to the sofa. "Make yourself comfortable—you can remove any restricting clothes and your shoes."

"The atmosphere in this room, the fragrance...everything is so peaceful and relaxing." Kuri inhaled and exhaled slowly.

"Good, Kuri." Melanie sat next to the sofa and gestured toward the tray of healing stones and crystals. "In India, I learned that ancient cultures from around the world used stones and crystals not only to balance energies but also to improve, to activate, and to guide. I will now place some of those on you, explaining each one's purpose. Their energies will interact with your own electromagnetic field throughout our session."

Melanie warmed the small amber in the palm of her hand, then gently placed it on Kuri's forehead. "This fossilized resin comes from ancient evergreen trees and has seen many eras. May it bring you courage through your journey and defend you emotionally. May it free your curiosity."

She placed an amethyst opposite the amber. "This stone symbolizes the wind element. May it activate your higher mind and assist your going inward while traveling through time."

She put two tiny jade stones on Kuri's closed lids. "Listen to these green stones as they whisper to you. Capture the messages; they will help you see and explore."

As she continued adding stones and crystals on the seven chakras of Kuri's body—the crown, third eye, throat, heart, solar, sacral, and roof—Melanie explained the jet would open the doorway into the past and into other dimensions; the lapis lazuli was to relax and open the mind in order to connect unconscious wisdom with the conscious mind; the moonstone was a source of wisdom and the clear quartz crystals were to bring perception while breaking through the barriers of time.

Once Kuri's body was thoroughly relaxed, Melanie softly rang the Tibetan bell.

"While I guide you back through time, your conscious mind may interfere and question whether what you see, hear, and feel is real or a product of your imagination. Let it go. There is no evaluation, no censure, no verdict."

She rang the Tibetan bell again.

"Inhale the splendor. Exhale the trouble. Relax deeper." She rang the Tibetan bell again, more softly this time. "Deeper...go deeper...you're deep in a state of calm...so deep, you now feel your multidimensional being." Melanie finished her last word with another silky tone of the bell.

"I will help you as you go back in time. You will grasp and comprehend all that was and make sense of all that is. If you experience sorrow and suffering on your journey, acknowledge it but do not dwell on it. Allow it to enable you to understand how to live your present life more valuable—more complete."

Melanie rang the Tibetan bell again, then calmly placed two fingertips on the amethyst and amber resting on Kuri's forehead.

Finally, she lightly tapped on the other stones and crystals while reciting a saying by Swami Vivekananda.

"Before the sun, the moon, the earth,
Before the stars or comets free,
Before e'en time had had its birth,
I was, I am, and I will be."

Chapter Twenty-Eight

Kuri was fully conscious of Dr. B's presence next to her, yet the amount of space between them felt like units of astronomical distance as the therapist's soothing voice guided her into a state of perfect relaxation. Freed from tension, she barely was aware of her body while her mind projected clear images from Dr. B's promptings.

She saw herself standing on top of a tall staircase, slowly taking steps down. It was like she was watching a movie of herself. She heard Dr. B's voice counting her down each stair. "Ten-nine-eight-seven-six-five-four-three-two-one."

Kuri felt a tapping on her forehead and listened as Dr. B. invited her to envision a door ahead. Kuri observed herself opening the door; a bright, beautiful light welcomed her. When she walked through the light, she began to speak out loud. "I see myself," she said. "I am a tiny girl, between my mother and father, holding their hands." It was a vision of utter joy, and she could feel the energies of countless other happy moments folded into it.

Suddenly she shivered as she viewed herself in cold, sterile rooms surrounded by white-coated doctors talking over her in their perfunctory, forceful tones. She felt her parents' concern; their reassuring words took away her panic and suspicion. She wanted to tell them what plagued her, but she was still too young to explain the magnitude of her night terrors.

She watched herself crawling into Aimi's bed. As always, Aimi's presence and determination kept chasing the demons away. "I love you, sweet baby sister. I won't let anybody hurt you," she heard Aimi reassure her. Kuri laughed when she saw Gavin clowning around; her brother always knew how to make her feel good, especially after she came back from the hospitals, the visits with the doctors.

Suddenly she heard herself cry out, feeling the sharp pain of a needle that Ethan jabbed into her small arm. She whimpered when hot milk from the bottle burned her tiny tongue and the roof of her mouth. She watched Ethan hovering over her crib, pinching and shaking her violently, holding his hand over her mouth to smother her cries.

She heard the Tibetan bell and Dr. B's calming voice. "You don't have to remain in this moment of fear and pain. Go back to the white light, and I will guide you deeper."

Kuri felt the therapist's hand as it gently touched her upper chest and abdomen. "Allow the light to fill your physical body; let it enclose you like a protective shield." Dr. B's soothing voice suddenly seemed far away.

Kuri felt the tap-tap-tap on her forehead and a warming hand on her chest. Tap-tap-tap. And then she heard the distant ring of the Tibetan bell.

"Ten-nine-eight…go deeper with each number," Dr. B. told her. "Seven, six, five…imagine yourself in an oasis of total freedom where glorious light offers unconditional love. Four-three…you are going deeper. Two…all is pleasant, peaceful, perfect. One…you are there."

Tap-tap-tap…Kuri perceived Melanie's fingers on the moonstone and on the clear quartz crystals, followed once more by the sound of the bell.

"Where are you now?"

"So beautiful. So tranquil. I hear melodies…singing…but there are no voices. I sense loved ones around me—their presence comes in vibrational forces. Beautiful light, colors I have never seen before. Everything is clear, everything is familiar…I am home."

"Can you explain 'home'?"

"I have no words; there is no vocabulary to describe this splendor, but I am able to communicate with all that is."

"What do you look like?"

"I have no body but I am. I have free will and I am making decisions. I am choosing the life I need to live."

"Do you know why you chose your present life?"

"To complete a mission. But I must go further back to understand the purpose."

"Are you ready to go deeper?"

"Oh, yes. I want to find the awareness of what was."

As if from very far away, Kuri heard the Tibetan bell and sensed light tapping on the jet and jade stones.

"You are floating, carried by the white light. I will count you down. Five…the light guides you. Four…you move through spectrums and dimensions. Three…you arrive on the other side of the light. Two…find yourself. One…be there."

Far, far away, the Tibetan bell tolled.

"Look at your feet. What do you see?"

"I see feet in white socks and shiny patent-leather shoes."

"Can you look further up your body?"

"I see my legs, a plaid skirt. I see a white blouse; the collar is tied with a blue ribbon, but the ribbon is coming loose."

"What else do you see?"

"I am jumping rope. I am good at it. I have copper hair and my braids are bouncing while I jump. I am counting. I am laughing. I am happy."

"Are you by yourself, or is someone with you?"

"A friend is here. A girl. She has thick blond braids, and she wears the same skirt and blouse as me. She's very pretty."

"Do you know her name?"
"Erika…her name is Erika von Schloßhauer."
"Where are you?"
"In front of my house."
"Where do you live?"
"In Berlin-Schöneberg."
"Do you know your name?"
"Yes, my name is Judith Rozenblum."

Chapter Twenty-Nine

1938

Neunundvierzig... *fünfzig*... *einundfünfzig*... I keep jumping my rope. Erika is making a face. She only made it to thirty-nine, and I'm already over fifty and know I can do more. Erika is my favorite friend—we're both eight years old.

Every day, on our way home from school, Erika is allowed to play for one hour at my house. Then she gets picked up by her nanny and has to go home; she lives in a villa only three blocks away. She has one older brother and a younger sister. Erika's father works for the government. I think the von Schloßhauers must be very rich. I don't like to play in the big von Schloßhauer home—everybody there is too serious, and children only are allowed to play board games and we must always be quiet.

My parents own the apartment building we live in. Five other families live there; our apartment is on the top floor. I have no siblings, but I have Struppi, my little terrier dog. Erika likes visiting me because in my home we can be loud and laugh and run and nobody complains. We chase Struppi through the rooms, and

Mama doesn't even get mad when we slam a door or when a chair gets tipped over; she enjoys laughing with us. Sometimes Erika and I help Mama bake cookies. We stand near the oven and can't wait for them to be ready; we love eating cookies while they're still warm. I have fun when Erika comes to my house.

Papa and his brother, my uncle Salomon, own a furniture store. They have many customers; even the von Schloßhauers buy furniture from the Rozenblum Brothers. On some days when I don't have school, Papa takes me to the store with him. I wear my prettiest dress, and Papa smiles when I stand by the door to greet the customers.

Uncle Salomon and his wife, Bela, don't live too far from us. I get to play with my three little cousins all the time. Esther and Elias are four years old, they are twins. Miriam is eight months old—she is the sweetest baby in the world. My cousins love when I read to them, and they laugh when Struppi performs the tricks I taught him.

My parents tell me how proud they are that I am a good student and that the teachers praise my work. When I grow up, I may want to be an educator, just like my teacher Frau Littenhoff; she is very, very smart. But I also want to be a dancer, and I've been taking ballet classes since I was five years old. My whole family and many of our friends like to attend my ballet recitals; a few times even Erika and her sister have been there with the nanny. When I dance, I forget where I am and who I am; I turn the stage into a fantasy world of my own.

I don't understand what is happening. Two months ago, Papa and Uncle Salomon sold both of the apartment buildings where our families live. Why? I hear them say they're lucky that during these times they even came close to getting their sale price. Then the adults talk about investing in England—I don't know what all of that means. Lately everybody seems worried, and they always talk in hushed voices. Now Papa and Uncle Salomon say they must sell the furniture store. When I ask questions, Papa pulls me on his lap. "Mama and I are working on a new life for us—all for a good reason," he says. I still don't understand.

There's a lot I can't figure out. The last time I saw Erika was many weeks ago. Why isn't she allowed to play with me anymore? Her brother Martin walks by our house with some friends; they watch me jump rope and then Martin calls me a name I never heard before and says that my family is un-German. That makes me very angry, and I push him. Martin is furious; he calls me a dirty Jew and hits me so hard with a stick that I need stitches on my chin.

Today Mama walks with me to the ballet studio, but the doors are locked and nasty things about Jews are written on the door. Another parent tells Mama that Frau Levi, my ballet teacher, and her whole family were taken away. I am very sad and very confused because I don't understand why so many Germans dislike the Jews—aren't we German, too?

On rare occasions my parents and I take Struppi to Weißensee, a Jewish cemetery—one of the few places where Jews still are allowed to take walks. On our way back home, I see other children, and I wish I could play with them in the public gardens, but Jews are barred from everything now. Papa can't even take me to the museums anymore.

Mama and Papa tell me that we will move to England where Aunt Bela has relatives. Papa says he is in the process of making travel arrangements. I want to stay in Berlin, but Papa explains that life in Germany will never be the same for us. Mama hugs me—her soft arms and soothing voice always make me feel better. She smiles and assures me that Struppi will come to England with us.

❄

This week I'm really sad because we prepare to leave what until recently was our building, but Herr Professor Juhnke and his wife, who live on the third floor, insist we move in with them. Their apartment is very big, even bigger than ours. Mama and Papa say that they cannot accept Herr Professor's generous offer, but he stresses that we have to stay with him and his wife. "Where else will you go?" he asks. "The other two Jewish families in this building left—nobody knows what happened to them." He points to the wheelchair by the window. "My wife will never be the same after the stroke; I have bad gout, and it gets harder and harder for me to take care of her," he says. "Let's help each other through these difficult times."

Mama and Papa finally agree to Herr Professor's offer. I see them shake hands. Papa tells me as soon as our papers are ready, we will move to England; until then, we will stay in two of the back rooms of Herr and Frau Professor Juhnke's apartment.

Summer break is over, and I am very happy; I've been counting the days for school to start. Mama and Papa tell me that I'm not allowed to attend classes anymore, and neither can the other Jewish girls. I don't understand why—I have so many friends and all the teachers like me. I go into one of the back rooms and cry. Mama and Papa try to comfort me, but it doesn't help.

Herr Professor Juhnke offers to teach me. Papa says that the professor is very smart and many people in Germany hold him in high regard for his accomplishments. When Herr Professor was younger, he taught science and mathematics at the university in Göttingen. He also wrote many books. He's retired now. Herr and Frau Professor are not Jewish. I don't have grandparents, so I make believe Herr and Frau Professor are mine—I like being with them.

I often hear the word *Judenbann,* and I ask Herr Professor Juhnke, "What does a ban on Jews mean? Why can't we go to parks, playgrounds, and swimming pools anymore?"

He looks at me with sad eyes and says, "Throughout human history beasts and devils have always existed. They were in relatively small numbers compared to the masses of ordinary men who chose to be blind followers, who avoided making inquiries or who were too lethargic to educate themselves."

"You mean people did things they really did not want to do?" I ask. "Why?"

He bends down to me. "Exactly," he says. "If somebody forced you to kick a dog, would you?"

"No! I could never hurt a dog or any animal!" I protest. "But even bad people who don't care about animals, why would they kick the dog? Wouldn't they know the dog might bite their leg?"

"You are very smart, Judith," says Herr Professor, and continues talking in a quiet voice. "In Germany today, we unfortunately have rulers and policy makers who can't even understand their own decisions; they are neither concerned nor capable of calculating the consequences of their actions." Herr Professor shakes his head and wipes his glasses clean. "And, once again, there now are hordes of simpletons who'd do anything they're being told; they trust and swallow false promises."

"Why? And what will happen to all these people who are followers?"

Herr Professor shrugs his shoulders. "We don't know yet, but history will tell one day. Meanwhile, these people are blinded by their excitement. It's like they stare into a black hole, totally unaware of what they're being sucked into."

"That is so dumb," I say, because recently Herr Professor showed me a book on astronomy and taught me about black holes.

Herr Professor takes my hand and leads me into his study. I love that room; it's wall to wall full of beautiful books. He reaches up and pulls out *All Quiet on the Western Front*. "We'll read it together," says Herr Professor, handing it to me. "It's a tough book to read, but you are very smart for your age. You'll learn that uncertain times and war can breed conflict between people who held no resentment against one another before. Feel free to ask as many questions as you want. I will explain whatever you don't understand." He looks at the book's cover. "I'm afraid this book might not be around for much longer."

I am not sure what Herr Professor means, but I am eager to begin reading.

❄

Today is the eleventh of November, and I don't understand what is going on or why. Two nights ago, our furniture store was looted and vandalized; all the big windows were smashed in. We waited day and night, but neither Papa nor Uncle Salomon returned home. A friend tells Mama and Aunt Bela that Papa and Uncle Salomon were arrested. Nobody is sure where they were taken. Mama, Aunt Bela, my cousins, and I, we all cling to one another and don't let go. I never felt pain in my heart before—it hurts so much.

1940

Aunt Bela and my little cousins left for England shortly after Papa and Uncle Salomon disappeared. Their papers were ready, but ours still are not. Mama says it's for the best because she hopes Papa will soon return home. "Where else but right here will he look for us?" she says.

Mama now cleans and cooks for Frau and Herr Professor; today they both turn eighty years old. I think it is wonderful that they were born on the same day and in the same year. Mama and I bake a delicious cake, put candles on it, and surprise them. I have a special gift for them. I secretly put on my tutu and toe shoes. When Mama sits at the piano and starts playing "The Sugar Plum Fairy," I come into the room and dance for Frau and Herr Professor.

Even though we now are in hiding, Herr Professor tells us not to worry—he has high status with officials in the Nazi regime—but for our own safety, he prefers we stay indoors. Now he goes daily to shop for groceries and always takes Struppi along. Mama continues to cook, bake, and clean; she also bathes and dresses Frau Professor and assists Herr Professor with tasks he can't do anymore.

Every morning for three hours, Herr Professor teaches me in his study. He often pats my shoulder and tells Mama I'm a genius in mathematics. He says I'm like a sponge when it comes to reading books. Each day I learn more about the world and the customs of other societies. My favorite book in Herr Professor's rich library is Shakespeare's *Romeo and Juliet*; it now has a special place on the second shelf where I can easily reach it. I am reading *Romeo and Juliet* for the third time and know many quotes and passages by heart. On most nights, before I go to sleep, I make Herr Professor laugh when I put drama in my voice, clutch my chest, and recite, "Good night, Good night! Parting is such sweet sorrow, that I shall say good night till it be morrow." And Herr Professor raises his voice and almost sings his response, "Did my heart love till now? I forswear it, sight! For I n'er saw true beauty till this night." That makes me giggle all the time, and I go to sleep with happy dreams.

Mama and I never go outside anymore. Whenever the weather is nice, we sit on the balcony because we like the sun and the fresh air. But we have to make sure the concrete walls and flower boxes are shielding us from the views of neighbors. In the evenings, we read our books, and before we go to sleep, we say our prayers, hoping for Papa to come home. We pray for our family in England; we are thankful for the kindness of Frau and Herr Professor.

1942

There is hard knocking on the door, and I hear Herr Professor argue loudly with other men. We hear him shout, "Get out of my home!" Then the door slams shut.

Mama and are I hiding in the larder. Mama is holding her hand over my mouth. My heart is beating fast.

Soon there is louder banging against the door; more thunderous exchanges of words. The front door slams shut again. We hear shuffling footsteps and know it's Herr Professor. He looks defeated when he opens the door to the larder. He explains that someone in the building informed the Nazis about Mama and me. "I showed them the papers from my friends in government, granting permission to have you live with us as household assistants. I showed them authorization from the doctor that my wife and I depend on your aid, but neither the documentation nor my arguments mattered;

these scoundrels will be back tomorrow." He wipes his eyes. "I am so very sorry."

The next morning, when they come to take us away, Mama and I wear our nicest dresses under our best coats. We each carry a suitcase. I can't turn around to look at Herr Professor, who stands with Struppi under the entrance door of our building. I'm afraid if I turn, I'll run back. I hear my little terrier bark, and the pain in my heart is unbearable. I keep swallowing my tears.

We are on a transport to Ravensbrück, an all-women concentration camp. Mama says it's only eighty kilometers from Berlin; I see a brief flicker of hope in Mama's eyes. But the moment we arrive at this camp, every bit of faith and belief in us is crushed.

As we stand in line with the other women and children, a guard commands me to step forward. She looks me up and down and runs her fingers through my curls. She sneers, "*Rote Haare, Sommersprossen, sind des Teufel's Artgenosen!*" It upsets me that she ridicules my copper hair and my freckles and compares me to the devil in front of everybody; but I know better, and I control my tears and swallow my pride.

I keep thinking about the books I read with Herr Professor as our heads are shaved and our clothes are taken away. When we are given striped uniforms, made of very thin material, I think of Herr Professor's encouragement to be proud of my heritage no matter what.

All the Jews are identified by the yellow triangle on our uniforms. But I see countless other women with different colored triangles. Mama explains this way the Nazis can put their finger on our ethnicity and political beliefs. I soon learn that the Gypsies wear black triangles; political and Soviet prisoners wear the red triangle.

A woman in our barrack tells Mama that most prisoners in the camp are Polish women and children, but that there are more than twenty nationalities imprisoned in this camp. Every day I am confronted with new facts—horrible things that Mama would like to protect me from hearing, if only she could. I also find out that prostitutes are thrown into the same barrack as intellectuals. I learn about the beliefs of Jehovah's Witnesses and why the Nazis tell the Romas that they are racially undesirable. Even though the different colored triangles are supposed to distinguish our national or cultural tradition, we all are the same; we are human beings; we all treasure life.

Mama tries to shield me when other prisoners whisper about terrible medical experiments. But I do hear about the *Kaninchen,* women and children who are selected for brutal, unnecessary surgeries and research. The German doctors smash their bones, cut wounds in them, and then deliberately infect those wounds over and over again. Pregnant prisoners are taken to what is callously called *Kinderzimmer;* as soon as the babies are born, they are taken away and... Mama holds her hands over my ears. I'm glad she blocks out the rest. I don't want to hear anymore.

Some of the female guards are pretty, but all are coldhearted. In their mouse-gray jackets, culotte-style skirts, and black leather boots, they all look dark and grisly. They make us stand for hours in rain and cold temperatures during roll call; oftentimes they whip us or send their dogs after us for no reason whatsoever.

Strangely enough, we prisoners hardly recognize some of the guards when they're off duty. These beasts suddenly wear beautiful dresses, have their hair coiffed, smile, and carry the flowers they picked in the forests. We hear stories that they work hard at making themselves attractive for the male SS with whom they go boating and often partying all night long.

Who are these women? Who taught them to be so brutal? Who do they listen to? I think of what Herr Professor said, "simpletons who believe false promises, who blindly stare into a black hole, totally unaware of what they're being sucked into."

The Jewish women in our barracks form a tight bond. I now consider myself a woman. I am only twelve years old, but I definitely don't feel like a child anymore. Mama apologizes that I have to grow up so fast, but I am glad because I like to help rather than be helped. Together with the other women, I create games for the children and arrange schooling—I teach them things I learned from Herr Professor.

Even though the rations are so little, I often share my food with some of the younger children who keep crying because of hunger. Two women in our barrack are doctors; they show me how I can aid the sick; there's a lot of illness in the Ravensbrück prison. I quickly learn what can be done for those with diphtheria, dysentery, tuberculosis, or typhoid…all these illnesses run rampant here. Sometimes there are outbreaks of lice. In our barrack, we keep ourselves and everything else as clean as possible, hoping to avoid contagion.

1943

One of the head guards is Hedwig Mollke. She's small and cold-blooded, and with her tiny beady eyes she looks like a reptile with lipstick. Her voice is nasal and monotone. When she talks or yells, she flicks her tongue a lot; when she does that, she reminds me of a lizard who uses its tongue to sniff out its surroundings. Everybody is afraid of Mollke—even some of the other guards.

Mollke finds out that Mama is multitalented when it comes to sewing, cooking, and other personal improvements. Mama praises my skills and insists she needs my help. Mollke orders us into the SS hierarchical housing quarters, where she condemns us to whatever drudgery she can think of. The good thing is, we are instructed to take regular showers and keep our uniforms clean at all times. Mama says we have become Mollke's slaves, but at least now we don't have to stand for hours during roll call and we are spared from becoming victims of the other guards' appetite for cruelty. Our hair is growing back, and because we now cook for some of the high-ranking members of the SS, we even get more to eat.

Mollke tells us that male officers in senior and important positions will inspect KZ Ravensbrück; there will also be an elegant dinner and entertainment.

She hands Mama yards of silky material and orders her to design a dress. Mama works the sewing machine like a professional, and I finely stitch the hems by hand. When Mollke sees the finished dress, she smiles—something she's never done before. She shows Mama a picture of a beautiful woman in a magazine. "Make me look like that," she requests. While Mollke is under the hair dryer, Mama and I start preparations for three big cakes. I continue in the kitchen while Mama styles Mollke's hair, plucks her eyebrows, and puts on makeup. When the cakes are in the ovens, I clean my hands, fold the apron away, and walk into the next room. I know my eyes grow big when I see Mollke; she actually looks attractive and…I dare tell her. She smiles for the second time.

"Your mother tells me that you had ballet training. I want you to perform after the dinner tonight. Your mother will play the piano." Mollke warns us that everything has to be perfect. "Don't embarrass me, or else…"

"But I don't have a tutu. I don't have toe shoes," I demur.

"You'll wear what I'll give you and dance barefoot."

❄

Mama and I sit on a hard bench in the rear of the commandant's headquarters. We hear loud music and roaring laughter.

"They're consuming a lot of alcohol," Mama whispers. She's wearing a formless black dress and clunky dark shoes, something Mollke gave her. It doesn't matter, Mama always looks beautiful.

I'm still in my prison uniform when Mollke comes in. "Hier." She hands me a silky see-through blouse, a wispy shawl, and tiny pink underwear. "Put this on." She gives the cosmetic container to Mama. "Turn her into a little temptress," she orders. When Molke sees horror spread over Mama's face, she warns, "No protest! You do what I tell you, or I'll see to it that both of you end up with the *Kaninchen*."

Mama starts playing from sheet music given to her, a beautiful tune but nothing I've ever danced to before. My instructions are to enter the small stage as soon as I hear the first notes, but I remain frozen behind the door, staring into the mirror—it's not me I'm seeing.

I hear loud voices and rhythmic clapping and then somebody pushes me through the door into the smoke-filled room to loud whistles and laughter. I don't want to look at the SS men and women, so I lift my eyes and stretch my arms to the white ceiling as if reaching out for help. I hear Mama's voice in my head: "We must obey their orders yet never lose our dignity…that's how we'll survive."

I tune out the noise and begin to move to the music, imagining myself in a far-away place. I begin to move through the beautiful scenery I see in my mind's eye. I sway like palm trees and pirouette like wind-blown bougainvillea blossoms; I leap like a gazelle and pretend to fly like a graceful sandhill crane. In this trancelike state, I am free again and never want the music to stop—when it does, I sink to the floor like the dying swan from Swan Lake. I remain in that position and pull the shawl over me, trying to hide from the ruthless reality that suddenly surrounds me again.

"We found our own little Mata Hari," I hear a man shout near me. The applause and the laughter get louder, accompanied by thumping of heeled boots. Somebody pulls me up. "Smile and bow," hisses a voice; it's Mollke. I obey, trying to ignore my naked body, visible under the sheer fabric.

When I raise my head, I freeze. There's Werner von Schloßhauer, Erika's father, in his SS Ober Gruppen Führer uniform. He stands by one of the front tables and points to me. "*Komm her, Du kleine Juden* Mata Hari," he booms. Mollke pushes me forward.

"You've grown up nicely, you little red fox." He roars with laughter. He turns to the other men and women at his table. "This fetching Jew-girl used to be in school with my daughter Erika…only until we cleansed, Aryanized, and privatized the institute," he guffaws, and I can smell the alcohol on his breath.

He turns around to the other tables and shouts, "Shall we have our Jewish Mata Hari perform another exotic dance?" The SS men answer him by stomping their boots and howling approval.

"You are lucky they like you," he slurs, and hands me a glass of wine. "Drink up!" he orders.

The wine makes my head spin, and I feel tears welling up in my eyes. I step back onto the stage toward Mama at the piano and see the pleading expression of sorrow and regret in her eyes. Then, through a hint of a smile and quick nod I hear her silent encouragement: "Never lose your dignity…that's how you'll survive."

Suddenly there is commotion behind me; I turn around. An inebriated female guard is trying to pull Mollke off von Schloßhauer's lap; he roars with laughter as Mollke kicks the other guard. The situation is almost comical, but the laughter gets caught in my throat when I see the drunk guard punch Mollke in the face, one, two…three times. I forget where I am and how sparsely I am dressed. I run and thrust myself between the two women. "Stop! Please stop!" I shout, catching the guard's arm before she can punch Mollke again.

As soon as I realize how stunned and surprised the other officers and guards are by my actions, I hurry back toward Mama.

"*Stehenbleiben!*" The intoxicated female guard almost loses her balance as she stumbles after me. She grabs at the sheer fabric covering my body and rips it off. "You little Jewish whore!" I feel the first strike across my face and then she hits me harder and harder; I fight the pain but remain standing, trying not to flinch. I notice uniformed arms grabbing the drunk guard by her shoulders, yanking her back. She glares at me and hisses, "I'm not done with you," before she staggers away.

Mama stands in front of me, trying to block my nudity when von Schloßhauer walks up and orders Mama to take care of Mollke, who looks pale as a ghost. He covers me in a white tablecloth and pulls me through the door.

"You still need to complete a dance," he says, grinning. "Your next performance will be only for me," he mutters.

❋

The sun rises over the horizon when I walk back to our barrack. I feel torn up inside and every step hurts. *How could he do this to me?* I ask myself. *I am his daughter's friend—we're only thirteen.* Tears stream down my face and, like snails, they leave their trails in the remnants of my makeup.

When I stumble into the barrack, Mama rushes to my side; she's acting brave, but I know she's crying inside. Other women try to soothe both of us; one of them folds both Mama and me into her arms. "Remember," she says, "righteousness is of no virtue among this species. *You* are not part of their breed!" Another woman gently touches my cheek. "Don't lose hope," she says. "A quitter never wins—a winner never quits."

Chapter Thirty

Kuri looked at the face of the French Morbier clock in her parents' living room. "I don't understand; he promised he would be here," she said. "Let me try one more time." She called Ethan's number for the fourth time that afternoon, and once again there was no answer; her most recent text message still remained unread.

"I really was hoping to see my Ethan today—it's been too long. I hope he's all right," Teruko said. "I miss him."

"Punctuality has never been Ethan's virtue," David said, "even though our son probably has one of the fastest cars in the state."

"Dad, I believe he already sold the McLaren." Kuri looked at her father. "That's why I asked Stan to give Ethan a ride."

Kuri's phone dinged, and she quickly glanced at the screen. "Speaking of Stan…" she muttered. After taking a moment to read the message, she looked up. "He waited forty-five minutes in the courtyard outside Ethan's building. The doorman called upstairs, but no one answered in Ethan's apartment."

"What about his fiancée…what's her name…ah, yes, Irina? Can you contact her?" Aimi wondered.

Kuri slapped her forehead. "Irina! Why didn't I think about her earlier?" She called, and after the seventh ring, she disconnected and sent a text message.

"She's not answering either," she said, after waiting a couple of minutes. "Something important must've come up for them that they can't make it today."

"But everybody is glued to their phones these days," Gavin grumbled. "Unless he and Irina broke all ten of their fingers or are lying unconscious on the sidewalk someplace, there's no excuse."

"Well, then once again we shall have a family meeting without Ethan," David said, with sadness in his eyes. A few moments later, he looked at Kuri. "You asked for all of us to come together to share an extraordinary experience. Shall we begin?"

"Let me start from the beginning," she said, as everybody found a comfortable place to sit. Kuri was excited to finally be able to tell her loved ones about the breakthrough she had achieved with Dr. B.

"As you know, for years the medical world was unable to give us an explanation for the terrors that haunted me as a child; they misdiagnosed all my psychological and physical symptoms. But now I've met Dr. B! For the first time, a therapist actually can hear, see, and understand me." Kuri was pleased that she had her family's full attention. "Through Dr. B's excellent ability in the field of past life regression therapy, she helped me make sense of the nightmarish visions I've endured. Her guidance took me to the source of my suffering."

As she began to talk about the techniques Dr. B. had used to regress her into a previous life, Kuri told her family every detail about her existence as Judith Rozenblum; the carefree life she had in Berlin-Schöneberg that ended when she became a young victim of the Nazis.

Sharing this newfound knowledge with her family, Kuri felt her anxieties subside, just as they had drained away in her discussion with Dr. B. after their session had ended. "My whole body feels lighter; my mind is clear—free of burden," she said.

The chime of the antique French Morbier clock startled Kuri, and when she turned her head toward the sound, she realized her family had let her talk for more than an hour, without interruption. Now they all looked at her silently.

Her father cleared his throat. His words came haltingly. "I've never given thought to the supernatural—most likely because those are parts of life some people can't perceive—I am definitely one of them. He paused pensively. "I have to admit, I am definitely lost for words."

"I'm not," Gavin interjected, leaning forward. "No offense, Kuri, but how can you know that this past-life experience is actually real? You are a highly artistic and inventive person. What if those memories are just a product of your creative imagination?"

"Well, according to Sufi Al Ghazzali, a Persian philosopher from a past century, imagination travel is instant; not that one is traveling physically anywhere but rather into another world that is like a mirror of this one. Al Ghazzali said a higher world is a spiritual mirror of a lower world. And when we journey through either our visionary or imaginal world—as I did through hypnotic guidance—we can actually move into another reality."

"What? How? This is way over my head."

"I understand, yet the intensity of my feelings is almost impossible to explain; the details that emerged from Dr. B's hypnotic regression were so precise and vivid…" Kuri stopped talking, losing herself in thought.

Teruko reached for her youngest daughter's hand. "We all forget the most important question: Has this experience brought you relief? Just recently, you had recurrences of your old symptoms. Have they become less severe after what you believe is an awareness of a past life?"

"Absolutely! It is most astounding that I understand the connection between the symptoms now. During my regression therapy, as I saw myself being Judith, I felt the ice-cold sensations and the darkness, heard the voices and experienced severe pain. It was identical to the same suffering that plagued me when I was a little girl, sensations that even haunted me until very recently. And now, because I know where it all came from, the captive chain has released me."

Kuri fell quiet, allowing herself to think before she continued. "I like the ancient philosophy of the spiritual mirror; I envision it as an infinity mirror that recedes into never-ending distance, casting back reflection after reflection after reflection." She paused again, then added softly, "I absolutely can feel that I lived before."

"Wow!" said Aimi. "That is beyond incredible." She exhaled loudly. "Wow," she exclaimed again, "I have so many questions; where do I start?"

"This is a whopper of a supernatural eye-opener; it's like science fiction," Gavin said, scratching his head. He forked his fingers through his hair. "I'm skeptical, but weirdly enough, I want to hear more."

"Is there more?" asked Teruko.

"There has to be," Kuri replied, nodding. "What happened to Judith? Did she survive the war?" Unable to sit still, Kuri got up and walked behind her chair, resting her hands on its back. "I am going to have another session with Dr. B—maybe even more than one. I need to find the answers; it's essential for me to know. It's imperative to find real proof."

"How will you possibly do that?" asked Aimi.

"While I was under deep hypnosis, I distinctly recalled names and places. I will look in the official records for those names. One way or another, I have to discover what happened to Judith Rozenblum." One by one she looked at her family and said softly, "I will have to find a way, confirming that Judith lived. I will find the answers to why my dreams and visions have led me back to her."

Her phone dinged. She sighed and blinked herself into the moment, looking at the text message on her phone.

"Is it from Ethan?" Teruko asked hopefully.

Kuri shook her head as she saw her mother's smile fading. "No, but it's from Irina; she says it's urgent."

Chapter Thirty-One

Irina picked up immediately, and before Kuri even was able to say a word, she heard the extreme distress in Irina's voice.

"Oh my gosh, oh my gosh, Kuri! Ethan...he's on floor; there's blood. You must come here and help. Please, Kuri, I not know what to do."

"Is he breathing?"

"I not know. I'm trying...it just happened."

"What happened?'

"I think he overdose with bad drugs...oh my gosh!" Irina's voice grew from panic to hysteria.

"Call 911, Irina. Call now!"

"No, no! I can't. I'm afraid police will find—"

"You must call 911, Irina. Hold on..." Kuri turned to her alarmed-looking family members in the room. "Irina believes Ethan overdosed."

"I'll get the car," Gavin shouted as he ran out the door. "I'll call 911."

"Irina, are you there?" Kuri asked, signaling for Aimi to assist their parents.

"Oh my gosh! Wait, wait..."

With the phone pressed against her ear, Kuri rushed behind her sister and parents through the house, then into the garage. Gavin already sat behind the wheel; the engine was running.

❋

"Irina, please calm down. We are on our way, but I don't know how long it'll take to get to the city. We called 911. The ambulance is on the way."

Kuri heard a rattling sound, and Irina's voice in the background kept repeating, "Ethan? Wake up. You hear me? Ethan! Oh my gosh... Ethan!" Then, she began screaming frantically in Ukrainian.

"Irina! Irina? What is happening?"

"I think he... yes, he breathing again."

"Thank God! Irina, please, stay with him. Did you hear that we called 911?"

"Oh no, oh my gosh, no! I not want to be here alone with him when police come. I can't—"

"Irina, please listen. You have to stay with Ethan. I'll be on the phone with you the whole time. I'll help you talk to the paramedics. We will meet you at the hospital."

"No, please, not! I not want to be here when they come. He did something bad. I warn him, but Ethan never listen to me. I think he did bad heroin, was maybe laced with fentanyl. Oh my gosh... I not want to get into trouble."

"Trouble for what?"

"Because..." Irina whimpered, "because I give him something..." the rest of her words were swallowed by sobs of despair.

"Irina, what did you give him?"

"I always carry syringe with antidote because Ethan take lots of drugs and I worry about him. What if police ask me how come I have syringe with Narcan?"

"Narcan? That's exactly what he needed. You saved his life!"

"Yes, but will police ask why I have Narcan? Oh my gosh, Ethan always force me to pick up drugs for him because I..." Heavy sobbing smothered the rest of her sentence. "Oh no, someone at door."

Kuri heard voices and clatter in the background.

"People coming; they bring stretcher. You will talk to them? Here…"

"Who am I speaking to?" a woman asked.

"I am Ethan Berger's sister Kuri. My brother's fiancée found him unconscious; she thinks he overdosed on heroin, maybe laced with fentanyl; she—"

Kuri heard a thud, followed by clamor. "Hello!" she called out. "Hello!" There was screaming; she knew it was Ethan. Then she listened to increased commotion.

"Hello…"

"Kuri? Oh…no!" Irina sounded frantic. "Ethan fighting ambulance man," she whimpered. "They give more medication; now put strap around him. It's so terrible."

"Irina, you must go with them to the hospital. Keep me on the phone as long as you can. We will be there shortly."

Chapter Thirty-Two

Twenty-four hours earlier...

Ethan had not seen Irina since she returned from New York. He was furious. How long had she been back in Chicago? He couldn't remember. It didn't matter, he certainly would let her know of his displeasure. Who did this ungrateful bitch think she was? Only one hour ago had he finally received a text from her, letting him know she was on her way.

"Well?" Ethan asked when he saw her coming through the door.

"Well what?"

He could tell there was something different about her; she acted more secure, more self-important. He didn't like it.

"Well," he said again. "Are you well or not well? You're like a stone wall carved with hieroglyphics. I can't read you."

She returned his remark with an indifferent expression. "You had long time to learn how to read me," she scoffed, then shot him an icy look so glacial it made Ethan shudder; he wasn't used to it.

"Get over yourself," he shouted defensively. "Just because some New York modeling agency is giving you a contract is no guarantee that you'll be on the cover of *Vogue*! And who the fuck got you through their doors in the first place? If it wasn't for me, you'd still be picking up dog shit and working your ass off at catered affairs. Stop acting so fucking superior and show me some gratitude." He walked over to the bar area, then poured himself a drink.

He watched her squat next to Lolli, petting the dog. She definitely looked transformed, and he had trouble taking his eyes off her. Gone was her previous seductive appearance with lash extensions, scarlet lipstick, and tight-fitting clothes. Without the enhancements of cosmetics, she looked younger, even prettier in the slim white jeans and a simple black T-shirt. He wasn't used to this new style, but in a puzzling way, it turned him on. "Hey," he said hoarsely. "I had a rough night. Sorry for being an asshole." He held up a glass. "What can I pour for you?"

"Nothing! Thanks. I made decision to change. I come today to tell you in person." She let go of Lolli and straightened. "I have no drugs, no alcohol since last time I see you…the day Kuri was here. To tell you truth, I not miss it. I feel great!" She walked closer and looked at Ethan. "Everything more vibrant to me now; I like new clarity of life! You must try. Everything can be better for you, too…for both of us, if you want."

Ethan swallowed. He couldn't believe he actually envied her. He desperately wanted to feel better than he felt at that moment. *Am I that fucked up?* He did not like questioning himself. He looked at the drink in his hand. *Fuck no! I helped that bitch in so many ways—she wouldn't even be here or look like this if it wasn't for me.*

"Really?" he yelled. "Did my goody two-shoes sister fuck with your brain?" He let out a mirthless laugh. "Trust me, you'll never make it in her world; it simply ain't gonna happen!" He grabbed Irina by the shoulders and squared her in front of him. "What's wrong with the life I can give you? Look around. This is as good as it'll ever get for you." He tried to lift her onto the counter, but she wriggled out of his arms.

"Why you say that?" She blinked her tears away. "I not like the way you treat me; I not like be at your mercy all the time."

A mix of desire and fury swelled in Ethan. When he tried to pull her toward him, she stepped away.

"What the fuck?" he shouted. "What did my fucking sister promise you?"

"Nothing! She promise nothing to me." As if looking for protection, Irina crouched next to Lolli again. "Your sister is very good woman; kind and generous. She also very honest; whole time I was with her, I feel guilty that you say so many lies to her."

"Fuck! You didn't tell her, did you?"

"I tell her nothing. You are the brother; I think you must tell her truth. You owe her to—"

"*You* shut the fuck up because my sister owes *me!*" Ethan's eyes kept burning into Irina's as he walked backward toward the bar. He ignored the glass waiting to be refilled; instead he lifted the bottle to his lips and took a giant swig. With the bottle still in one hand, he wiped the drops of liquor from his chin with the other. "Where's my stuff? I need it."

"I not know—I have nothing for you. Whatever left from last time, you still must have here…somewhere. Yesterday, you text me to go to your dealer to pick up your supply, and I text you back that I never go there again." She frowned at him. "You not remember? Go read my texts." She watched him as he quickly bent over his phone.

"No!" he said angrily. "I probably couldn't even understand your lousy English."

"Oh my gosh! I text you how I make fresh start; how I have new career and that I want live healthy and better life now. You even sent back angry text. You tell me I must pick up your stuff or else…" She shook her head. "You not remember?" she asked again. A soft sadness spread over her face, and she looked at him pleadingly. "Ethan, you must change life, too. It will be good for future. It also save you lot of money. You can live happy."

"Really? Did you forget who paid for all your shit? Who has been your ATM machine?" Still holding the bottle in his hand, he squared himself in front of her. "You really want to cut off your source of finding honey? Well"—he laughed—"then stop buzzing like a bumblebee." He belched and with an awkward thump, he put the empty bottle on the counter.

He snapped his fingers. "Hey, you!" he shouted when he realized Irina wasn't looking at him. "If you think you'll be singing la and di and da in New York, forget it! You better practice wailing boo-hoo right here in Chicago because without me, you're nobody and you'll never have anything!"

Unsteadily, he walked to the side table and grabbed Irina's tote. "Aha!" he crowed, and like a trophy, he triumphantly lifted Irina's cosmetic bag into the air. He turned it upside down. "What the fuck? Where is it?" He kept staring at the spilled contents: a bottle of Tylenol and a few cosmetic items.

"I tell you," Irina said. "I am done. I will not watch you do wrong things anymore."

"Fuck! What happened to all the money I gave you?"

"I never took money you give me last time or time before; I left all of money in drawer by your bed. Go look—it's all there," Irina said in a small voice as he passed by her.

"Speak up! Can't hear you!" he shouted. "Fuck, whatever…I don't really give a shit."

"You drunk, Ethan. If you want, I make you coffee," Irina said tonelessly.

"Bah!" He turned and stared at Irina, still squatting next to Lolli, gently caressing the dog behind her ears.

Ethan muttered something totally trivial and pushed past them on his way to the bedroom. Halfway there, he turned to see if Irina or Lolli would follow him. His chortle subsided when, to his surprise, he realized that neither paid any attention to him. "Ah, fuck you both," he snarled, and slammed the door to his bedroom suite behind him.

❄

He woke up early the next morning with a pounding headache; his mouth was dry. "Hey, Irina Czarina, where are you?" he yelled.

He got out of bed and unsteadily walked into the living quarters. "Hey," he shouted again, moving toward the bar. He took a glass from one of the shelves above the wet bar, filled it with water, and opened the cabinet where he kept a bottle of Advil. Just as he gulped six tablets down, out of the corner of his eye, he saw the note on the marble countertop.

"You pass out! I feed Lolli—I know you will not walk dog tonight or whenever you wake up. I take Lolli with me and bring back tomorrow. Please think about what I tell you. You and I can have good life together. XO."

Still standing by the bar with the half-empty glass of water in his hand, he tried to piece the events of the previous night together.

Did I snort more than two lines and pop a few OxyContin*?* He wasn't sure but remembered screaming insults at Irina when the last bottle of Gran Patrón Platinum slipped from his hand to the floor. He thought it funny when she cut her foot on a shard of glass and recalled laughing at her; he also had mocked her tears when she cleaned the floor.

A hint of regret tried to trespass the outer limits of his brain, but given the condition he was in, he didn't know what to do with that feeling.

He looked around the living space. Except for some chairs and a few odds and ends out of place, everything appeared fairly fastidious, but when he walked back to his bedroom suite, he despised the mess in the morning light.

Since matters of cleanliness always were of great concern to him, he wished that either Irina or his housekeeper were present to bring structure to the chaos. On the other hand, he didn't want them to see the empty liquor bottles or the vomit-soaked sheets and towels. He grabbed two large garbage bags and threw everything into them that offended his critical eye, including the towels and linens from his bed.

The back entrance of his unit led to the building's garbage chute; he dumped the bags without giving it another thought. When he reentered his kitchen, he scrubbed his hands and forearms like a doctor before engaging in surgery.

The silence in his spacious condominium irritated him. "Alexa," he ordered. "Play 'Kim' by Ryan Adams."

As he listened to the music, Ethan groaned. It was hurting his head. "Lower the volume," he demanded.

He thought of Lolli, suddenly missing the dog. More thoughts popped into his head. "No-no-no!" he yelled when images of his childhood tried to creep into his distant memory.

"Alexa! Stop!" he called out and sank into the sofa. For a moment, he sat quietly, listening to the pounding in his head. Then he tried calling Irina, reminding himself to speak kindly. She did not answer. He texted her and stared at the screen, waiting for a reply. Nothing!

"Damn!" he shouted, and furiously threw the phone into the cushions. As soon as he stood up, his heart started to thump so hard, it frightened him. He felt dizzy, and as he reached for the bottle of Hendricks on the table, he realized his hands were trembling. "Fuck," he groaned, realizing the bottle was empty. He staggered into the bathroom, where two other empty bottles greeted him. He vaguely recalled having searched drawers and cabinets during the night for drugs. He leaned against the wall and groaned. Suddenly, he spotted an oval-shaped white tablet on the floor. Was it Vicodin or Xanax? It didn't matter. He scooped it off the marble tile and swallowed it with the last drops from a bottle of Patron sitting on the vanity. He took a glimpse in the mirror; he looked like a boxer who'd just been through the losing side of a twelve-round fight. He kept staring at his image, suddenly realizing he still was wearing only boxer shorts. He shivered and lurched into the shower. The pulsating power spray hurt his skin, so he adjusted the pressure to a soft mist spray, then stood as still as he could between the fine water droplets.

When he was done, he dried himself and fumblingly made his way to his walk-in closet. Naked, he stood in the middle of the large space and gazed at his many dress shirts and suits, meticulously hanging color-coordinated on the racks. On the opposite side, the generous range of casual attire was accurately hung in specific groupings—everything arranged for each of the four seasons; even his shoes were lined up like soldiers, classified by their brand. He had difficulty concentrating and wished his head would feel as organized and methodical as the items in his closet.

He pulled a pair of Ralph Lauren jeans and a distressed cotton chambray shirt from their hangers and got dressed. Barefoot, he walked into the kitchen and opened the refrigerator. When he looked at the various groups of food, his stomach turned. With a twisted face, he slammed the door shut. He grabbed a Coke from the pantry, drinking it straight from the can. The loud burp brought slight relief. Even as the fog in his head slowly began to lift, he still felt rotten. *Maybe if I add rum to the Coke, it will fix things.* But when he looked through the various cabinets and pantry, he realized he'd gone through whatever alcohol had been left. He closed the door to the pantry and sagged against it. *Didn't I place a liquor order recently? Maybe I didn't. Did I ask Irina to buy alcohol? She said something I didn't like... what was it?* His brain did not cooperate.

"Concentrate. Concentrate," he muttered to himself. "Booze won't be enough anyway; I need something harder." He walked over to the sofa and took his phone. "I'll call..." It scared him that suddenly he couldn't think of the dealer's name. "Fuck, what's his name?" He scrolled through his entire contact list. Nothing. He leaned back. "Dammit! What the fuck is his name?" He scrolled through his contacts again—and there it was, finally: Marco Mendez.

"*Bueno.*"

"Marco? Ethan Berger. Can I come over?"

"You yourself? No shit. What happened to your *mamacita caliente linda?*"

"Ehm... she's out of town."

"Did *mamacita* tell you I moved in with my *hermosa*? I'm not at the Washtenaw address anymore."

Ethan wrote down the new address, relieved he did not have to go to that sleazy house on Chicago's northwest side.

"Get here fast. I gotta leave in an hour."

Thirty minutes later an Uber took Ethan to the address on North Sheridan Road. Ethan was shocked when he entered the neglected lobby of what he assumed must have once been a respectable apartment building. Reluctantly, he entered the elevator and gagged from a stench that reminded him of rotting fish. He started breathing again when the elevator door opened on the fifth floor. He found the apartment number and knocked on the door.

Mendez stuck out his head, quickly looked left and right into the hallway, then motioned Ethan to come in.

"Well, dude, you're a sight for sore eyes," Mendez said, sneering. A cigarette hung immobile on his lower lip; he flicked its ashes off. "So, whaddaya need today?"

Ethan pulled a piece of paper from his pocket. The dealer raised his brows when he looked at the handwritten list. He smirked as he disappeared into another room.

Alone in the living room, Ethan peered at the cheap, dated furniture; he noticed clumps of cat hair on the worn-out wall-to-wall carpet.

A while later, Mendez returned with baggies. "You got the money?"

"Of course," Ethan said. "How much?"

"Last time I saw you, you pissed me off because you complained about the price." Mendez snickered. "My price has gone up…no more discounts for you!" With a gleam of devilry in his eyes, he held the baggies up, shaking them.

"How much?"

"You got a lot of pure quality stuff here," Mendez said with a toothy smile. He put the assortment on the shoddy-looking table, and as if blessing the selection, he laid the palms of his hands onto the bags filled with syringes, powder, and pills. "Mmm…let me think." He rubbed his forehead. "I let you have it for eight fifty."

Ethan suspected he was being taken advantage of, but he was

desperate for a fix, so he paid, swiped the drugs off the table, and put them into his backpack. Back on the street, he pulled his baseball cap low onto his face and hailed a taxi.

"Clybourn and Willow," he told the driver, who, in a foreign language, kept talking on his Bluetooth throughout the ride.

"Wait here, I'll be right back; keep the meter running," Ethan said, and groaned as he climbed out of the car—his whole body was hurting. Slowly, he walked into Binny's Beverage Depot. He felt unsteady, and rather than spend any time looking for his favorite brands, he just grabbed two bottles from the closest shelf and went to the counter to pay. As he took his credit card out of his wallet, he again noticed the tremor in his hand. He wiped the cold, sweaty palms on his jeans before putting the bottles in his backpack. He couldn't wait to get home, to kill the pain, to feel numb…to sleep.

❄

"Ethan! Oh my gosh…Ethan!" He heard Irina's shrill voice, could feel her body looming over him even with his eyes closed. When the hell did she get back? He wanted to push her away, but he had no power, couldn't even raise his arms—he felt totally lifeless. He struggled to open his eyes. Her face—wide-eyed and distraught—floated over his. Strands of her hair stung his skin like porcupine quills; the stupid cow was rambling in Ukrainian.

"Piss off," he said through clenched teeth.

"Ethan…oh my gosh. You overdose with what? Really bad stuff? I give you Narcan."

"Get off me or I'll piss in your ugly face!" He saw her move away from him; he heard her talking on the phone.

"Oh no, oh my gosh, no…I not want to be here alone with him when police come. I can't…"

"Who the fuck you talking to?" He heard himself slur the words. "Goddammit!" he groaned as he heard Irina mention the police.

He wanted to stand, but he was unable to get his brain and legs working together. The pain was unbearable. He did not want to feel the way he felt; more than anything, he just wanted to go numb again. He vaguely remembered stashing oxycodone in his pocket; it took a tremendous effort, but he managed to slide a hand down and retrieve it, then reach up so he could push the pills between his lips; he swallowed.

"Oh my gosh... what you doing?"

He felt Irina's fingers part his lips, but it was too late. He bit down hard and heard her sharp cry of pain. His own laughter echoed through his brain; like a parrot it kept mimicking the cackle and got louder and louder until the ear-shattering squawk pushed everything out of his consciousness.

He passed out again.

Chapter Thirty-Three

"We have a few options," Dr. Berliner told the Berger family outside Ethan's hospital room. "I believe natural detox isn't a viable option for Ethan. From what you told me and from his medical history, his drug abuse is severe—an ongoing and longtime habit that could be life-threatening." The doctor paused; he rubbed his earlobe, then continued to speak. "I recommend a supervised medical detox where patients like Ethan, with significant risk factors and psychiatric symptoms, are monitored and cared for around the clock until they're balanced enough to move to the next stage in recovery."

"Knowing Ethan, he will want to get out of this hospital as soon as possible—he's done it before...twice," said Aimi. "What about rapid detox, followed by a family intervention while he's still in this hospital? If he gives the okay, he'll go straight to a rehab facility that is away from Chicago."

"Rapid detox is by far the most dangerous and controversial of the different types we offer here. We would have to put Ethan in a medically induced coma with an anesthetic or sedative, speeding up the detox process with naltrexone to reduce the body's physical cravings while he's unconscious. However, that procedure won't cure Ethan's mental addiction."

"Anesthesia is a health risk, isn't it?" Teruko said.

"It is," Dr. Berliner said. "And rapid detox can still be painful for the patient, even while he's unconscious. But you need to understand that, right now, your son's addictive behavior is already one of his greatest health risks."

"Let us think about it, Doctor. Meanwhile, we'll stay with Ethan until he wakes up." David looked through the glass into the room where his son lay hooked up to intravenous tubes.

"We are giving him sedatives because he was quite aggressive when the paramedics brought him in," Dr. Berliner explained, seeing David's worried expression. "He'll wake up very soon, and depending on his reaction and condition, let's wait to make the next decision."

The doctor turned to Irina, who, like a schoolgirl being punished, stood pressed into the corner of the hallway, watching everything fearfully. "You did the right thing when you gave Narcan to your fiancé—that saved his life," he told her. The doctor faced the family again. "Because Narcan is short-acting, Ethan even needed an extra dose of naloxone to counteract the fentanyl overdose. The paramedics found syringes and open baggies with pills and cocaine. We don't know what he took or how much of it—he refused to tell us."

Kuri walked over to Irina. "I'm glad you told us what really happened between you and Ethan. I am sorry he made you do things against your will. You must have been scared when he kept warning you about the outcome of your immigration status. I can imagine your anxiety when he kept threatening you with deportation; all because this Ukrainian man brought you into the US with counterfeit travel documents when you were only a teenager." Kuri put her index finger under Irina's chin, lifting her face to make eye contact. "Many mistakes were made, but now is not the time to dwell on them. You arrived in time to save Ethan's life—that's what matters right now." She took Irina's hand. "Come, don't stand here by yourself; you are part of our family."

"I am sorry, Kuri. I not have been honest with you; there still is more. Ethan tell you many lies..." Irina's voice trembled as she tried to swallow her tears. "I want to tell you truth in New York, but I was scared of what Ethan can do. And now..."

"Now is not the time," Kuri said. "Whatever it is, you can tell us later. Not here in the hospital." She pulled Irina into the group.

They sat around Ethan's bed, talking softly. Teruko was holding Ethan's hand when he opened his eyes. He groaned when he saw his family.

"Fuck," Ethan moaned, reaching over, trying to pull the peripheral IV lines from his arms. "Get the fuck away from me!" He sat up and jabbed his elbow into Gavin's face as his older brother attempted to hold him down.

Aimi ran out of the room, calling for help, and two nurses immediately rushed into the room to restrain Ethan as he thrashed on the bed, cursing his family.

"Get the fuck away from me! Get me out of here." With surprising strength, he kicked the sheet away, his foot aiming for the abdomen of one of the nurse's.

"You fucking blew my high! You moved me out of my home against my will." Writhing in fury, his arms knocked equipment off the hospital bed table.

"All of you, please wait outside!" the nurse said brusquely.

As Kuri and her family scrambled into the hallway, Dr. Berliner rushed toward them. "We will have to put Ethan into restraints again," he said before he went into the room. "I'll talk to you once we have him hooked up." He shut the door behind him.

Dismayed, the Berger family watched the activity through the glass window.

Fifteen minutes later, when Ethan had finally been restrained and sedated, Dr. Berliner stepped out of the room to speak with the family, but before the doctor could open his mouth, David raised his hand. "We made our decision," he said. "After witnessing this, we can see rapid detox is the only viable way to get my son through his initial withdrawal. By then, we will have picked a treatment center and brought in a therapist so we can give Ethan his options during the intervention."

Chapter Thirty-Four

She woke up in the middle of the night and stared into the darkness of her bedroom, trying to make sense of what caused her to be wide awake. What was that? Kuri turned on the light and reached for her journal but was unable to convert her mind's sensations into words. She would have to talk to Dr. B. about this.

She flipped the light off, then tossed and turned, experiencing difficulty falling asleep again. Frustrated, she reached for the phone on her nightstand and looked at the time; it was only 4:45 in the morning and still dark outside. She yawned and closed her fatigued eyes and, surprisingly, fell asleep.

Less than one hour later, she sat bolt upright in bed, looking around until she realized where she was and who she was. Totally flabbergasted by the experience, she grabbed her journal again; this time she was able to immediately write down every detail of her dream—she couldn't wait to tell Dr. B. later today.

After breakfast she let her parents know she preferred to stay home because of work-related issues. "See you later this evening," she said, and watched the car pull away from the house. She admired her father's determination to stay active in the business but felt sad for her mother, knowing she would spend the day sitting at Ethan's bedside, holding his hand while her son lay in a medically induced coma.

Sitting down at her father's desk in the library, Kuri called Aimi and Gavin. In a conference call, the three siblings talked about different rehab centers for Ethan. "Thank you for doing all the work," Kuri said after the next steps were discussed, then disconnected the call. Satisfied Gavin and Aimi would carefully do their research and come up with the best option for Ethan, she opened her Apple MacBook Pro to look over parts of the studio contract again. "Ridiculous," she muttered after she had examined it carefully. She closed the laptop and reached for the hard copy of a screenplay she had put on the side table, curled up on the leather sofa, and began to read.

At noon sharp, the phone rang. Kuri felt prepared to speak with her agent and lawyer.

She noticed it was already past one o'clock when, still engaged in the three-way-conference call, she again brought up alternative options regarding the project.

"Well, it will be a breach of contract, and Prime Pictures will take you to court," said Anton Hill from the law firm of Hill, Brown, and Cooper. "You're at the top of your box office powers—they can't replace you."

"Anton, you need to remind them that so far I only verbally agreed to the contract because I asked for screenplay rewrites. They neither have my signature, nor do they have my screenplay approval," Kuri protested. "Right now, I must deal with a family emergency…plus I need time for another personal conflict. As I mentioned before, I have no idea how long it will take to deal with both of these matters."

Anton Hill sighed. "I understand, but you know the studio—you're their main attraction."

"We need them to agree to delay shooting, and we have good reason!" Kathi Kemper, the agent, interjected. "Why would Prime Pictures already want to announce a release date when the screenplay is not yet finalized? I think Kuri is on the right track to wait until her demands are met; this will allow her the time she needs for her personal affairs."

Anton Hill cleared his throat. "Okay, we'll go back to the drawing board. Stand by."

Kuri walked outside—she needed fresh air. Shaded from the afternoon sun by the Altura cantilever umbrella, she leaned into the loveseat and put her feet on the ottoman.

Her eyes drifted over glistening Lake Michigan, and she marveled at its Caribbean-clear-blue color. She remembered reading that over the last twenty years the change in color from its former brownish green was due to the arrival of zebra mussels and quagga—its invasion had killed off a significant amount of phyto-plankton.

Everything in nature is so unique and interesting, she thought, and closed her eyes; she felt tired and ready to doze off in the still-ness of nature around her.

When she opened her eyes again, she gasped; hundreds, maybe thousands, of starlings appeared from the north and whirled between earth and sky in the ever-changing pattern of murmura-tion. Each bird seemed connected to the other and, en masse, they turned simultaneously—even the birds at the end of that enormous flock whirled in unison.

"This is awesome," she whispered into the wind when the swooping and diving mass of birds turned to the south and in their aerial ballet, like an ever-shape-shifting cloud, moved their unpre-dictable formation toward the west and disappeared from her sight.

She wished she could've shared this natural wonder with someone and immediately thought of Adam. The time on her phone let her know he wouldn't be able to talk at this hour; she decided to send a text.

Nature just gave me a gift: a murmuration of starlings. It was so beautiful, and I thought about you! I have an appointment with my therapist early evening. Can we talk later tonight? Around ten o'clock? I have so much to tell and talk about! I love you and miss you. ♥

Sofia was busy cutting vegetables when Kuri came to rinse her coffee mug. "Are you preparing dinner already?" she asked. "I can't believe I forgot all about lunch."

"I did not want to disturb you, but I made a chopped salad and grilled ahi tuna earlier for you," Sofia said. She dried her hands and opened the refrigerator.

"That looks so good," Kuri said as the bowl was placed in front of her. "*Gracias,* Sofia. *Por favor siéntate. Necisito practicar mi Español.*"

Later, after her parents returned home, it was Kuri's turn to be driven into the city. As Stan had done several times before, he dropped her off in the alley by the rear entrance to the office building. "I'll text you when I'm ready to come downstairs," Kuri said, pulled the floppy hat closer to her face, and dashed into the building.

"I really worry about my parents," Kuri said, after telling Dr. B. the events of the previous day. "They went through so much with me when I was younger, and Ethan has given them problems ever since…"

"Since you were born?" Dr. B. asked, when Kuri stopped talking.

Kuri nodded and sighed. "I hope the intervention will work. Once Ethan is in a treatment center, I believe my parents will be able to renew their hope again. Right now, everything is so uncertain…so dark."

"Speaking of…earlier you mentioned your strange dreams. Tell me about them."

Kuri took her journal from the backpack. "I woke up from one dream I can't even explain. Everything was in this sepia kind of color, like old photographs. But there were no images, except I had the feeling I was above myself, looking at my body lying in bed."

"You said there were no images—how then could you look at yourself?"

"I didn't see anything—it was more of a strong sensation of myself, enveloped in this reddish-brown color." Kuri rubbed her forehead. "What could that have been?"

"I am not sure, but have you heard of out of body experiences or OBEs?"

Kuri nodded. "If it was... why and how did it happen?"

Dr. B. smiled. "OBEs have captivated humanity's attention for centuries. From a scientific standpoint, there has been research on strong G-forces, on sensory deprivation or overload, on hallucinogenic drugs and much more. On the other hand, OBEs also are explained in folklore, mythology, and spiritual beliefs. Given your history and your recent recognition of a previous life..."

"This may be more evidence of the soul—proof of life after death," Kuri interrupted excitedly. "I recently read about renowned people who also believed in the same, like Johann Wolfgang von Goethe. He wrote, 'I am certain I have been here as I am now a thousand times before and I hope to return a thousand times.'"

"Even in my profession, there are some who believe in life after death," Dr. B. said. "For example, Carl Jung, the famous Swiss psychiatrist. He wrote, 'I could well imagine that I might have lived in former centuries and there encountered questions I was not yet able to answer; that I had to be born again because I had not fulfilled the task that was given to me.'"

"Incredible," said Kuri. "Since my own experience, I started to read books about hundreds of instances where children remembered a past life—many of them in India, others in Asia. Why, in our Western world, is it considered childish fantasy when young kids speak about such connections?" For a second, Kuri closed her eyes to think. "On the other hand," she continued, "from my own childhood experiences, I know how hurtful it was when nobody was able or didn't try to understand me, especially those in the medical field. What will it take to bring or accept proof?"

"Time, Kuri. Time will tell," Dr. B. replied. "As for right now, let's focus on the way you perceive things—that eventually may help you connect event to event." She paused. "Let's go back to yesterday; you had a lot going on. Many unsettling events were uploaded into your brain; it's difficult to process all the streams of sensory information. Give yourself time to connect the incidents."

Kuri reached for her journal again. "Maybe I am beginning to see how I can do this." As she was turning the pages, looking for her last entries, she said, "Last night, after the OBE or whatever it was, I fell asleep again for a relatively short time. When I woke up, I actually didn't know who I was or where I was!" She stopped to reflect. "This happened many times before, and it used to terrorize me, especially when I was younger," she continued. "But this time I was so calm—I was totally unafraid." She looked at Dr. B. and smiled. "I know it is because of the past life regression that I am able to connect the dots between the then and the now. These dark dreams don't frighten me anymore." She looked at her journal and turned over another page. "Here it is! I tried to write it all down—there were many, many terrifying and sad impressions; I will try to detail my abbreviated impressions."

Kuri took a deep breath and began to read and elucidate.

Chapter Thirty-Five

1944

Whenever von Schloßhauer pays his so-called inspection visits, I become his prime target. Even though I keep myself clean on the outside, inside I feel forever defiled and contaminated. Mama's arms are around me. "My sweet, innocent girl," she whispers. "There is an eternal twine of love that binds all of us together. Some of the twine may fray from sins and evils, but I have hope that a new era of good and love will approach when the twine can be woven together again." Mama pulls me closer. "I believe that a new generation will lift up those who are down and show them how to walk again." Even though Mama's consoling words caress my senses, they do not remove the assault that I suffer. Will I ever experience the beauty of life again? Will I ever be able to find trust in humankind?

I am sure Mama knows about the pain and shame that von Schloßhauer inflicts on me; the distress on her face is unbearable. So, I keep quiet about von Schloßhauer's assaults. *One day,* I keep telling myself, *punishment will fall upon all who have wronged us.*

Today is my fourteenth birthday, but instead of celebrating I mourn.

It is early in the morning, and I am on my hands and knees scrubbing the kitchen floor. When I hear the cracking of a whip, I dare to sneak a peek through the window in Mollke's house.

"I have to protect the fatherland against its internal enemies," shouts Irma Meier, the most feared SS guard during roll call; secretly, the Ravensbrück prisoners call her *die schwarze Mamba.* "Keeping discipline and lawfulness in this camp is as crucial to our Reich as is slaughtering our enemy on the front," the poisonous black mamba yells as she slithers back and forth, inspecting her victims. She stops and thrusts her stick into a prisoner's chest, but the woman doesn't flinch. "You all are whores!" She spits into another one's face and moves on. "You are godless delinquents, and there's only one way to keep you in control." She cracks her stick over an old woman's head, then slams it across another prisoner's back. "The enemy must be beaten!" she screams, and strikes a young girl on the kneecaps. "That's the only way our foes will capitulate."

❄

We find out that hundreds of women will be transferred from Ravensbrück. We are among them. "Where to?" I ask Mama, but she doesn't know.

Mollke cracks one of her rare smiles before Mama and I are dispatched to the cattle car with the rest of the prisoners. "Well," she says, grinning, "now Herr SS Ober Gruppen Führer von Schloßhauer will have to replace his little Jew wench." I see jealousy in Mollke's eyes, but as she is stonehearted and mindless of others, she has no idea how I loathe von Schloßhauer and all the rest of the SS ogres.

As we ride to our unknown destination in the dark, cramped cattle car, Mama leans her head against my shoulder, and I enfold her in my arms. She's lost weight, and I know she's not feeling well, but Mama never complains. "Sleep," I whisper, and I hum the lullaby she used to sing to me.

The September sun blinds my eyes when the cattle car doors open. "*Raus! Aussteigen!*" SS men bark their orders, commanding us off the train while their dogs are growling and fletching their teeth.

ARBEIT MACHT FREI it says mockingly across the big iron gate at KZ-Dachau. As we walk through, a pungent smell in the air snakes up my nostrils. A sick feeling overcomes me, and I can taste the vomit rising in my throat. I gag and swallow, swallow and gag, afraid to even wipe away the watery saliva that drools from the corner of my mouth as we continue forward. Mama is weakened; she clings to me for support.

Men in prison outfits come toward us. I take hurried looks through my long damp lashes. Hollow cheeked and rawboned, all the male prisoners have vacant expressions on their faces; we pass by each other in total silence. And then, my eyes hook into those of a young man, and an unfamiliar awareness overtakes my sense of being. Suddenly, the moment seems unaffected by the surroundings and I feel as if I'm flying through infinity in a whirl of emotions; I feel dizzy and can't breathe. But something makes me turn, and as I slowly look back, the young man turns and looks at me at that very moment. The second our eyes reconnect, I perceive a brilliant beam of energy pass between us—there is a feeling of unknown elation.

The barrack Mama and I are assigned to is already overcrowded; Mama and I share a hard, narrow bunk. Our food rations are less than minimal, and Mama's health deteriorates day by day. She only wants to drink; unable to hold down any food, she smiles sweetly as she passes me her portions. I am fearful because Mama barely is able to stand during roll; other prisoners and I hold her up as best we can to avoid beatings. When we go to sleep, Mama puts her mouth onto my forehead and lays her hand over my heart. I pull her tightly into my arms—we keep each other warm.

I wake up and I shiver. Mama is still in my arms, but she is cold and lifeless. "*Mama, meine liebe Mama,*" I cry out, and hold her beautiful face between my hands. "Don't leave me here—I want to go with you."

"Sh-sh-sh." Rose, a kind older woman, pulls me gently from the bunk and folds me into her bony arms. "Your mama told me she had no more strength to go on. Her death is a blessing." Rose lays the palm of her hand on my upper chest, near my heart. "She wants you to know that she'll always be right there; she'll guide and watch over you."

Chapter Thirty-Six

Conrad Capperton swung his long legs off the contemporary black leather lounge chaise in Adam's office and swiftly stood up. "That was a long and stimulating session," he said, his booming voice filling the room. "On my flight to Dubai, I have plenty of time to rethink my strategies about the merger."

"I leave for Arizona tomorrow, Capps. If you need to talk, I can be available most evenings."

Already halfway through the door, Capperton turned around. "Look outside," he said, grinning. "They're waiting for you by the garage again."

Adam didn't bother to look through the large tinted window; ever since his visit to New York, the news of his liaison with Kuri had made him a paparazzi magnet. Instead, he cleaned his desk, organized hard copies into their respective folders, and locked the file cabinet. Finally, he made sure everything he needed was backed up on his computer and, on his way out, he said good-bye to few other late-working employees.

As soon as the garage door opened, a photographer tried to block Adam's car. Driving at a slow speed, he steadily kept moving forward until the photographer was forced to step aside. Adam shook his head at the two reporters walking alongside the car. He mouthed, "No comment," as they kept knocking on the windows, shouting their questions. Gradually, Adam increased the speed and drove from their sight.

He wasn't surprised when, the moment he parked the car near his house, a couple of paparazzi came rushing toward him; he recognized their faces.

"Adam!" one of them yelled. "Will you be accompanying Kuri to the MTV Video Music Awards?"

"Are you okay with Kuri presenting the award to Tommy Nova?" screamed the other, shoving the microphone into Adam's face.

Before he unlocked his front door, he turned around and held up his hand. "Guys, guys…" he said calmly. "If you think I have different answers to the same questions you keep asking day after day, you're wasting your time!" He ignored another reporter who tried to get his attention by shouting, "Adam! Adam! Adam!"

"Guys, enough!" he said, vaguely smiling at the group. "Go home, get some rest." He stepped into the house and locked the door. Just then, he felt the tap vibration from his phone.

"Hey, Mom. What's up?"

"Hi, darling—I put you on speaker," said his mother. "Dad and I know you're leaving tomorrow and want to wish you safe travels. We drove by your house just an hour ago; when we saw the reporters, we kept going. Are they still there?"

"Of course. Same thing most days. It'll be nice to get away from them for four weeks—by the time I return to Boston, let's hope they have lost interest."

As he spoke to his parents, he walked from room to room to lower the bamboo shades on the windows facing the street. Before he closed the wood blinds in the kitchen, he saw that his trash cans outside had become search items for the media. He couldn't help but laugh. "You know," he told his parents, "I feel as if I've been transported into a world of satirical fiction, like Truman Burbank in

The Truman Show; every one of my movements is being described by strangers where my preferred laid-back existence is being metamorphosed into the spotlight."

"Be glad your attitude remains so even-tempered," said Adam's father. "I'm not sure I could handle this craziness."

It was almost ten o'clock in the evening when Adam finished packing for his trip. He sat down in one of the two dark red leather chairs—the pair that had been purchased by his paternal grandparents in their younger years. Adam appreciated the comfort of the aged and slightly worn French art deco chairs; he also liked how they accentuated most of the other contemporary décor in his house.

Just when he was about to pick up his phone to call Kuri, it rang. *Once again, mental telepathy at its best,* he thought when he saw her name on the screen.

With great interest he listened to Kuri's detailed account of what had transpired during the past few days.

"I am so sorry how painful this continues to be for you and your family," Adam said after she finished talking. "From what I hear, Ethan has deeply rooted problems, and it will take patience and understanding from all involved." Adam hesitated before he continued. "I know you and your family have already talked to therapists and I clearly don't want to interfere, but I am here to assist, whenever you want."

"Thank you, Adam. We are working with the doctors to find a rehab facility for Ethan," she said. "Once a decision has been made, I'll let you know—perhaps then you'll give us your professional opinion." She inhaled sharply before continuing. "Speaking of therapists…I've had another eye-opening session with Dr. B."

"Anything you'd like to share?" Adam asked softly.

"Yes and no. There's a reason I feel hesitant to tell you some of my deepest and most personal things over the phone," she said.

"I understand. You told me about celebrity hacking and that it happened to you before. Perhaps next time we see each other we can talk about it."

"Hopefully it will be sooner than a month from now. You have no idea how much I miss being with you, Adam."

❄

The following morning, Adam took an early flight from Boston to Phoenix, rented a car, and arrived at Rancho del Sol in Sedona, just in time for the late-afternoon meeting with other therapists participating in the monthlong workshop. Given the two-hour time difference between Arizona and Illinois, it was too late to call Kuri, but as before, he sent her a long text.

The next day, Adam's schedule was filled every hour on the hour with consultations, treatments, and study groups. During brief breaks, he tried to call Kuri but each time had to leave a voice message.

It was already past five o'clock in the afternoon when Adam decided to skip dinner with other therapists and instead drive to Bell Rock, a nearby red rock formation that had a reputation as a powerful vortex where spiritual energies coalesced. Once he arrived, he chose a moderate climbing route that would take him to the base of the upper slide area. There were no other hikers going up the trail at this late-afternoon hour, though a middle-aged couple making their descent greeted Adam warmly and told him to be prepared for spectacular views.

On his climb, Adam's eyes feasted on the arrangement of the rock, forms and figures that were the work of nature's elements over the course of several million years, long after the sea had receded.

In this phenomenon of a physical world, where peacefulness didn't end and where stillness began to merge with another dimension, Adam chose a spot to sit down, wanting to enjoy the images and humbling colors of Mother Earth.

He was overcome by happiness as he thought of the mysterious cosmic forces believed to emanate from the red rocks. He wished he could experience this moment in its endless beauty with Kuri. He desperately wanted to talk to her, better, share the glorious sunset with her on FaceTime, but in such savored solitude, there was no electronic signal this far out.

He saw her magnificent face in the setting sun, and he imagined her willowy body moving like the tall grass swaying gracefully in the summer breeze; each rush of wind seemed to carry her honeyed voice. When he heard the calls and songs from a yellow-throated vireo, a black-and-white warbler, and three hummingbirds, he imagined hearing Kuri's clear, contagious laugh. He intensely missed her, and his heart ached because too many hours would have to pass before he could hold her in his arms again.

Would Kuri's schedule allow her to come to Sedona for a few days when he was finished working at Rancho del Sol? He wondered if he should reserve a creekside cottage under a canopy of sycamore trees at L'Auberge de Sedona; he had stayed there before and loved it. He would ask her.

Adam rose from the smooth boulder and walked closer to the rock's edge. A unique light filtered through the sky, illuminating the red rocks in intense colors; their shades of deep purple, pink, and amber coalesced with the flames and flickers from the setting sun. *Another majestic overture to a new dawn,* he thought.

Chapter Thirty-Seven

"Gavin and I have spoken with representatives from various treatment centers," Aimi said. She purposely had waited for the family to finish eating lunch and for Dale to take the four children from the kitchen to play hide-and-seek outside. "We believe we've found the right place."

"And Ethan's doctors had only good things to say about this rehabilitation center." Gavin handed the brochures to his parents and Kuri. "Rancho del Sol in Sedona should be the best place for Ethan to receive a new chance at a healthy life."

"Sedona?" Kuri, who had just stood up, attempting to clear the table, sat down again. "Adam is working at a treatment center in Sedona right now."

"It must be Rancho del Sol then," Aimi said. "That's the only rehab center in Sedona."

"Didn't you tell Adam of Ethan's condition?" David rubbed his tired eyes. "I'm surprised he didn't recommend Rancho del Sol or another treatment center."

"I didn't ask him to. He knew Aimi and Gavin were looking into it. Adam wants to respect our family's privacy."

"Well, it sounds like we may have an opportunity to meet Adam sooner than we thought," Teruko said thoughtfully.

Bewildered by this remarkable coincidence, Kuri nodded and, in shared understanding, locked eyes with her mother.

"Anyway," Gavin said, "Ellen Rogers, the representative from Rancho del Sol, will meet us tomorrow morning at White Birch to talk about the intervention. Obviously the five of us will be there; Ellen also wants us to ask one or two of Ethan's friends to be part of it." He looked at his mother. "Who can we call?"

Teruko shook her head. "At a recent charity function, I ran into a few mothers of his once good friends. They told me that their sons and daughters many times in the past tried to keep in touch with Ethan, but his behavior and drug habits were too off-putting; they distanced themselves in order to move forward." Teruko's voice was thick with emotion. "Your father and I have yet to meet any of his new acquaintances, but from what we learned, I'm not sure we would even want them near Ethan."

"But there's Irina," David interjected. "What about her?"

Aimi threw her hands in the air. "She isn't even his fiancée—they both lied to us."

"That is not fair, Aimi!" Kuri said, defending her friend. "Irina talked to all of us—she came clean! Do you have any idea how hard this must've been for her?" Kuri gave her sister a challenging look. "If anyone lied and corrupted, it was Ethan! He misled Irina about having political connections that could get her a green card. Meanwhile, he falsified letters that threatened her with deportation whenever he wanted her to do things against her will." Kuri grimaced. "Poor Irina was terrified of being sent back to Ukraine."

Aimi lowered her head. "Okay. Sorry. But it still is difficult for me to understand that she tolerated, even enabled Ethan's drug dependency. How could she fall all this time for his crap? She doesn't strike me as a stupid girl! She probably developed her own dependency…" Aimi stopped, and began rubbing her right thumb repeatedly over the tip of her index and middle finger. She raised her eyebrows. "Money talks," she said. "Irina became addicted to his lifestyle."

"Stop it, Aimi," David said. "You seem to have difficulties understanding how Irina's life changed when she lost her parents and, with no other relatives, ended up in an orphanage. The poor girl was still a kid—never even got to finish school when she fell into the hands of a crook who practically smuggled her into the United States."

Teruko nodded. "And from what she told us, her life became even more complicated in this country. And then she met Ethan, and he promised to turn things around for her..."

"Well," Gavin interjected, "given Ethan's addictions, his false promises and odd behavior shouldn't surprise any of us. Meanwhile, we still have to know more about Irina."

Kuri, who had walked to the open terrace door to inhale the soft summer breeze, turned around and looked at her family. "Whatever your thoughts, Irina now has become part of the process!" she said determinedly. "And I can't shake the feeling that she came into Ethan's life for a reason."

"You're kidding! What might that reason be?" questioned Gavin.

"It's a feeling I can't explain. Like you said, we still have to know more about Irina."

"Let's focus on Ethan," Teruko said. "What if he walks out of the intervention—like he's done before? What can we do should he refuse to go through the program in Sedona?"

"If he chooses that route, then we all will come to the agreement to cut him off!" David said, placing both of his palms on the table. "No more financial help! No more emotional support! We all must let go of our instinctive feelings and be resolute about our reasoning and knowledge."

Chapter Thirty-Eight

Adam glanced briefly at the new resident arrival sheets before setting the folder aside; he would look at each patient's confidential data later. He first wanted to type up his notes on the mood and anxiety disorder lecture he'd attended in the morning. As soon as he opened his laptop, several message notifications popped up—all from Kuri.

The instant he saw her name, something clicked in his mind, and he reached for the resident arrival folder again. Among the five names, one immediately leapt out: Ethan Berger. How did he not notice that before? And how, since he and Kuri had never discussed treatment options for her brother, did her family pick Rancho del Sol at the same time he was here? It was almost as strange a coincidence as learning that Kuri knew a woman named Irina Messing, who was just the right age to be Golda Messing's granddaughter. Adam thought of the brief moment he passed Irina in the lobby of Kuri's apartment building. Ever since then, he'd desperately wanted to see Irina again; he had so many questions for her…but where and when would he ever meet her again? And if so, how could he possibly approach her?

Lost in thought, he pinched the tip of his nose. What was keeping him from telling Kuri about his past life regression? Why was he hesitant to tell her about how he had uncovered the connection between his visions and Shimmy Messing's tragic life? Adam wished he could open up to her, and yet, unsure of how she might react, he instinctively kept holding back.

Fascinated by synchronicity, Adam leaned into the chair and thought of the remarkable concurrence of events in the recent past; were they fate or fluke? Adam thought about the Swiss psychologist Carl Jung, who defined the word *synchronicity* as "the coming together of inner and outer events in a way that cannot be explained by cause and effect and that is meaningful to the observer."

Jung must've been correct, Adam pondered. *This phenomenon where synchronistic events go against all logical thought has long fascinated humankind.* Still deep in thought, he pinched his nose again. *There absolutely is no sensible interpretation by the natural laws of cause and effect.*

Suddenly Adam was unable to remain sitting still. He leapt from the chair and paced back and forth in the room, then made the decision to call Kuri. Just when his finger was about to press Kuri's number, the phone lit up—it was her! *Again, another amazing coincidence,* he thought.

"Kuri! When your name appears on my screen, it inevitably makes me smile."

"Same here, my love! I know how busy you are, but do you have a moment? I have so much to tell you."

"Of course. I was about to call you because there are certain thoughts and beliefs—matters I really want to share with you..." Adam paused, suddenly feeling uncertain again. He took a breath, then said, "But, please, you first."

"We just finished the intervention, and I can't even begin to tell you how terribly traumatic those hours were. Ethan was beyond aggressive and verbally attacked all of us present; several times, he attempted to storm out of the room. It was brutal!"

"I am sorry that you and your family had to go through this

experience," Adam said. "From what you told me earlier, Ethan was hostile to any idea about rehab and treatments. Did he change his mind?"

"Well, in the end—and to no surprise—it was all about money. At one point, during another one of Ethan's fierce explosions, my father calmly stood up and said he was done! He told Ethan he wanted nothing more to do with him; he would revoke Ethan's trusts and the entire family would withdraw from his life. But as soon as the rest of us stood up to leave, Ethan metamorphosed from an angry adult into a child crying out for help."

"How did everybody react?"

"My mom's composure worked miracles. She held Ethan's hand throughout the rest of the session and was able to keep him calm! Only when my dad offered to take care of my brother's debt and ongoing expenses did he perk up. It was like a business negotiation and, in the end, Ethan agreed to rehab."

"Besides your parents and siblings, did any of his friends partake?"

"Sadly enough, Ethan has no friends. We asked Irina, his ex-girlfriend—they had been dating for more than a year."

"Irina?" Adam held his breath. "How did that go?"

"Horrible at first—he kept insulting and blaming her for everything that's wrong with him; at one point he even tried to strike her. Thankfully, the therapist had prepped and prompted Irina prior to the session. Despite being nervous, she turned out to be a real trooper; she stood her ground."

"That's good." Adam paused. Having just heard about Irina, he desperately wanted to tell Kuri about the possible connection between Shimmy and Irina but…how could he? So much more needed to be said and explained beforehand. He cleared his throat. "I want to tell you about the treatment center where I am working now—"

"I was just going to ask you!" Kuri interrupted. "Is it Rancho del Sol? Please tell me it is because that's where Ethan will be arriving later today."

"It is," said Adam. "I saw Ethan's name on the arrival sheet just moments before you called; I couldn't wait to tell you."

"Adam…this is amazing; it's unbelievable! Do you realize that I will be there in less than two weeks? You'll meet my family. But more importantly, I will see you—be with you! Isn't this the strangest development of events?"

"Even under these unfortunate circumstances involving your brother, nothing can make me happier," Adam agreed. "Serendipity at its best once again!"

Chapter Thirty-Nine

For most of his life, Ethan had considered himself an expert when it came to masking the truth to people. Lately, though, he'd been off his game; he felt as if he was being choked by a pack of conspirators but unable to get rid of them. Even now, he was stuck on an airplane to some fucking institution in Arizona. He hated confined spaces and wanted to scream as he sat wedged between his mother and Ellen Rogers, the bitch therapist, who, with her grating voice, aquiline nose, and sharp piercing eyes reminded him of a hawk.

"Enough," he warned himself. "No more mistakes! Time to stop fucking around," he hissed through downturned lips. He closed his eyes when he felt his mother take his hand into her own. Her touch actually made him feel better—but then, where had she been all those years he'd longed for her soothing presence? Why did she not shield him from all the shit that caused him to suffer? Behind closed lids, Ethan saw his mother hover over Kuri instead of him; he saw how she would calm her distressed husband when she should have comforted her youngest son. Ethan groaned and yanked his hand free, but his mother gently retrieved it again and he felt her lips kissing his fingertips.

"Everything will be fine, my sweet Ethan. You are surrounded by love."

He loved his mother's tranquil voice; he desperately wanted to believe in her promise. But life had taught him not to trust anyone other than himself. He suppressed another groan and shifted, trying to make himself comfortable in this hard, narrow seat, but the pain in his head and the aches in his body seemed to steadily worsen. He couldn't believe his father had not overruled Ellen Rogers's idiotic idea to book coach when there was a private, luxurious plane waiting to be used. Yet the fucking therapist had insisted the family needed to stop pampering Ethan. *Like they ever fucking pampered me in the first place,* he thought, and suppressed a chortle. *And the old fool listened to this fucking bird-of-prey therapist.* Ethan shuddered, overcome by disgust at his father's stupidity. He coughed loudly, trying to camouflage another grunt. God, he could use a drink, better yet, drugs…anything to numb himself so he would not have to put up with this shit in the insane world around him.

He turned his head, released his hand, and smiled at his mother. "I need to go to the bathroom," he said, unbuckling himself. "Don't get up!" he said, and lifted his long leg over Ellen Rogers. He forced a smile as he stepped right over her into the aisle. He felt a tug on his sleeve and saw her pointing to his middle seat.

"Why don't you sit down again," she said, and it was clear from her tone she didn't mean it as a question. "There are two people waiting back there already."

Ethan wanted to punch her in the face, do some damage to that hawklike nose of hers, but instead he kept his crooked smile locked on tight. "I have a cramp in my calf," he told her. "I'm going to stretch my legs, if that's okay with you." He walked away, knowing her eyes would be following him.

He was up next for the bathroom and, just in case the therapist bitch was watching him, he barely turned his head toward the flight attendant in the galley when he asked for some painkillers. "Advil, Aleve…whatever strong thing you have for headaches," he said softly, playing up the sick passenger routine.

As soon as the lavatory door opened, Ethan stepped into the galley to let the other person squeeze by. Being out of Ellen Rogers's sight, he took four packets of Advil from the medical emergency box the flight attendant held open. He thanked her and then locked himself in the lavatory. He sagged against the wall. One after the other, he ripped the packets open and swallowed eight Advil capsules dry. He stared at his image in the mirror. "I can't believe I have to go through this shit again," he grumbled. "All those fucking sessions with compassionate-my-ass therapists!" He shuddered when he thought about those endless hours of therapy, especially group, where he would have to sit and listen to everybody's bullshit. "I hate it!" he hissed, still looking at himself in the mirror. "I don't give a fuck about anybody's anxieties and fucking disorders."

Ethan washed his hands and took a small palmful of water to rinse his mouth, making sure to spit it all out—he'd read someplace that the water tanks on airplanes were insufficiently cleaned and could hold bacteria. He wiped his mouth and looked in the mirror, realizing how tight the muscles in his face had gotten from all this stupid stress. "Shit!" he said, thinking about a previous experience where he'd had to share a room with a weirdo in a Malibu rehab facility. He spat into the bowl again and dry heaved, suddenly unable to breathe in this confined lavatory space. He quickly opened the door and couldn't believe his eyes. There was Ellen Rogers, the fucking hawk, waiting for him.

"Are you okay? You were in there for a long time."

"Really?" It took all his strength to control the fury. "Well, certain bodily functions take longer than others. If you don't believe me, feel free to take a sniff!"

Back in his seat, he took his mother's hand. "I'm glad you came along, Mom. It means a lot to me." He squeezed, giving her his best smile. "Don't worry about me. I will be okay."

Teruko pressed her cheek against the back of her son's hand. "You know I won't stay in Sedona. I'll see you in fourteen days during family week, but I'll fly home again tonight." She caressed his arm. "Since there are no more commercial flights—the company plane will pick me up."

Ethan cringed. "Now isn't that generous? Tell Dad he is"—Ethan almost choked on his thick words—"a truly awe-inspiring man." He slumped into the seat, overcome by more resentment and anger. Without looking at his mother, he said, "I'm really tired now." He folded his arms across his chest, unaware that his hands were closing into tight fists. Behind closed lids, he schemed his revenge.

Chapter Forty

She sat in the waiting room, eager for Dr. B. to open the door to her office; Kuri really wanted to talk about recent events that had formed a source of new problems.

Twenty minutes later, after telling Dr. B. about the difficulties during Ethan's intervention and its outcome, Kuri took a deep breath and added, "You may not believe this fluke of circumstances, but Ethan currently is undergoing rehabilitation at the same center where Adam happens to be working this month! Don't you think it is a bizarre coincidence that they're both at Rancho del Sol in Sedona at the same time?"

When she saw Dr. B's surprised expression, Kuri asked, "What?" Do you have an unfavorable opinion of Rancho del Sol?"

"Not at all!" Dr. B. couldn't resist a chuckle. "Rancho del Sol happens to be a very good choice for Ethan," she said. "I'm smiling because it also is the same center where I will be lecturing in another week."

Kuri leaned forward. "No, c'mon! Now, that's beyond weird," she exclaimed. "Could this be a mysterious cosmic clue, trying to connect the individuals?"

"Well, Kuri, when you speak of cosmic clues, think of the possibility that the universe might actually take notice and nods at us from time to time, hoping we'll perceive the signals."

"Hmm." Kuri crinkled her nose. "Adam recently tried to explain synchronicity to me. He said that synchronistic events are like small miracles, and if we pay attention, they can lead us to a place where we might understand more about the core that connects everything." She tilted her head, intently looking at the therapist. "What do you think?"

"Nobody has been able to give proof to synchronicity or explain it properly. But perhaps people and events that link us together become the reason for our desire to go deeper so we can peek through the crack of the door the universe leaves open for us."

Kuri sat quiet for a moment, gazing into space before she looked at the therapist again. "Wow…that's profound. I think I'm beginning to grasp the basis of what you and Adam are trying to say."

"The mystery of life never ends, does it?" Dr. B. said, adjusting her position in the chair. "Tell me, have you had any recent upsetting dreams and visions? You haven't brought it up lately."

"I still have them, but because of the recognition I gained through PLR, I now understand why I hear the voices, why I feel the suffering. The horrible visions definitely don't scare me the way they used to; they are beginning to make sense. Yet, something is missing—something I still need to discover about Judith…" Kuri looked fixedly at the ceiling, then shook her head. "I am unable to put into words what I perceive," she said. "I really hope my next PLR will help me through this enigma."

Dr. B. nodded. "We will do this in due time. Meanwhile, let's shift back to current events. You mentioned Irina earlier. Despite some of your family's doubts, you feel a rather strong connection to Irina."

Kuri nodded. "When she stayed with me in New York, we spent a lot of time together, talking. I heard about her life in Ukraine and the problems she had to face when she came to this country. She also told me all about her relationship with Ethan—they fed on each other like bacteria on sugar; it reminded me of my own relationship with Ethan when I was a little girl. Just like Irina, I allowed Ethan to use me, hoping to win his love. Even though Ethan held the deportation threat over her head, Irina now deeply regrets having been the errand girl for his drug addiction. She also confessed to her codependency and financial reliance on my brother."

"You said earlier, you feel Irina is somehow connected to what you're trying to discover about yourself. Why do you believe that?"

"Ever since my past life regression, I've been making an effort to learn more about the Holocaust." Kuri leaned forward. "Irina told me she was raised Catholic but had Jewish roots! Her grandmother Golda had survived by hiding the fact she was Jewish; she was living with a Polish couple who pretended Golda was their daughter." Kuri began to fidget with her hair. "This is where it gets interesting…Irina told me that Golda had a brother who was sent to Auschwitz and then to Dachau!"

"Hmm! In your past life regression session, you saw yourself as a prisoner in Dachau. Is that why you feel a connection with Irina?"

"I can't shake the feeling that it must mean something, right?" Kuri was unable to sit still; she kept twirling a strand of hair around her finger. "That's why I want another PLR session as soon as possible, hoping it will shed light on more details about Judith's life. I just know there is more—I need to discover something that will prove my past life was real."

"Did you share any of this with Irina?"

"Oh God, no! It may freak her out! On the other hand, I desperately want to talk about this with Adam—I believe he really would be open to all of it, but so far, the time hasn't been right."

"Because of your interest in the subject, does Irina know what happened to her grandmother's brother?"

"She has no idea. Her parents tried to search for him but died before they had any answers. Of course, Irina never had the financial means to follow up; I promised I would help."

"Isn't she curious why you have such an interest in the Holocaust and why you want to know about her ancestors?"

"She did ask, and I explained that when we were filming in Germany, I visited Dachau. I explained that, ever since, I simply needed to educate myself more on the subject."

Dr. B. nodded, then reached for the calendar on the side table. "I know how eager you are for your next PLR session, Kuri. Those appointments require extra time. Unfortunately, I can't fit you in before my trip. Let's find a time after we both return from Arizona."

Chapter Forty-One

Adam rushed out of his casita and ran across the desert path into the main building—he was fifteen minutes late for the two o'clock afternoon meeting. He opened the door to the conference room and apologized to the other therapists, quickly making his way around the table to the only empty chair.

Deirdre Mullins, the director of the trauma recovery program, handed Adam two pamphlets, opened one, and pointed to the second page. "Don't worry, we just started," she whispered.

Anton Wills, the director of liaison psychiatry, continued to talk about treatment options for one particular resident, a new patient at Rancho del Sol who had a history of love and relationship addiction. "Adam," he said, "you met with Paula yesterday. What are your impressions?"

"Paula seems to reflect on intense fantasies. She has trouble living in reality, but she's aware how much she projects her desires on people she barely knows. She claims it's the only way she can create a chemical high in her body. I feel she's lacking the ability to be honest and truthful; Paula needs work on building her confidence."

While several other therapists continued to discuss the patient's intimacy issues and inabilities to talk openly about fears and other topics, Adam took notes.

"That brings me to another patient," said Anton Wills. "Josefina Herrera! This morning in group therapy, I encountered some difficulties with her."

Deirdre Mullins nodded. "I worked with her the last time she was here—a little over a year ago. Despite her small frame, she's a powerhouse and can be rather challenging." Deirdre looked at Adam. "What's your feeling? You also worked with her last year and have already seen her twice since she arrived."

"Last year I introduced Jo to hypnotherapy, to which she took favorably. Jo agrees it relaxes her to the point where she now can talk about the accident that took her mother and brother's lives and crippled her father. I believe hypnotherapy will also help her with the mood and eating disorders she developed after the accident."

"Excuse me for interrupting," said Phillip Pastor, the spiritual counselor and grief therapist. "Has anyone noticed that Jo Herrera and Ethan Berger have developed a friendship? I see them together whenever they have a moment of free time."

Two therapists nodded, some others shook their heads or shrugged.

"Well, Ethan Berger's name is next on my list," said Anton Wills. Some of you have worked with him already. Who wants to start?"

"He's tough," said Brenda Isaacson, the primary therapist. "He's like a secured vault where the combination is locked up inside."

"Yes, I agree. Ethan is a blanket of secrecies. One has to be very patient and prudent with him," said Juan Franco, the psychiatric nurse practitioner.

Anton Wills nodded. "Because of Ethan's substance misuse, his recent overdose, and dual diagnosis, it's clear he still needs medical-assisted treatment."

"In group therapy yesterday, Ethan at first came across quite Pollyannaish, and then out of nowhere he insisted the others were judging him, and his behavior changed from excessively cheerful to cocky and obstreperous," said Brenda Isaacson. "Today, however, Ethan was perfectly even-tempered and occasionally even peppered the session with humor. I have the feeling it had something to do with Jo Herrera being present."

Adam sat quietly as other therapists exchanged their impressions about Ethan.

"What's your take, Adam?" asked Anton Wills.

"I've recused myself from Ethan Berger's treatment," Adam reminded his colleagues.

"Why? Do you know him?" Deirdre Mullins said.

"I am close to someone in his family."

"Let's move on, then," said Anton Wills.

As the meeting continued, Adam noticed Deirdre Mullins stealing glances at him, quickly looking away whenever he turned his head in her direction.

"I'm sorry for gaping at you during the meeting," Deirdre said later, catching up with him in the hallway. "I was able to put the pieces together when you mentioned you knew someone in Ethan Berger's family." Deirdre smoothed her skirt, then tightly folded her arms across her chest. "I might not look like someone who is infatuated with celebrities of any kind"—she kept shifting from one foot to the other—"but I am a huge fan of Kuri Berger, and I remembered seeing footage of Kuri and you on television. I read you've been dating for some time." Deirdre blushed and smoothed her skirt again. "I'm embarrassed to confront you with this…"

"It's okay." Adam smiled. "I was hoping nobody here would make the connection; up until now I was lucky." He leaned toward Deirdre and spoke softly. "I'd appreciate if you kept it quiet, though—I don't want this stuff to interfere with my work."

"Of course." Deirdre beamed.

After returning to his casita, Adam changed clothes—he had just a little under three hours to get in a bike ride before attending a lecture on "The Pros and Cons of Hypnotherapy for Treating Anxiety Disorders" later that evening.

He headed out for the Soldier Wash trails, one of his favorite short rides; it was the ideal ending to a September day. As with every early evening, the still, cloudless sky already revealed a pensive mood. Over the horizon, the slowly disappearing sun backlit the red Sedona mountains, illuminating the landscape so it could sparkle like clear crystals. In this magnificence of nature, Adam opened his sensory faculties to the scents and sounds of the desert. Pedaling at a steady but comfortable speed, he enjoyed noticing fine components in the environment. He heard the variances in the wind, he tasted the air, smelled the flora and fauna, and occasionally got off the bike to touch grasses and plants he'd never noticed before.

He felt revived when he finished his ride. After taking a shower, he quickly went over the notes he took during the day, then checked his messages. Finally, he closed his laptop. It was time to call Kuri; talking to her had become the highlight of Adam's day.

Today their conversation focused on the family-oriented portion of Ethan's treatment and Kuri's impending visit to Rancho del Sol with her parents and siblings.

"Even though I can't wait to see you again, this wasn't the way I anticipated it," she admitted. "I've been through family week with Ethan twice before when he was in rehab. A lot of painful stuff comes up, and I know it's going to be hard on my parents again."

"I understand," said Adam. "And we should be discreet while you're here. At least one of the other therapists knows that you and I are seeing each other; however, Ethan has no idea who I am or what my relationship is with you."

"It's better that way. Knowing my brother, he would twist it around and claim it to be a conspiracy…" She stopped and gasped.

"What? Is everything okay?"

"Yes, everything's okay, but I just realized I have to tell you something really interesting! You and I recently talked about simultaneous occurrences and how life can miraculously work in bringing people together. Now, listen to this…my therapist is headed to Rancho del Sol."

"Wait, what?" Adam had purposely avoided asking Kuri about her therapy; he respected her privacy and felt it was up to her to share any details when she was ready. But this was yet another astounding link between the two of them; the web of coincidence was becoming impossible to ignore. In his mind, Adam quickly ran through the names of the visiting therapists at Rancho del Sol; none of them, as far as he knew, were from Chicago. And then it hit him. "Melanie Brichta is your therapist? She is brilliant!" he exclaimed. "I'm a huge admirer of her work. In fact, she's actually speaking here tonight."

"Unbelievable, isn't it? Obviously, Dr. B. knows all about us—you've become such an important person in my life. When I told her that you have a working engagement for the month of September at Rancho del Sol, she said she would be there as well."

Adam thought he could sense uncertainty in Kuri's voice. "Don't worry," he said softly, "the relationship between a psychiatrist and the patient is based on trust—confidentiality is paramount; Dr. Brichta and I would never talk about you behind your back."

"I appreciate that, but whatever I tell her, I want you to know as well. Remember, I recently told you that I had a very special treatment with Dr. B. where I discovered some things about myself that I'd like to share with you; but as I said before, I can't do it over the phone. I need to be near you, see you, and feel your reaction."

Adam realized he was holding his breath. He knew that Melanie Brichta was an expert on past life regression as well as hypnotherapy. Could that be what Kuri wanted to share with him? He, too, was waiting for the right moment to tell her of his own past life regression and his subsequent discoveries in Bavaria. Was Melanie Brichta meant to be the conduit to bring them together? He felt his heartbeat accelerate.

"You're quiet," she said. "Did I say something wrong?"

"No, my love. We will definitely find the right moment in time—just the two of us—where we will tell each other everything."

There was an instant of silence, and Adam wondered if the connection was lost.

"Are you there?"

"I am, but I am confused; too many thoughts keep racing through my head."

"Anything I can do to clear things up?"

"Well, for one thing…how is it going to work after we arrive in Sedona? I know you can't be part of our family sessions with Ethan. But how shall I react when I run into you at the treatment center? People may recognize me—I don't want to compromise your work there."

"Don't let that bother you. I think you and I just need to let our stars guide us—whatever is meant to happen, will happen. There should be no reason for us to hide behind barriers that shouldn't be there in the first place."

"You said that beautifully, Adam. You know what I really look forward to?"

"What is it, my love?"

"I can't wait for you to meet my family and to introduce you to Irina."

"Irina?" Adam's back straightened. "She is coming to family week?"

"Yes, we felt Irina is the only non–family member that knows Ethan well. Despite their rather complicated relationship, my folks and I feel blessed that she agreed to come along."

Adam chewed on his lower lip as wild thoughts raced through his head. *Wasn't I just wondering if I would ever see Irina Messing again? Is the universe reading my mind?* The web of synchronicities around his life seemed to be drawing tighter and tighter. He was aching to find out what it all meant.

Chapter Forty-Two

"Up until last week, you were reluctant to invite some of your family members. How do you feel now that they're here?" Dr. Wills asked.

Ethan stopped jiggling his foot and tried to project an aura of calm by putting his hands behind his neck, leaning back, and plopping his feet onto the small table in front of him. He broke eye contact with Dr. Wills and fixed his gaze on the four-armed saguaro cactus outside the windowpane.

"You led our family session yesterday—don't you think it went well?" Ethan gave a one-sided shoulder shrug and scratched his neck.

"Your mother had a very calming effect on you—have you always been close to her?"

Ethan faked a smile and did his best to show this fucking shrink a caring and convincing attitude. He was sick of talking about his feelings, his memories, his relationships, his goals, and all the rest of the never-ending bullshit—he'd been through two weeks of this investigative nightmare already, and there were still another two weeks looming ahead of him. It was all so pointless.

Granted, he was beginning to feel better, but he almost knew he'd start using again when he got out; he really missed the high from the coke and the buzz from the alcohol. This time, he'd really have to hide it from his family; commitments were made, and he needed his debt to be paid off. *Fuck! There is so much goddamn family money—am I not entitled to my share? I hate the way the old man rules over what rightfully belongs to me! And now my damn family pretends to offer moral support? Fuck them all! I don't give a splashy shit about their moral support.* Ethan cringed and tried to think of something different, and immediately her face popped into his mind's eye.

Jo Herrera! He had met her shortly after his arrival; getting to know her had transformed yesterday's forlorn life into a sanguine situation. He tried to spend as much time with her as possible; they used every chance to get away from the therapists' prying eyes. Jo was the one bright spot in this entire shit show.

Sitting on the sofa, lost in thought, Ethan heard Dr. Wills asking him something about his siblings. Ethan exhaled. "What about..."

"You used to get along well with Aimi and Gavin, but that changed when Kuri was born. You refused to talk about it yesterday; would you like to talk about it now?"

"Kuri!" Ethan slapped his thighs. "Poor thing was sick from the beginning. Her mental... uhm..." He stopped talking. *Don't do that, Ethan,* he warned himself. *Play nice with this asshole doctor, make him believe you've forgiven your siblings for all the shit they put you through. Better yet, do it with some humor.*

He cleared his throat and smiled broadly. "You know," he said, "looking back, I compare my older siblings to the characters in the Harry Potter books. My brother, Gavin, was like Harry, pretending to be brave, obsessive, and witty, and my sister Aimi tried to be like Hermione—always logical and self-assured. But both of them had the same goal: they were trying to outwit and double-cross Voldemort... a.k.a. yours truly." Ethan threw his head back and laughed at his own quick wit. "But I didn't mind—I always admired Aimi and I respected Gavin. I had some trouble dealing with Kuri's weird behavior when she was a little girl, but that all has changed. Hey, I love my siblings...too bad they don't get it!"

He kept spinning a few more tales about his childhood and early adult life and believed his delivery sounded remarkably honest—he almost convinced himself. "You know, Doc," he finally said, "I've learned so much already at Rancho del Sol during the past two weeks. I am truly grateful for the treatments here."

"Let's talk about your friend Irina—there was a quite a bit of tension in the room yesterday; you kept disagreeing with her."

Ethan wanted to explode out of the chair but instead took his feet slowly off the table and straightened his back. He cleared his throat. "Irina is not my friend, Dr. Wills! She brought me drugs, and we had sex. Period! That's not friendship!" He snorted softly, then continued. "Irina took advantage of my vulnerability and my money—too bad my family has trouble seeing that." He dismissively waved his hand. "That's it, though! That fucking bi—" He caught himself and said, "Sorry! I mean, that fraud is out of my life!" He quickly added, "Don't get me wrong; like everybody, Irina deserves to be happy. But not at my expense and not at my family's."

He averted the therapist's eyes and turned his head to the window, staring past the statuesque four-armed saguaro cactus into the remoteness of nature; the desert suddenly looked uncomplicated and appealing to him. Instead, he had to be cooped up in this small space of a room where he felt as if he was in a straitjacket. *When is this fucking session over? What is the point of it all?* He wanted to scream but urged himself to keep cool. *Control yourself!* He took a deep breath and turned his head back to Dr. Wills, rewarding the therapist with a broad smile. *Be careful of this nerdy therapist,* he warned himself. *He may look like a soft schmuck, but I think this weird little fucker can be a bomb thrower.* Ethan intensified his smile and said, "Doc, there's a lot you don't know about me. For one thing, I happen to be very smart and always have been praised for my creativity. I recently developed a great new product that can transform someone's life! I put together a team and worked on my creation day and night. But nobody cared about the obstacles I had to face by myself to get this project up and running. Only now do I realize that the stress, the lack of sleep—often panic—set off the downward spiral that brought me here."

He paused, expecting a response from the therapist. When nothing happened, Ethan continued. "I know I still have a lot of work to do, especially for my family to see that I've changed. I'm ready to face challenges! I used to turn to the wrong people, just so someone would listen to me. Well, that's over! I won't do that anymore." Ethan nodded, hoping Dr. Wills was buying his bullshit. "I sincerely want to heal myself and prove to my family that everything is going to be better from now on."

Unable to interpret the therapist's expressionless face, Ethan forced a smile; he felt his bile rising. As soon as this damn session was over, he was going to track down Jo. If he couldn't actually get high, Jo would be the one to lift his sour mood.

Chapter Forty-Three

David had rented a house for the family, just fifteen minutes away from Rancho del Sol by car. After another day of emotionally draining confrontations with Ethan, it was a relief for the family to return to this temporary oasis, cradled in the grandeur of the Red Rock Mountains.

One after the other, everyone came outside to relax quietly by the pool. Teruko sat on a chaise lounge with her eyes closed while David gazed at the Coconino National Forest in the distance. Aimi was at a table, writing in her journal, as Gavin, with half-closed lids, sat under a California fan palm tree in a meditative pose.

Kuri was bent over her cell phone, answering emails and text messages until it struck her that she should separate herself from the outside world and simply let herself be in this peaceful setting. Just as she leaned back to relax, she noticed Irina sitting by herself on the shallow side of the pool, staring at her feet in the water.

Kuri walked over to her new friend. "Are you okay?" she asked quietly. "I know Ethan was rough on you this afternoon."

Irina kept wiggling her toes, creating tiny ripples in the water. "I am thinking how wonderful to have big family. I am grateful you include me to come to Sedona—you open my eyes to many things." She looked at Kuri. "I today realize that every time I'm near Ethan, I must defend myself because I not like to please him anymore." She pulled her feet from the water and hugged her knees. "The things Ethan always say to me make me pain." She pointed at her head. "His insults and demands feel like dirty sand that sift through every cranny and nook of my brain and settle in there like sentiment... no, sorry... not right word." She looked at Kuri for help.

"Sediment?"

"Yes, thank you. For long time already, I want to get rid of that dirty sediment." Irina wiped her cheek. "In Chicago, I say to him many times that I not like what he doing to himself and what he doing to me. I ask him to let me go, but he always laugh and say, 'Fine! Go!' He say that without his money, without his connection... immigration men will find me and send me back to Ukraine! Ethan know how to scare me, and so I keep doing what he tell me," she whispered, wiping her other cheek. "I always feel so alone—that's why I love him in sick way and make bad mistakes for him; I make many mistakes for me, too." She shook her head and sighed. "Then I meet your family and I learn he not just trick me, he trick everybody. I now have no feeling for him anymore." She pulled her legs tighter into her chest. "Oh my gosh... I talk too much. I'm sorry."

Kuri reached for the small towel next to her and dried Irina's tears. "You saved Ethan's life, and we are grateful to you!" She put her arm around Irina's shoulder. "I also believe that Ethan was meant to be the conduit so you and I could meet." She gently lifted Irina's chin to make eye contact. "The greatest value of pure friendship is to appreciate and be appreciated," said Kuri. "You and I have found that in each other."

Aimi squatted next to them. "I overheard your conversation," she said, laying her hand on Irina's back. "I know I was skeptical at first, but once I learned more about your life and what you had to go through all by yourself, I ask you to, please, accept my apologies, Irina! You are not alone anymore, you have found a family of friends."

"Come sit with us, you guys." Gavin pulled another lounge chair into the round. "By the way, Ethan found new targets for his anger after he drove you out of the room earlier," Gavin said to Irina while adjusting the back of the lounge chair for her. "We're all used to his insults and antics. Today he called me a tasteless nothing burger." Gavin chuckled. "That actually was a compliment compared to the names he usually has for me—sometimes I just have to find some humor in it all."

Aimi matched Gavin's laughter. "In the cafeteria earlier, when I slipped on a wet spot while carrying my lunch tray, I almost fell! Ethan saw that and mocked me, saying I looked as graceful as a filing cabinet falling off a truck." Aimi giggled. "I couldn't help but visualize that scene, but when I laughed at his mockery, his insults worsened."

"Remember how disgruntled he was last year when he first read about Kuri's relationship with Tommy Nova?" Teruko shook her head wistfully. "Ethan said Tommy's voice reminded him of a castrated coyote during a full moon."

"Ethan always thought of his sarcasm as comical," Kuri said. "I once invited him and a couple of his buddies to a venue in Chicago and after the concert took them backstage to meet Tommy. Ethan introduced us to his friends, saying, 'Hey, Tweedle Dee and Tweedle Dum, come meet Tweedle Dim and Tweedle Dumber.' I thought the comment was not only stupid but also totally inappropriate; I showed no reaction, but Ethan and Tommy laughed so hard they actually snorted!" Kuri rolled her eyes. "Two peas in a pod," she said.

"You all know how much I enjoy a good laugh!" exclaimed David. "But I don't get Ethan's grotesque kind of humor—it's become very difficult to laugh with him."

"It saddens me too, because laughter is meant to be the warmth that can drive coldness from the heart," Teruko said. "Despite the many heavy and sad discussions during the past three days, I want to believe there might be a positive side to everything." She looked at her husband. "What's your impression of Ethan's new friend Josefina?"

"I know of her father, Julio Herrera. He is on Forbes's list as one of the world's billionaires."

"Hey…I already Googled him," said Aimi. "Did you know his ancestry is Spanish? He was very young when he inherited a ton of wealth and moved to Mexico. It was there where he kept adding to his fortune."

David nodded. "Herrera owns a huge holding company that presides over big businesses like insurance, agricultural companies, and department stores. The man also established a big science and technology firm."

"Yup!" Aimi said. "I also read he's known to be merciless when it comes to making a deal. On the other hand, he is respected for his philanthropy."

David agreed. "Herrera founded a university and built schools and programs for children. I give him a lot of credit. Unfortunately, he was met by tragedy."

"Oh my gosh!" Irina said. "What happen to him?"

"Hang on…" Aimi bent over her iPad and read out loud: "'The Herrera family was in their private jet en route to Tegucigalpa, Honduras, when the plane crashed during a difficult approach. Investigative reports determined the crash was due to bad weather and low visibility. Toncontín International Airport, with its extremely short runway, has long been considered to be one of the most difficult and dangerous landings because it is surrounded by mountains and residential neighborhoods.'" Aimi inhaled, looked briefly at everyone around her, and continued. "'Marisol Herrera (sixty-three) and son Felipe (twenty-two) were killed in the crash, as was the pilot Juan Marquez (fifty-seven). Julio Herrera (seventy-six) and his daughter Josefina (thirty-four) survived the accident; they were transported via medical air ambulance to Houston, Texas, where Julio Herrera was listed in critical condition; his daughter Josefina was listed in stable condition.'"

Aimi looked up. "That was two years ago. Meanwhile, there have been rumors that it was Josefina who was flying the Gulfstream... if that's true, no wonder she suffers from trauma and needs therapy."

"How's her father now?" Irina asked.

"From what I know, he was severely burned and suffered spinal cord injuries. The whole thing is tragic." David stiffly got off the lounge. "I've never known Ethan to volunteer or care for those who are physically or mentally in need, but he seems very concerned and protective over Josefina... or Jo, as he calls her. I am hopeful he's beginning to understand what the word compassion means."

"I think it is a good omen. My mother used to say that when the agony of others keeps echoing through you, that's when you learn how to understand someone else's feelings." Teruko also rose from the lounge and stood next to her husband, gently elbowing him. "I can tell someone is ready for dinner. Who else is hungry?"

"But shouldn't we wait for Adam?" Gavin wondered.

Just then, Kuri heard the vibration alert from her phone and smiled when she read the text message. "He'll be here any minute," she said.

Chapter Forty-Four

Adam was grateful Kuri's family had made him feel welcome in their lives from the moment they first met. Given the tight work schedule at Rancho del Sol, he only had been able to spend short periods of time with them during the past three days, but their affection and warmth for each other was easily extended to him. His earlier concerns that Kuri's parents and siblings might press him for details about Ethan's case or have questions about how the other therapists thought he was progressing was easily erased because the family showed great respect for Adam's professional discretion.

As much as he enjoyed spending time with the Bergers, he felt especially euphoric about the moments he and Kuri were able to devote to each other. The past three nights had been magical and, as he rode his bicycle to their rented house, he looked forward to another blissful evening with her.

He left the bicycle at the rear entrance and walked around the house toward the pool area; the terrace door was open. He followed the voices that led him into the great room.

"Adam!" Kuri got up from her seat and ran into his arms. "We just sat down; everybody is starving." She pointed to the seat next to her.

"You've only met Irina in passing at Rancho del Sol," said David, and after making the introduction, he lifted his wine glass. "I'd like to toast to my family and to our new friends."

Throughout the lively dinner conversation, Adam risked a few peeks across the table. He was hoping for an opportunity to engage with Irina in conversation. But how should he approach her in order to learn more of her family's past? Would she be able to confirm any of his research, especially of Shimmy's life? His mind raced as he contemplated the possibilities; it filled him with wonder how on this often chaotic, huge planet, unexpected connections might cast light on uncertainties and expose some of the world's limitless secrets and wonders.

"I have an announcement to make," Kuri said as everyone was finishing their meals. "You all know that I was asked to be a presenter at the MTV Video Music Awards. You also know that, after the ugly episode with Tommy, my first reaction was to decline, but after another crazy run-in with the paparazzi, I changed my mind. I now believe it'll be good for me to go out there and prove the tabloid stories wrong."

Gavin gave his sister a thumbs-up approval. "But won't it be awkward since Tommy is one of the nominees and also one of the featured performers this year?"

"Not at all! It'll be the only way to show I hold no ill feelings; my presence will prove that I moved on."

"Good for you," Teruko said. "These reporters need to be straightened out; they keep coming up with new nonsense—I still don't know how they found out we'd be in Sedona!"

"Yeah...and how about them asking Kuri if she was suffering from relationship disorders and checking herself into Rancho del Sol—all because of the breakup with Tommy?" Gavin grimaced. "Endless crap."

"They even brought up Kuri's childhood medical history

again…more fabrications! Who feeds this poison to the media?" Teruko's usual silvery voice had taken on gruff undertones.

"Who cares," David said. "The tabloids make their money from folks who thrive on rubbish." David rolled his eyes. "This morning I had to call the county sheriff's office again to have paparazzi removed; they completely blocked the gate to the house." He took a sip of wine. "I want respect for my family's privacy. Is that really too much to ask?"

Aimi returned to the table with a second helping of chicken enchiladas and cornbread. "What about you, Adam? Were you followed again today? Too bad you're being dragged into this media frenzy as well."

Adam shook his head. "Even though the reporters soon realized Kuri came as a visitor to Rancho del Sol, not as a patient, they kept hanging out to get my attention; but strict new county sheriff injunctions prohibit the media from being on or near the grounds now. Apparently, Rancho del Sol is used to problems like this—they've had celebrity patients."

"Speaking of paparazzi…of course, I would've loved if Adam was able to escort me to the awards ceremony, but since he'll still be working here in Sedona, Irina now will be my date." Kuri leaned across the table to high-five Irina.

"Oh my gosh. Can't believe anything like this possible in my life." A pink tinge spread over Irina's face. "I not remember being so excited…ever in life."

"Meanwhile, we have another couple of days before family week ends, let's try to make the best of it." Kuri stood up and started to collect the dishes.

Aimi looked around the table. "Anybody still want anything? Otherwise Kuri and I'll do the dishes and prepare a very special dessert."

Irina asked to be excused from the table and walked outside. "Bad habit, I know," she said, holding a cigarette sheepishly when she saw Adam following her. "I will stop the smoking soon. Past few days with Ethan make me very nervous." She inhaled but turned her head away to exhale. "I try to not give you secondhand smoke," she said, tapping the cigarette and watching the ash tumble into the tray. As if talking to herself, she mumbled, "I now completely understand that Ethan and my relationship was bad one; I not was good for him but…he also not good for me."

Adam nodded. "From what I heard, you're facing fresh beginnings with an exciting new life ahead. I'm very happy for you and wish you good luck."

"Thank you," she said with a smile and extinguished her cigarette. "You know, many years I wait for green card, and like miracle I got it just recently. I can make brand-new start now; I come long way."

Adam shifted in the chair and cleared his throat. "Kuri told me you were born in Ukraine. I visited your country and also have been to Poland because…" He paused, trying to find the right words, finally settling on, "To study the people and their culture."

"You been to Rivne, maybe?" Her eyes lit up. "I was born there. My mother Ukrainian but father's family come from Poland. Actually, before World War II, father's family live in Germany." She faced Adam and smiled. "Kuri say you are Jewish, right? You know, I am half-Jewish; Mother was Catholic but Father Jewish. My father…"

Without any more promptings, Irina launched into her family's story.

Adam did not move—he was spellbound by Irina's narrative, as every detail he had read in Sarah Goldstein's research fell into place. His soul swelled in jubilation, and the very moment Irina mentioned the names of Golda and Shimmy Messing, it was like an old forgotten melody coming to life again.

"My father always talk about his mother, Golda. He tell me many stories. He tell me she had beautiful voice. My father sing her favorite song to me many times. I remember all of melody but only some words—German words. I not know what they mean."

And just like that, Irina began to sing.

"Roter Mohn, warum welkst du denn schon?
Wie mein Herz sollst du glüh'n und feurig loh'n.
Roter Mohn, den der Liebste mir gab . . ."

"Forgot rest of words, but melody is always in my heart." She continued to hum.

Adam couldn't believe he was listening to the song he'd heard time and again in his dreams—well before his past life regression therapy in India had set him on the path to understanding what it meant. Without realizing it, he began to hum along.

"You know this song?" Irina looked surprised.

Adam nodded tensely. "Yes. An old friend from my past used to love this tune—I have not heard it in a long time."

Irina sighed, looking into the evening sky. "I think how nice would be if I could share my new life with Mother and Father. I miss them. I miss Father's stories. So sad that everybody . . . my whole family is gone."

She pointed at the stars and said something in her native tongue. Without taking her eyes off the firmament, she explained. "My father always say that when old stars die, new ones are born. I wonder if true for people, too."

Adam had trouble controlling his emotions. He wanted to tell Irina what he knew, but he couldn't—not yet.

"There you are!" Aimi stuck her head through the terrace door. "You better come in now to taste Kuri's and my culinary concoction; everybody already is digging into our homemade magic. If you guys don't hurry up, our divine chocolate soufflé might be gone!"

Later, after everybody had gone to sleep, Kuri and Adam still remained side by side outside. They watched the sparks from the firepit table rise, slowly blending into the darkness of night. In the distance they heard the short, high-pitched yips and howls from a pack of coyotes.

"I almost forgot," Kuri whispered as she snuggled closer into Adam's arms. "What do you think of Dr. B?"

"Dr. B . . ." Adam repeated, reflecting on the earlier lecture. "Dr.

Melanie Brichta is wonderful," he continued. "She's a fountain of knowledge! I am learning so much from her."

"When you're finished with your work here, do you think you can arrange a quick visit to Chicago?" Kuri asked, sounding drowsy. "I'd like you…" her voice was trailing off. "Special session with Dr. B.?"

"What do you mean, my love?" Adam's heartbeat quickened. What was she trying to tell him?

"Let's stay here tonight," she breathed, barely audible. "So peaceful…"

He realized she had fallen asleep in his arms, and he pulled her closer to him. "I love you," he murmured as his lips brushed against hers. "Even though this night ends with unanswered questions, there'll be a new sunrise with answers."

Unable to sleep, he gazed into the starlit skies, reliving the impressions from the previous day.

Chapter Forty-Five

Eight hours earlier

Dr. Melanie Brichta's lecture on "The Power of Your Past through Hypnotherapy" was followed by a short question and answer session. It was already late in the afternoon, and since Adam had no more appointments, he purposely stood last in line as his colleagues were shaking Melanie's hand, complimenting her on another stimulating presentation.

When it was his turn, he stepped forward. "Thank you, Dr. Brichta, for sharing your in-depth knowledge about the subject," he said. "Your speech brought new insights to me—to everybody." He hesitated to continue but quickly changed course. "The incredible information on your studies in India elevated my own special interest in the subject because, years ago, I also studied hypnotherapy in Mumbai."

"You did?" Melanie looked at him and cocked her head. "*Years ago?* You must have been quite young when you studied there," she said, with smiling eyes. "May I ask where in Mumbai?"

"I spent several months at the Institute of Life; Darshita Khatri was my mentor."

Dr. Brichta held onto the edges of the lecture stand in front of her. "Now, this is a surprise! Darshita Khatri became my most influential teacher and spiritual leader when I lived in India—that was over twenty years ago, in the early nineties." She closely looked at Adam. "I noticed you standing in the back of the room yesterday during the focused awareness demonstration. However, we have yet to be formerly introduced..."

"Oh, I do apologize!" Adam said, feeling himself blush. "My name is Adam...Adam Gold. This is my third year at Rancho del Sol; every September, I participate in the symposiums and workshops here." He held out his hand to shake hers. "Again, I am so sorry for not introducing myself first."

Dr. Brichta cocked her head again. "Mmm...I thought it might be you," she said, now smiling broadly. "Back in Chicago, Kuri told me to look out for Adam Gold. She thought of it as quite coincidental you and I should meet here."

Adam nodded. "After your first talk, I didn't have the guts to approach you. I thought it was inappropriate to be so forward and blurt out the connection. Now, I'm thrilled we met, and if at all possible, I really would like the chance to talk more about your knowledge and the experience you had with patients on past life regression." Adam cleared his throat. "I had my first PLR in Mumbai...it was an eye-opener that led to awesome discoveries; I'd like to share those findings with you and hear your thoughts, Dr. Brichta."

"Please, call me Melanie—and may I call you Adam?"

"Of course, with pleasure!"

"It truly is coincidental, that the same spiritual leader in Mumbai played a part in both of our lives. I think it would be interesting to hear about your experience, Adam." Melanie began to collect the remaining material on the lecture desk. "Do you know the Meditation Ramada?" she asked. "At this time of the day, nobody will be there. I could meet you in fifteen minutes."

Adam was the first to arrive at the open shade structure, used daily during early mornings and before sunset for guided meditation and relaxation. Just when he was about to lean against one of the four columns, he heard his name.

"Adam! Do you come here often?"

"Actually, it's my first time this year…I haven't had the time."

He waited until Melanie placed herself on one of the thick floor pillows. After she relaxed her back into the built-in bolster, he made himself comfortable across from her.

"Have you seen Kuri since you arrived?" Adam asked.

Melanie shook her head. "Back in Chicago, Kuri and I agreed that we'd be at Rancho del Sol for different reasons. The Bergers are here for a demanding family week, and my three-day work engagement is strictly geared toward a particular group of therapists with a very specific agenda. I'll be leaving tomorrow afternoon already; I doubt Kuri and I will get a chance to connect." Melanie reached for another pillow to support her arm. "What about you, Adam?"

"Since the Bergers arrived, I've spent the evenings with them," Adam said. "I very much enjoy getting to know Kuri's family—it's been a wonderful experience, even under difficult circumstances for them."

"Let's shift gears," Melanie said. "I'm interested to learn about your past life regression in Mumbai that led you to research and discoveries."

Since Adam knew Melanie was a prominent expert in the studies of hypnosis and past life regression therapy, it was easy for him to talk about the recurring visions he'd had for the first twenty years of his life. He elaborated on those pleasant dreams where a girl kept singing the same song, and he detailed the complicated dark visions of pain and suffering behind barbed-wire fences.

"But the most powerful phantasm was of another girl—young and fragile—with beautiful copper hair. In my dreams, I was with her at the farmhouse…in a barn. And, over and over again, I kept seeing a green meadow, a brook, and a big old tree. Those visions were so commanding, they had etched themselves onto my brain, and I did not rest until I found an expert, a police artist, who produced composite drawings from my memory." Adam paused and had to blink himself back into the present. He saw Melanie leaning toward him—her eyes were wide open.

"You said your first past life regression brought some answers," she said softly. "How? What can you tell me about them?"

"Of course," Adam said. "Not only did Darshita Khatri bring clarity to my confusion—she convinced me to set foot onto a path of retrieval."

Adam continued to elaborate that the dark visions led him to study more about the Holocaust. He detailed his visits to former concentration camps in Europe, always searching the archives of municipalities for answers. His explorations, he said, less than three months ago, led him to the Bauer farm in Bavaria where all things of importance finally matched his memory mold.

Adam could tell he had Melanie's attention. "I am transfixed by your story," she said, sitting upright. "Please, go on."

Adam talked about the old woman who, decades ago, tried to save the girl and the boy—escapees from the Dachau death march. He talked about his emotions when Max, after sharing his mother's memories, led Adam to the oak tree where he was able to unearth the metal box.

"Everything I just told you is only known to Max Bauer, his mother, and wife in Bavaria," Adam said pensively. "I'm still in awe that I actually was able to find witnesses and a handwritten document from 1945. To me, this record authenticates that I lived before—I was Shimon Messing! Every dream and vision that shadowed me throughout my life suddenly made sense." Adam wiped his eyes. "I get emotional when I think of it as my past life," he apologized. "Shimmy had a family—they lived honest, happy lives before Auschwitz and Dachau." Adam swallowed, then locked eyes with Melanie. "Shimmy was only sixteen years old when he died, and the copper-haired girl he loved was only fifteen—her name was Judith Rozenblum."

Adam saw Melanie sink back into the bolster, closing her eyes. After a long silence, she looked at him and said in a low voice, "Thank you, Adam, for sharing your incredible experience with me. I can't begin to tell you of the valuable insight this has brought to me."

"I know some of your patients have had past life revelations. Can you tell me if anyone else has been able to validate these supernatural disclosures?"

Melanie took her time to answer. "My studies have shown that trauma, illness, or emotional fears of any kind can have a connection to a past life; I've been able to heal several complex issues through regression therapy."

"I am aware of that," said Adam. "I've read most of your publications. Only in yesterday's lecture you spoke about a young man with severe migraines who, under your guidance, remembered a previous lifetime where he had suffered a fatal head injury. Due to this new awareness, his migraines subsided." Adam leaned closer. "But what I really want to—"

"Forgive me for interrupting," she said. "What you really want to know is if any of my patients remembered names or places from a past life. You want to know if those names and places could be fact-checked, like you have been able to, due to your diligent discoveries."

Adam nodded, looking at Melanie with a contemplative eye. "I think I know what you're going to say next," he said.

"We both are professionals and, unless we have the permission of our patients, we cannot disclose their very private and sensitive information," she said with a fixed hint of a smile. "At this point, are *you* prepared to go public with your remarkable story?"

He shook his head. "No! At least not yet. I feel as if the account of my past life events has not been completed; something still is missing."

"You know, Adam," she said thoughtfully, "we both experienced our first regression therapy in India. I became aware of Darshita Khatri more than two decades ago; you found her some ten years later, also searching for answers. And since you shared your story with me, I think it's only fair to tell you some of mine."

Melanie lowered her head and, with her left index finger, gently began massaging the area right above the eyebrows in the middle of her forehead.

Is she waking up her third eye? Adam thought, recalling specific studies in India, learning that some individuals believe in the mystical concept of an invisible eye. Was Melanie one of them? Was she able to perceive the significance of this concept?

In a gentle voice, she began talking. "In this life, I didn't get married until I was thirty years old. My husband and I were deeply in love. He wanted children and had no idea I continued following a strict birth control regimen. When he found out, it broke his heart. Still, he remained patient and hopeful. But whenever he brought up the subject of creating a family, I became panic-stricken. I was convinced that, once we had children, something terrible would happen to all of us. I went to see two different therapists; neither was able to help me. Five years later, my marriage fell apart. It left me extremely distraught; I needed answers. My journey took me to India, where I found Darshita." Melanie paused. After a few deep inhales and long exhales, she continued. "Through her guidance, Darshita helped me embrace my spirituality; I soon discovered the essence of my subconscious and gained perception beyond ordinary sight."

Melanie closed her eyes but kept her index finger on the junction above her eyebrows. "In a past life, I was of a Native American tribe," she said in a huskier voice. "My husband was strong and powerful—a true leader. We had three happy children. When the soldiers came, my husband fought fiercely to protect us; he killed two of the soldiers…"

For a fraction of an instant, Adam thought Melanie would change her mind and stop her narrative, but after another long exhale, she continued in a low, thick voice.

"My children were forced to watch the soldiers batter their father to death; they saw me being assaulted. Then, together with others of the tribe, the soldiers bludgeoned us into the big river. The water was icy—many froze to death, others drowned. I heard my children cry out for me, and I kept their heads above the water until I took my last breath. Then I pulled their bodies down with me."

Melanie slowly removed the finger from her forehead, slightly lifting her chin while her eyes remained closed.

Knowing she needed time to settle her thoughts, Adam sat still until she opened her eyes. "Did you recall names? Do you know when and where you lived?" he asked softly.

"Like you, I followed my strong impressions, and through research of historic documents, I now believe in a past life I lived with the Shoshone of Bia Ogoi—which now is Idaho. A massacre of the Shoshone took place there in 1863 at Bear River. Everything I researched became a counterpart to what I saw in my past life regression."

When Melanie adjusted her position on the thick pillow, Adam realized she was trying to stand up. He sprung to his feet, offering his assistance.

"From the moment I understood the cause of my fears, I knew what I needed to do in this life and how I could help others!" she said. She laid her hand on Adam's shoulder. "By the way, and in case you wonder…I never remarried, but my ex-husband, his wife, and their two children have become my dearest friends."

Melanie looked at her wristwatch. "Oh my," she said. "Time for me to go."

Side by side they walked back to the main building.

"I am so grateful you made the time to get together. It meant a lot to me," he said, shaking her hand.

"What we told each other, we keep to ourselves," Melanie said softly. "Perhaps one day we will be able to openly talk about it to others. I have the feeling we will meet again, Adam."

He watched Melanie walk into the main building. He knew that two resident therapists had asked for a past life regression with her. Adam wondered if they'd be open to their own spiritual journey. If so, what would they learn?

Thirty minutes later, as he was riding his bicycle out to the Bergers' house, he hoped the time they'd spent with Ethan during the last several hours had been more pleasant and promising than on previous days.

Chapter Forty-Six

"Yeah? Empathy my ass!" Ethan blew out his cheeks. "Ever since she became famous, Kuri has treated me with nothing but contempt! That is, should she bother to speak to me at all!"

"But only yesterday, you told the group that when everything else had failed and no other family member came to your rescue, Kuri was the only one who helped you financially. You also said you were appreciative when she decided to make her loan to you a gift." Dr. Mullins raised her eyebrows. "Didn't you consider that an act of empathy?"

"Well," Ethan muttered, rubbing his head with his knuckles to tamp down his rage. He really wanted to tell that chunky shrink she was one of the 99 percent of therapists who gave the rest a bad name but quickly decided to bypass the question. "Well," he said again, "I invited Kuri to participate in this program because I consider her an integral part of the family. Should I not be disappointed when she told me earlier this morning something important had come up and she had to leave? Should I not be sad that her aim for greater stardom always is more critical than my recovery?" Ethan sniffed loudly. "My famous sister probably couldn't handle certain truths that surfaced during family sessions. How convenient for her to suddenly claim that La La Land needs her for"—he huffed out his irritation—"for whatever nonsense!"

Gritting his teeth, he again wished for nothing other than to get this whole therapy-rehab shit over with.

❄

Later, as Ethan sat with his parents and two siblings around the lunch table, he kept quiet. What more was there to say? Everything from the past had been chewed up and regurgitated again and again. He put the napkin over the untouched food on his plate. It sickened him to watch his family chewing and swallowing like cows their cud.

Even though he had promised himself to ignore his sister's sudden departure, he needed to blow off steam. "Am I the only one who's surprised that Kuri decided to leave early today?" he blurted. "Doesn't she understand how much she still could've contributed to my healing process?"

"I am confused," Teruko said. "Earlier this morning, after Kuri profusely apologized for having to leave, you told her you understood. You saw how annoyed she was, receiving the call about the studio's decision to reshoot some scenes."

"I don't care," Ethan huffed. "She very well knew family week was a five-day commitment. So now, after three short days, she suddenly disappears like a fart in Tornado Alley?" He grinned at his vivid imagery, but once again, nobody else around the table seemed capable of appreciating his wit.

David cleared his throat. "Your mother and I have been talking," he said, turning to Ethan. "We know you love to travel. Say the word, and wherever you'd like to go when you're finished here, we will take you. It'll be a good opportunity to recharge and spend quality time together." Tapping his fingers together, David sat back in the chair waiting for a response.

Ethan couldn't believe he was hearing this. The last thing on his mind was to go with Mommy and Daddy on vacation.

"It's a great idea," he said, "but because of all the therapy and the work I've done so far, I've had the opportunity to do a lot of thinking; I now have some plans for myself, and for that I need to be on my own." He suppressed a chuckle when he saw uneasy expressions on his family's faces.

"After what you've been through, would being on your own be a wise choice?" Aimi asked. "You're still going to need medical-assisted treatment after you're discharged from here. You may want to be close to people who love you and support your best interests."

"I disagree. I feel much stronger mentally, and I'm committed to maintaining a healthy lifestyle. I will make sure that I only surround myself with people who are beneficial to my growth and wellness." Ethan clasped his hands behind his neck and puffed out his chest. "I know what's best for me. The time has come where I want to rely on myself."

Gavin cocked his head. "Forgive me for being blunt, Ethan, but what you just said makes no sense. How can you know what's best for you? Only three weeks ago you overdosed and almost killed yourself! It's impossible for anyone to make perfect decisions on their own under these circumstances."

Ethan stood up abruptly and, without looking at anyone in particular, pushed his chair under the table. "I'm telling you again, I know what I want!" He gave the chair another shove. "I'm done here," he said, and had to make an effort to calmly stride out of the cafeteria, keeping a tight lid on his fury.

He went into his room and dropped onto the bed, staring at the ceiling. He knew he had to pull himself together. In another fifteen minutes, he'd have to leave for equine-assisted therapy. Actually, the interaction with the horses was the only activity he appreciated. *At least the horses don't unload their shit on me, like everyone else here,* he thought. But above all, he was looking forward to the only person who knew how to brighten his day…Jo Herrera.

Ethan had met Jo soon after his arrival at Rancho del Sol, and each day, as they took the twenty-minute walk to the stables and the forty-minute hike back from the pastures, he learned more and more about her. He certainly liked everything he heard and slowly grew to love what he saw; even with her long dark-brown hair and short stature, Jo was the physical opposite of anyone he had ever been attracted to.

She had told him about the airplane accident. Some of the marks on parts of her body were faint but still visible. There definitely were some lovely angles in her face, but unlovely ones as well. A pale pink scar ran from her left temple down to her chin, and when she smiled, her mouth turned somewhat crooked. He didn't like hearing about the skin grafts and plastic surgeries necessary to fix her up again, and if he was being honest, her slight limp would probably always bother him. Other than that, Jo had a distinct sex appeal. Her firm, round ass defied all explanation; her shiny espresso-colored eyes under brow-skimming bangs were bewitching, and her low voice with its Mexcian accent was sensual and pleasing. At first, he resented having to compete with Jo's brainpower, but soon he acquiesced. He looked at it as a vast improvement over Irina or the other dumb blonds from his past—as a matter of fact, since he had met Jo, he didn't want to think about the younger, taller, and stunning chicks who once gave him a distinct testosterone tug.

But most importantly, from the moment he heard about Jo and her enormous wealth, Ethan was ready to overlook any and all of her flaws or imperfections. The prospect of a pristine, lavish life immediately had transformed Jo, several years older than he, into his perfect new picture of the ideal woman.

Ethan would have liked to hold her hand as they walked to the stables, but from previous experience, he knew that specialists in the recovery and addiction fields frowned at patients developing amorous relationships during rehab. And since he detested living by rules, he clearly did not like having to keep his new liaison on the downlow.

"How did it go today?" Jo asked. "I saw you with your family in the cafeteria earlier. You didn't look too cheerful."

"You know how I feel; I can't wait for them to leave—I'm better off without them." He realized Jo was moving closer, and he felt an instant shiver running down his spine as her bare arm brushed against his.

"I'm getting to know you more and more each day, and I realize we have a lot in common," she said. "For as long as I can remember, I couldn't stand my unavailable, conceited mother who deviously cheated on my father; I'm convinced Felipe wasn't even my father's child—that's why I intensely disliked my *brother.* And then I find out how you detest your rigid, power-hungry father and loathe your siblings. Yet, we both adore one parent: my father means everything to me, and you still crave your mother's attention." Jo kicked a pebble with her stylish studded-leather hiking boot, creating a small cloud of dust. She looked at her boots. "Shit."

"What's wrong?"

"Weird," she muttered, still looking at her feet. "Sometimes I do things that make no sense."

"Huh?"

"Why do I wear these expensive Alexander McQueen boots in this dusty desert when I prefer my footwear to look perfect?"

"Well, I can top that!" he replied. "I buy expensive sports cars, then get pissed off about the tight interior." He started to laugh. "We're like two peas in a pod, huh?"

"And neither of us like when things backfire or when others see through our insincerity," Jo said, and kicked another pebble out of the way—this time with more force. "I think it's time to sharpen our technique whenever we act suspiciously simpatico; let's find more clever ways to hide our real selves."

Ethan teasingly poked her with his elbow. "C'mon, little girl! Fuck all this therapy shit! Birds of a feather like flocking together."

"Birds of a kind are of the same mind."

Ethan stopped walking and quickly looked around. Ahead, the five other residents and therapists already were entering the stables, and when he saw that nobody was behind them, he grabbed Jo's shoulders and turned her toward him. Being almost six feet tall, he towered over her; he liked how this provided him with the toxic masculinity he needed to defeat any subliminal self-doubt.

They crushed their lips together, almost knocking the wind from each other's lungs while lighting their own brains on fire. In a swirl of emotion, they obliterated all thoughts of torment by opening the door to lust and lechery.

As soon as her cool hand slipped under Ethan's shirt and touched his bare back, his endorphins made him feel drunk—he craved that feeling and wanted more. He pressed her body into his and felt the adrenaline speed up his heart rate. He trembled when he heard her say, "I promise you more... much more."

"This is only the beginning," he rasped into her mouth. "I want you."

"No! You need me!"

When they heard voices nearby, they disengaged from the embrace, and Ethan quickly pretended to brush something off Jo's shirt.

"Yes! I want you, and I need you," Ethan whispered into her ear.

"I do have a plan, *mi amor*!" Jo said as they started walking toward the stables again. "Meet me at ten o'clock tonight in the Meditation Ramada; I'll tell you of my ideas then." She winked at him and with a naughty grin added, "We also might find some other use for the meditation cushions."

"The Meditation Ramada? That might not be safe. What if the night patrol guy sees us there?"

"So what!" she scoffed. "What's the worst that could happen? We get kicked out of the program here at Rancho de Mierda?" A disparaging smile formed on her lips. "Perfect! That only would speed up my goal."

Chapter Forty-Seven

Ethan had no idea it was almost midnight when, completely exhausted, he rolled onto his back. "Holy fuck," he said hoarsely, "that definitely was the most exotic thrill ride I ever had." He reached for the T-shirt next to him to wipe the sweat off his face and chest. Without turning his head toward Jo, he muttered, "With your acrobatic performance, you ought to consider joining Cirque du Soleil—you'd be their star attraction."

"I prefer a tête-à-tête show," she said. "I don't need a crowd or applause to tell me how good I am!" And, just like that, she straddled him again. "Did I tell you that I have a thing for Eurasian guys?" She moaned as she ran her index finger over the contours of his face. "You really turn me on, Ethan Berger—you're even hotter than Henry Golding."

He shivered with excitement as he felt her long fingernails scraping down his neck to his torso. "Stop," he whispered. "Please stop." When she fiercely pinched his nipple, he didn't push her hand away; he wanted her to win the battle. *Why am I not having a problem being subdued?* he wondered. *I've always been the one who likes to be in charge. Why does it suddenly feel so good being sexually passive?*

He groaned when her hand squeezed his groin. *Ow… mmm… I can't even distinguish between pain and pleasure anymore.*

"Nothing is sexier than a guy who's strong enough to let me be in control," she rasped into his mouth. "I love how easily you submit to my demands and positions; but your stamina…it's beyond incredible!" And just like that, she rolled off and assumed another position. "You're one sexy hunk, *mi amor,*" she said.

Ten minutes later, as he was still trying to catch his breath, lying next to her on the meditation cushions, Ethan grumbled, "Man, this fucking desert air! My mouth is as dry as a kangaroo rat's. Is there any water left?"

"Here." She handed him the half-full, crunched-up plastic bottle. "Drink up—I need you to listen to my plan."

Even though he was dead tired, he felt obligated. "What's your plan, *dulce niña?*"

"Knowing as much about you as I do…I think you will greatly appreciate what I'm about to offer."

Through half-closed eyes, he saw her slip into her leggings. "What is it?" he asked drowsily.

"Don't you fall asleep on me!" she said matter-of-factly while donning her T-shirt.

The tone of her voice alerted him. He sat up and reached for his own clothes. "What is it?" he asked again.

She remained standing and waited until he had zipped up his shorts. "Kneel down!" she said, and then, in one fluid move, stretched her left arm toward him.

Close to his face, her small hand appeared as a seamless branch of her arm, and her curved fingers looked as graceful as those of a ballerina.

"Ethan Berger," she said with a confident smile on her face, "I am offering my hand in marriage to you!"

Totally stumped, and without conscious thought, he took her hand into his and pressed his lips to her fingertips, feverishly seeking for words. "You…eh…" he cleared his throat and looked up. "You beat me to it," he rasped, and kissed her hand again.

"Well?" she demanded. "Does that mean yes?"

"Yes, of course! Yes!" Ethan rose and, overcome by a sudden head rush, he almost lost his balance. "Being with you for the rest of my life would make me the happiest man on earth," he whispered as he steadied himself in her embrace.

"Stop with the platitudes, *mi amor.* We're a perfect match."

With his index finger under her chin, he gently lifted her face. "The moment we get out of here, I'll buy a magnificent ring and—"

"No need," she said, and wriggled away from him. "My papi gave my mother a huge emerald-cut diamond ring on their twentieth anniversary; it goes without saying, the bitch never wore it! Because Papi is gravely ill, I want him to see that ring on my finger before he dies. It'll prove to him that I finally found what I've been looking for." She tapped her index finger on Ethan's chest. "I found you, *mi amor.* You!"

Ethan watched as in one swift move Jo sunk to the floor cushion again. "Sit," she ordered, and patted the cushion next to her. She put her hand on his inner thigh and gave it a light squeeze. "I'm only continuing with the program here because I made a promise to my papi." She gave Ethan's thigh a tighter squeeze. "And you're staying in the program so your daddy will pay off your debt." Jo smiled smugly when she added, "But now you won't need your daddy anymore—you got me! I will change your life dramatically, and I know you will enjoy it!"

Ethan coughed nervously. "I'm passionately in love with you and don't want to leave your side, but I need to straighten out some things once I'm done here. Will you come to Chicago with me? I can…"

"Where's your passport?" she cut in.

"It's together with all my other stuff they're keeping at the office here."

"Good. As soon as we finish the program, you come with me to Mexico; no need for you to go back to the Windy City. I have very competent people working for me—they will take care of everything." And without further ado, Jo elaborated on how she'd planned their future together. At the end of her delivery, she moved closer to him. "I assume you like what you heard," she said.

Ethan nodded; he knew he was beaming. He took her face between his hands. "You're such a fucking straight shooter; I can't help but adore that backbone of yours."

She pulled away from him to sit up and motioned him to do the same. She pointed at the night sky. "You know what that is?" she asked, but didn't wait for his answer. "That's the Milky Way, and we dwell in that galaxy. It has over two hundred billion stars and enough dust and gas to make billions more." She tilted her head. "I'm like the Milky Way; I'm already worth billions but have enough energy to make more." With a broad grin, she winked at him. "Because you have an appetite for opulence, you can help me achieve my goals." She looked at the sky again and determinedly added, "We shall do great things together."

Ethan swallowed. He couldn't believe his luck. From the day he had met her, he'd been scheming how to finagle his way into her life, and now, this night, without him having to make any effort, his target was being offered on a shiny silver platter. He pulled her onto his lap. "*Tu me completas, mi carino,*" he said in a low voice. Then, with an unknown acceptance of surrender, he kissed the woman who had become his lottery ticket.

Chapter Forty-Eight

"These separations are killing me! They get worse every time," Kuri said, pressing her face into the silky comforter while kneeling at the end of her parents' bed. "I can't ask him to give up his job in Boston. What would he do? Come to the set and watch me work?" She took a tissue from the Kleenex box her mother handed her. "Adam is a brilliant psychiatrist and loves his profession." She blew her nose. "Maybe I should move to Boston and—"

"Moving to Boston is not a bad idea, but you'll still be in and out of the country for months at a time," Teruko said.

"If only there was a way I could get out of the contract," she groaned. "On the other hand, it's such a great role!" She sniffed into another Kleenex. "Darn, that sounds selfish and makes no sense, because I'm willing to give everything up for Adam."

"Your lawyers are working on it; let's see what will be." David sat up slowly. "Argh," he grunted, "my joint stiffness is at its worst in the mornings." He put on his robe. "Look," he said, "worse comes to worse, you go ahead with the new project. If there's one man that can tolerate seeing you with other attractive men in love scenes, it's Adam. He never seems fazed by any of the gossip around you, and he even manages to stay out of the spotlight." David raked his fingers through his thick silver-gray hair. "You know," he said, "Adam strikes me as beyond secure in this relationship; I believe he'll support you whatever your decision will be."

"Of course! That's why it hurts so much when we're apart." Kuri wiped her eyes. "For years it felt as if I was moving through life without a part of my soul. And now that I've found…" her voice trailed off; she stared at the ceiling.

"Go on," Teruko said after a minute.

"I thought about something already in Sedona; I realize what I must do next."

"Which is?"

"Instead of me going to Boston next week, I'm going to ask Adam to come here." Kuri straightened and rubbed her hands together. "He already met my therapist in Sedona. I'd like him to be present when Dr. B. guides me through my next PLR; I just hope there's no professional conflict." Unable to remain still, Kuri sprang to her feet. She put her hands on her chest and nodded to herself. "Adam greatly respects Dr. B's wisdom and skills—my heart tells me it will be the perfect time to involve him in my search for the mysteries that still elude me."

"Good idea," Teruko said, sending her daughter an encouraging smile while belting her favorite, hand-painted peacock kimono robe. "Keep following your instincts, Kurisutaru—my crystal child."

David opened the bedroom door. "Aaah, coffee—I can smell it all the way up here. Anyone else besides me ready for Sofia's huevos rancheros?"

They were sitting around the table when Aimi, still in her riding attire, rushed into the kitchen. As always, she looked quite the equestrian in her white shirt, tight red-and-black-plaid pants, and dark leather boots.

"What a beautiful morning. I got up at five to ride Ebony for two hours," she said, and thanked Sofia for the mug of steaming coffee. She looked at her father's plate. "Wow, looking at this makes me drool. Can I get some of it, Sofia?" Aimi loosened the white-and-black polka-dot scarf around her neck, then unfastened the helmet and placed it on one of the chairs.

"Where are the boys?" David asked.

"They had a sleepover with Millie and Max last night. Dale and Gavin plan to take the four kids to Six Flags Great America today." Aimi made room on the table for a plate of Sofia's special recipe. "*Muchas gracias, Sofia. Que se ve delicioso!*"

When she finished eating, Aimi leaned back. "I have some breaking news for you guys. You want the good or the bad first?"

"Always bad first," David said.

"I had a few phone messages late last night and, just on my way over here, made necessary follow-up calls." She crossed her arms. "It's official: Ethan relocated to Mexico! Our lawyers received word from him. Well…not directly from Ethan but from his new lawyers across the border."

"Really?" Wide-eyed, Teruko leaned forward. "What else did you find out?"

"Ethan found himself a sugar mama in Jo Herrera and now resides in a sprawling Shangri-la."

"Good for him," David said, smiling broadly. "If that's the bad news, then the good news must be extraordinary."

"Yeah! Supposedly, Ethan is conducting himself very well in his new role."

"What do you mean?"

"Gavin made some inquiries, and from what his Mexican sources revealed, Jo is showing Ethan off in her high-society circles, but more so, she has him sitting right next to her in boardrooms. Rumor has it, he's her puppy on a training leash."

"Well, that actually sounds promising," David said. "I can't recall the last time Ethan showed up for any of our board meetings. If Jo can do what none of us could accomplish, then more power to her." He turned to Teruko. "He texted you a few days ago that he's very happy, right?"

Teruko nodded. "I'm the only one he apparently wants to communicate with. He let me know that I never need to worry about him anymore; he said Jo made his dreams come true."

"Lucky dog!" Aimi said. "Whereas he rejected anything this family ever tried doing for him, Josefina Herrera apparently has more luck. With her barely five feet of height, she might be tiny, but she's got the reputation of a powerhouse with almost masculine traits."

Teruko tilted her head and frowned. "I seriously doubt Ethan will be able to tolerate any kind of dominance."

"Of course he will. He definitely cut the cord with whatever life he led before," Aimi said. "His condominium was under contract only days after coming on the market, and we know he sold his car to pay off his gambling debt."

"Except," David cut in, "I found out there's additional debt." He clasped his wrist with the opposite hand and massaged it. "A new lawsuit was filed against Ethan by one of the creditors."

"A lawsuit? Does that mean he can't come back into the country?" Teruko looked pleadingly at her husband. "If so, what can we do?"

"Don't worry about Ethan—I'm certain he's got it all figured out!" Kuri moved closer to her mother. "You and Dad have done all you could. You've given and forgiven so many times while Ethan was incapable of seeing what you sacrificed for him. Perhaps Jo will know how to open his eyes and his heart."

"Absolutely!" Aimi said. "Ethan's surprise new liaison might be a blessing in disguise. His financial obligations are chump change to Jo Herrera—she'll pay that off in a jiffy. She's in charge of her father's empire and is running it with an iron fist; she definitely won't let anyone besmirch her family's reputation. But I have the feeling she'll make Ethan pay for her freehandedness."

"How so?" Teruko's worried expression intensified.

"Mom, it's exactly what Ethan needs. He will live in obscene luxury, but she'll control him all the way; the Alpha woman has found her Beta boy."

"But why? Of what benefit will he be to her?"

"Ethan always has been a chick magnet; he's beyond darn handsome. Jo Herrera has found her younger trophy! I'm sure she'll train him right where she wants him to be, and in my humble opinion, Ethan is long overdue for this type of a drill."

Chapter Forty-Nine

Unable to concentrate on her work, Melanie didn't quite know what to do with the suspenseful excitement she was experiencing. *Why am I wasting my time sitting here when I can't focus on writing this article?* And with that thought, she closed her Mac. *I really need to distract myself from this restlessness . . . but what should I do?* Then, abruptly she made a decision, quickly walked into another room, and opened the closet that held all her photo equipment. She put two of her cameras and three different lenses into a large camera backpack, and after making sure she had everything, she closed the doors to her apartment, hoping to leave the tension behind.

She considered herself lucky because traffic was light on the Kennedy Expressway; it got even better once she merged onto Eden's Parkway. But while she was driving north, new theories and fresh ideas kept racing through her brain again; like monkeys they bounced around, always trying to outsmart each other.

Melanie couldn't silence the replay of the conversation she'd had with Adam at Rancho del Sol when he told her how his dreams and visions had linked him to actual locations and real names. She shuddered, remembering how difficult it was to control her shock and awe as Adam's story crystallized with Kuri's recollection during her first PLR session when, under hypnosis, she spoke the name of Judith Rozenblum. Only weeks after at the ranch, Adam mentioned that very name as he had read it in Shimmy's letter. Needless to say, Melanie's professionalism did not allow her to share this incredible piece of information with either her patient or with Adam. Instead, Melanie hoped for the universe to make the connection. Her trust worked; just days ago she had received a call from Kuri, asking for another past life regression session, requesting Adam to be by her side.

Melanie felt the tingle in her spine again, and being caught up so deeply in reverie, she didn't realize that she'd veered her car into the left lane. A loud angry horn from an SUV speeding down the highway ripped her back into the moment; she gasped out loud and quickly corrected her mistake; she forced herself to pay attention until she exited the expressway.

When she arrived at the Rivertrail Nature Center, she pulled into the first open parking space, slung her backpack over both shoulders, and walked the short distance to the entrance. Even though she did not like caged habitats, the animals, some too injured to be released, at least were able to move freely in their natural environment. While strolling along the river through sugar maple woods, she took advantage of several excellent photo opportunities. As she had anticipated, nature gently unwound her eagerness, diverting her thoughts from what she hoped, or better, what she seriously wanted to believe was predestined.

Melanie never scheduled appointments on weekends, but for this Sunday, she had made an exception. Kuri's request for having Adam present while undergoing hypnotherapy had been on the forefront of Melanie's mind, and knowing what she knew, she was more than eager to find out if two souls from a previous life might reconnect. In less than a few hours, she would know.

When she opened the door, Kuri and Adam stood hand in hand,

looking at the framed photographs that lined the walls of Melanie's waiting room.

"Dr. B! You and Adam clearly don't need an introduction." Kuri's light-green eyes sparkled like brilliant emeralds. "I am so grateful you allowed us to come on a Sunday."

Melanie always had been fascinated by Kuri's almost unearthly beauty, but when she saw her young patient standing next to Adam, Kuri emitted an additional pristine glow.

Even Adam, whom Melanie had grown to admire for his competency, depth, and joie de vivre, looked more princely than she remembered; he also radiated excitement.

Melanie composed herself. "Come through," she said, and gestured them into her office, asking them to be comfortable.

"Before we start, I want to make sure I have your consent for the upcoming session," she said. "Both of you, individually, have undergone a past life regression and understand the intricacies and sensitivities of what is considered a perplexing field." She paused to inhale. "None of us are prepared for what we might experience, and there's no guarantee you will be pleased with the outcome. However"—she paused to take another deep inhale—"you need to be sure that you are genuinely ready for this."

"Yes," Kuri and Adam said in unison, and nodded.

"Is there anything either of you would like to discuss first? We have time."

They looked at each other.

"You first," Adam said.

"Inasmuch as we know so much about each other, Adam is aware that I held back about what happened during my past life regression therapy." Kuri turned to him, smiling apologetically. "Because I feel so close to you, it may seem ridiculous that I haven't been able to share the magnitude of the discoveries that resulted. My memories were so unreal and so personal, I simply needed more time to regard the experience as real and not as a fantasy or delusion." She squeezed his hand. "I am grateful you're here now.

I'm ready for you to become part of my journey—that is, if you will trust what you may hear."

Adam put his arm around Kuri's shoulder, pulling her close when he addressed the therapist. "I told Kuri that she changed my existence and has become the singular and foremost substance in my life." He cleared his throat. "I know this may sound corny, but if there truly is a Book of Life for each one of us on this planet, then I believe it will validate that having met Kuri in this lifetime will be my most beautiful chapter."

Melanie sat still, looking at the young couple across from her. After a moment of silence, she said, "Our paths continuously take us to intersections of two or more roads, and the decisions of which roads to take can be endless."

"How true," Kuri agreed. "After what I experienced in my PLR, I now understand there is no end; we have free will, and because of it, we can choose to walk a new path of life all over again." She smiled at Adam, then looked at Dr. B. "I'm ready for my next exploration."

Chapter Fifty

The room into which he followed Melanie and Kuri gave Adam an overwhelming sensation of déjà vu. The layout, the quietude, and the fragrance from the incense sticks took Adam back to the place in Mumbai where, years ago, he'd had his own past life regression. He immediately recalled that Melanie also had her first experience of the same kind there. Once again, he found it stunning how through Darshita Khatri's techniques, they both had recovered memories from another incarnation. As he already had done before, Adam couldn't help but think of this remarkable concurrence of events as another addition to the many recent miracles of synchronicities.

"Dr. B?"

Kuri's voice broke his reverie.

"Thank you for allowing Adam to participate in the guidance," she said as she laid down on the sofa. She closed her eyes and began to breathe deeply.

"I believe this was meant to happen," Melanie said softly as she prepared the stones and crystals. "Adam has had his own experience in Mumbai and recently observed a session at Rancho del Sol. He'll be quite proficient."

"Are you nervous?" Kuri asked him.

"Not at all." He sounded calm but felt his heartbeat increasing.

"You have such a soothing voice; everything feels right."

As Melanie talked about the purpose of each stone and crystal, she placed them on Kuri's body. Then she handed Adam an amethyst and two jade stones and nodded for him to proceed.

"As you travel through time, may this assist you," he said, and placed the amethyst on Kuri's forehead.

"May these open your eyes to all the exploration on your journey," Adam said, putting two small jade stones on Kuri's closed lids.

Melanie and Adam took turns guiding Kuri through the relaxation of her body.

At Melanie's hand signal, Adam rang the Tibetan bell. He watched Kuri and could tell she was going deeper and deeper as Melanie's calm voice shepherded Kuri through space and time.

"Before the sun, the moon, the earth,
Before the stars of comets free,
Before e'en time had had its birth,
I was, I am, and I will be."

Chapter Fifty-One

1944

Together with many other women who came with us from Ravensbrück, Rose and I now work at Agfa-Commando, a satellite camp. Rose tells me she's impressed by how quickly I learn to assemble ignition timing devices for bombs and artillery ammunition. Every day, I do my work in silence. While losing myself in memories of the past and dreaming of the future where I see Papa again, I ignore my hunger and thirst. But during meal distributions, Rose reminds me that I must keep my strength; she watches me closely and nods encouragement when she sees me finish my rations.

Will I ever breathe freedom again? Will I hear my heart sing again?

A voice interrupts my thoughts.

"You! Go over there and help that prisoner with his electrical work," a woman SS guard orders. My eyes follow her outstretched arm and her pointed stick, and I see the young man that looked at me when we passed each other under the gate! Our eyes lock again. Standing beside me, he wordlessly indicates what tool he needs. I hand it to him, and his fingers touch mine. Enigmatic vibrations rush through me. I believe he must feel them too, because we both hold our breath.

"*Los... weiter... arbeiten!*" The guard orders us to continue with the labor before she turns her attention to other workers.

"*Ich heisse, Judith,*" I dare to whisper; speaking softly, he tells me his name is Shimmy.

Every day now I look forward to working at Agfa Commando. The days I don't see him are endlessly long, but the days when I'm ordered to work with him end too soon. We have so much to tell each other, always making sure we keep a small distance between us. We speak only in whispers and hardly move our lips because the guards are forever hovering nearby, waiting to justify an attack. Like birds of prey, they see everything; like bats they are of extreme hearing.

I don't know how, but Shimmy receives extra portions of food. When nobody is looking, he pushes some of it into my sleeve.

My heart sings again, and wherever she is, I know Mama is smiling.

1945

There's an outbreak of typhoid in the women's barracks. I keep myself as clean as possible. Rose and I now share a bunk. I tell her about Shimmy, and she often stands guard when he and I meet by the fence that separates the women and men's barracks. He continues to hand me food, and many times I share it with Rose; her tremendous willpower and positive attitude is awe-inspiring and is giving me strength. She is confident that freedom and a better life are waiting for us.

Spring is here... I don't know what month it is, but it feels like April. Rose is sick—like so many others, she's contracted typhoid. She turns away from me at night and tells me not to touch her. "I'll get better," she promises. We both still work at Agfa-Commando, but Rose is struggling. This time, it is I who encourages her to eat and drink, but she has no appetite and frequently gives me her ration.

I meet Shimmy at the fence; he looks troubled. Hurriedly he tells me the SS will march us to an undetermined destination. Our hands are touching through the small opening on the bottom of the barbed-wire fence. He kisses my fingertips and gives me a thick piece of bread. We hear a voice nearby. "Go," he whispers. "I will find you again."

I want to warn Rose, but she is so ill, she barely acknowledges my presence. I know she's not able to walk with us, and I pray that God will call her home before the Nazis beat her to death.

My prayers are being heard; during roll call Rose tugs on my sleeve and whispers, "Good-bye, my sweet Judith—God is waiting for me. I must leave you now." With a smile she sinks to the ground.

❋

It is already evening when they line us up—prisoners in their worn-out uniforms as far as the eye can see. We are given another meager ration of food; they tell us that it will have to last for days.

My stomach has been hurting all day, and I think I may be feverish. I ignore the pain and rely again on Herr Professor's inspirational teachings; I can hear his voice, "*Der Geist triumphiert über die Materie!*" Over and over I mesmerize myself and silently repeat, *I can do it, I can do it; mind over matter, mind over matter, mind over matter; I can do it, I can do it...*

It truly is amazing how the intellect can control a sick, fragile body. I recall the books I read in Herr Professor's study where famous people overcame all kind of obstacles. I think of Beethoven, who lost his hearing and still composed the most sublime music. When I hear that music in my head, I am able to ignore the cramps, the weakness, the headaches. I leave the darkness and slam the imaginary door to lock away three years of Nazi horror. In the sunshine, I find Shimmy; I see us skipping over green meadows while gentle winds and warmth caress our skin.

We walk all night and all the next day. The sun is setting again, and dusk is falling rapidly. All of a sudden, I see Shimmy. He towers over most other prisoners and is stretching his neck, turning his head back and forth. I know he's looking for me.

"Shimmy." My voice is weak, but he hears me and then he's walking next to me, interlacing his fingers with mine. I find the strength to squeeze tightly, never wanting to let go of this link of love.

"We must escape from here," he whispers, and as if the angels hear him, suddenly there is howling havoc ahead of us. Two of the nearby SS aim their rifles and run toward the tumult. I feel a strong push and tumble with Shimmy into the dark woods.

When he hears me fight for my breath, he scoops me up and continues forward through the dense forest. I feel his hot breath on my neck and know he's struggling for air. Unexpectedly we both fall into a large depression in the ground. We're holding onto one another, barely breathing; we're afraid someone is chasing us. But instead of feared human voices, all we hear is the tranquil sound of nature. In this absolute absence of light, I can't even see Shimmy's face, but I feel his beautiful presence when he covers me with a cloak of petals and leaves.

His kiss wakes me, and I see sunrays filtering through the branches of trees. I want to stay here forever with Shimmy, but he picks me up again and carries me away. He holds leaves to my lips, and I gratefully lick off the raindrops. I drift in and out of consciousness. I feel hot, but I shiver uncontrollably and have strange hallucinations; the abdominal pain is getting worse. I'm afraid I caught the typhoid fever that had spread throughout the camp. I won't tell Shimmy, though. He has enough to worry about.

"I must rest a little." I hear Shimmy's voice, but it comes from far away. He lays me on the ground and collapses next to me. I don't know how long we sleep. When he wants to scoop me up again, I tell him I can walk.

The sun has already set when suddenly, like a curtain in a theater, the forest opens and presents us with a beautiful scene; it's like a painting filled with brilliant colors. A gently babbling brook curves through a meadow that is saturated with spring flowers; a majestic oak tree with new young leaves seems to wave at us, inviting us to come closer. But Shimmy points to a barn next to the farmhouse. We keep close to the ground and slip through the door into the warm shelter. I fall into thick piles of hay and think of Hans Christian Anderson's story about the princess and the pea; her piled-high soft bedding could not compare with my cozy bed of mown grass.

I hear voices, someone is talking German and it frightens me. Did the Nazis find us? I want to sit up and warn Shimmy, but he gently pushes me into my warm bed of straw again. I immediately drift into sleep.

❄

I feel a cold compress on my forehead, and I thirstily drink the water from the cup against my lips. My lids are too heavy to lift, and I have no strength to object when hands strip off the loathed prison jacket and pants.

Oh, how I welcome the softness of clean clothes on me and the luxury of being covered by a thick blanket. Again, I feel the cup on my mouth, and I gratefully drink. Am I hallucinating, or do I see a young woman by the door? I hold my breath, but she's not in a uniform; she wears a dress and an apron, like Mama when she didn't want to get her pretty dress dirty. The woman smiles at me. It takes all my strength to raise my hand and wave to her. "*Danke*," I whisper, and drift off again.

Is it a dream, or am I dancing in my favorite tutu and pointe shoes? Distant divine music, like thousands of harps, permeates the air. Where is it coming from? I open my eyes and search. More happiness fills me when I see Shimmy coming through the barn door. But his handsome face is pale, his eyes look tired and glassy. He lies next to me. "I need to rest," he says. "I will feel better soon, I promise." He kisses my lips. His body is hot, but he shivers.

"Don't be afraid," I tell him. "This is a special moment, it's a birthday of a new life. Just listen..." As the heavenly music comes closer, the beautiful sound is taking away my pain. I feel good and strong again. I am surrounded by love.

"Look...the light. Can you see it?" I ask Shimmy. "Do you hear the music? I've never heard sweeter melodies." I search for his hand. "Dance with me," I whisper.

I hear his voice. "We are free—we're floating on air." His words are lyrical and gentle. I feel his fingers connecting with mine as he whispers, "You and I...forever."

Chapter Fifty-Two

It is time to return now." Dr. Melanie Brichta spoke softly, touching the stones on Kuri's body. "You now will come back to full waking consciousness."

The voice she heard was familiar, but she moved away from it; she was not ready to leave the feeling of bliss where pure love sparkled in the brilliance of a golden light. Why would she want to leave this splendor while dancing with Shimmy? Wasn't it here where they were meant to delight in the magnificence of vibrational forces forever?

"As you turn around, you will see the door you came through when you entered this life."

She felt a pull but resisted.

"See yourself walk back through the long passage of light. You may leave all the bad memories behind. Take only the good ones with you. Go through the door, and close it tightly behind you."

She heard another voice. She wasn't sure but knew it was her own. "No. I'd like to keep dancing. It is so beautiful here; so serene."

The therapist gently tapped the stones and crystals, speaking slow and soft. "It is time to return. Take the soothing memories and the splendor with you—they are yours to keep. Thank your subconscious for the awareness of your past, and hold on to all of its beauty."

She pulled away from the instructions, her desire to defy gravity was more intense than the distant voice she heard. Oh, how she loved dancing in the majesty of light and vibrations.

❄

As if hypnotized himself, Adam stood motionless by the sofa. He stared at Kuri—or was it Judith? His own memories from a past life had formed a single entity with what he had just witnessed. *I found the proof,* he thought, spellbound by his comprehension that his life was bound to Kuri's by their shared experiences as Shimmy Messing and Judith Rozenblum, two teenagers robbed of their families by a cancer in history.

Amid the horrors of Dachau, we found each other, only to have death steal from us the life we dreamed of living together, Adam reflected in stunned silence. *Our past life memories fused so they can fit into the spiritual universe. We both became aware of the absolute importance of our journey—the passage that took us into spheres beyond earthly reality. Our souls transcended oblivion, and in the mystery of all existence, we found each other again as Kuri Berger and Adam Gold. Life gave us a new chance to fulfill our mission and to complete the love that had remained incomplete.*

Still gazing at Kuri, he was unaware that due to this continuous flow of data, epochs of unshed tears spilled from his eyes. He felt a hand on his shoulder; he heard Melanie's voice. Though distant, he detected urgency in the tone.

"Adam! Can you hear me? Kuri needs to know you are here; that you are waiting for her."

He wiped the dense mist from his eyes and saw Melanie's face close to his.

"Your voice will draw her back, Adam."

He noticed insistence in her voice and willed himself to wake from his trance. "I'm sorry," he mumbled. "What must I do?"

"Kuri…no…I believe it's still Judith who desires to remain in the spirit world; she's impervious to my guidance."

"Oh, no! She has to come back!" Adam bent over Kuri, feeling for a heartbeat, any sign of life. "Oh, please, no!"

"Your guidance will bring her back," Melanie said calmly. "She needs to hear your voice."

Adam lightly put his hand over the stones on Kuri's chest; he watched his teardrops fall through his fingers onto her skin.

"Please feel my touch," he said softly. "Please hear my voice. I am here, waiting for you." He lowered his head very close to hers and then he whispered,

"Your soul is united with mine
No one can tear us apart
Eternally our lives shall entwine
Together, forever in heart."

A sharp inhale parted her lips, but she remained silent.

He brushed her lips with his. "I am here…waiting for you," he said again.

There was a muscle twitch in her beautiful face.

Adam tapped on the stones under his fingers. "You are still in the long passage of light. Walk to the end of it. A beautiful big door is slowly opening, inviting you to move through. When you are on the other side, close that door behind you."

Adam paused, allowing for her to pass through space and time. A smile of relief spread over his face as his hand felt a strong heartbeat beneath the stones on her chest. He leaned closer to her face and murmured, "I've been with you throughout time." He saw eye movement under her still-closed lids; her lashes fluttered gently.

"Take this moment to say farewell to your spiritual being," Adam told her, "but know that the harmony of your eternal life will always be with you."

She took another breath, this one more forceful than the last.

"I am going to count you up into the state of your current existence. With each count you will become more and more awake." Adam waited so she could absorb the information, allowing her to adjust to the moment in time.

"One, two, three...you are slowly becoming grounded in your body again. All remains in harmony. All is beautiful. All is very peaceful." Gingerly, Adam removed his hand from her chest.

"Four, five, six...you are in complete control of your body and mind. Little by little you are waking up—becoming more aware."

With the hand that had felt her beating heart, Adam wiped the last of his tears away.

"Seven, eight, nine...you can feel your body resting on this comfortable sofa—everything is peaceful, ever so beautiful."

Adam took a deep breath.

"Ten..." he said. "You may open your eyes whenever you are ready to return to the state of being awake."

As if in slow motion, Kuri lifted her lids. Her eyes immediately found his.

"Adam," she murmured, as a tender smile formed on her lips. "You heard everything? Can you believe where I went, what I saw, and what I felt?"

He nodded. "I not only believe, but I was there; I lived that life with you."

Her puzzled look caused him to pause, and when she slowly tried to sit up, he took her hands into his. "Just as I am here with you now, I was with you before," he said.

The frown between her brows remained, but her eyes suddenly shone with expectancy. "You know more about the mystery behind it all, don't you?" She looked around the small room. "Where is Dr. B? I'd like her to hear—"

"She left just a few minutes ago—the moment you opened your eyes," Adam said as he sat next to Kuri on the sofa. "Only now do I realize that Melanie has been aware of your and my previous connection, but she had to keep it to herself. She is giving us the privacy for what I need to tell you," Adam said tenderly.

"There's such a wellspring of emotion within me," she breathed, searching deeper in his eyes. "You do know my soul to the core. Please share with me what I need to know."

Holding on to both of her hands, Adam began to talk…

Chapter Fifty-Three

The therapist had quietly closed the door that separated the hypnosis room from her office. For a brief moment she stood immobile, holding on to the doorknob. She took a deep breath, then slowly walked over to her desk and sank into the chair. Unable to hear their voices, she imagined Adam was taking slow steps, unraveling the extraordinary evolution of events to Kuri; information that only had been shared with Melanie in the Meditation Ramada in Sedona. She closed her eyes to recall Adam's reaction as he heard Kuri evidence their existence together in another life: disbelief was mixed with an overwhelming expression of joy; his lips kept moving, speaking silent words until he whispered, "Destiny decided for this to happen long before we met again."

Melanie was certain that Kuri and Adam, currently in the process of absorbing their connection in the indefinite progression of life, were oblivious to the space, the time, and the reality around them.

Melanie was grateful she had made this appointment on a Sunday where time was of no essence; no other patients were scheduled, and even her phone was silent. On weekends, a message center took all the calls, only notifying her in case of emergency.

A smile of pure accomplishment spread over her face; it remained there as she began to document her thoughts on the enigma of past-life memory. Even though she was well aware her assessment was going beyond conventional scientific thinking, it was of great importance to chronicle this new information about the profound mysteries of the material universe.

I gave Kuri's psyche full permission to follow its own resonances during the deep memory process, and she was able to arrive at a place where she could confront and understand her symptoms by grasping their origin. While everything was still fresh in her mind, Melanie quickly made a record of her many impressions in more detail than ever before.

Sure, in her long practice, she had witnessed remarkable hypnotic regressions with other patients, and she definitely had gained a wealth of knowledge during her long career. Yet, nothing compared to the day in Sedona when Adam revealed the findings of his own deep memory process to her. The moment he mentioned names from his former life, Melanie was able to connect the dots between her patient, Kuri Berger, and the young man with whom she had conversed in the Meditation Ramada.

I wish I could publish this phenomenon—it's clearly nonpareil to anything I've ever experienced in the field of pseudoscience, she thought while her fingers kept flying over the keyboard.

Just like her, several other of her colleagues also had pioneered the study of altered or nonordinary states of consciousness. Some had been given permission to publish their patients' past life experiences, withholding identification.

On the other hand, Melanie was well aware of controversial articles that either debunked the whole concept of past life regression or even questioned certain practitioners' theories and approaches in the process of mind-body healing.

Not only did I witness firsthand how Kuri was able to alter her state of consciousness and access higher realities, she and Adam brought absolute proof that they had been in this physical world before. Their power of recall was more than astounding. In my presence, and without the knowledge of the other, they individually described the same images. As the images became more lucid to them, they not only recalled their own names, but they remembered each other's names from a previous life.

Melanie's thoughts kept racing ahead as she typed her assessment. *Because Adam had been able to draw his visions on paper over a decade ago, his enhanced drawings led him to the location that matched his sketches. He produced names and cities that tallied with the images in his dreams. All of his recollection of persons had been identified through the specificity of information. Finally, Adam's abundant evidence and Kuri's recollection during deep memory process sessions coalesced; it gave testimony of their past life core: they had lived and loved one another once before.*

Melanie didn't know how long she had been typing, but when she believed every detail was documented, she relaxed back into the desk chair and stared at her last sentences: "Unbeknownst to each other, in unconnected past life regression sessions a decade apart, they recalled crossing paths in Nazi Germany; Kuri remembered her life as Judith Rozenblum, and Adam recalled his as Shimmy Messing. As a separate entity, they both called to mind the same sentence they spoke when they died in each other's arms. 'Dance with me,' Judith had said. 'You and I… forever,' Shimmy had answered."

Melanie heard the soft knock against the door. She swiveled around in her chair and saw Kuri and Adam walk side by side into her office; they looked enlightened, their eyes were luminous with joy.

Kuri walked up to her. "Dr. B.," she said in a low voice, "it must have been difficult to keep everything to yourself. You waited so Adam and I could make our own discovery. Because of what just transpired, I seem to be at a loss for words, but… we are so very, very grateful to you."

"Thank you," said Melanie in a thick voice. "My goal for you was to gain direct experience of yourself as your soul journeyed through time; my aim for you was to grow and find healing." The therapist blinked through a tear and with a smile continued. "You not only found healing, you found your love—your soul mate again."

"From the moment I met Adam, I felt there was something, like a preexisting bond," said Kuri. "Of course, I couldn't comprehend this mystifying phenomenon."

"Yes," Adam chimed in. "And the instant Kuri opened her eyes under the tree in Dachau, I sensed an inexplicable link. Two days later, I read Shimmy's letter and couldn't wipe away a divine vision." He looked at Kuri. "I so badly wanted Judith to be you!" He took Kuri's hand and looked at her in awe. "My vision... my hope came true today."

"It's extraordinary how the essence of our souls connected us again," Kuri said, speaking softly. "During my hypnotic regression, I sensed the deep love for Shimmy. I feel as if I woke up from a long slumber, and now this love became alive, vibrant, and so full again."

Melanie delighted in their togetherness; she did not want this day to end when the exchange of countless impressions seemed to fill all the empty spaces with light. She looked at the two young people sitting across from her and, once again, marveled at the many great secrets of time and life.

Chapter Fifty-Four

All the way on their ride to the Lake Bluff home from the therapist's office in the city, they couldn't stop talking; they spilled their deepest thoughts and emotions—impressions they had been unable to express before. For the first time, as they bared their souls to each other, they knew they were completely heard and understood. They hung onto each other's words and finished each other's sentences. They'd never felt so alive and couldn't wait to share with both of their families what had transpired during the past few hours.

Later that evening, in an extended FaceTime call between Boston and Lake Bluff, the Bergers and the Golds kept declaring their fascination in the subject matter as they listened to Kuri and Adam's pure excitement and complete joy detailing their newfound awareness. Plans were made for the two families to meet in New York City before the end of the month.

The following morning, before six o'clock, Kuri and Adam were on their way to Chicago Executive Airport-PWK in Wheeling. Together they would fly to New York City, where a private car was to take Adam straight from the airport to his work in Boston.

Right before they boarded the chartered jet, Adam received a text message from Max Bauer; the two men had stayed in regular contact since they met in Germany almost four months ago.

"Uh-oh, you look unsettled. What is it?" said Kuri.

He showed her the text:

> Adam: Hope life is treating Kuri and you well. Eva and I took great pleasure in meeting her via FaceTime. As soon as you have a free moment, would you get in touch with me, please? Thank you!

"You may want to call him right away," Kuri said, handing the phone back to Adam. "It sounds urgent."

Adam nodded. "Strange, when we talked to them just a few days ago, they were in their usual jovial mood…something must have happened since then." He tapped on Max's mobile number.

"Adam, my friend. That was quick; I only sent the text a few minutes ago. Thanks for calling me right back. Wherever you are, it's got to be early in the morning, right?"

"I've been visiting with Kuri; we're heading back east. I was going to call you with some very, very exciting developments. But it can wait. First you, your message sounded important. Is it okay to keep you on speakerphone?"

"Of course!"

After Kuri and Max exchanged greetings, she, carefully and in her usual gentle manner, asked him what was wrong.

"It's about Mother," Max said. "Adam, you do remember that she's had trouble speaking, but as of recently, she's been getting more and more feeble. However, just two days ago, she suddenly grew very anxious, muttering words, urging us to take her to the grave under the apple tree." There was a crack in Max's voice before he continued. "Mother only calmed down when we brought her there in the wheelchair. She prayed in silence for a long time—she did not want to leave."

Adam and Kuri looked at one another with eyes wide open.

"Until today, the weather was sunny and fairly mild for October, but this morning, it started to rain, and it's quite chilly. Mother refuses to understand why we can't take her outside, back to the apple tree and the grave. She's so fragile..." Max's voice was filled with emotion. "Eva and I can't believe how Mother turned listless so quickly; now she also refuses to take her medication. The doctor says we may have to prepare ourselves that she's ready to go." Max paused. "I know she's old—we've been blessed having her with us this long." He sighed and added softly, "Adam, because you told me you hoped to see Mother again on your visit next spring when you want to bring Kuri along...I thought I'd let you know, she might not make it till then."

While on their flight to New York, Kuri and Adam made quick decisions, choices they assumed could very well result in work-related consequences; however, in the course of what just moments ago they'd heard from Max and what had come to light only two days prior in Dr. Melanie Brichta's practice, they knew there was no alternative.

Kuri also called her family, as well as Dr. B., letting them know that, at this point, nothing was more important to her than to meet Resi Bauer, the only person who actually knew Judith and Shimmy.

"I just have to meet this kind woman so I can thank her for her righteousness and understanding—I hope I'll get there in time."

❄

After all the necessary arrangements had been made, later that evening, Kuri and Adam fell asleep in each other's arms on White Birch's brand-new corporate jet as they flew through the night across the ocean into the sunrise over the European continent.

"In another sixty minutes, we'll land in Munich. Temperatures today are forecast for fifty-nine degrees with clear skies," said the flight attendant when she placed two mugs with freshly brewed coffee on the table. "Is there anything else I may still serve you?"

As so many times before, Adam once again could not take his

eyes off Kuri; she was holding the mug between both hands, gazing at the endless firmament through the airplane window.

"You know," he said softly, almost as if to himself, "it didn't really surprise me when Max called. What he told us seems only like another meaningful coincidence that wants to make the point in the synchronous incidents of the many recent happenings."

Kuri, still looking at the white, fluffy blanket of clouds below, slowly turned her head toward him. "You're right," she said, "another incident that may have no apparent causal link, but for both of us it could turn out to be remarkably connected. I wonder if this latest development might close the circle."

Chapter Fifty-Five

A previously arranged private car waited for them at the Munich airport. During the one-hour ride toward the Bauer farm near the small town of Kochel am See, Kuri found it increasingly more troublesome to control her emotions; the moment the farmhouse came into view, she whispered in disbelief, "Omigod, it feels as if I'm arriving in another reality." Her left hand clutched the sweater across her chest. "No matter how much I think I'm able to make sense of the whole concept…this is otherworldly." Unable to turn her head away from the scene, her right hand found Adam's. "I was here before," she breathed.

She was unaware of the driver removing two small carry-ons from the trunk and handing them to Adam. She did not hear the sounds of tires crunching and bumping over gravel and cobblestones as the car slowly pulled away, nor did she notice Eva and Max coming from the house.

Transfixed, Kuri stood in one spot, staring at the border of the forest. Slowly, as if following the course of a bygone path, her eyes found the old barn, and in a trancelike state, she walked toward it. She opened the big, heavy door and held her breath when she perceived the sounds of creaking floorboards under her footsteps. She gasped in disbelief when she heard the rustle of hay as she leaned against a stack. And then, the dusty, slightly sweet-smelling, earthy barn air miraculously opened up those brain regions responsible for her power of recall; she dropped onto one of the haystacks and gave complete freedom to the sentiments of her heart, permitting her soul to travel back in time.

❄

A young woman is entering the barn. For a moment I think she is one of them, but she's not in a uniform. She's wearing a blue dress with tiny white flowers under an apron. "Mama?" I whisper. I can't think clearly; I am so weak, so very tired.

"Ich bin die Resi," the pretty woman says, and gently touches my cheek with the palm of her hand. "Don't be afraid, mein Engerl, you are safe here."

"Mama?" I love when she calls me her little angel and runs her fingers through my hair—her gentle touch always gives me comfort. I want to look at her, but my lids are so heavy, I can't keep them open.

"Judith, my little angel." I hear sweet music in the distance. So many harps; where are they? I feel myself rising, ready to dance in my favorite tutu and pointe shoes, when the sound of shuffling feet pulls me back. I am so tired but as soon as I manage to open my eyes, my heart begins to sing because I see Shimmy walking toward me and then feel his body next to me again. His handsome face is so pale; his eyes look tired and glassy. "I need to rest," he says. "I will feel better soon... I promise." His lips touch mine.

Somebody else is here. I know it's Resi when a cold compress is put on my hot forehead. "Danke," I whisper, and smile.

"You can hear me?"

I nod.

"I believe God brought you to me for a reason," Resi says, gently caressing my hand. "I kept praying for a miracle to make you and the boy well again, but God must have other plans for you." Her voice is so peaceful. "I trust that a beautiful journey is upon you." I feel her

fingers combing my hair. "Before you go, would you please leave me something that'll keep us connected?"

"Of course," I murmur, "but we have nothing to give you."

"You do have something very special; a strand of hair from both of you?"

I smile and nod.

I hear two snips from scissors and then feel her soothing hands on my cheek again. I hear her say, "Pfiat Gott." Through half-closed lids, I see her kneel next to us; she's praying.

I notice Shimmy's labored breathing. "Don't be afraid," I tell him, as I suddenly feel so light and energized. "This is a special moment, it's a birthday of a new life." I can hear the heavenly harp music coming closer; magically it takes away all my pain. "Shimmy, listen..." I touch him, and he opens his eyes.

"Look...the light. Can you see it?" Shimmy's eyes are wide open now.

He nods. "Oh yes," he says. "So beautiful."

"Do you hear the music? I've never heard sweeter melodies." I search for his hand. "Dance with me," I whisper.

"Yes," he says. "We are free—we're floating on air." His words are lyrical and gentle. I feel his fingers connecting with mine as he whispers, "You and I...forever."

Chapter Fifty-Six

Kuri blinked twice. Was she still dreaming? No, this was real; Adam crouching next to her and Eva kneeling in front of them was extraordinary! Didn't she just have that same vision of others in a barn? Was it here; in this very place? She blinked again and tried to push herself into a sitting position. She felt disoriented.

"Kuri, are you okay?" Adam said. "You vacantly looked at me and kept talking, but I couldn't make sense of the words." He lifted her chin so he could look into her eyes. "What happened?"

"I…I believe I went back in time again." She looked around the barn, as if searching for something. "How did I get here?"

"You walked into this barn, almost as if you were programmed to do so."

She closed her eyes and rubbed her temples. "Since I don't remember, how long was I *out*?"

"No more than a minute."

"Really? That's all? I had so many distinct impressions." She shook her head. "What did I say?"

"Your eyes were wide open; you smiled at me, but I was unable to follow your words."

"I could understand," Eva offered calmly. "You talked indistinctly, but I heard what you said...you spoke in German."

"What? How? I don't speak the language."

"You did say *himmlische Musik,* and you whispered, '*Tanz' mit mir.*'"

Kuri looked from Eva to Adam and back to Eva. "I don't even know what those words mean," she murmured. "This is so surreal." As if trying to focus herself into reality, she blinked again, then looked at Eva and extended her hand to the other woman. "I certainly imagined our first meeting to be different; I must apologize for this awkward situation."

Eva smiled. "Please, no apologies. Since last June, Adam's story gave my husband and I a lot to think about. We allowed new horizons to open, and ever so slowly, we fathomed that there are no limits to probabilities. Something profound occurred when we met Adam a few months ago, especially for Mother. It'll be a true gift for her to see him one more time."

"Of course, yes!" Kuri said. "This is why we came here. And I really, really want to meet Resi for so many reasons."

Up until that moment, none of them had been aware of Max, who was leaning against the frame of the open barn door, silently observing. His face brightened when they walked toward him.

"My dear young friend, how kind of you to come," Max said, and enfolded Adam in a tight embrace." Then Max turned his attention to Kuri and clasped her right hand into his. "It's wonderful to finally meet you in person." Smiling, Max kept shaking Kuri's hand. "Adam told me so much about the young woman who completes him."

"May I?" Kuri asked, and without waiting for an answer, she first flung her arms around Max and then embraced Eva. "Ever since our FaceTime call, I couldn't wait to get here, but neither Adam nor I knew we'd see you this soon."

"Yes, your call coincided with something extraordinary that happened last Sunday, something we must share with you," Adam said.

"Let's go inside and see Mother," Eva said. "After all, she's the true reason for your visit."

Quietly they followed Max and Eva into a bedroom where gabled ceilings and wood paneling gave the interior space a true Alpine loft feel. All the old pinewood furniture was kept in pristine condition—decades ago, the headboard, the armoire, the peasant trunk, and wooden chairs had been hand painted with a decorative Bavarian décor by a local artist. Soft rays from the midday sun filtered through white lace curtains onto Resi Bauer; the old woman's eyes were closed, her soft breaths were shallow, somewhat irregular.

Max pulled two additional chairs to the other side of the bed and, in a hushed voice, asked his friends to sit opposite from Eva and himself.

Kuri could not take her eyes off Resi. Strands of her neatly braided hair almost blended into the color of the white linen pillows; her thin arms were covered by long sleeves of a blue and white nightgown with floral lace; her hands, scattered with sun spots and lines, lay folded atop the goose-down duvet. She looked beautiful and serene.

"Is she…"

"She's sleeping," Max said when he saw Kuri's worried face. "She was restless most of the night; Eva gave her medication to calm her down."

"Is she in pain?"

"She has no pain," Eva said. "But since the day she insisted to go to the grave by the apple tree, she's been acting more anxious; the urgency in her behavior became immediately clear to me." Eva nodded when she saw Adam and Kuri's quizzical expressions. "I studied nursing in Australia." she explained. "After Max and I married, I continued my studies in Germany; for many years, I've been licensed for in-home hospice care. I learned about and witnessed many people's last days; their final moments often tell what they see and hear." Eva touched her mother-in-law's cold hands and gazed at her lovingly. "Even though I believe she's ready to let go of life, I feel she's choosing her moment to die. It seems she's still waiting for something..." Eva looked at the two young people sitting across from her.

"Did she have any idea we were coming?" Adam wondered.

"Yes," said Max. "We told her right after you called from the plane." He shifted in his chair. "You mentioned you had rather exciting things to share with us."

"Yes, but should we talk here?" Adam looked from Max and Eva to Resi. "Now?"

"Absolutely," said Eva. "Even if Mother already is crossing the threshold between this world and the next, she can still listen; hearing is thought to be the last sense to go."

"Whatever you're going to tell us, does it have to do with what you uncovered under the oak tree last June?" A glimmer of hope flickered in Max's eyes.

Kuri and Adam nodded in unison.

And then, Adam began to talk; from Kuri's and his first meeting in Dachau to her last hypnotic regression session, only days ago, in Dr. Melanie Brichta's meditation room, Adam elaborated on every fact that so miraculously had taken place.

"Under hypnosis, Kuri recalled the same scenes and spoke the same words, exactly as I remembered them from my own visions and past life regressions," Adam said at the end of his delivery. "She remembered being Judith Rozenblum and talked about her death in a barn with Shimmy Messing." Adam's lower lip quivered, and his eyes glistened when he said, "Separately, Kuri and I recalled the same details, all identical to Shimmy's words that were written over seven decades ago, in 1945."

"Holy dooley..." Eva breathed. "Even though I was a bit hesitant, I did believe what you told us in June, but I clearly did not expect that the two of you..." Eva wiped her eyes. "It's... it's simply divine."

Max, this burly man in his midsixties, suddenly looked like a little boy as he leaned over his mother's bed, also wiping his eyes. "You always knew! You always knew!" And then he added, even more gently, "I'm so sorry for doubting your awareness, Mother.

Your intuitions and spirituality often were beyond my perception."

After a long moment of total silence in the room, Kuri cleared her throat. "There still is more," she said softly. "As soon as we arrived here today, I experienced a powerful déjà-vu—it was a familiar vision with a new facet."

Eva, Max, and Adam looked up.

"Do you feel like talking about it?"

"I'm very emotional right now," she said in a low voice, dabbing her cheeks. "What happened during that brief moment in the barn might yet be another piece to complete the puzzle."

Kuri looked at the old lady and took a deep breath.

"I saw everything through Judith's eyes—I was her when I died in Shimmy's arms. I saw a woman asking permission to cut a strand of hair from each of us." Kuri swallowed. "She said her name was Resi, and she wanted to be forever connected to us." Kuri leaned over the bed, closer to the old woman. "How curious that I should have that vision today in your barn," she said almost inaudibly. "You connected with us throughout the years. We returned."

A sound of air escaped Resi's lips. Her lids fluttered, and slowly she opened her eyes, focusing on her son and daughter-in-law. "They came," she rasped in her unmistakable Bavarian dialect. A faint smile formed on her lips.

Was it the golden sunrays still sifting through the lace curtain, or did her skin suddenly begin to glow as if color was returning to her pale face? When she attempted to sit up, Max and Eva sprang to their feet, quickly adjusting the thick pillows behind their mother's head and under her back.

"Yes, Mother, they came back," Max said. "You always knew." And then he gently turned her head to the opposite side of the bed.

"Angels," Resi said hoarsely, and in a weak attempt tried to stretch her arms toward Kuri and Adam; they each took one of her hands into theirs.

"*Die Keksdose,*" Resi rasped.

Simultaneously, Kuri and Adam turned their heads to Eva and Max and asked, "What is she saying?"

"She's asking for the tin cookie box. I wonder why." Max got off the chair, walked to the foot end of the bed, and with both hands raised the heavy dome lid off the old peasant trunk. He searched for a moment, then removed a vintage Haeberlein-Metzger tin cookie box and put it on the table next to the bed.

"My father gave this to Mother many, many years ago," he explained. "As soon as the cookies were gone, it became Mother's treasure. She called it *mein Gedächtnis Behälter,* which means my memory container." For a moment, he stared at the blue tin box where painted garlands of flowers framed images of couples in their traditional costumes from various regions in Germany. Gently, he unfastened the latch and opened the lid.

He took out his father's clay pipe and a Hohner harmonica from the cookie box and showed them to his mother.

Barely noticeable, the old woman shook her head.

Max held up a little silver rattle and tiny spoon. "These were mine," he said softly, and laid the items next to the pipe and harmonica. As if to himself, he added, "You kept what reminded you of all your most precious points in time." He looked at a small, burgundy lacquered container, and as soon as he opened it, he beamed. "Look at this," he said, and showed the contents to Eva and his guests. "Mother even kept my baby teeth."

One after the other, small memorabilia were placed on the bedside table, but Resi kept shaking her head. The moment Max lifted a flat needlepoint pouch from the very bottom of the tin cookie box, Resi nodded and visibly relaxed into her pillow—she looked exhausted, but her face seemed to glow and her eyes shone. Without lifting her hand, she pointed a finger at Kuri and Adam.

"I think she wants you to open this," Eva said, and handed the needlepoint pouch to the young couple.

Carefully, Kuri untied the pouch and removed pages of a handwritten letter. She looked at them. "It's written in German," she said, and handed it to Max. "Would you please translate it for us?"

Chapter Fifty-Seven

May 1945

The horrors of war might be over, but our world seems to continue transforming into a wilderness. How can Germany live with the guilt over the atrocities that were carried out by so many madmen?

My nights continue to remain sleepless. When I hear approaching thunder, I still fear new bomb attacks. When there are knocks on the door, I am afraid the Wehrmacht or SS are outside, pointing their rifles at us. Instead, hungry people from the city are standing outside our door, offering to trade whatever they have left of their possessions for food. We share with them what we can give, but our supplies are already low. I think about the countless people who not only lost their homes and all of their belongings but also were stripped of their dignity. I think of the men, women, and children who never again will feel the nearness, the warmth of loved ones—millions of innocent people's lives were brutally taken.

And yet, a new spring has come, I see the bursting of buds; new flowers and leaves are blossoming again in warm sunshine. And when I look into the sky, I tell myself that, even after so much cruelty and suffering, a new life, a new world, a new beginning will return.

Two days ago, my in-laws and I laid two beautiful young people, a girl and a boy, to rest. My kind father-in-law dug the grave in a special spot, close to the brook. I picked daisies, marigolds, and dandelions from our meadow, now in full bloom. I covered the dark freshly turned soil on the grave, creating a beautiful thick blanket of spring flowers. Today, as I sit in front of their resting place, writing my thoughts onto these pages, I think of the two angels sleeping below the blossoms; their sweet faces will forever be etched on my mind. Yet, I will never know their names, their ages, their families; I will never know whom to contact and tell them they died in each other's arms, peacefully and surrounded by love.

The moment these two young people arrived at our farm—adolescents so emaciated, so sick, and so fearful of more torture—I heard a voice from deep within me. My soul spoke to me and guided me to return the quality of self-worth to these innocent youngsters; give back, even if only a small piece, of what had been taken from them by granting them the respect and honor they deserved.

In their last moments of life, I followed the guidance and asked the girl for permission to leave me a strand of hair from each; a connection that one day might rectify doubts about the immortality of the soul. For I believe it is the mystery of the universe that all things continue—they do not die, they only withdraw temporarily and then return again.

My deep spiritual and religious beliefs make me feel connected to a Supreme Intelligence. I have no doubt that there is a profound purpose for being and that there is an explanation for everything that happens to us. Yet, words fail me to explain my deep-rooted, inexplicable awareness.

Because of the times we live in and the many human misgivings, I believe it is best to keep my way of thinking to myself.

❋

May 1951

Six years have passed. Many wonderful things have happened.

Two years ago, Alois, my beloved husband, returned home from captivity in the Soviet Union. I missed him so much, and during the moments when he plays his harmonica for me again and when I watch him smoke his precious clay pipe, I am very grateful that my Alois was not among the millions and millions of those who lost their lives during that terrible war.

Last year, God blessed us with a beautiful baby boy; we named him Max, after my father.

Right after our baby was born, I planted an apple tree by the grave in the meadow, and we carved two Stars of David into the young trunk of the tree. Now, one year later, the little apple tree is sprouting nicely, just like my sweet baby boy. And when I look at the two Stars of David, I am awed by their mystical significance.

Whenever the weather is nice, I carry Max down to the brook; he loves to watch the water flow over the stones, and he squeals with delight when I imitate the chirping birds. Then, I sit with him under the apple tree by the grave and sing lullabies, rocking my baby until he falls asleep in my arms. In this beauty of unbound nature around us, I feel abundantly connected to all creation and grateful for the limitless dreams that enrich our current lives. I can't help but wonder if there also are limitless lives we may have lived before or may enter again. When Max is older, I will start explaining my own convictions to him, that our existence is simply like one of the thousand dreams that come to us while we live this life. And, just like dream after dream, the energy of our soul has no end. Not until the wondrous spark of divinity within us is being called home to the one energy that is true and real, the intelligence behind all that exists.

Today I shall put the two strands of hair that I kept in a matchbox by my bedside, together with these written pages, in a needlepoint pouch I just finished making for this purpose alone.

I hope to be blessed with a long life. And when the time comes to close my eyes forever and return to the life of all creation, I pray the strands of hair from two nameless angels will have found their connection to two new young lives.

Chapter Fifty-Eight

I had no idea…" Still glued to the last sentence, Max's eyes filled with tears. He looked at his mother and returned her smile. "*Es ist wahr geworden,*" he whispered, and wiped his eyes. "Your trust, your beliefs came true." Max folded his mother's hand into his. "I had no idea," he said again.

Without moving her head, the old woman's eyes slowly moved from her son to Kuri and Adam before resting on the needlepoint pouch.

"I think she wants you to know there's something else in the pouch," Eva said.

Kuri handed the bag to Adam. "My hands are shaking," she said. "I am overwhelmed by the significance of this moment."

Adam slowly lifted the flap, carefully reached into the pouch, and removed an old matchbox. A blue dried cornflower and white daisy were glued to the top of the matchbox. Adam swallowed and looked at Resi. "May I open this?" he asked in broken German.

Another smile spread over the old woman's face; she nodded.

He laid he matchbox on the white linen duvet and slowly pulled the inside holder from its housing.

Gasps escaped four mouths as four pair of eyes gazed at two strands of hair: a bright copper lock and a dark-brown wave, lying side by side.

For several minutes, in the absolute silence of the room, only thoughts were given their individual freedom.

Suddenly, Resi's arms reached up. "*Ja, ich bin bereit,*" she said.

"Mother?"

"So many angels…right here. I see them," Resi said, her voice distinctly stronger as she looked past the four people in the room. "Yes, I have connected; my work is done. I am ready to come home."

"I believe she's seeing another physical presence," Eva explained. "She's seeing whoever she's talking to."

"She looks so radiant, so happy," Kuri murmured, holding the matchbox with the strands of hair to her chest.

Eva nodded. "I've witnessed this before. It's beautiful—I believe a connection to the next world is taking place." She touched her husband's arm. "I think it's time for us to say whatever we want her to take with."

Together, Max and Eva leaned over their mother and for minutes took turns whispering to her. Then they each kissed her forehead and, without hiding their emotion, they thanked her, telling her how much she was loved.

A long exhale escaped Resi's lips, but seconds later there was another intake of breath.

Resi opened her eyes and looked at Kuri and Adam. Slowly her lids closed, and with her last breath, she said, "Two angels…Life brought you back."

Standing at the bedside, Kuri and Adam sensed a sudden aura of lightness as a cool breeze seemed to drift over them. They looked at each other, and at the same instant, both declared, "Yes—I am here."

Acknowledgments

This novel greatly relied on the time and understanding many wonderful people were willing to give me.

My complete thanks go to Ruth Hornung and Dr. Arnold Clevs. Both of you generously shared your stories with me about the difficult and emotional times you endured during the grueling years of World War II. Your powerful testimonies deeply touched my emotions and intensified my aim to acquire more knowledge of and from this history.

I will always be grateful for having paid attention whenever the late Bella and Sidney Miller and the late Samuel Beider talked about the way of life as it was for them in Europe before and during the war. As Elie Wiesel wrote, "The past belongs to the past and the survivor does not recognize himself in the words linking him to it. The survivors of the Holocaust who tell their stories bear witness, transmit a spark of the flame, tell a fragment of the tale, and remember for those who begged them to tell the story."

I am indebted to all of your voices of wisdom!

I owe special thanks to Ron Hogan, editor extraordinaire! Your talent and guidance provided the encouragement I needed and enriched my imagination. I could not have hoped for better.

Greatest thanks to Olivia Geyelin, Samara Rubin, Daniel Beider, Kathy Peisner, Lynn Wiese, Aimee Carbone, Anita Durkovic, Anna Franklin, and Georgia Curtin for your various contributions, providing me with knowledge about things I still had to learn and understand; and to Noah Beider for your young spirit and encouragement.

A tight grateful hug to my dear friends Barbara Heinz and Libby Cummings for reading the first draft of this novel. Your approval and enthusiasm gave me the necessary boost to keep going and improving.

I tip my hat to Lori Conser, Susan Wenger, and Mindy Burnett at Wheatmark; I greatly appreciate your help, support, and patience.

Here you go...DAK! Your insistence for the past two decades finally has come to pass; I pay homage to the man and his acclaimed DAK straw hat.

And even though a cliché, I must say that I couldn't have done this book without...all of my kindred spirits who held my hand throughout the amazing process of writing. I am grateful for your support, your patience, and your understanding whenever I sequestered myself.

As always to my amazing family: Fran, Jackie, Kenny, Kelly, Mike, Danny, Olivia, Samara, Andy, Hal, Cody, Darilyn, Jacoby, Noel, Jonah, Skyler, Noah, Ellee, Payton, Alani...I Love You!

Made in the USA
Coppell, TX
21 March 2020

17345583R00185